THE SIX AT
CHESTNUT HILL FARM

A Contemporary Novel

REBA RHYNE

The Six at Chestnut Hill Farm

Thanks to:

Cover Photo by Robin Rhyne Greenlee of Wonderful Blessings Photography of Walland Gap where the railroad ran on the left and the road to the right of Little River which flowed from Townsend, Tennessee. In the background is Thunderhead Mountain in Cades Cove.

Thanks to Cousin Philip and Susan Whitehead for posing for the cover. He is an Executive Pastor of Living Waters Church and grandson of Burl and Melvina Tipton Whitehead. He lives in Kentucky.

Layout of Front Cover and Back by Ken Raney
Editing by Kim Peterson and Sara Foust
Dawn Staymates, my formatter, and Cheri Cowell of EA Books Publishing

Published by EA Books Publishing a division of Living Parables of Central Florida, Inc. a 501c3
EABooksPublishing.com

Contents

Introduction

The two themes in this book involve families and trust.

Families are made up of many different characters. First, the father, whose personality steers the destiny of the whole. He can be domineering, forgiving, loving, trustworthy or any number of characteristics. The mother, who is in charge, more or less of the household and daily interactions when the father is at work or at home, can be nurturing, or so busy all she has time to accomplish is to work at a job, cook, and clean.

Then, here come the children. Mix their personalities into the family — the perfect one, who can do no wrong, the one who stands up for himself and takes a beating for the rest of his siblings, or the one who runs for safety when things get loud and disagreeable.

Some families are a recipe for disaster or the framework for a major work of God's love. The two families in this book are very different, even though they have attended church, and some profess to believe in God. That profession doesn't make them perfect, just ready for their Heavenly Father to take his pruning tools to them, which He does. Who will change? Who will stay the same, get better, or get bitter?

Real friendship and love demand trust. Trust is earned a little bit at a time, and once it's earned, should last a lifetime. An old Irish proverb says, "when mistrust comes in, love goes out." At least, it stops love in its tracks until suspicion and doubts are resolved.

How many people can you say you truly trust? Can you count them on one hand or two?

Relationships are about trust. Without it, love is insecure. Without it, families are unstable and broken. There are two families in this book—one with trust and one without.

I love this verse from Isaiah 54:16. It says, *Behold I have created the smith that bloweth the coals in the fire, and that bringeth forth an instrument for his work.* I've worked the bellows, making white-hot coals which purify metal and make it pliable. God's fiery work in my life does the same—burns away faults and makes me trustworthy in my relationships with family and friends.

MY HOPE: If this is your family, it is my hope that your heart will be pricked to make changes in your approach to your mother and father or brothers and sisters. If this happens, then 105,158 words on paper and countless hours of work will be worth it.

MY PRAYER: May the Holy Spirit give power to these written words and use them to bring glory to Jesus Christ and the Father in Heaven … amen.

THE SIX AT CHESTNUT HILL FARM

REBA RHYNE

CAUTION

One of the characters in this book is Grandpa Puckett. He loves jokes or as he calls them "funnys." When the phone rings, the call could be a friend from church with the latest. So just to caution you ahead of time, here's one of his funnys.

A duck, a skunk, and a deer went out to a local restaurant one night to eat. When it came time to pay the receipt, the skunk didn't have a scent and the deer didn't have a buck, so they put their meal on the duck's bill.

Don't say I didn't warn you. RR

❧ Chapter One ❧

Manda Weathers

"Manda, have you ever thought about marrying again?"

I was sitting across from my pastor with his expansive, paper-filled desk separating us when this question came like a bolt out of the blue. Thank goodness, I was in complete control of my body, or my mouth would've dropped open. He was a happily married man so why the question?

"I, uh, uh, thought about it several years ago after Todd passed. Since then, I've learned to live alone and enjoy my singlehood." Was singlehood a word? I couldn't remember and, being in shock at that particular moment, I didn't care. One moment I was relaxing in front of his desk, talking about our youth's planned mission trip out west, and the next my mind was a jumble of conflicting thoughts. What on earth had brought that question into our conversation?

Seeing the surprised expression on my face, my pastor gave a short chuckle. "I know my question is very personal and seems strange, and maybe I'm not the right person to ask it. But wouldn't you agree that we're very good friends?

1

"Yes." I'd known my pastor for twenty years. I confided in him, and I trusted him.

He continued, "And very good friends can share anything?"

"Yes." *Almost anything.* Where was this going?

"Here's the dilemma. Our pastoral staff has been praying and wracking our brains for an answer to Luke's problem."

Luke's problem rolled through my mind like a mini-earthquake.

Luke Avery was the music minister of Church-on-the-Hill. His wife, Peggy, passed away of breast cancer four years ago, and he was raising his nine-year-old son, James. Luke was thirty-six and another *very good* friend of mine, whom I respected for his commitment to God and his love of music — a commitment and love which I shared. Our relationship was, well, comfortable.

A year or so after his wife passed, I offered to become his helper on Mondays. We worked at various jobs in the music department, sorting music for the choir and replacing the last Sunday's selections. I knew with his heavy schedule, the mundane processes often were left for later. After our work day, he'd pick up his son from school, and I'd meet them for dinner at one of the local restaurants. Sometimes, he'd drive to my house and pick me up. I accepted his invitation as *quid pro quo* for my weekly help. He was single, and I was single. So, why not?

On our last workday, he hadn't mentioned and didn't appear to be having any difficulty, and I was someone in whom he confided.

"Manda?" Pastor had leaned forward with his elbows on his desk.

"I wasn't aware that Luke had a problem, Pastor Lane. He hasn't uttered a single word about it to me."

"We haven't announced it to the congregation, because we weren't sure it would be necessary. Do you remember when his brother, sister-in-law, and baby niece were killed in the plane crash on 911? They were in the one which crashed into the Pentagon."

"Of course, I do. It was a terrible shock to Luke. Our whole church supported him during the terrible aftermath." Church-on-the-Hill members had poured their love on their music minister.

All except Charles (Chop) MacGregor, who didn't seem to like anyone. He stalked the halls, looking for something to complain about. Chop had a habit of making people miserable. Most men in the church tried to be friends. He'd rebuffed their attempts, except for one or two. When the vote came to approve Luke as music minister, he'd voted no. Why? No one knew.

Pastor Lane continued, "Luke's brother had three other children: Clint, Marcus, and Marybelle. They went to live with their paternal grandparents."

"Yes, I recall that. Didn't they live in Texas?"

"Longview, Texas, to be exact. To make a long story short, the grandmother has recently been diagnosed with dementia and can no longer care for the children, although they're still in her house. None of the other brothers and sisters can afford to take all of them on a permanent basis, and the family is adamant about not splitting them up.

"Luke feels God is leading him to care for his nephews and niece. He can swing the finances, but the responsibility and workload of three more children along with his hectic schedule here at church—" My pastor spread his hands in a something's-got-to-give gesture.

"Whew! I had no idea. What a difficult situation." Meanwhile my mind churned through several months of old conversations. So that's what's wrong with his mother. He'd said on his last trip home—Christmas, wasn't it?—she'd seemed confused at times, and evidently this had been going on for some time. Later, he'd told me he felt his father, realizing she had a mental problem, kept her condition from everyone in the family, including his sister Agnes Freeman, who lived nearby in Kilgore.

"Luke's not one who likes change. Although he's made the decision, the magnitude of this adjustment has him walking the floor at night. Since he's the most even-tempered man I know, I think he can manage the responsibility of three more children, but not without help."

Playing dumb, I asked, "So what does my not being married have to do with Luke's decision? Does he need a babysitter?" I wasn't sure I wanted to hear the answer.

"Our congregation doesn't have many eligible women, especially one whose qualities could handle circumstances like this. I thought about you." My pastor laughed. "Now don't get me wrong." He threw up his hands in a defensive gesture and stood. "I'm not taking up the job of matchmaking."

Really.

He came around and leaned back on the front of the desk, immediately facing me.

His comfortable, office couch, had now turned into a hot seat, and this was where I sat. "You're a great helper in Luke's music department, and whether you know it or not, he talks about you continuously—has for several months. He doesn't show interest in any other single woman in the church, and I believe he has more feelings for you, than he cares to admit to himself. He'll never forget Peggy, but he doesn't mention her like he used to."

"Peggy was a unique and lovely woman." I did agree with him. I hadn't heard Luke mention his late wife for some time.

"Yes, she was." Pastor looked at me, expecting a comment.

"Luke's easy to be around, and I admire his talent—his dedication to the church." My confusion increased with each moment the conversation continued. My pastor knew how to throw a big wrench into life.

"Luke doesn't know we're having this discussion. I wanted to talk to you in private and find out your feelings, if any, for him."

If I had feelings for Luke, what was he going to do then? "I—I'm not sure I have any beyond being his good friend. The thought never entered my mind—" Well, if it did, it was a fleeting thought. "I'm comfortable around him, but, Pastor, I'm older by a few years."

"In this case, I don't think age makes much difference and a wonderful togetherness certainly will. So how *do* you feel about Luke?" he gently pressed the issue. He was as casual as if we were still talking about the trip, we *had been* planning for the youth on summer missions, which was exactly why I was in his office. His gray-blue eyes seemed to bore into my brain, trying to extract an answer.

I sat wordless, something no one would ever accuse me of, with my mind going in circles as I looked at him. It was plain as the nose on your face. My pastor wasn't talking about a babysitter. He had determined I was a good candidate for Luke's wife.

But, my thoughts screamed, Manda your plans are to remain single the rest of your life. Remember the good times we've planned and all the trips we're going to take.

"Pastor, I'll have to get back to you. It's been a long time since I've examined a man with thoughts like you're invoking." I felt like we were discussing the latest model of washing machine at Sears. Was the decision to love and be married no more complicated than that?

"I know this is sudden, but think about it and pray about it."

Perplexed and confused by this turn of events, I murmured a few words of goodbye and stood. It was past time to go—way past time.

In the hall, I hurried past Luke's office and out the door of our church's administrative wing. "We didn't finish our talk about the trip," I said as I opened my car door. I turned to go back, but the possibility of running into *him* or Luke was too great. I needed quiet time in a remote corner somewhere. I needed to think, and think seriously.

I knew just the place—a familiar place—a safe, private place.

Picking up some KFC, I headed for Townsend, Tennessee, and Cades Cove in the Great Smoky Mountains National Park—only a thirty-minute drive away. Townsend, a sleepy, mostly unchanged town, sits at the western entrance of the park. Distant ancestors, the Tiptons were once involved in the lumber company, which became the motivation for its settlement. Once I arrived there, seven miles of curvy, uphill road separated me from my mountain destination.

Often when I needed space, I drove the familiar route to the cove and spread my blanket in a favorite grassy field off Hyatt Lane. There, I ate my meal and rested on my back, while watching the white, puffy clouds floating high overhead. I couldn't wait to get there. Being a weekday, it would not be crowded, and peace would reign.

Several minutes later, I dropped off the last hill into Cades Cove, arriving at the upper end entrance. Tourists stop here to pick up an information booklet, but being a local, I continued slowly through the gate and past the volunteer who usually mans the center.

Rolling down my windows and breathing in a lungful of clean mountain air, I noticed a lone black crow flying above, cawing as it headed for a convenient branch in a tall, pine tree. The black bird watched as I slowed down and drove by. Its raucous calls filled my ears as I sniffed the mountain breeze. Ah, there's something different about the smell of oxygen in the Smokies, and the scenes unfolding before me were expected and certainly not threatening—not like the rest of the morning.

I mashed the brakes hard as a squirrel skedaddled across the road in front of my car. "Fellow, don't cross the road with a car coming. You'll get killed," I told his scampering backside as I passed by. Inching along, I watched him climb a tree, where he sat on a branch, barking at my intrusion into his lunchtime.

As I continued driving, tall, green mountains surrounded me on all sides. The Loop Road is narrow, one-way, and blacktopped around the scooped-out valley. Wild, fat turkeys pecked at grain or bugs in the open fields. One tom turkey strutted his stuff around his harem of hens.

Looking to my left, a string of trees followed winding Abrams Creek, which flows through the lowest area in the middle of Cades Cove and after several miles out of the valley over Abrams Falls through Happy Valley into Chilhowee Lake. The stream had taken this same course for centuries.

The day was perfect. The sun shining, and the familiarity and peace of the place started to calm my troubled spirit.

I drove on a road which makes a curving loop around the valley, passing various log cabins left by the earliest settlers almost two hundred years ago. At the lower end, the overshot Cable Mill still turns, grinding meal for visitors to buy. Becky Cable's white, frame home, one of many which once stood in the cove, is close by — a remnant of this affluent community just before the land was incorporated into the national park.

I'm not driving that far.

If I don't want to travel the whole eleven-miles, two roads cross the valley. Sparks Lane and Hyatt Lane provide a shorter route. I turned my dark-blue, Toyota

Avalon left onto the second one, Hyatt Lane. To the right, the dark, crowded forest of tall spreading oaks, pines, and bunched up maples pushed against the path. To the left, fields stretched to the blue mountains, these high hills included old Thunderhead, the towering sentinel of the cove, reaching to the open sky.

Even though I drove slowly, my tires kicked up wisps of dust on the dry, rocked road. Pulling carefully off the path onto the edge of one of the many open fields found in the cove, I stopped my car. Sliding off the tan, leather seat, I got out and popped the trunk, grabbed my blanket, drink, and lunch box of chicken, and headed toward a favorite spot. The field, recently mowed, smelled of pungent cut grass, and round bales of hay dotted the expansive field.

The sharp sound of my red blanket snapping as I flapped it open disturbed the silence near me, causing a covey of quail to leap into the air and fly noisily away. I sat, smoothed the blanket with my open palms, and flicked off some pieces of grass from my last visit here.

Closing my eyes, the historic ambiance of Cades Cove surrounded me. I imagined whispers of its former inhabitants, and heard the laughter of the children as they played under the hemlock trees next to rushing, gurgling Rowans Creek. Across the road, man and horse plowed a field. He stopped, bent down, and picked up a handful of dirt, letting the rich, dark soil flow through his fingers, while wiping the sweat off his brow with his checkered handkerchief. A woman, dressed in flour-sack, gingham printed with flowers, scrubbed her clothes on a wooden washboard on her front porch, while the smells of wood burning and stew cooking on her woodstove floated through the air.

As I sit here, with muted sounds on all sides, somewhere in the stubble around me, a black cricket raked its leg against the other. The distinctive, melodic chirp of a red bird came from faraway in the thick forest behind me with the cicadas playing rhythmic albeit rasping backup. In the short stubble, there's a rustle of a small animal, maybe a rodent or rabbit. I didn't get up to find out.

Another sound surprised me. A rumble from my stomach area reminded me that I was hungry—hungry as one of the black bears, ambling through the autumn huckleberry bushes or high in a wild cherry tree, availing itself of their sweet nourishment. I laughed at the old saying as I reached for the box of food, the smells coming from inside making my mouth water.

Bears are plentiful in the cove, and, there's a good chance of seeing one or two as I drive through.

As a youngster, I learned these black marauders would raid campsites. My parents told stories of staying in a tent at Chimneys Camping Area and hearing them, during the night, knocking over coffeepots, metal coolers, and anything smelling of food. No campers at the Chimneys now, only picnickers.

When I hiked overnight in the Smokies as a young adult, I tied my food in bags and strung it high on tree limbs to keep the curious black animals at bay.

My stomach rumbled again. I sat cross-legged, opened the red and white box, and dug into my fried chicken, potato salad, and green beans, thinking food eaten in the mountains tasted twice as good as sitting at a kitchen table.

My reflections rambled on—anything to not address the events which happened earlier in the day. They could wait.

My thoughts turned to Todd Hughes Weathers.

I'd met Todd on one of our church group day hikes in the Smokies. Hilly Church Hikers was made up of college students. On this particular walk, we were going to Spence Field, an arduous trek starting from the picnic area at Cades Cove.

Spence Field provides a wonderful view of North Carolina and Alcoa's Chilhowee Lake.

At the bottom of Chilhowee Lake lay the foundations of my Tipton ancestor's mercantile store, barn, and old cornfields.

Plus, the remains of the old road and the trestles of an old railroad track were covered in the water, both used while the Aluminum Company of America was building dams up the Little Tennessee. On a clear day, I could see the lake from Spence Field.

After making the difficult trip up the mountain, my group was sitting in the grassy field, enjoying the view and eating a sack lunch of sandwiches and chips when Todd appeared from the trail behind us. I listened as he explained his itinerary to our group.

He had hiked alone to Spence Field and planned to stay at the night shelter. The next day he'd make a detour up to Thunderhead Mountain, come back down, and continue on to Russell Field. Later in the afternoon, he'd return to the picnic area at Cades Cove and drive home. I knew this itinerary well. My father and I had done the same.

Todd carried a pack big enough for a week on the Appalachian Trail, and I was curious as to why he did this, since so much baggage wasn't necessary for a one-night stay. When it was convenient, I went over and asked.

"Oh, I'm practicing for the big one." He smiled, and his eyes twinkled with blue highlights.

"The big one?" I questioned, sitting down beside him so we could talk.

He laughed, showing perfect white teeth. The sound he made was a deep baritone chuckle I didn't expect, and then he replied, "It's a private joke between me and my hiking partner, Jim Peabody. We're always planning the big one. Means we would like to hike a bigger portion of the Appalachian Trail and stay several nights." From his pack, he pulled out a sandwich, tomato, and can of A&W Root Beer. This wasn't normal fare for overnight stays in the Smokies. Real food added pounds and was subject to being mashed in your pack. Carrying perishable food was okay for day hikers like our group.

Seeing my raised eyebrows, he enlightened me. "I have dehydrated food and a filter for drinking water on the rest of the trip." He grinned, seeing my interest and knowing that walking light was important on serious trips into the mountains. A forty- or fifty-pound pack was plenty to lug up and down the rough trails, without adding the unnecessary weight of heavy food.

"I see, I think. So, when are you going to do this—walk the AT?"

"Good question. I just don't know. I do know one thing. We're not going to walk the whole AT. My devotion to hiking doesn't go that far. Does your group hike a lot?"

"We try to hike once or twice a month in the spring and summer. Seems like it's harder in the fall and winter, because most of us are in college."

"Could a non-church member join your hikes?" He was munching on his tomato, eating it like an apple and leaning over as juice squirted in all directions. Pulling out an orange handkerchief, he swiped at his chin.

"Sure," I responded. We'd take this good-looking, blond, blue-eyed stranger with the deep voice. I found myself rather attracted to him, but my trust of other people wasn't impulsive. Trust must be earned.

"I don't like to hike by myself, so having company would be great." He flashed his white smile again. "Jim works a lot."

"Are you a University of Tennessee fan?" I pointed to his orange handkerchief.

"My blood runs orange," he said emphatically.

That clinched it.

Todd was a hit with our group, so we'd made arrangements for him to join us on our next trip. He asked for my number, which he stuffed in his jean's pocket. When I graduated from college, we were in love and within six months we were married.

Children? Yes, we wanted them, but for some reason God didn't allow this blessing. And then, Todd was gone, unexpectedly of an aneurism of the aorta. His father had had the same problem and passed early. After the death of his father, his mother had married again and moved to Cody, Wyoming, with her new husband. On one wonderful road trip across America, Todd and I'd visited their ranch and celebrated our love for each other.

So many sweet memories of Todd, I thought.

The emotional effect of the morning's conversation and a full stomach was taking its toll, and I relaxed under the sun's loving touch, while wrapped between the safety of the mountain's comfortable arms.

"Okay, Manda. You can nap if you want to." I wanted to. I rolled over on my stomach, put my head on my folded arms, and went to dreamland.

My dreams were about Luke—Luke coming toward me. Luke looking in my eyes, Luke's arms around me, and Luke...no, no, no! My pastor's voice, "How do you feel about Luke, Manda? How do you feel about Luke?" echoed again and again throughout my sleeping mind.

I awoke with a jolt and sat straight up. I was a traitor to the wonderful memory of my former husband. My mind was playing tricks on me. I'll never sleep again, I promised myself.

I'd never had a dream like this about my music minister. The morning's discussion must have prompted it or triggered it. My pastor, yes, our talk might change my whole life.

Folding my knees up to my chin, I wrapped my arms around them. Bowing my forehead on my kneecaps, I thought about my relationship with Luke. I *was* rather attracted to him. I had to admit his appeal. Had I refused to acknowledge his increasing charm, because of—because of what? Manda, Manda, have you been fooling yourself about this man? Is it possible you could fall in love with him? Or are you smitten already?

I couldn't—or wouldn't—answer this question.

Four children … I let that inconceivable thought sink in. I ticked off the years. Some of them must be teenagers. Good heavens, an instant family. My solitary, quiet life would be gone by uttering two little words. I closed my eyes and whispered a prayer.

"Father, this day has certainly been a strange one, and I don't know where You are going with this. One thing's for sure, I trust You, and I'll follow your leading."

At the age of forty-two, I was a widow. My four-bedroom home did not have a mortgage. My sweet Todd made sure of that with a generous insurance policy. I loved my job as a beautician, and my life was simple. I liked to travel and did so at will. The question was twofold. Did I want to love again, making life complicated, *and* take on the responsibility of four children with a younger man? The whole thing was preposterous.

Then it hit me, Luke's decision was as life-altering as mine. Here I was thinking only of myself. What he must be going through. What did my pastor say? Walking the floor, wasn't that it?

"But, that's just like Luke," I murmured, "willing to sacrifice his time, money, and …

I drew air into my lungs and let it go in a long sigh. Where *was* God going with this? I stood, shook and folded my blanket, collected the remains of my lunch, and headed for my car. I opened the rear door, threw the blanket and box on the back seat, and shut the door.

Glancing up, I saw Thunderhead Mountain towering over the other surrounding hills. It looked down on me and seemed to say, "Manda, don't rule out anything. You've been here and conquered me. I'm the *worst hill* around. Don't worry, but wonder what God has in store for you."

Really, Manda, mountains don't talk.

As I buckled my seat belt to drive home, the thought occurred to me, if Luke didn't know of my pastor's talk, then he might not be interested in pursuing a relationship with me at all. Okay, so this intrusion in my life might not come to anything. I relaxed and decided it was so.

At least it was so, until it was unso. Was unso a word? Probably not.

❦ **Chapter Two** ❦

Luke Avery

"Good morning, Luke," Bess Myers greeted, as she headed for the doors of Church-on-the-Hill.

I had opened the double, glass doors to let her hurry into the building. "Welcome, Bess."

"Might rain," she threw over her shoulder as she rushed on by.

The last Sunday in May, and she was late again. "Bess, you may be right about the rain. Where's Caitlyn?" I turned and called after her, but not soon enough. She had disappeared through a door leading to the upstairs classrooms. Caitlyn, her cheerleading daughter, went to William Blount High School. My question echoed down the empty halls of Hilly Church, as the members affectionately called the place.

The other members were in their classrooms.

Smiling, I turned around. Some things never change. Bess would never be early.

I continued to look out of the double, glass doors toward the parking lot. Overnight, it had clouded up, and the leaden skies threatened to drop buckets of rain at any second—not a good sign on Memorial Day weekend, which was always designated the first official boating weekend in East Tennessee. I'd turned down an invitation to ride on a pontoon boat, do some fishing, and cook out on Tellico Lake later that day.

It's a good thing James didn't know about the invite. He'd have been greatly disappointed.

On holiday weekends, we didn't hold church on Sunday night, preferring the congregation to enjoy family time.

I might have gotten in some fishing.

Fishing was my favorite occupation when not leading music or performing other ministerial tasks. Bass tournaments were popular in East Tennessee. I was a novice at learning the art of catching the big fish from one of the other church members.

Today, additional problems crowded my mind. I wouldn't have enjoyed the lake. I'm glad I'd turned down the invitation.

Pushing open one glass door, I stepped outside under the roof of the passenger drop-off. The lot wasn't full. Several families had left on vacation as soon as school dismissed last Friday. Looking at the closest cars parked in the front row, I mentally named the occupants of each, coming to the last one.

Manda *always* parked in the last spot on the first row, closest to the office wing, where she usually entered the church. Her dark-blue Avalon was in its usual place.

"I didn't see her this morning," I murmured, realizing I missed her Sunday morning visit.

Manda was a ray of sunshine each time she entered my office, and she usually came by on Sunday before she went to class. "Strange that she didn't stop by." I laughed at myself. *Did I come outside to make sure she was here?*

"Well, she's here, Luke," I muttered, waving my hand in the humid air as I walked through the front entrance. I turned around to keep the heavy door from banging shut as a gust of wind blew against it.

Large, quarter-sized drops of rain splattered on the concrete outside. The sky-buckets turned upside down, and the wind blew sheets of rain under the overhang and against the door. Momentarily, hail rained down from the dark, gray skies. This usually signified a cold front moving into the Tennessee Valley, but in late May the drop wouldn't be very noticeable.

I buttoned my sport coat, shivered slightly, and caught a movement or reflection in the glass panels of the door.

The image revealed my prematurely gray, salt-and-pepper colored hair and dark eyes with crinkles at the side from smiling. An almost unnoticeable circle appeared under my eyes from a few sleepless nights of late. My face was more-or-less square. I called them squirrel pouches, those protrusions on each side of my short, pointed chin. They reminded me of a squirrel with two pecan nuts stuffed in their cheeks, one on either side—a sight I saw often in the Piney Woods of Texas, where pecans and oil wells were plentiful and where I was born. I wasn't unhappy with my looks, but I didn't call myself handsome, although some might.

A flash of lightning followed by a loud boom reminded me of the storm raging outside.

Rain and hail brought back many pleasant memories of Texas ranch living and some not so amusing—like when my family and I ran for our storm shelter as a tornado raged nearby. Or when I rode Scout, my horse, pell-mell toward home to avoid being drenched by a downpour or pummeled by ice. Years later, my parents had sold their ranch and moved into town.

The most important memory concerned Peggy. We'd gone to the movies to see a sob story—chick flick to be exact—and she'd cried. Go figure. When the movie was over, I steered her toward the front entrance. Rain poured onto the parking lot, and after waiting several minutes for the storm to subside, we dashed into the downpour and into the car as ice rained from the skies. The picture of her hair in wet strands, eyes shining with excitement, and red lips wide with a smile loosened my tongue.

"Will you marry me?" I'd said in a moment of deepest love. The hail beating on the roof of the car drowned out my words, but Peggy knew exactly what I said.

"Yes, yes," she shouted above the uproar.

I'll never forget that special night or the kiss that followed. Strange I should think of her this morning, with all the complications of the last few days, when my mind is consumed with thoughts of my brother's children and the decision I'd made to raise them as my own.

I sighed, thinking how quiet it was in the foyer, even though a storm raged outside. Surely, God was here. I often felt His presence while walking the many corridors of Hilly Church.

Even though I'm in His presence and trust Him in all things, I'm lonely. Lonely as a man can be who is alone. Yes, I have James to love, but it's not the same as having a companion to hold and love as a man should his wife. I'd thought about marrying again, but hadn't pursued the idea with passion, although I had someone in mind. The recent circumstances within my family caused the idea to become primary in my life.

"What a dilemma," I said to the reflection in the glass. "You should have said something to *her* months ago."

I watched the rain pelt the concrete. No one moved outside or inside. At fifteen minutes to ten, the choir members would quietly slip out and hurry to the choir room to practice this Sunday's special music. When the warning bell sounded at exactly ten, six hundred or more members would stream into the hall and fill the pews in the sanctuary. More than one hundred children would head for children's church. Fifteen minutes after ten, the church service would start. At eleven-thirty, everyone would be leaving the church for lunch, that is if Pastor Lane managed to end his sermon on time, which wasn't a given.

I wonder where the greeters are this morning? Two people usually stayed at each of the three main entrances, handing out bulletins, opening doors for attendees, and escorting visitors to classes or empty pews in the auditorium. Church security roamed the halls and parking lot.

I turned and headed down the main hall of Hilly Church, the heels of my high-topped, zipped-up boots echoing in the empty area. The boots reminded me of my favorite cowboy boots — the worn, comfortable ones I'd packed away and placed in the back of my closet at home. Putting them there was like placing my Texas heritage on hold for future reference. I always dug them out and wore them when I returned home to see my parents.

Passing the corridor leading to the administrative wing, I heard voices and saw several people headed in my direction. I waved a salutation at the lost greeters and security people, realizing they must have been attending a quick meeting in the minister's office.

I hurried on toward the music room and a coffee stand in the hall. Stopping, I poured a cup of high-test and mixed a bit of creamer into the black liquid. I need this, I thought as I stirred with a slender, red stirrer. I watched absentmindedly as black and white swirled together, blending until they became one color—like courtship and marriage.

"Luke, you've got a one-track mind these days," I whispered into the cup as I tested the hot liquid.

I blew on the surface of the brown mixture, then took a careful sip.

Taking the hot coffee, I crossed the hall and entered the music room. The patriotic music sheets for the sixty or so choir members needed to be placed on their seats. I busied myself with accomplishing this small task, noticing at the end of one row, several small boxes sitting in a corner.

One of my fellow students at Bible Theological Seminary, who was now the minister of music at a large church in the Dallas area, periodically cleared his shelves and sent his overflow of choir pieces to me. The mixed-up music sheets needed sorting before they could be used.

"Hum-n, I've got to ask Manda if she'll have time to help me sort through the new boxes of sheet music on Monday." I mentally made myself a note.

Manda was my proclaimed volunteer assistant. She'd organized and labeled the whole music department, and I had joyfully accepted her help even having fun on the occasions I could join her. What a pleasure to put my finger on any item in seconds. Not that I'm a sloppy person. My position included visiting the sick as well as helping with the seniors and children's worship. Somehow, I couldn't find the time to do everything. Organization in the music room lagged behind, and Manda supplied the time and know-how.

Finished with arranging the music, I sat at the piano and slowly touched the keys.

My sister Agnes had called that morning. "Luke, mother's worse."

This was exactly what I needed to hear on Sunday morning. I'd hurried to fix breakfast for my son, James, and when the phone rang, I was tying my tie in front of the bathroom mirror.

"When Pop missed her on Friday, she'd walked out of the house and down the street toward the main road. He was frantic, when he called me."

"Then she is worse. She hasn't done this before, has she?"

"No. Pop called me in a panic. I rushed over, and mind you, we found her sitting on the front porch of the pink brick on the corner in a rocking chair," Agnes had exclaimed. "Thank goodness, the people weren't home."

"Did she know you, Sis?" I sat on my recently made queen-sized bed, not sure how long this conversation would be or what course it would take. My sport coat lay beside me.

"Not at first, not until we brought her home and into her kitchen. Then she was fine, if you can call having dementia and going in and out of reality fine. I sat Pop down and had a long talk with him. He's finally admitted that she can't be left alone, but he refuses to make a decision that would mean placing her where someone could watch her each day. He's still determined to deal with it himself—no assisted living or nursing home for Mom."

"How did she get away from him?"

"Pop said he just went outside to water some tomato plants he was growing—five or ten minutes at the most. When he went back into the house, he washed his hands, and went to the bathroom. That's when he went to look for her and couldn't find her. Luke, something's got to be done, and I can't persuade him."

I heard the tears and concern in my sister's voice as she continued. "I'm afraid she'll hurt herself or leave a pot on the stove while in a memory lapse and burn the house down."

"It's hard for me to imagine Mom with the problem she's facing. She was our rock, our solid rock. She was there when Pop went on sales trips. There at our basketball and baseball games. She ferried us to and from school. She was always there. I feel like I'm losing the last earthly stabilizing force in my life, especially since Peggy died." My voice trembled with emotion.

"I'm sorry for your loss, brother, but Peggy is gone and life goes on." Agnes was good at stating realities. She continued, "I'm going to take the children home with me for the summer. My house will be crowded, but we can't trust Mom to keep them now."

"Thank you, Agnes." I hoped the relief I felt didn't show in my voice as I drew a ragged sigh. "I'm not prepared for them to come and live with me, not yet." I fiddled with the red alarm clock on my nightstand, moving it back and forth.

"I recognize that, but they'll need to move before school starts, because I'll go back to work. This is only a temporary solution."

"I know, I know," I'd said lamely, realizing the truth of her statement. So many important decisions needed to be made. "I'm working on it."

~

"Luke," one of my choir members clapped me on the back, bringing me to the present.

I started backward and almost fell off the piano bench.

"I didn't mean to scare you," said elderly Don Jackson, looking very apologetic as he grabbed to steady his music director. "What were you thinking about?"

"I *was*," pausing I looked straight at him, "I was looking at my new music and thinking Manda was going to have to help sort it." I stood and pointed toward the boxes in the corner. Maybe that wasn't all the truth, but at present, it was enough.

"Did I hear my name mentioned?" Amanda Tipton Puckett Weathers — or Manda, as she preferred to be called — smiled at us.

Both Don and I turned and stared at her.

I saw a woman in a summer-yellow, paisley print dress accented with blue, dangling earrings, necklace, and blue belt. Mauve lipstick lined her perfect mouth, and her sandy brown hair, with straight bangs, which touched her suntanned forehead, was pulled back behind her ears. Add wide brown eyes and a heart-shaped face and she was a vision of loveliness.

My heart skipped a beat. I hadn't seen her wear this outfit before, and I *would have* remembered it.

"What's wrong? Are you guys tongue-tied?" She looked down at her outfit, tugging at a seam. Her smile grew wider revealing her even teeth.

"No, sweetheart," said Don who was in his seventies. "I just wish I was twenty years younger and single." He laughed. Don called most of the lady's sweetheart. "Now, here's a young man who is single and 'bout your age." Don's statement *wasn't* uttered in complete innocence.

I looked at my choir member. Why did throttling Don come to mind?

I'm sure that doing away with a choir member is definitely not in the Scriptures, but I'm not going to let him use his seventy-five years and gray hair as an excuse. "Don that was entirely unappreciated and uncalled for." I might as well have said this to the clock face on the wall.

Knowing his words had accomplished their intention, Don looked out from under his bushy eyebrows at his embarrassed prey, a sly grin on his face.

Can he read my thoughts?

During the ten years I'd led the choir, Don's wife excused his motormouth saying, "My husband's tongue often runs into ruts and needs to be pulled out. Sometimes, I want to do it literally." At their fiftieth wedding anniversary, she'd pulled me aside and confided, "I've quit trying to warn him about his embarrassing statements." This was after he'd made several gaffes during the evening. Weird and discomforting moments seemed to follow the man around.

Both Manda and I blushed. "Take your seat, Don. You've said enough," I said abruptly. I stepped to Manda's side, took her by the arm, and led her into the music library where a table sat in the middle of the room. Looking back, I watched an obedient Don take his designated choir room seat.

"He never changes," I said, shaking my head.

"Aw, Luke, we're used to Don and his comments. Hilly Church wouldn't be the same without him. He always tells the truth, and no, he's not the least bit inhibited."

"Those are supposed to be assets, but in Don's case, well ..." I hurried on trying to cover my confusion about Don's statement. "I was just telling him I need help sorting the new sheet music from Dallas and hoped you might have some extra time available," I continued quickly, noticing Manda's amused look.

"Sure, I'll come in a little bit early tomorrow. We'll get it done."

The sounds of more arrivals and loud talking in the music room ended the conversation. I escorted Manda to the choir room and took my place in front of the group, rifling through the music on the stand before me. When I looked up, Don was grinning at me.

"Luke, I've sorted through my tools at home. I've got some extras. I'll bring them to you one day next week." Don always made amends for his blunders quickly.

I nodded.

"Okay, everyone, let's get down to business.

CHAPTER THREE

Manda

I arrived at Hilly Church a little past eight on Monday morning, having taken a quick detour by the beauty shop to make sure all was secure.

Pastor's office was empty with the light on. Luke sat at his desk. Everything appeared normal as I walked in. "Good morning, Luke."

"Manda, I was just thinking about you," he said, his chair rolling easily on the carpet as he stood and came around his desk.

"Are you ready to start the exciting task of sorting sheet music?"

Luke was smiling as we walked out the door and past the office of our pastor, who now sat inside talking on his desk phone.

Putting his hand over the receiver, he called as we passed his door, "Manda, it's nice to see you. When you finish in the music library, I have some new books that need sorted and labeled for our book library." He was kidding, of course, because other people manned our church library and bookstore. I helped on rare occasions when traffic was heavy or when a staff member was on vacation.

Luke paused, as we both stood framed in the doorway of our pastor's office. I had no way of knowing our pastor was taking a mental snapshot of the moment or that his matchmaker's juices were again stirred.

Luke said, "We'll be in the music library."

"Enjoy your day. I may come by to visit, before I make my run to the hospital."

Luke was quiet as we walked the tile-lined corridors. Our destination was on the other side of the church, through the foyer, and past several Sunday School classrooms. The sound of our footsteps echoed through the empty hallway.

I glanced at him from the corner of my eye. Normally, we would fill the long walk with light chatter. "What did James think about not going to school today?" I asked as we walked through the choir room into the music library.

Yesterday's storm had caused a large oak tree to fall across power lines near his school, knocking out electricity in the immediate area. According to news reports, crews had worked all night and were still in the area this morning. The reporter had said the problem should be cleared for school on Tuesday.

"We didn't even talk about it. He thought he'd get to sleep in this morning. He was a little disappointed until I told him he was going to Mrs. Docksets for the day."

Luke lifted the small but heavy boxes onto the polished surface of the table and helped me open them. He started removing the contents.

"Will she keep him for the summer?"

"Yes. She called and volunteered. And I forgot to tell James. I'm so forgetful lately." Luke seemed exasperated that he'd forgotten.

"He told me he likes Mrs. Docksets."

"Yes, he'll be perfectly okay with it."

"Mrs. Docksets is an amazing woman. She exudes love. The children recognize this, and they love her back. Even those who've grown up and married come and hug her each Sunday. I wish I could gain their trust and love as easily."

"Manda, some people would say you do just that." Luke looked across the table at me.

I read something different in his eyes this morning—an unusual gentleness—warmth I hadn't noticed before. Or had I?

The heat was on my cheeks as I blushed and dropped my eyes. "I love children," I said, electing not to analyze his glance and changed the subject. "I wonder if your friend in Texas has any sheet music left. We've unpacked several different songs—not to mention cantatas for Easter and Christmas."

Luke cleared his throat, jerked his hand in the direction of the tabletop, and answered, "We do have plenty. My seminary buddy has one-hundred-and-twenty people in his choir. I think I'll go phone the music director over at Johnson's Chapel. His choir isn't as big as ours and maybe he could use what we don't need." He hastily left the room to make the call.

That was abrupt, I thought, looking after his disappearing figure. What's going on?

A sudden feeling of disquiet came and went. On purpose, I became absorbed in sorting the sheets before me. I wonder why the music comes in such an unorganized mess. Are all music ministers the same?

I laughed. The sound echoed strangely in the room.

A different, business-like Luke soon returned. "Manda, let's pull out the *"Remember Me"* series of cantatas we sang last year. I'll take them to the chapel along with the overflow from this group we're sorting."

"I know exactly where they are." I walked to the floor-to-ceiling cabinets and opened two doors. "I'll need some help though." I was glad everything was back to normal.

Working side by side, the stacks for the choir grew higher, as we chatted and shared the relaxed companionship to which we'd grown accustomed.

～

Shortly after noon, I ate a leisurely sack lunch while Luke rushed to the hospital and the local medical transitional care units to visit sick church members and grab a bite to eat. He planned to deliver the sheet music to Johnson's Chapel while he was out. It was almost three o'clock when he returned.

"Did you give up on me?"

"Oh, no. Ministers usually arrive on time, but I've noticed their return home or to church after visitation is always iffy."

"It took longer at the hospital than I thought it would, and I needed to tell the pastor of Mrs. Griffitt's return. She fell at transitional care this morning, and her daughter thinks she's had a stroke. You're almost done," said Luke, a little surprised and glancing down at the bare surface of the table. "I'm sorry I didn't get back to help."

"This is the last stack." I walked to one of the music library shelves and placed it inside, pausing to straighten the pile and checking the rest of our work. I turned around smiling. "I'm not sorry the sorting is done."

"Do you have plans for later? I was thinking we might go to China Cuisine tonight for dinner."

I never made plans for Monday night, preferring to spend the time with Luke and James, and Luke always asked me.

"That's perfect." I would be glad to go there. The Chinese place was quieter and any conversation could be heard without shouting, especially if we went early, which we always managed to do.

"I'll pick you up about five-thirty."

"Are you rushing me out of the building, Mr. Avery?" I teased.

Luke's eyes and mouth smiled. "You know better than that."

Picking up my purse, I waved goodbye from the door. "See you at five-thirty," I called over my shoulder. I stepped around the tiered levels of the choir room and headed down the main hall. Luke's footsteps followed me to the choir room door. He was watching me leave.

～'

My mother and father were shelling peas on their glassed-in back porch. A ceiling fan cooled the area.

"Hi, girl," my father greeted me. "Pull up a chair and help pop-the-peas."

"That's exactly what I wanted to do on my visit," I teased him, laughing and looking toward the backyard of the large lot in the subdivision, where a huge garden grew in abundance. My parents supplied their neighbors and church friends with fresh veggies during the summer.

From the backyard, a faint outline of the Smokies could be seen through the branches of a huge oak.

"Oh, come on. You can help. You're good at this." Dad held up his hands saying, "My fingers are so big, they get in the way. We don't have many left to go." He gestured at the bushel basket sitting on the floor.

I peeked in. No, there weren't too many.

"I can't stay long." I pulled a wicker chair from its place at the table, where the two often ate breakfast, and made myself comfortable.

Dad got up and went to the kitchen.

Mom and I heard him rummaging through the drawers, looking for a knife and mumbling.

Mom shook her head. "Knives are easy to find around here, but he likes to search and fuss." Her expert hands flew over the pods, pulling strings, separating the halves of the pods, and stripping the small peas into her bowl. "Is everything okay, dear?" She assumed something was wrong, since I was visiting. She paused momentarily to look my way. Everything had to be okay for Mom to continue working.

"Life is beautiful," I explained, as Dad reappeared.

"Here we are," said Dad, cutting off our conversation and holding up a paring knife. "I had some trouble finding this little escapee. It was playin' possum behind an eggbeater." He handed me a bowl and some newspapers.

I spread the newspapers on my lap and set the bowl securely between my knees. I watched Dad's big hands scoop up a large amount of the long, green beauties from the bushel he'd picked that morning. He placed them in my bowl along with an empty container which rested on a table between my mother and me. "I think these are the best peas I've grown. It took watering them almost every day to get a good crop. Don't know why we're having such dry weather. *El Niño*, maybe?"

I picked up a pod from my bowl, broke it open and stripped the round green vegetable from its secure womb into my cupped palm. The peas I dropped into the empty container he had placed beside me. The hollow sound of them hitting the empty metal bowl was one I remembered as a young child.

We worked for a while, talking about family happenings until, "What would you both think if I married again?"

This bombshell caused my father to drop his paring knife in the floor, and my mother stopped shelling peas and stared at me.

"Well, this is a well-kept secret. Who's the lucky man?" Dad managed to say.

"There isn't one, yet."

"But there could be?" he insisted. He knew me so well—had since I was a little girl, getting into scrapes around the house and school.

I drew in my breath sharply. My hands were suspended in the air as I continued. "A situation has come up. I can't say more than that."

"My dear child," said Dad, "you don't marry situations. You marry a human."

"Are you in love with someone, Amanda? You're very mysterious about him." My mother always called me Amanda when she was shocked or angry.

I sat with my hands stationary over my half-empty bowl as she continued to stare. All work had suspended for the moment. "Possibly, maybe, I don't know." I ran my fingers through my bangs and looked up toward the revolving fan. "Mom, Dad, nothing may happen, but if it does, what would you think?"

Dad spoke as if thinking out loud. "Are we opposed to another marriage for you? We've gotten used to you being single, but your mother and I've discussed this possibility. You've waited a long time to decide to get marry again, and in the meantime, you've become rather independent, especially these last few years since Todd passed. As such, will you be able to include someone else in your life—change your life drastically? The poor guy would have to fill two very big shoes," my father observed.

He was right. I had made a life of my own and managed to handle any problem coming my way. "I've thought about this very thing. My Todd was the best husband one could ask for, and I missed him for so many years after he was gone. Now, all I have are sweet memories of his presence in my life."

We were back to popping peas, and Dad had retrieved his fallen knife from the floor. "Will this man measure up to your standards for a husband? That's something you've always been adamant about. What about the trust factor?"

"I don't think there's any question about his qualifications, and I don't think you two will have a problem with him."

"When will we meet him?" asked Mom.

"You already know him, but nothing may happen. I only wanted to keep you in the loop just in case."

"So, he's from church?" My father was grasping at straws.

"Yes, but we need to change the subject."

Dad grinned. "Talk about shock and awe. Our former president doesn't have a thing on you." He knew better than to press the subject and respected my wishes.

We continued to pop peas for several minutes, talking about the weather, their neighbors, and my work as a beautician, until my father decided to tell one of his rib-ticklers. "I know a funny."

"Oh, here we go." Mom, rolled her eyes.

"Now, Margaret, this won't hurt a bit."

"That's a matter of opinion, my dear." The last pea was popped and in the full bowl.

He continued, "Why did the elephant eat a light bulb?"

"Hum-m, why did the elephant eat a light bulb? I can't imagine. Was he hungry?" I put my hand to my mouth, thinking. "Mom, do you know?"

My mother smiled her knowing smile. Dad had already run this one by her, and she wasn't telling on peril of losing her life.

I gave up. "I have no idea."

"Because — because he wanted a light lunch. Get it. Light lunch." My father threw back his head and guffawed at my obvious stupidity. "Gotcha." He shot his finger gun at me.

"I'll have to remember that one for church Sunday. The children will love it." We sat in comfortable camaraderie for a few more minutes until I stood to leave.

I almost opened my mouth to say that Luke was coming, and I needed to dress for our dinner. But I didn't. I realized saying those words seemed so natural—like the normal thing to do.

Instead, I continued with, "See you Thursday." I hugged each one and left.

～

"Where's James?" I asked as I slid onto the soft leather seat of Luke's black Chevy Tahoe. I'd changed to black pants and paisley-printed, red blouse—an outfit I knew he liked.

"He's staying all night with the Docksets. Seems he had a great time today. Her grandson came over, and they spent time together reading, jumping on the trampoline, and playing games on the computer. And, they all went to his favorite Maestro's Pizza for lunch. I have to admit it's a bit unexciting at our house."

Luke started the truck and pulled out of my driveway onto the main road of the subdivision. The eating place was only minutes away.

The traffic was heavy on the main highway, and Luke had trouble changing lanes, so I didn't speak again until we'd parked in front of the restaurant. Luke came around to my door and opened it.

Wow, he looks nice in his open-at-the-throat white shirt and navy-blue sport coat.

"Lady Manda," he said, bowing deeply and giving a swoosh of his arm. "We have arrived."

Had he gone completely crazy? He was flirting, something he never did.

"Thank you, kind prince." I laughed, flirting back with the feeling of disquiet returning. During the day, our relationship had changed. Was it the reality I'd seen in his eyes earlier in the day? "I'm glad our carriage arrived in one piece."

"The horse traffic was a bit heavy, milady. Too many horses out there—horse power that is." He offered his arm as a group of passersby pointed and smiled at his antics.

"Twenty years ago, Maryville traffic wasn't so bad," I observed. "But our area has added new companies, and many people come here to retire. Being a bedroom community of Knoxville doesn't help either. I'm sure you've heard the residents complain that we need a bypass."

"Longview, Texas, is not far behind Maryville," Luke observed as we walked across the parking lot and down the sidewalk to the door of China Cuisine. "We do have a loop which helps alleviate congestion. Let me rephrase that. It's supposed to help with the traffic, but during the morning and evening rush hour the traffic still moves at a snail's pace."

Luke opened the door to China Cuisine, and a waitress asked to seat us.

"I've never been to Longview. What's the area like?" I asked, as we were led to a table.

Luke seated me, and we gave our drink orders. "Longview isn't like East Tennessee, that's for sure. There are no tall mountains in Texas unless you go to the Guadeloupe Mountains on the Texas-New Mexico border or Big Bend National Park on the Rio Grande, and Big Bend's seventy miles from civilization. You'd better have your tank full of gas when you head for Persimmon Gap.

"Where I lived, we have a few pitiful hills compared to the Smokies and lots of long-needled pines. Our wildflowers, although not the same varieties found here in the mountains, are well-known and beautiful in the spring. We have miles of driving trails where the best showing can be seen. Lady Bird Johnson, who by the way was born in East Texas, was instrumental in preserving the wildflower heritage of Texas and the nation."

"I've heard of and seen pictures of the Texas bluebells."

"We don't have many of those in East Texas. You'll find large fields of them in Central Texas, below Dallas. My mother always insisted on visiting the area when the bluebells were in bloom. We'd take a picnic and eat it along the way. Those were fun days."

"Is it a long trip to your hometown?"

"Less than a thousand miles. Eight hundred and fifty, I think."

Luke paused while the waitress placed the sweet tea on the table. After she left with their dinner order, he continued, "It's not hard to get there. I drive to north Georgia and into Alabama on I-59. This road connects with I-20 which runs west straight thru to Shreveport, Louisiana. When I reach Shreveport, I always get excited. I'm only a little more than an hour to home."

He was looking at me with that new special light in his eyes — the same one as in the morning.

"Where does I-20 end?"

"The road dead-ends into I-10 before you get to El Paso. I-10 stops in San Diego, California."

"I've been planning a driving trip all the way to the West Coast."

"Do I-20, and you'll drive right through the area where I was born and raised. Are you going by yourself? Isn't that dangerous?"

"No, Paw. And yes, I usually go by myself," I teased. "I don't do stupid things when I travel."

"How can you manage to take off so much time from work?"

"Being a beautician has its perks, and I schedule time off during slower periods. Other people take up the slack of my not being there. Most of them are grateful for the extra work."

"I've always wondered about your choice of career. You graduated from college with a BA in history to work on dirty hair?" Luke teased right back. "Shouldn't you have become a teacher?"

"My parents used to say the same thing. Guess I like making women beautiful. I make enough money, and I'm happy doing it. What else is important? Don't you do the same?"

"Yes, I do." Luke continued to smile, making slight dimples in his cheeks.

Pushed by an overhead fan, his aftershave floated in the air. My heart beat a bit faster as he continued to look at me with his dark eyes. Luke squeezed the lemon into his tea. The silence was punctuated with the tinkle of the ice teaspoon against his glass as he stirred.

"Do you plan on going back to visit Longview this summer?" I knew this was a loaded question, but I wanted to know the answer. Timidity doesn't solve problems, my father always said.

"I'll be going at the end of summer." Luke's smile was gone as he looked up at me.

I met his eyes without hesitation and wondered if he would tell me why he needed to make the trip.

When Luke didn't continue, I asked, "Can you drive to Texas in one day?"

"Yes, but it's a tiresome trip for one person. Manda, there's something I want to share with you." He leaned forward, elbows on the table, and hands clasped together. His voice was husky as he continued. "Do you remember when my brother, sister-in-law, and baby niece died on 911?" He waited for my answer.

"I do remember. It was a hard time for your family, because Peggy was close to delivering your son."

"That's true. My brother had three other children. They were with my mother and father in Longview when the plane crashed. My parents elected to keep them and send them to school there. It's been hard on Clint, Marcus, and Marybelle." Luke stopped to clear his throat.

"I can understand how they must have been hurt and confused. Surely, they've adjusted by now." I will not rush ahead and tell him I know the problem.

"They have, but something's happened, something that will tear up their lives again." When the waitress came with their food, Luke pulled back and waited.

The tinkle of silverware and rustling of napkins prolonged the disruption as we prepared to eat.

I tasted my food. "Hum-n, they make great General's Chicken. How's your Shrimp Kung Pao?"

When he didn't answer, I looked up.

He sat motionless, looking down at his food, his hands resting on the table.

Embarrassment flooded me at my lack of sympathy. I put my fork down and reached across the table. I placed my hand on his, and his long fingers wrapped around mine. "I'm sorry, Luke. What has happened?"

Luke squeezed my hand and held on. In the restaurant's dim light, I was sure his eyes glistened with tears.

"Will you excuse me for a moment?" Luke's chair scraped against the floor as he rose and hurried to the men's room.

My appetite for food suddenly vanished as I pushed my plate away. "How could you be so insensitive, Amanda Weathers?" I scolded myself. "Luke has hardly been himself all day. He's been quieter than usual." I sat patiently waiting until he returned to the table.

"This whole dilemma has me so upset," he said when he returned and seated himself. "I've agonized over it for several days."

"I can see that. Just tell me what's going on."

Luke drew a deep breath before he continued. "First things first," he said, looking at me.

"Peggy died four years ago. At first, I thought I would never get over it, but the Lord had other plans. He sent someone else to comfort me in my loss. That person has become more important to me each year."

I recognized the look he was giving me.

When I started to speak, Luke raised his hand, "Please hear me out before you say anything. If you stop me, I may lose my courage." Luke paused, trying to choose his words carefully.

"I don't know why I've waited so long to speak about my feelings for you. Guess I was content to maintain the *status quo*, or maybe I'm ready for Peggy to be a sweet memory in my life."

Again, I placed my hand on his.

Luke gripped my fingers and continued, "But now, I hesitate to say anything to you, because of the dilemma I'm in. Before you tell me I'm out of my mind, let me tell you what's happened. I've told you my mother has been acting strange, she's been confused at times. My sister, Agnes, you met her when she came to visit two years ago, she persuaded my father to take Mom to the doctor in Dallas. The doctor determined she has dementia. She's on medication, but her mental deterioration seems to be progressing rapidly."

I listened carefully as Luke echoed the words our pastor had spoken last week, and then he told of Agnes' conversation on Sunday. "She sat my father down and told him the certainty of the situation. There's no cure for Mom's problem. She will ultimately not know him or us, and she'll be totally dependent on round-the-clock care. But Pop's adamant. My parents decided years ago that they weren't going to a nursing home. They've heard so many horror stories about old people being abused and not cared for properly." Luke shook his head. "My father is a stubborn man."

I nodded, agreeing. Mutterings from my parents went something along the same lines.

"But that's not the issue I'm concerned about. It's my brother's children. Agnes packed them up and took them to her home in Kilgore. She's going to keep them for the summer, and I plan on bringing them home to Tennessee before school starts. Their permanent home will be here with me." Luke paused to let this news sink in. "Do you understand?"

I nodded. I wondered if the love I felt for him showed in my eyes as his was doing.

"Do you see why I hesitate to mention that I'm learning to love you. I've waited too long. I can't imagine any sane women wanting to get involved in this sticky situation." He placed his other hand over mine and held on. "So, here's the question. Is it possible ... or could we see each other with the idea that our relationship or courtship might become permanent? I'm not asking you to marry me, but to come to know me with the idea of marriage in the future. Could you ... would you ... consider this?"

Decision time was here, and I had weighed the pros and cons of the situation for days without coming to a resolution. My mouth wouldn't open with my response.

The silence was deafening.

"Please, say something," Luke pleaded as his eyes searched my face.

"Yes," I said, realizing that if my pastor hadn't spoken to me earlier, I might have said no, especially knowing the impact of becoming the mother to four children. But because of him, I'd had time to consider the idea of being married again and becoming a mom at the same time. The Lord works in mysterious ways.

"Yes, what," replied Luke, leaning forward.

"Yes, I would like to pursue your idea of a relationship or courtship with the possibility of marriage in the future." Did I say that, I thought after the words were out of my mouth? But Luke was talking—

"Thank you, God." Luke's head was down, but when he raised his eyes to mine, I saw that they were happy, and his face wore a huge smile. "I've agonized over the words to use when I talked to you. Even today in the music library, I wanted to blurt out my feelings for you, and my escape was to make the telephone call to Johnson's Chapel."

So that was why he'd left so abruptly. "Did you say I would be crazy to get involved in your life?" Manda teased.

"I did, but I hoped you might want to join me in my madness. Do you think I've made the right decision? To bring the children to Tennessee? The children understand their lives are changing, but I don't know how they feel about this second disruption of everything they hold dear. I haven't had a chance to talk to them face to face. Blending families may be easy or the most difficult thing I've ever done."

"Time will tell, Luke. But we will pray for God's guidance and lean on His promise to help in times of testing and change."

"Manda, I just felt a rumble in my stomach area. I think I may be hungry."

"Shall we eat?" I picked up my fork.

"Let's say grace," Luke replied. "Maybe the good Lord will warm up the food."

"Where's a microwave oven when you need one," I countered.

❦ CHAPTER FOUR ❦

Manda

Two weeks later on Tuesday, I walked out of the house into my garage. A blast of heat hit me squarely in the face. I punched the garage door opener and went outside. The thermometer read ninety degrees. The local news station predicted ninety-six for the day's high, unusual for middle June. "Thank you, God, that I don't have to work outside in this heat and bless those who do."

I opened my car door, deposited my purse on the passenger seat, and dug into my blue Capris for the car keys. Sliding onto the driver's seat, I started the car and drove across town to work.

Suds and Styles, a five-chair hair salon, was located in a typical strip mall, containing a large grocery chain store called Food Plus, Peter's Quick Pizza Delivery, and Your Personal Financial Services.

Customers who walked into the beauty shop saw nothing different from similar ones in the area. The customary waiting area contained out-of-date magazines and dog-eared hairstyling books placed on a convenient stand. The smell of shampoo, permanent solution, and hair spray permeated the air. The usual hair washing basins were at the back of the room. Each work area was neatly divided, giving some privacy to the operator and customer being served.

The difference in Suds and Styles and the other salons located in town was the personal, intimate service the hairdressers gave. Our ladies often put down their combs and prayed for customers, whose problems became known in the course of washing, cutting, or styling their hair.

I unlocked the door and opened the business to customers. Bells attached to the inside handle jingled to announce my presence.

The contrast in the outside temperature and the air conditioning inside caused me to suck in my breath. Looking around, I noticed condensation on the front windows and made a mental note to wipe it off.

Tuesday wouldn't be very busy. Most of the customers were walk-ins. I turned on the "Open" sign, the overhead lights, and walked to my much-cherished station at the back of the room. My low heels tapped on the surface of the black and white tile floor, echoing in the open, empty room with its high ceilings.

I'd earned my place at the back. Newly hired stylists were placed in the front positions. They usually handled the newcomers, trying to build up their own clientele.

Twenty years is a long time, I thought as I placed my purse underneath my work shelf and headed for the coffeepot. Taking out the coffee can, I measured the grounds into the white filter and placed the filter into its basket. The carafe I filled with water and poured into the top reservoir. Then I mashed the on button.

Picking up a broom, I quickly gave the floor a once over, answered the ringing phone, and checked the bathroom, making sure it was clean.

The smell of fresh coffee and my first walk-in customer greeted me as I returned to my work area.

At twelve o'clock, June Masterson, the shop's manager, joined me for the afternoon shift. "Have you been busy?"

"Three cuts and a style," I replied, as my last customer passed June coming in the door.

June was a long-timer also, having leased the salon for twenty-five years. Her station was the last one at the rear. She opened a drawer and deposited the "suitcase" she carried for a purse. She was fifty-five years old, tall, skinny, and a talker. She looked like an out-of-the-seventies hairdresser—wearing a pale green smock coat, matching pants, and white shoes.

When the girls kidded her, she always said, "I was trained in these clothes. I started my first job wearing them, and I plan on continuing to put them on each morning, period—end of discussion." Her red hair was streaked with lighter shades of beige.

I hadn't seen June's roots for so long, I couldn't remember her original color before she bleached and colored it.

June was a sweetheart, friendly and giving. She kept threatening to retire and *give* the shop to me—joking, of course. I was absolutely positive they'd carry her out of the place in a box some day in the future.

Suds and Styles was June. She created the ambience because of her Christian faith, which was plainly noted by the cross symbol on the door next to the bells. As the customer walked into the business, foul language and dirty jokes remained outside.

"I'm going next door to the deli at Food Plus to buy a salad. Do you want me to pick up something for you?" I asked, searching for money in my purse.

"No, I'm fine. I ate with Mom before I came to work. My mother makes the best vegetable soup in the world."

"How would I know? You didn't bring me any." I placed my hands on my hips and pretended to be indignant.

"I should have, Manda, but my mind's been preoccupied with Mom's medical problems." After several fainting incidents, June's mother had recently been diagnosed with diabetes.

"How is she feeling?"

"Not too bad, but she'd be better off if she'd eat the right kinds of food. Chocolate ice cream and New York cream cheese cake aren't on her diet. Her eating habits harken back to when dad was alive. He always had to have dessert after his meal. She still fixes something sweet when she invites us kids over, and she helps us eat it, even though we nag her not to cook it or eat it."

I nodded. "She'll get used to eating less sugar. Your mother is a strong woman who can handle anything."

"You mean strong-willed, don't you, but I hope you're right. Otherwise, she could have serious medical problems." June shook her head in resignation.

I stood at the front entrance, my hand on the door handle. "Sure you don't want something—coke, chips, a large hammer to use on Mom."

June laughed. "I think it would have to be a sledgehammer. No, I'm fine, but thanks anyway."

~

"Manda, how's your sweetie doing?"

I stood drying my hands on a multi-flowered, paper towel after finishing my lunch. "Do you mean Luke?"

"Of course, I mean Luke. It's not like there's a thousand men running around after you. Not that there shouldn't be. I just know you don't encourage any of the eligible ones of my acquaintance, like Brad Hixon. Whew, what a hunk. I only wish I were younger. Whoo, whoo." June threw her fist in the air and slung it round and round like she was turning an old-fashioned ice cream churn's handle, cranking the homemade kind.

"Oh, get over it, June. Brad's a…" There was no way to put it delicately. "Brad's a lady's man to use an old-fashioned term from *your* age group." Age group existed as a private joke between us.

"What's wrong with that? He's a real hottie, and that's a more recent term to describe a good-looking guy."

"You should be ashamed."

"Hey, just because I'm older than him doesn't mean I can't admire a good-looking man. I am unmarried, and I'm not dead."

We started laughing.

"To answer your question, Luke's fine. His schedule has been busy lately, and the pastor has him working on a lengthy project. He's directing a special cantata for July Fourth with speaking parts, so he's rehearsing the actors, making sure they learn the parts."

"When do you see him?"

"We do dinner Monday and Wednesday and, usually, Friday. On Sundays, we get together for lunch after church. He always calls me if for some reason he can't come. He gives me some space in our relationship. I need that after being alone so many years."

"Sounds so structured, unemotional …"

"No, not at all. I love to hear his voice on the phone, and we talk for hours. He's attentive, instinctively knowing exactly what I want or think. It's uncanny how we think alike."

"My husband and I were like that. Do you think couples grow alike as the years go by, and isn't it a wonderful feeling? Did you ever think you would find another soul mate like Todd?"

"Never. I felt fortunate to have loved once; twice must be ordained in Heaven."

"Have you told him that you love him?"

"I haven't even told you that," I stated forcefully.

"Aw, it's written all over your face. I can see that love-glow."

"It's true. I think I've been in love with him for some time."

"I always say, you must give yourself permission to love again, and especially after the wonderful marriage you had with Todd."

"Yea, verily, wise-on-love woman. I agree. It's true."

June laughed as she looked at me. "It's amazing how that feeling bubbles to the surface, and shines on someone's face."

"Really?" I looked in my hair station mirror. "I don't see anything different." I turned my head from side to side.

"Silly." June came over and gave me a quick hug. "You're not supposed to see it."

"Sometimes, I sit on my couch and wrap my arms around my knees, imagining that envelopment is Luke's love."

"He'll make a fabulous husband."

"Whoa, there. Don't get the cart before the horse. He hasn't even kissed me yet."

"Don't worry, he will."

"I think the protocol of being a minister will hamper our physical involvement, but being kissed and held would be nice."

"I love where you are in your relationship now. Once you admit your love to each other, the aura, uncertainty, and excitement of not knowing is gone. Your future together is established, and your thoughts turn to your upcoming marriage and completing your love."

"Wow, that's deep, June. I didn't know you had it in you."

"Huh. You don't know anything yet. I may write a book on L-O-V-E." June spelled out the word for emphasis.

"I want a signed copy."

June answered, "Okay." The front door bells jingled again. "Speaking of the eligible …"

Brad Hixon with all his good-looking male attributes walked in the door.

～

Around three o'clock the phone rang.

"Suds and Styles," June answered.

"How are you, Luke?" During a brief pause, June raised her eyebrows at me. "Oh, sure, she's here."

June placed her hand over the receiver. "It's your sweetie," said June, handing me the portable phone.

I made a face and took it. "Good afternoon, Mr. Avery." The minute I heard his voice, I knew something serious was happening.

"Manda, Mom's had another episode. I'm afraid this one will necessitate her children's involvement."

"Oh, Luke. What's happened?"

"It's a long story. I'll tell you tonight. This time, Dad had to call the police to help find her. I'll pick you up at six. Is that all right?"

"Rather than go out to eat, I'll cook. We can fix burgers on my grill. The only thing I need is fresh buns. I'll grab them here at the grocery store—and a dessert." I felt it was important for Luke to take a break. My den was blessed with a large overstuffed sectional—perfect for lounging in a relaxed atmosphere. We'd snuggle down, chill out, and watch TV.

"That sounds great. James and I'll be over at six. See you then."

I clicked off the portable phone and handed it back to June.

"Has something terrible happened?" asked June.

"I'm not sure. His mother must have gotten lost again. Anyway, Luke said his father called the police to help find her."

"It sounds like she's getting worse."

"Yes. It does."

The phone rang, and June answered it. "That was Luke. He said to tell you he'd pick up a movie to watch. Do you need to leave early, Manda?"

"Would you mind?"

"No. The afternoon's been slow. Go about four-thirty."

The front door bells jingled and another customer walked in for a haircut.

～

"You're early," I said after opening my front door to admit Luke and James. They were dressed in walking shorts, and James carried a ball and bat.

"We were just sittin' there staring at each other, so we decided to come on," James answered in his Tennessee drawl, while Luke stood smiling at us both.

"Come on in, so I can shut the door. This has been a scorcher of a day."

"Yeah, even Mrs. Docksets's dog was hot. Manda, you should have seen him. He went down and waded in the creek at the back of her house and came out slinging water and mud everywhere. Man, he was wet and dirty. She wouldn't let him come onto the screened-in porch. He was put out—went around with his tail tucked between his legs the rest of the day."

Luke laughed. "He was literally *put out*, son, so he pouted."

"I didn't know dogs pouted," I added. I hadn't had a pet in years. Working did not lend to having one unless you had a fence. I just couldn't see penning one up.

"Take my word for it, they can," said Luke as they walked into the den.

"Manda do you mind if I go to the upstairs bedroom and look for a board game we can play? And, I want to put my extra ball and bat in the entrance closet. We might want to play some later."

"Not a problem. Go ahead."

"It's too hot to play outside today, son." Luke's voice had finality to it as he shook his head.

"Okay, Dad," James nodded and headed for the stairs. "Manda, we'll play another time," he called from the staircase.

"Sure," I tossed after his disappearing figure as I returned to my kitchen.

Luke followed along behind me. "Something smells good." He put his nose over a pot on the stove which emanated smells of brown sugar, mustard, and onions. "Baked beans. I haven't had homemade ones in forever. Do you make them from scratch?"

"I do. I start with canned pork and beans and use my own easy recipe. The burgers are ready for the grill." I indicated the meat piled on a metal platter."

"You must have been busy today." Luke put his arm around me and gave me a quick hug, while checking out the rest of my preparations for our meal.

"Not, really. June let me leave work early, so I got a head start on dinner. I only need to set the table. Are you hungry?"

"I am." Luke picked up the burgers. "Where's the lighter for your grill?"

"Look in the middle drawer over there." I pointed to the opposite side of my kitchen and watched as Luke went around the center island to the exact spot I'd indicated.

Reaching for the gold knob on the cherry wood drawer, he opened it, rummaged around, and held up his orange-colored treasure. "I think this is it. Tennessee orange, hmm. I wonder if a transplanted Texas man can handle one of these."

I loved my kitchen. The convenient layout was what sold me on the house years ago. I could move quickly from counter space to stove to sink, and I loved the small window over the double sink. It overlooked a huge private deck where the grill sat. I waved my hand to indicate the window. "I'll raise the window, and if you need anything you can let me know."

Luke nodded as he rounded the center island, carrying the plate of perfectly flattened patties. He left through the French doors off the kitchenette, calling over his shoulder, "We'll have cooked hamburgers in a heartbeat."

I busied myself with placing the plates, silverware, and napkins on the table in my small dining room. From there, I could see Luke as he efficiently maneuvered the burgers on the grill—one hand on his hip and the other holding the turner. His movements in cooking the burgers were fluid, like when he directed the choir, smooth and sure. The confidence in his actions attracted me more than any part of his physical body or facial features.

I slipped through the door onto the deck. This would be a good time to talk about his Mom's problem.

Luke turned to greet me. He held out his hand to welcome me and encircled me with his arm. "How do you want your burger cooked?"

This was a first for us, cooking burgers together.

"I prefer mine medium-rare, pink in the middle."

"Me, too." Luke put the turner under one of the patties, pushing it out of the flames; leaping from the bottom of the grill.

"Do you need a squirt bottle of water?"

"No, I'll just move them around."

"I thought this would be a good time to talk about your Mom."

Luke dropped his arm and turned slightly to face me, but kept one eye on the cooking meat. He shook his head. "According to Agnes, my Pop has his hands full. Being here in Tennessee, I'm not exposed to the everyday happenings, just the most important or harmful ones."

"Does your father depend on Agnes?" I wondered about the other siblings.

"She gets the full brunt of major problems and hears a running report of each day's troubles. I feel guilty not being able to help more." Luke shook his head, again.

"Are you and Agnes close?"

"Of Mom and Pop's five children, we are closer." Luke thought a minute. "It's probably because our age difference is only two years.

"Who's the oldest?"

"My brother, Robert, who was killed when the plane crashed. Duane was born five years after him and three years lapsed before Agnes came along. Tony was born about three years after me."

"Do they live in Longview?"

"No, the others moved away like I did—all but Agnes. Her husband Mike works in the oil drilling business in East Texas. He follows the drilling rig, and there are times he isn't at home for a week or more.

Right now, he's working close by. Tony is in Houston and works as an engineer at NASA. Duane owns a business in Dallas. He lives the closest to Longview, but rarely comes home. He and Dad didn't get along."

"Why?"

"My Pop can be hard-nosed and stubborn. When he gets something in his head, he's going to have it or do it, and he laid down his brand of laws to his children. He and Duane had some knockdown, drag-out fights about mostly insignificant stuff. They never came to blows, but words ..." Luke lapsed silent, remembering.

"I've often wanted brothers and sisters."

"It's okay when you're young. But personalities emerge, and then the fun starts, especially when the family isn't rooted and grounded in Christian principles. My Pop never darkened the door of a church."

"So, what happened to your Mom?"

"Yesterday, Pop went to the drugstore to fill Mom's medicine. Mom wouldn't get out of the car and created a scene. Mom never acted like this before she got sick. So, to pacify her, he made her promise to stay in the car and left it running. It's hot in Texas, hotter than here."

"I don't like the sound of this already."

"Well, Agnes told me that Mom must have decided to drive next door to a gift shop she loved to visit." Luke turned to look at me saying, "Mom and I've been there many times, and it's only a few feet away from the pharmacy. They stock western and Navaho décor." He turned back to the grill and flipped the frying burgers. The sound of them sizzling and their delicious aroma filled the air.

"Anyway, when she got there and parked out front, she evidently couldn't remember why she was there. Instead of going inside, she must have walked out of the parking lot into the large subdivision behind the business. It's easy to do, because from where the cars park, a graveled walkway leads to this cluster of homes—maybe a hundred houses in all. She kept walking down the hot streets in the afternoon sun until she got tired and thirsty." Luke stopped, checking the frying meat.

I'd been watching his face. It alternated between sorrow and disbelief. And at times, an almost imperceptible shake of his head. He was having a hard time coping with the reality of the inconceivable words coming from his mouth. During his pause, he was turning something over in his mind.

I waited, not saying anything until he was ready to talk again.

"Manda, I'll bet she confused that graveled walkway with the one behind our house. It leads to a walking trail and park where she always took us to play and, later, her grandchildren to exercise."

"That sounds reasonable, but who knows what goes on in a muddled, cloudy mind? You and your mother were very close." It was a question and a statement. I felt like I knew the answer, but wanted him to confirm it.

James stuck his head out of the French doors. "Manda, can I turn on the TV?"

"Be my guest, honey."

The door shut, and James disappeared into the dark interior. Soon, the low sounds of voices floated through the open kitchen window.

Luke answered my question. "Very, very close. I didn't realize her favoritism until I was older. At times, her partiality caused a bit of jealously among my siblings. I always got the best piece of chicken or the front seat in the car, if it was available." Luke laughed.

"What happened next?"

Luke cut into a round patty and ducked his head to check its doneness. "Agnes told me the police's scenario. Mom found an unlocked shed behind one of the houses. Inside was a dirty fireside chair surrounded by all kinds of junk. She crawled into it and went to sleep. She'd walked almost a mile from the drugstore."

"Why did your Pop not know about her actions? Couldn't he see her from the pharmacy?"

"If I remember correctly, the prescription counter is in the back, so he couldn't see the car, and the pharmacist was busy. Dad told him his problem, but it took twenty minutes before the prescription was filled. When he came out, the car was gone. He panicked. He looked for the car in the parking lot, found it, and rushed inside the gift shop. Mom wasn't there. Realizing she could be anywhere and in the ninety-eight-degree weather she could become quickly dehydrated, he called 911. By the time they found Mom, every police officer in Longview joined the hunt."

"I can only imagine how your Pop felt. He must have been worried sick."

"He was. When Agnes arrived, she said he looked like a man life had beaten—ashen of face and desperate—terrified." Luke drew in his breath and let it out in a gush of frustrated air. He continued in a softer tone of voice. "I hate to think of Mom in this sad state of affairs. She's always been the foundation of our family and a strong woman in that way. She deserves better."

Manda stepped closer to Luke and put her arm around his waist. "How long did it take to find her?"

"After they organized the search—about two hours. The police called an ambulance and insisted she go to the hospital. The emergency room doctors kept her overnight. That was yesterday. Today, she's home again and lucid. Thank God for that."

"Yes, you can. So, what happens next?"

"I'm flying to Longview after the morning service on Sunday. The rest of my brothers will be there. On Monday, we've decided to confront Pop with his alternatives, and let him choose which one he likes best."

"Kind of an intervention, huh?"

"Exactly."

"What alternatives are you offering him?"

"We'll discuss that Sunday night. Agnes is checking them out this week." Luke moved to pull the burgers off the grill. "Time to eat. The burgers are done."

~

"Manda, it's eleven o'clock."

"I didn't realize it was that late." I stretched my arms over my head and got up from my warm nest in the den couch.

"Time flies when you're enjoying yourself. James, we need to head home." Luke shook his boy who had gone to sleep during the movie. "Here, go unlock the truck. I'll be there in a minute." He handed his sleepy son the keys.

James rubbed his eyes and shuffled toward the front door.

I picked up the TV remote and turned it off, following Luke.

"The dinner was wonderful and the company extra special," he said, pulling me to him in a gentle hug and letting his cheek rest momentarily against my forehead. "I'll see you at church tomorrow night." He let go and waved goodbye.

I shut the door.

The house was quiet, too quiet. I walked to my front window and watched the black Tahoe pull out of the driveway.

A tug, a longing I'd forgotten came over me as the truck disappeared from sight. It would be nice to have a man's arms around me again. I smiled as I turned off the lights and walked to my bedroom.

❧ **CHAPTER FIVE** ❧

Manda

I looked at my watch and at the line going through the checkpoint scanners at McGhee Tyson Airport. People took off their shoes, pulled computers out of their bags, and emptied pockets of change in preparation for heading through the arch. Occasionally, the foghorn alarm sounded rudely in my ear. I saw someone stop, turn around, and start the process again.

I remembered how it was before, when you, your relatives, and friends could walk to your gate and say goodbye. We never thought about bombs, terrorists, or killings. We'd saunter down the halls, rummage through the gift shop, or lounge in Tennessee rocking chairs, before our final leave-taking. Not now. Not ever again. 9ll changed all that.

I knew that 9ll had changed Luke's life too. He'd lost his oldest brother, sister-in-law, and baby niece. Even though he'd been at Hilly Church only about a year, our congregation had supported and encouraged him through the terrible ordeal. His son, James, was born shortly after.

I looked at my watch again. In ten minutes, Luke would head for Gate 5 and proceed through the line.

Where we stood, the windowed walkway slanted upward toward the scanner area, and several couples remained on the incline, each prolonging the inevitable goodbye. Luke and I stood about halfway, looking out the tall, glass windows. We watched the mechanics bustle around the airplanes sitting on the tarmac.

"I hope they're extra careful servicing my airplane," Luke said quietly.

I nodded, thinking the same thing.

The noise of the two waterfall fountains behind me broke into my thoughts. I turned to look and let their soothing sounds calm me. Twenty feet long, the level, open rectangles overflowed with cascading water. Green plants and round, gray rocks were arranged artistically in the middle of each tank. The falling water greeted travelers on their way to and from the airport gates.

"Luke, I wonder how hard it was for the workers to set those huge tanks and level them?" What did this have to do with today's happenings? It was thought-altering small talk. We both needed it.

Luke turned. His hand bumped my hand. He wove his fingers through mine.

A thrill ran through me. It was the first time he'd held my hand.

"I can't imagine setting them. I'll bet they held their breath the first time the water flowed to the top and over the edge." He fell silent, looking at the falling water.

I wondered if he was thinking about saying goodbye?

I remembered the last time I'd heard a waterfall's sound. In Cades Cove, I'd stopped at Rowans Creek on my way home from eating my KFC and listened to its rushing water. It was a favored spot, because in the years before the park was established, my family had lived there and known people who lived up and down the creek.

The stone masons at the airport had replicated the sound of rushing water but not the scenery.

I closed my eyes and saw the gigantic hemlock trees, making cool, shady areas underneath their drooping branches. The air was pungent with the smells of the forest. In the distance, gray-blue mountains overlooked the once plowed and planted fields. A small cemetery, sat out of place, stark and alone in the middle of the expanse.

I started to raise my arm to look at my watch, and realized Luke was still holding my hand.

"You don't need to look. It's almost *time*." He said the word time as if we would never see each other again. Luke dropped my hand and turned to look through the glass windows. I turned with him, and he put his arm around my waist.

Standing with my back to the stone art behind me, I glanced at the man beside me. He was the reason for that frantic trip to the Smokies. Was that only a month ago? It seemed like a lifetime. I thought about our relationship. I couldn't think of a future without him. "How quickly life changes," I murmured.

"Did you say something, dear?"

"No, just thinking out loud," I responded.

I'd taken June's advice and given myself permission to love again. Released from its bonds, my love for Luke had rushed to the surface from the depths of my heart and soul. The ferocity of its coming had taken me by surprise. No fetters, no strings were attached to its approach. Whatever happened in the future we would face it together. But Luke didn't know my decision yet. He hadn't asked that important question.

Luke's flight was on time. He needed to go.

I watched him as he picked up his backpack, placed it on his shoulder and adjusted the bag so it was comfortable. Inside were his computer and other personal items.

"I'll e-mail you while I'm in Texas. Thanks for keeping James while I'm gone."

"I'm sure he'll be spoiled rotten by the time you get back, especially if he goes to the shop with me. June will see to that."

We were standing, facing each other. For a minute, Luke hesitated like he was confused about what to do next. He took his free arm and placed it around my shoulders, guiding me a few steps in the direction of the checkpoint, and then he turned.

I thought he was going to hug me, so his lips met the side of my mouth.

"Goodbye, Manda. I'll see you Saturday." I saw that he was embarrassed after his awkward attempt to kiss me.

"Goodbye," I called after his retreating figure. And then I thought; that wasn't much of a kiss. I wanted one better than that. A kiss should mean something. "Luke."

He stopped and turned around.

The expression on my face must have told him volumes as I ran to him.

When he realized my intention, he slid his computer case to the floor and encircled me with his arms. I raised my face and felt his lips on mine. I was being thoroughly kissed. Gripping him tightly, I thought I might faint as he held me close. I'd waited a long time for this.

"I love you, Sweetheart," he whispered in my ear.

Angel talk out of Heaven couldn't have touched my heart more. "You are *my* Sweetheart, and I love *you* better."

"We'll discuss that when I return," he said, holding me to him. "I don't have time at this moment."

"I'll look forward to it, Mr. Avery."

Luke let me go and picked up his backpack. At the scanner line before he started to empty his pockets, he turned to wave goodbye.

❧ CHAPTER SIX ❧

Luke

I sat down in the crowded waiting area at Gate 5. In ten minutes, the Delta flight would load, and I would head first for Atlanta and change planes for Texas. Running my fingers through my hair, I thought about what awaited me on my arrival—Agnes for sure. And then there was my stubborn Pop. What would be the conclusion of this hurried trip to Longview?

Manda and I had prayed for the outcome which was in God's hands.

Shrugging off further reflection, I decided to change my focus and enjoy the flight down to my hometown. As a kid, I'd flown to visit my maternal grandparent's home in Tulsa, Oklahoma, where I spent at least a month each summer after school was finished. I found I loved getting on an airplane and flying to any destination. Even today's flight, with the clouds hanging over my head, I felt no different. I was excited.

Manda's kiss. Now that was thrilling. I'd held off for weeks not wanting to rush things until she was ready. But today, as she stood looking at me in her green outfit, I wanted to kiss her, and my awkward attempt at getting a little closer had landed askew.

"I love you better," she'd said softly. But I noticed, her brown eyes were filled with love before our lips met.

Seeing love in her eyes reassured me, and I let my pent-up emotions loose when I kissed her, holding her in a tight hug, feeling her warmth against me, and never wanting to let go. Ah … Manda. There was an important question I needed to ask her upon my return. I thought I knew her answer.

"We are boarding at Gate 5," the PA system broke into my pleasant thoughts as the rustling of the people around me indicated they'd heard the gate attendant's words.

I stood stretching my arms and legs to the amusement of a woman sitting across from me. I'd noticed her when I sat down, and we'd nodded to each other. She was gathering toys and giving directions to her two children, a boy and a girl.

She smiled in a friendly manner as she observed my exercise. "Better do it now. I think this flight's full."

"Sardines, huh. I've always wondered why they couldn't give us a little more leg and knee room."

"My husband says it's called profit." She laughed.

I nodded to agree and shouldered my backpack. "Are you going to Atlanta?" I asked, continuing the small talk, and being friendly.

"No, I'm going on to Dallas, then Kilgore." She stopped to look back at their former sitting place, checking for straggling objects.

"Really, that's where I'm headed," I said. "We should be on the same flight."

"Jacob, you've left your DS." She let go of her son's hand and gave him a push toward the seating area. "Go get it, and I'll wait on you. Hurry."

"Maybe we'll see each other later," I said as the line moved forward, and I walked ahead to the airline's ticket agent.

I checked out my flying companions as I entered the airplane and looked for my seat. One fellow traveler turned his carrot-topped head and watery eyes in my direction, giving me a friendly, toothy smile. I nodded as I passed, shoved my carry-on into the overhead compartment, sat down, and buckled my seat belt. Within minutes, we taxied down the runway and took off to the north in the opposite direction from Atlanta's Hartsfield-Jackson International Airport.

The prominent ALCOA tower, sitting on the Aluminum Company of America's land, disappeared out of view. Wendy's, Applebee's, and West Chevrolet passed by. A few minutes later, the airplane's wing dipped sharply right to head east and then south. The measureless Smoky Mountains stretched to the undulating horizon. It was a breathtaking view of white clouds, mountains, and lakes in the distance. Roads snaked across and around the hillsides. Flashes of water glistened in the tree-lined hollows and ran jubilantly toward the Tennessee River and manmade Loudoun Lake. West Knoxville drifted by on the right.

Atlanta, here I come.

∼

Two hours later, I shoved my backpack into the open overhead bin on the Dallas flight, noticing that another bag declared "I Bow Hunt." My sardine companion on the window seat was the red-headed, paunchy guy I'd seen on the flight from Maryville. He sniffed his nose, daubing at it with his blue-checked handkerchief, which he still held in his hand. A small, black Stetson rested on his knees.

Oh, wonderful. I'll have the flu before I get off this flight.

Hunched over with his elbows resting on the seat's armrests, his nose was buried in a *Sports Illustrated* magazine. I guessed the bag in the upper compartment belonged to him. Sliding into my aisle seat ripped his attention from the sheets he was reading. He turned his watery eyes my way, as I buckled my seat belt with a loud click.

"Howdy, Partner. You goin' to Dallas?" My seatmate sniffed again and jabbed at his red nose with his large bandana—Texas sized I thought—both of them.

"No. Longview," I replied, hoping I wasn't in for continuous conversation all the way to the Lone Star state.

"I've hunted around Longview. Piney woods, right?"

"Yeah, sure enough." I nodded to concur and pulled the flight magazine out of the pocket of the seatback in front of me.

My seatmate was silent.

I scanned the contents and nothing of interest jumped out at me. Folding the pages together, I replaced it in its hiding place, noticing the barf bag stuffed inside. Texas airspace was notorious for being rough and bumpy, but I rarely had any trouble with the roller-coaster ride through the Texas-sized storms. I left the bag and pulled out the safety sheet.

"Didn't find anything of interest myself," replied my companion, trying to restart the conversation. It was halted by the flight attendant's announcements of safety procedures. I checked the safety card and returned it to the pocket.

"Guess we aren't goin' to have a seatmate," the red-haired guy indicated the middle seat as the attendant made the last check, going up and down the aisle. Moving sideways, he placed the black Stetson and Sports Illustrated in the vacant area.

"I'm not unhappy about that. Are you?"

"No. My names Frank MacDill." He held out his hand. "Sorry, I have allergies." He indicated the handkerchief in his left hand. "I'm headed to Parker County — the city of Weatherford, Texas, to be exact. I have friends there who own a thousand acres of prairie and rolling hills. We're going to campout, chuck wagon style, on their fifty-acre lake and scout the deer and turkey population for huntin' this fall."

The planes jet engines roared loudly. My new friend was suddenly silent as we taxied down the runway. I leaned over to look out the window as the aircraft took off.

When the plane righted itself and the magnificent view of the Atlanta skyline was gone, I said, "Glad to meet you. My name's Luke Avery. So, do you bow hunt?"

"How'd you know? Oh, my bag in the overhead compartment." Frank answered his own question. "Yes, I've hunted with one most of my life. Lot's of skill involved in bow huntin'."

"I can imagine. As a young man, we did some hunting with rifles when I lived in Texas, but I prefer fishing in Tennessee. Seems bass fishing and tournaments are the outdoor pastime among the sportsmen there."

"Do you fish the Thursday afternoon tournament out of Tellico Dam?"

"Not much, I'm not that good." I could've said my fishing buddy always did, and that he won more than not. I went when his regular partner couldn't go.

"I do fish, but for crappie. They're good eating. Now, my pal over in McMinn County, his name's David, has a catfish pond, about three acres. That's about an hour's drive from Maryville toward Chattanooga. When he feeds them, they swarm to the surface, and they're easy to catch. I get enough for my freezer and come home. I help him out by buying fingerlings for his pond. Do you fish for crappie?"

"I have once or twice. My life is pretty busy."

"Really. What do you do for a living?"

"I'm the music minister at Church-on-the-Hill."

The airplane had continued to climb over the red-dirt hills of Georgia. The pilot came on the intercom and announced, "We're at 32,000 feet. We'll have smooth flying to Dallas. Arrival expected in about two hours. Sit back and relax. Enjoy your flight. If we can do anything to make your trip more enjoyable, please let a flight attendant know. Thanks for flying Delta."

As soon as the pilot finished Frank exclaimed, "Hilly Church! Well, I'll be doggone. I thought I'd seen you before. Been there a few times for special services. I know one of your members, Don Jackson. He's some kin to my wife."

"Yes, Don's in my choir."

"He always was a good singer." Frank thought a minute and, before I could say anything added, "And a talker."

Talker is right, I thought. But I decided to ignore this part of Frank's statement. "I need him in the tenor section. Where do you go to church?"

"Out at Johnson's Chapel."

"It is a small world. I know your choir leader. We have lunch at least once a month."

The flight attendant, serving snacks, interrupted the conversation. "Would you like some peanuts, Sir? Cola?"

"No peanuts, but apple juice, please. How about you, Frank?"

"That sounds good to me. Don't need to get peanut pieces under my teeth." He indicated a lower partial plate.

"What do you hunt with your bow? When's the season open?"

"October, and we hunt deer and turkey. The season opens on the same day for both."

"Do you eat the animals you kill?" I handed Frank his juice and napkin.

"Yep, we field dress the deer and take them to a processing house close by the Doc's place. The turkey we have smoked."

"Your friend is a doctor?"

The attendant handed me my drink and pushed the rattling cart down the aisle several seats.

"Sure is." Frank started laughing, "Dr. William Blind, works on eyes. Get it! Blind! Works on eyes." Frank guffawed, slinging his hand and almost upsetting his cup into his lap. He grabbed at the cup while several people around stared at him and me.

I felt a little warm from embarrassment. Frank was not perturbed.

When he settled down, I asked, "Does he specialize?"

"Yep, he's a retinal specialist. Well known, as a matter-of-fact. People come from several states to consult with him."

"How did you get to know him?" Somehow, I couldn't imagine Frank being the friend of a serious medical man, especially one with the meticulous but important job of working on a patient's eye.

Frank turned serious, "Aw, a buddy of mine started having trouble. Couldn't see out of his right eye. Well, he could see, but he didn't have all his vision. His doctor referred him to Doc Blind. They'd gone to med school together. My buddy's a senior citizen on Medicare. He couldn't afford to fly. So, I volunteered to drive him to Texas. We went twice. The second time, we stayed about a week. That's when the Doc operated to put a band around my friend's eyeball."

"I understand that's a tedious surgery."

Frank nodded. "That band's stitched in place. I'm glad my eyes are good." Frank shivered. "Anyway, the Doc put us up in his lodge. It's a beautiful place and set on a knoll amongst huge trees next to the spring and creek which feeds his lake. You can see several miles in all directions, and there's plenty of walking trails. And if you aren't into the foot thing, there's always a horse."

I sat watching as Frank squirmed his overweight body around in his seat and pulled out his billfold. Flicking out some cards, he handed me one. Mesquite

Lodge was emblazoned in blue on the white card with a list of amenities and the address. A picture on the back said it all. Double-storied with huge wood posts, it looked quiet and peaceful.

"Beautiful place," I said, as Frank replaced his billfold.

"You can have it." He indicated the card. "Maybe you can stay there in the future. Doc has a manager who takes care of the place. Lots of honeymooners take advantage of the huge rooms, and meals are included. He has a well-stocked library in the cavernous lobby and a cozy fireplace. I'd take my wife, but she won't leave Tennessee."

"Maybe so." I replied, thinking honeymooning was a possibility.

Frank continued. "While we were there, the Doc took me huntin' with a group from Fort Worth. Every year he asks me to come down and go scoutin' with him. We really hit it off."

The subject ended, and Frank was quiet.

I stuck the card in my shirt pocket.

During the lull in the conversation, the flight attendant picked up our trash.

"Frank, I think I'll close my eyes for a few minutes." I hit the chair lean-back button and listened as Frank continued speaking.

"Okay, Partner. I'll read the rest of my article." Frank opened his magazine and buried his nose inside.

"Sure," I said and closed my eyes, wondering if he couldn't see well and needed to see Dr. Blind himself. I smiled in spite of myself. It *was* a strange name for an eye doctor.

Hiding behind my closed eyelids, my thoughts continued with the coming events of the next few days. I would, of course, see the children. No, not *the* children, I corrected myself. They would soon be *my* children. Adoption proceedings were underway. This was important to me. For some reason, I felt the legal measures would make them truly mine.

Assuming this responsibility was a gigantic undertaking. I'd agonized over making the decision for several days, until I understood the results both good and bad of my choice. I knew from past talks with my mother that my brother's life insurance would help put the children through school and college. The transfer of these monies into an account I'd opened up for that purpose still needed to be made. They weren't at my house yet, and I didn't anticipate a problem with the exchange. Even with this money, there would still be significant financial responsibility, but I could handle that. I thought about my brother's children.

Clint was tall and lanky. He looked like his dad, who looked a lot like me. Anyone would think he was my son. Clint was sixteen with athletic graces in all sports, especially baseball. A natural pitcher, Clint's ease of motion drew the attention of men and women alike. On the occasions I'd had a chance to see him play, girls hung onto the chain-link fencing around the diamond, calling his name.

We would have that in common, because I was a star basketball player at Longview High School. I had my share of friends, including several admiring girls.

I'd noticed he was the self-proclaimed boss-father of the three siblings, even going behind my parents' back to control his brother and sister. I wondered what our relationship would be like. Was he ready to give up the father role and accept me as such?

Agnes's input would be valuable regarding his stay with her. She was a good reader of people.

Thirteen-year-old Marcus was a quiet kid who loved the arts. Controlled by his brother, he dutifully followed along behind him. If Clint was in trouble, so was Marcus. During my last Christmas visit, he'd taken a pencil and roughed out a decent likeness of me. Drawing wasn't the only thing he used a pencil for, he could write poetry. Not that he flaunted this talent. His big brother ribbed him about his verses, so he placed them in a locked box his grandmother bought him to keep them safe. She was the only one he trusted to read and critique them. Marcus was studious and made good grades in school. I could picture him as a future architect or artist.

Marybelle was a blond-headed, clinging sweetheart. At eleven, she was two years older than my son, James. I wanted them to be friends. When she smiled, the room and everyone in it lit up—like Manda's presence did. She was a helper and loved sticking her nose into every happening, especially if it meant coming to the aide of another person. Her parents were killed when she was two. Mom was the only mother she'd known, and Maryb, as everyone called her, was my mother's spitting image, even in her actions. Because my mother was a servant to her family and those around her. Leaving my mother would be hard on the young girl, but I hoped she would learn to love Manda. Their personalities were so much alike.

There I go, assuming Manda and I would be married.

The thought was becoming more and more comfortable, and I hadn't even popped the question yet. "Luke, that's on the front burner when you get back home," I admonished myself. I pushed on the armrests of my seat trying to discover a more comfortable position. The airplane engine hummed as I settled down.

∽

"Sir, will you bring your seatback to the upright position?" The flight attendant's hand on my shoulder and voice in my ear startled me.

"Sure." I groggily fiddled with the seat control, realizing we must be about to land. I couldn't believe I'd gone to sleep.

"Did you have a good nap?" asked Frank.

I gave a two-chuckle laugh. "I must have. Didn't know I was that tired." But I did feel rested. I felt the airplane dip as it glided toward the runway.

"It's been a pleasure talkin' to you, Luke. The next time I'm at Hilly Church, I'll come by and say hello."

"Sure, you do that."

The airplane's tires bumped the hot tarmac. I realized I'd missed the spectacular view of the Dallas skyline and the numerous blue lakes surrounding the city.

As soon as the plane touched down and taxied to the gate, everyone scrambled into the aisle to open the overhead bins and retrieve their possessions. I pulled out Frank's bag and handed it to him and then grabbed mine.

Several minutes passed before the debarking passengers cleared the aisle in front of me. Stepping back, I made room for Frank to edge in, and soon we were moving toward the nose of the airplane. We walked toward the overhead tram.

"Guess this is where we part company, Partner." Frank stuck out his hand to say goodbye.

"I enjoyed your company."

The last I saw of the I Bow Hunt bag, it was slung over Frank's back as he headed for the luggage pickup area. He'd found another companion and was talking excitedly as they continued together down the gateway. For some reason, I felt neglected.

❧ CHAPTER SEVEN ❧

Luke

The part I always disliked at the Dallas/Fort Worth International Airport was getting from the regular terminal to the puddle-jumping area. The hike through the crowded hallways to a bank of escalators, down the escalators, and into waiting buses was long. In the buses, standing room only provided room for the sweating, ill-mannered, and anxious, as we rode to the gates for the next leg of our journey.

At the smaller terminal, planes loaded and unloaded for short hops to Texas cities where passenger traffic did not require or the runways accommodate the big jets. Travelers, like me, left from the crowded, noisy waiting area and walked out on the tarmac to board.

Today the airport was no better, busy, inside and out. The propeller-driven airplanes loudly announced their coming and going.

Every chair in the waiting area was full. I would have to stand, or sit on the dirty floor. Service men in khakis, cowboys in ten-gallon hats, women with crying children, and dark-skinned Mexicans stood in desperation waiting for the next flight out. After the flight was loaded, those left behind made a mad dash for a vacated seat.

My layover was almost two hours. I stood looking around, wondering where the woman with the two children could be. Sighting them in the mob became impossible. To pass the time, I picked out interesting people to watch and study — a favorite pastime of mine.

A gray-headed man with an expensive cane and his elderly, highly-coiffed wife with a huge shoulder purse caught my attention. They stood arguing in the center of the floor. He was gesturing with his arm, and she was in his red, angry face. They were yelling loudly at each other. "How could you be so stupid," he said.

"I told you, but you didn't hear," she shouted, gesturing toward the full seats at a gate, the over-stuffed purse threatening to fall in the flour.

I wondered what on earth she had in there. Did I see a dog's head protruding from the top? I moseyed over closer. Sure enough, it was a dog's head — a stuffed one.

She grabbed at the bag as he continued, "I hear just fine. You should speak up instead of whispering."

"You've got the tickets. How was I to know for sure?" she responded. Sounded a lot like an argument they must have had many times before, but with a different subject. I expected to see the purse and cane flying through the air at any moment. The problem was obvious. They'd missed their flight.

I chuckled to myself and turned my attention to another passenger, or at least to three-thousand-dollar, alligator-skin, cowboy boots. Shiny, show-off pieces, I thought. I stared at them, and when I looked up the owner was staring at me. I nodded, and he nodded. His white Stetson bobbed up and then down. Glancing toward my feet, I looked at my scuffed-up cowhide boots. I wanted to stick mine back under a chair out of sight, but since I was standing up this wasn't possible. I crossed one leg over the other.

I continued to glance around the crowded room. A service man with his khakis stuffed into his army boots sat with his duffel bag clutched in his lap. I decided he was on his way home. I wondered if he had a girlfriend or wife waiting where he would land. I didn't see a wedding ring on his finger.

Someone walked through the crowd and extended their hand. I couldn't hear what they said, but the smile and embarrassment on the young man's face said it all. I did understand the mouthed words of the soldier as his visitor left. "Thank you," he said. I noticed he left on a flight to Waco.

Ah, there she is. The woman and her two children sat by herself away from the gate area. There were two seats so the young boy, who appeared to be about James' age stood nearby. Stood wasn't exactly right. He was walking up and down in front of the other two. I walked over to greet them.

"You made it to the gate area," I stated the obvious.

"Yes, we stopped at TCBY in the main terminal for something frozen and took a potty break." She smiled and drew a long breath. "I'll be glad to get to Longview."

"This is the part of flying I don't like, waiting like this."

"I agree," she responded, swiping at a spot on the older boy's pants.

"I'm Luke Avery. I'm the music minister at Church-on-the-Hill in Maryville, Tennessee."

"I'm glad to meet you, Luke. This is Jacob," she waved her hand at her son, "and Sue. I'm Joyce Taylor. I'm a house engineer," she laughed. "Means I'm a housewife. My husband, Dan, is the director at Nightingale Place in Longview. Jacob, please settle down," she turned her attention to her pacing son.

"Where's his DS?" I asked as a flight to Abilene was announced at Gate 4.

Mrs. Taylor waited until the loudspeaker quieted down and then said, "The battery is dead. He plugged it into the wall," she indicated the outlet. "I wonder if it's charging."

I went to check and Jacob followed me. "Sure is. Looks like you'll be playing again soon, maybe on the plane to Longview."

Realizing he was bored I asked, "Why don't we look around this terminal? We'll go upstairs and watch the airplanes as they come and go. Would you like to do that?"

"Awesome," replied the skinny, dark-haired kid.

"We need to ask your mother."

"She's my adopted mom," stated Jacob.

A little bit shocked at his divulging this intimate information, I bent down and whispered, "That means she loves you more."

"Sure, I know that." Jacob ran over to his mother to ask permission. His sister Sue immediately wanted to go along.

"Sorry, I didn't mean to cause a hassle."

"We'll all go." Mrs. Taylor got up and the group trouped up the stairs with their carry-on luggage. She found a seat, and I stood before the windows with her children. We watched the smaller aircraft as they taxied to and from the terminal. Time flashed by.

"Mr. Avery, I believe we need to go back to our gate. Our flight will load soon," Mrs. Taylor said this as she looked at her watch.

I helped her with her luggage. At the gate, she realized Jacob's DS had been forgotten during the excitement of going upstairs. "I have the hardest time keeping up with his game parts. I hope it's still there."

Jacob looked like he might cry at the thought of losing his game.

"Son, you're old enough to take care of your toys. I don't need to be reminding you to do this." His mother was tired and annoyed at her son. "You're going to lose your game. Remember your father said he doesn't intend to replace it. You will earn the money for the next one."

"I'll go look." I volunteered. It was right where he'd left it.

Walking back down the steps, he came running toward me.

Handing Jacob his game I pointed, "Look. It's charged up, so you can play with it."

His smile was a great big thank you. I gave him the thin black rectangle and charger. He opened it up to play.

"Not now, Jacob. Stuff the charger and game in your bag. You can play after we board." His mother waited until he'd finished, with placing the pieces in their black bag. "Here's your ticket. Don't lose it."

At that moment the announcement came over the PA system, "We are now boarding our flight to

Longview, Gate 3. Please have your ticket available for the agent at the gate."

~

"Nightingale Place, what is that?" I asked after we were in the air. Longview was about one hour away. The aircraft wasn't full. The vibration and roar of the engines was loud, but the Taylors and I juggled our seating arrangements until we sat within shouting distance.

"It's the newest assisted living residence in Longview."

"Really, does it have an Alzheimer's and dementia ward?" She had my attention. I needed to know more about this place.

"Yes. Unlike older facilities for the elderly, that special ward is separate from our main building and attached by a short, glassed-in breezeway."

"That sounds wonderful. I visit the ones in Maryville, and they're all included in a wing attached to the main building. Every once in a while, a patient with dementia comes through secured doors and takes a walk outside the building. Just because they have a mental problem doesn't mean they aren't smart. We've already seen that in my mother."

"Precisely one of the reasons for separating the buildings, especially if one of the dementia patients has a crisis. I've seen them carrying a doll and crying because the baby is unhappy, or lying down on the floor, and fighting the caregiver's gentle efforts to return them to the ward and their room. It's not a pleasant sight and very sad."

"I know what you mean. I was visiting Regal Place Home last week. When I drove into my parking space, one of the dementia residents was hurrying down the parking lot, carrying her suitcase. She was followed by two workers running after her. I heard her tell them, she was going home."

"You can't lock the doors, and you wouldn't want to lock them for their own safety. The key punch system keeps most of the patients in the building. But, when a resident learns to lean on the handle for fifteen seconds until the door opens, you can't unlearn them. Dan does his best to give each one a pleasant and safe environment. It's not easy. One new innovation for our facility is the ability for husband and wife to stay with and care for each other. This reduces the cost on the primary resident, gives the patient a companion, and makes for more of a home atmosphere."

"Where is Nightingale Place?"

"It's on the loop, out from Mobberly Baptist Church about a mile. You can't miss it."

"I know where Mobberly's located. I've been to church there."

"That's where we go now."

"There's a reason behind my questions. My mother has dementia. The family will be meeting this week to discuss our options," I paused and then added, "It's my father. He's stubborn."

"Many individuals don't want to admit someone has dementia."

"It's hard for me to accept." Six months had gone by since I'd seen Mom. I cringed from the scene I expected to find.

"Please consider my husband's facility. I don't think you'll find one better elsewhere. There is a waiting list, I believe."

For several minutes, we sat in silence. I looked out the window at the scene below, where areas of trees were followed by grasslands. I-20 stretched straight ahead bypassing Tyler, Texas. Tyler was the biggest city around Longview, and we were flying over it— only a few minutes until we touched down.

"Joyce," I turned back toward her to ask my question. "Jacob said he's adopted."

"Yes, both my children are adopted." She brushed the hair out of Sue's eyes. Her head rested in her mother's lap. The noisy airplane had lulled her to sleep.

I gave Joyce a brief history of my situation concerning my brother's children.

"My children are the biggest joy of my life. I'm not saying it's easy. Jacob has learning difficulties, and it took months before Sue adjusted to our home. Both kids were in and out of foster homes. I think the biggest problem was them coming to realize that the move to our home was permanent."

"Are they brother and sister?"

"No, no relation to each other, until we adopted them," she smiled.

"Taking my brother's children from the only home they've known for years and traveling to a different state won't be easy on them."

"Attention and love mixed with a heavy dose of prayer will get you through. I don't know how many times I cried out to God in secret, but every problem we solved was worth it. My advice is to deal with each difficulty as it comes to light, and don't make it any bigger than it is, because it's easy to do that."

"Sounds like good advice."

"Please make sure your seatbelts are fastened. We'll be on the ground in ten minutes." The flight attendant passed down the aisle as the plane slowed its engines.

"I've enjoyed meeting you, Joyce."

"And I you. I hope your stay will solve your mother's problem." She dug into her purse. "Here, here's my husband's card."

I placed it in my pocket with the one Frank had given me, wondering if God had placed Frank and Joyce in my life for a purpose.

The pilot brought the airplane in with a smooth landing and taxied to the gate.

I unbuckled my seat belt and helped Joyce with her luggage. She and her children preceded me thru the door and down the steps to the tarmac. The hot, muggy air of Texas greeted me as I headed toward the gate at Longview. I was—no, I couldn't say home. My roots were firmly embedded in the soil of East Tennessee. My adopted home was there.

"Luke!" Agnes came forward to greet me.

❦ CHAPTER EIGHT ❦

Luke

Agnes looked tired. "Sis, what's wrong?" I asked as we waited for my luggage at baggage claim. Instead of jamming myself into the midst of the crowd, I hung back toward the car rental area where it was quieter.

"I didn't sleep much last night. Mike's working in Weatherford, and Maryb had the sniffles. She was stuffed up and couldn't sleep. I was up and down with her all night." Agnes gave a weak smile. "It's not serious though."

"Have you eaten dinner? Maybe we can go to Barron's and relax."

"Wonderful idea. Maple roasted pecan salad and tomato basil soup sound great." I saw her swallow hard and knew she was already tasting these gourmet delicacies, especially the tart soup.

"That's one thing I miss. I haven't found a tomato basil soup that compares with theirs at home." I watched as Mrs. Taylor was greeted by a tall man in slacks, shirt, and tie. He looked at her through silver, wire-rimmed glasses. Jacob and Sue ran to him, and he bent to hug and kiss both. Mr. Taylor, I presumed.

Agnes noticed my interest in the foursome on the other side of the room. "I've seen him somewhere recently."

"Could it be at Nightingale Place? His wife and I met on the airplane. She gave me his card." I dug into my shirt pocket and produced the plain business card, handing it to her.

"I've got one just like it. I did like his facility, although I found it a little more expensive than the others." She handed the card back. "The dementia ward has some companion rooms where two people sleep separately but share a common living area. The single person rooms are nice. I can't imagine Mom needing more than that."

The baggage carrier jerked and started its noisy rotation. The Taylor's luggage was the first to come out. Mr. Taylor loaded a cart with several suitcases, and the group left through the sliding, front doors. My luggage appeared last.

Agnes had parked fairly close to the door. "Luke, we'll go by my house and pick up Mike's truck. He said to make sure you used it while you're in town. He filled it up with gas before he left yesterday."

Longview's airport is located close to Kilgore and Agnes' house was two miles to the west toward the small, once famous oil town.

I hefted my suitcase and backpack into the trunk of her car and jumped into the passenger seat. "Mike's in Weatherford?"

"Yes, he's digging wells into the Barnett Shale. He says Parker County is like a boomtown, building up along I-20 at a rapid rate. The noise and brisk increase in traffic from gas and oil drilling is causing multiple growing pains, and there's growing concern about drinking water contamination. Almost two hundred wells have been dug in the vicinity in six or seven years. Not all of them are his. Some of the local population have expressed mounting frustration over environmental concerns. I'm sure the business people appreciate the increase in money flow, but in one small community close by his operation, there have been problems."

"What kind of problems?"

"The residents have shown their anger by rocking his equipment. As long as they don't rock the workers …"

"Rocking his equipment!" repeating her words, I looked at her in astonishment.

"Yes. He doesn't think the problem will escalate further than that, but it's something I'm concerned about."

"I sat by a hunter on my way down. He's going to Weatherford to scout animals for the hunting season this fall. He didn't mention the area as an oil and gas producing area or that there were problems between the locals and the drillers."

"There are always problems between the locals and the drillers. I don't care where you go to dig. Reminds me of the energy-producing wind farms of West Texas. I can't imagine a quieter, cleaner way to produce the energy the United States needs. But I noticed there's another lawsuit in Mike's latest issue of *Energy News*." Agnes pulled into her circle driveway where Mike's Ford truck sat in front of the garage. The house was a two-story, white colonial brick, with a beautifully landscaped yard. Around the mowed area, oaks and long-needled pines grew in happy profusion. Under the trees, a long line of neatly stacked firewood stood ready for the winter.

"I don't know if this Chevy guy can drive a Ford. Guess I'll find out quick enough. Where is Clint, Marcus and Maryb? Here at the house?" I wanted to go in and see them if they were nearby.

"No, they're at the park along with my two. I dropped them off in Longview with Clint as chaperone. I plan to pick them up this afternoon after we eat."

"Has there been any discussion of their pending move to Tennessee?" It was a loaded question, but one I need to ask.

"Not to my face, but I've overheard grumbling within earshot. Things like leaving their classmates, missing church functions, and missing their grandparents. Clint isn't doing anything to improve his sibling's fears. But we'll discuss him later. I'll meet you at Barron's. Do you remember the way?"

"Of course, I do." I faked indignation, grinning at her suggestion I might forget a favorite eating place and climbed into the Ford. The motor purred when I turned over the key. I motioned for Agnes to precede me, and we headed down the road toward Kilgore. Halliburton was on the left, as we came to the stop light at the four-lane highway between the two cities. Agnes turned right and soon we went under I-20. A few miles later and we passed the shopping mall, Red Lobster, and turned into the strip mall where Barron's was located.

∾

"Luke, it's not one big thing. It's lots of little ones that combine to cause frustration when it comes to Clint."

I sat across from my sister, spooning my hot, tomato basil soup as she answered questions about my future children.

She continued. "I tell him to do something one way, and he'll find a way to do it another. The results are the same, so it's hard to jump on to him for disobeying you. But he is defying me—defying me subtly."

"Can you give me an example?"

Agnes thought for a minute. "This isn't the best example, but it's the latest one. Yesterday, I asked him to carry in firewood and fill up the brick firebox in the den. I told him to bring an armload at a time, and be careful not to get trash on the carpet. My instructions were simple enough without further explanation, so I thought."

"Sounds easy enough to me."

"Several minutes later, I checked to see how he was doing. Imagine my horror when he passed the door of the kitchen with Mike's contractor's wheelbarrow loaded with wood. He'd enlisted Marcus' help in moving the den furniture, holding the door, and getting the large load up the back-porch steps." She shuddered. "For sure, he was getting the wood inside, and he wasn't getting trash on the floor. And the task was done in record time, because he could carry more wood. He totally ignored what I told him and did the job his way. I checked the door casings and they weren't scratched. I didn't jump onto him, but he realized my frustration. He loves doing this sort of thing."

"So, you're saying it's deliberate."

"Yes, he's cleverly defying us." Agnes nodded. "He's a bright kid for sure and a great baseball player."

We both sat silent for some minutes, munching on our salads and spooning soup.

"How's Pop?"

"Don't ask. That's another problem."

"Why?"

"He's on his high horse. I had to tell him about our meeting. He's not a happy camper."

"Oh," I groaned. "I hoped we could keep this get-together from him at least until you, Tony, Duane, and I had a chance to meet."

"No such luck. Now, he's wondering why you aren't staying with them. He's insulted before you even see him."

"I have a feeling our meeting will not be pleasant — not pleasant at all." My full stomach contracted and suddenly a walnut-sized lump appeared in my throat. Even at the age of thirty-six, the thought of a confrontation with my father was cause for uneasiness.

"Why do I dread our meeting with Pop? We're only doing this to help him, not hurt him." I grimaced.

"Temper," said Agnes forcefully. "Isn't that the reason? I can't remember when he didn't blow up at the least provocation."

"It *was* frustrating, mainly because the reason changed weekly."

"More like daily." Agnes rubbed her forehead in a frustrated gesture. "Poor Duane, he always got the brunt of it."

"I'm not hungry." I pushed back my bowl.

"I was just thinking the same thing."

"Do you ever wonder how Pop always knows everything. It's like he has ESP."

"I've never figured it out either. It's one of the mysteries of the Avery family."

"I'm sure there's an easy explanation for his perception."

"Right under our noses." Agnes placed her crumpled napkin on the table. "Are we ready to go?"

"I'll pay the bill, and let's go back to Homewood Suites. We can talk there in comfort." The Suites was one of the nicest places to stay in Longview. A living room, small kitchen, and separate bedroom, plus a manager's reception each afternoon all combined to make it very comfortable. I'd never stayed there before, but I'd visited those who had. The welcoming food was enough to substitute for dinner. The tired traveler need not go out for food.

"I don't have much time. I promised the children I'd pick them up around five and take them out for pizza. Maybe you'll want to go with us."

Pizza didn't sound very good at the moment but seeing the children did. "Sure, I'll go."

∼

Back in Mike's truck, I thought about tomorrow's planned meeting with my parents. In a way, I was glad that Pop knew what his children were planning to do. He didn't like surprises either.

I remembered one surprise when he and Duane had it out. Duane was a sophomore in high school and wanted to start dating—had in fact asked one girl out for a movie on Saturday night.

My father always insisted we come to him for his approval on practically every life experience. It hadn't always been that way. When Pop was on the road as a salesman, my mother made decisions for us. At least that's what I thought. I didn't know until much later her decisions were always run by my father in such a way that he agreed with her.

Life in our family was always easier with him gone. Things changed when Pop sold the ranch, and we moved into town. He quit his on-the-road sales job which he hated and took a pay cut, working at a local hardware store until he became manager of the place. Most of the hostility in our family started with our move into town.

Duane knew Pop's law, and that's where the trouble started.

He hadn't asked Pop for permission to date, and he didn't have a driver's license. Duane had persuaded Mom to take him, trying to circumvent our father. He knew she would ferry him and his date into town, and she wouldn't tell anyone. Mom often took us to school functions so this shouldn't stir up any suspicion.

Somehow Pop found out. The ugly scene started on the front porch.

"What's this I hear about you taking a girl to the movies on Friday night?"

"I—I didn't think it was a big deal. All my buddies are seeing girls." My brother knew he was in big trouble—again.

At the first sounds of loud shouting, I ran to the front window, crawling upon the blue-striped sofa so I could stare at the scene outside. Pushing aside the sheer curtains, I looked through the glass pane, concerned about my brother. I always worried when I heard my father yelling. Someone was being chastised—usually

Duane. But instead of hunkering down or hurrying to my room, this time I watched.

I saw Duane's defenses go up, and Duane saw me.

"Big deal, huh!" exclaimed my father who had to raise his scepter of approval before any of us could breathe. "What made you think you could go? You haven't asked my permission to date. And how did you plan on getting there? Your mother?"

"Like I said, all my buddies are seeing girls. Their fathers don't seem to have any trouble with it." Duane was shouting at Pop.

"Don't you shout at me, young man!" Pop's voice was rising as well. "I'm your father, and I do care! And I don't like this sneakin' around behind my back."

"If you weren't so rigid, I wouldn't try to go around you. You say you care, but isn't that an excuse to rule over everything I do? I don't see you harassing Robert or Agnes. Don't you care about them?"

"Harassing, huh."

I could tell that my Pop was so angry he couldn't think of a comeback. There was truth in what Duane threw at him verbally, and he knew it.

"Dad this is crazy! I'm old enough to go out with girls."

"Crazy, you say. Get in the house. We'll finish this discussion later." And that's the way the arguments always ended. At least, until Pop chewed my Mom out and finished the argument by grounding my brother.

The door slammed hard as Duane hurried through it.

"And don't slam the door, Duane." My Pop was livid, as he appeared in the hall. The veins stood out on his neck and forehead, and his fists were clenched as he came through the door into the foyer of our home. No one approached him when he was in "one of his moods."

"Luke, get off the couch. Don't you have something to do?" He yelled at me as he went by toward the kitchen.

I sure did, and I decided to get to it. I pushed off the couch and hurried to my room.

My mother would get it next. Mom would stand and take it. I pictured her at the kitchen sink, tight-lipped, continuing to wash dishes. She would be nodding her head and listening to his ranting. There was no eye to eye contact. Soon, I heard a loud noise as he thumped his fist on the kitchen counter—the period at the end of the conversation, if you could call it that. My Mom never said a word. Without saying a word, she could agree or disagree and my Pop never knew her opinion. Years ago, she'd found out it was better to keep silent.

Why he picked on Duane I couldn't figure out, but I knew Duane was right. He didn't pick on our brother, Robert, who was out of the house in college at Waco.

I couldn't remember any terrible squabbles between Robert and Pop. Of course, I wasn't very old when he left for school.

Being the firstborn, Robert couldn't do anything wrong. Since it was several years before Duane came along, my oldest brother was almost like an only child. Robert, well, he was the standard or gauge for each child. He made straight A's in school almost without effort. He was good-looking, tall, making him a standout in athletics. His numerous friends ran in and out of the house.

In Pop's eyes, Duane never seemed to measure up to his oldest son. My Mom said Pop and Duane were just alike, and that's the reason they butted heads.

Agnes did a good job of wrapping Pop around her finger. At least, while she was young. Now, they butted heads at times. She refused to let him run over her. By the time Tony was born, my father had mellowed out ... somewhat.

Of course, Pop's giant foot landed on all of us at times.

~

"Uncle Luke, Uncle Luke," Maryb came running toward me. Because her attention was engrossed elsewhere, she tripped over a rock on the playground and fell head first.

I hurried toward her with Agnes close behind. "Maryb are you okay?" I eased her into a sitting position, looking at her knees and elbows and swiping dirt from her T-shirt.

Two shining tears waited in her eyes but didn't run down her cheeks as she smiled up at me. "Help me up, Uncle Luke." She raised her arms to be pulled upright to her feet, while brushing the two suspended tears from her eyes.

As I stood stooped over, still examining her for scratches or blood, she put her arms around my neck and gave me a welcoming hug. I felt a sticky wetness on my neck as I squatted to embrace her. "Are you sure you're okay?"

"Yes, I am. I knew you were coming. Are you going to take us back to Tennessee? I can't wait to see the mountains. Aunt Agnes has told us about them, and the Cherokee Indians, and the log houses, and picnicking. I can't wait to meet the lady in your church who makes doll clothes. Do you think she can make some for my doll? Do you think she'll let me help?" Maryb stopped to get her breath, and Agnes took over the look-see as I released my grip and stood back upright.

"So many questions for such a small girl. I hope you will let me answer them later."

"Uncle Luke, are you here to take us back to Tennessee?" This question came from Marcus who'd run from the monkey bars to check on his fallen sister.

"Not this time Marcus, but before summer's end. We haven't set a firm date yet."

Marcus extended his hand as a relieved look came over his face. He was at that awkward just-turned-teen stage.

"Are you too old to give hugs?" I asked him, suddenly realizing he probably didn't remember hugs from his father. I intended to change all that. I shook his hand but placed my arm around his shoulder and hugged him at the same time. "Where's your brother, Clint? Shouldn't he be close by?"

"That's what I'd like to know," said Agnes, standing up from her check of Maryb and looking around the area. "He's supposed to be here with you two."

"Over at the baseball diamond, playing with the other guys."

"Hum-n," said Agnes, staring pointedly in the direction of the team sports area.

"Why aren't you over there?"

"Guess I'm not big enough to play with them." This was uttered with a disgusted look on the younger boy's face.

So, Clint had left his brother out of the game, because he wasn't old enough. "Let's go over and see what's happening. Do you want to come, Agnes and Maryb?"

Agnes answered, "No, we'll wait here and swing. Is that alright with you, sweetie?" Agnes looked down at her charge.

"Gr-r-eat," said a smiling Maryb, who was into Tony the Tiger's cereal.

"We'll be back with Clint in a short time." Marcus and I headed for the ball field. "I'm ready to go for pizza. Are you ready Marcus?" Hungry, I wasn't, but spending time with them was on my menu.

"Yes, Sir. I've been hungry for hours."

"I thought your brother was to watch over you here at the playground."

"Yep. But he gets bored, and the other guys know he's a good ball player so they check to see if he's here and pester him until he goes with them. Maryb and I can take care of ourselves."

I wanted to say his older brother needed to follow his Aunt's instructions, but I decided it would be better to say this to Clint. No need to draw Marcus into the discussion.

The city of Longview is like Maryville. Miles of walking and biking trails have been developed for the enjoyment of its residents. Parts of the trails are paved for people with disabilities, so Marcus and I continued to the end of the blacktop and then took the gravel path to the ball field area.

From where we walked, I could hear the yells of the players and the distinct sound of Clint's voice.

CHAPTER NINE

Luke

When Marcus and I arrived at the baseball field, Clint acknowledged our presence with a curt nod of the head. He stood at home plate, tapping it with his bat and waiting for his first pitch.

"Clint, we're ready to go eat pizza," yelled Marcus. The words did not deter his brother from his game.

The ball hissed as it flew through the air. Clint drew back and with the ease of a skilled veteran who took his sport seriously, he hit a line drive into center field. Throwing the bat into the dirt behind him, he sprinted toward first base, legs churning like the pistons in a well-oiled engine. The ball took a crazy bounce off the fielder's glove, and Clint continued to second base, sliding in on his left leg with his right one touching the plate. Dirt and dust flew in all directions. He'd beaten the ball by inches. Standing up he dusted his pants and waited for the next hitter, a huge grin on his face and "attaways" from every side. A hint of arrogance showed in his smile and pride in his stance.

When the next batter drove his run in, he said his goodbyes to his teammates and sauntered over to Marcus and I.

"Hello, Luke," he mumbled. "Guess we better go eat pizza, huh Marcus." He clapped his younger brother on the back.

There was no apology and no more comment by any of us on his actions of the afternoon. I really thought this one was on the house. The next problem would be dealt with in an appropriate way.

After meeting Agnes and Maryb for pizza, she loaded hers and mine up in her car and drove home. Before she left, we decided to meet in my room at seven to discuss tomorrow morning's meeting with Pop. She offered to call and notify everyone.

I went back to the peace and quiet of my room at Homewood Suites. This gave me some time to reflect on the afternoon's happenings.

I couldn't help but admire Clint's athletic ability. He was definitely his father's son. I said a quick prayer. *Dear Father, I'm willing to do whatever it takes for him to be mine.*

Would I regret my promise to God?

My thoughts were stopped by the hotel phone ringing in my room. My brother Tony was on the other end.

"Hi Luke," his familiar voice sounded in my ear. "I'm here, checked in at the Suites. When are we going to meet?"

"Hey, brother. How was your trip?"

"Just fine. Ran into a bit of rain north of Houston, but the shower was brief. Talked to Agnes. She plans on being here at the Suites at seven."

Classic Tony, I thought. Get right down to business. Not much for small talk. "You're supposed to come here to my room at seven, but if you wish, you're welcome to come over now. I'm going to freshen up a bit. The Texas sun was hot this afternoon."

"I'll get settled in. I need to unpacked and call my wife. What room are you in?"

"Room 208. Have you heard from Duane? Is he here yet?"

"No, not yet. I talked to him on his cell phone as I drove up from Houston. He is on his way. Didn't leave 'til late. I don't think Duane's in any kind of hurry to get here."

"I can understand that. I'm not looking forward to this meeting either, but it's one of those sticky situations people have to face in life."

"Pop's goin' to think we're meddling in his affairs."

"He'd be right, wouldn't he?"

"Yes."

"Come to think of it, I need to call him."

"Okay, Luke. I'll be up in a few."

I hung up the phone, paced around the room and then pulled the receiver off its cradle. I punched in the familiar number. Because the landline sat next to his recliner, Pop was quick to answer the call.

"Pop, it's Luke."

"How are you, son?" This was his classic answer. So far, so good.

"Just fine. I'm actually here in Longview." I wanted to say more, but decided to take it slow and see what kind of reaction he had to each piece of information.

"I know you are."

Short and sweet, I thought. There was a studied calm in his voice. "I'll be over to see you in the morning. It's been a long day, and I'm tired."

"I see."

"How's Mom?"

"You'll find out tomorrow."

"Um, yes, I'll see you then." I hung up the phone. That was the strangest phone conversation I'd ever had with my father, and I didn't like it. He was angry with a capital A. This didn't bode well for tomorrow's meeting.

~

The knock on the door woke me up. "Just a minute," I called. The hot shower had put me straight to sleep. Sitting up, on the room's couch, I ran my fingers through my hair. My mouth felt like it was packed with sawdust. When I opened the door, there stood all three of my siblings.

"Come in, come in." I stood back to let the group enter. "Wow, how did you all manage to get here at the same time?" I asked as I shook hands with the two men.

"It wasn't easy," said Agnes, heading for the small kitchen. "Tony made it just fine, but Duane got stopped by a Texas state trooper. He has a ticket for his efforts." She deposited a manila folder on the dinette table. "Luke, I brought a carton of soft drinks. Do you mind if I fix us a glass?"

"Heavens no. Go right ahead. I need one, too. I checked and there's ice in the refrigerator." I turned back to Duane.

"What happened to you?" I asked, motioning for him to take a chair. He turned around and sat in the room's recliner while Tony and I sat on the couch.

"Duane, do you want ice in your drink?"

"Sure."

Our discussion was suspended while Agnes drew ice from the ice maker, filling up four glasses. She poured the cola over it and brought Duane the first glass.

"Thanks, Sis."

Soon we were all sipping our drinks. Agnes pulled a chair from the dinette and sat down to join the conversation.

"What happened?" I asked again.

"Aw, just one of those things. I was late leaving Dallas, and I was driving too fast."

"He couldn't talk himself out of this one." Tony grinned at his big brother.

"No, you don't live in Longview anymore." Agnes joined in kidding him. "Duane can turn on the charm most times, but this wasn't one of them."

"Agnes, I don't think it was charm. He knew all the officers." Tony took a sip of cola.

"Sorry about the ticket, Duane. How's business?" I asked.

"I'm covered up, Bro. Hired another worker, and I just bid on another job that'll keep me busy 'til the end of next year."

"What will you be doing?"

"It's an apartment complex in South Arlington— ten units of twenty apartments in each."

"Hmm, that does sound like a big job," Tony responded.

"It's a plum. I hope I get it."

"So, how's NASA, Tony." Three sets of eyes turned on their thirty-three-year-old brother.

"Well, I can truthfully say I'm busy. I transferred to the RATS program."

"The what?" asked Duane.

"NASA's Research and Technology Studies.

"Oh, cute. What do you do, set out traps?" Duane laughed a little bit too sarcastically.

Tony laughed with him. "No, we're into testing rovers and robots for human space exploration."

"Really, I thought Obama put all that on hold," said Agnes.

"No, only our Moon Base. The President is into deep space exploration so this fits into his plan. I've been to Arizona twice this year."

"What's in Arizona?" Agnes asked.

"Our testing lab and grounds. We want to cover all possibilities — not make any mistakes."

"Sounds really exciting." I chimed in.

"It is. NASA has come a long way since Project Mercury."

Duane ribbed his brother. "Have you got a patch, yet? I understand you can't do anything without an embroidered symbol on your shirt sleeve."

"Yes, Bro. We've got a patch. It's got a four-legged rat on it."

"Okay, okay, you two. Let's get down to business. I believe Agnes has some information for us. Sis?"

Agnes pulled her manila folder off the table and distributed the neatly stapled info. "Look at the top page. There are two options when it comes to caring for Mom. First, she stays at home with a home care agency, and Pop takes over at night. Second, she goes to an assisted living facility and receives 24/7 care in the dementia section."

"Don't our parents sleep in twin beds?" Duane interjected.

"Yes," answered Agnes."

"Then I'm not for Pop caring for her at night. He sleeps through thunderstorms, and he would never hear her get up."

"Could someone stay all night?" asked Tony.

"Sure, we can get someone to do that. But it costs more than staying at an assisted living facility. I contacted two of these home care agencies, and I also talked to three people in my church who selected these two. Care-at-Home received the highest rating, and Hope Resources was the other choice. When I asked for drawbacks with in-home care, several were cited. I listed them for you to consider." Agnes paused. "They're in order of importance."

"Dependability. Don't these agencies do background checks on prospective employees. I would think the comments of their former employers and references would satisfy the fact of reliability. I sure wouldn't hire anyone without doing a thorough check." Duane looked at each one sitting in the room.

"Can't cook. Are you kidding me?" said Tony.

"One of my church friends said the sitters are young, and most of them eat fast food, canned, frozen, or TV meals. Hardly anyone in the young generation cooks."

"Light housework." I started laughing when I read Agnes' comment following this listing. One friend said their helper's idea of helping around the house was "dusting the couch, and she didn't mean with a rag."

"Inflating their hours. Oh, my goodness." Tony's voice sounded incredulous.

Agnes explained, "Evidently, this happens quite a bit, and then the agency bills the client who must keep good records of work hours. Once the sitter is caught, he or she is fired, and you're back to square one, training another person to take care of your loved one's needs. One of the other people I talked to has had six people within the last year. One only lasted two weeks."

"As far as I'm concerned the first option is off the table. Do you all agree?" The others nodded in consent. I wasn't thrilled with what I'd heard. "What's the second choice?"

"The second preference is assisted living. Assisted living means Mom will have her own room and as many of her possessions as she can get into it. Each home will provide and charge for the services Mom needs. There are three dementia wards in Longview. Each has a different set of rules pertaining to caring for their patients, but the dementia rooms are basically the same, except for Nightingale Place."

"I sat with the director's wife on my flight here, and it sounds like a great place. Agnes says it's a bit more expensive."

"It is, but we'll discuss that in a minute."

"Sorry, didn't mean to butt in."

Agnes raised an eyebrow at me and continued. "The other two I mentioned are basically hospital rooms with no medical paraphernalia. The staff is adequate but not excessive. I went online, and there's negative talk about inexperienced staffing or lack of staff at times."

Agnes shuffled her papers and pulled out one. She read, "'Nightingale's ward is called The Unit. It's the newest one in Longview. The Unit is separate from the main building, providing privacy for patients and visiting family.

"Rooms are lined with lots of windows, letting the sun inside and giving you the feeling that you are living with nature. And, in the common area, a huge cage with beautiful, multi-colored finches help create the illusion of being outdoors. There are lots of ornamental trees and plants to be enjoyed and watered by the inhabitants. In fact, the residents are encouraged to help take care of their facility.

"The Unit is attached by a long breezeway to the main facility where nutritious meals are prepared, transported to their own private dining room, and served in a community atmosphere. Mr. Taylor gave me brochures to distribute to you."

Agnes stood and gave out the literature. "The other flyer is from The Pine's Convalescing Care, and the last facility didn't have any information other than its financial data. I'll give you a few minutes to look over the pages, and then we can talk finances." Agnes got up and started filling the empty glasses.

I followed her to the kitchen to help. "Sis, you've done a remarkable job in getting all this information. I know it's time consuming."

Agnes nodded. "As you know, when something important hangs over my head, I usually fly into it, hoping to finish quickly. This time I paced myself. Made appointments and left time in-between each meeting to study my notes and the information given to me by each facility. Luke, there's going to be piles of documents to be signed no matter where Mom goes."

"Sign your life away, huh."

"Yes." Agnes turned around. "Are you guys ready?"

"Ready and waiting," said Duane.

Agnes handed out more papers.

"The charges for Mom's stay depend on how much she can do for herself. As she becomes more and more incapacitated, they will increase."

"Mom will be able to take care of herself now, won't she?" asked Tony.

"Pretty much. Medications will be handled by the staff nurse. There may be times when she will need to be taken to the dining room, but not often."

I sat listening to the back and forth of our group. My decision was made.

"Luke, you're quiet," said Tony.

"Uh-huh, I've made my decision. I vote for Nightingale's, The Unit."

"Can Mom and Pop afford it? That's my question." Duane threw up his hand in a familiar gesture we'd known since he was a teenager.

"Getting information from Pop on their finances is hard. But with both Social Security checks, and Pop gets a retirement check from his first job, plus he's been frugal as long as I've known him. Yes, I think they can easily handle the money issue."

The discussion went on for several more minutes and Agnes took notes.

"Aren't you overlooking a third or even a fourth option, Agnes?" asked Tony.

"What's that?"

"She could live with one of us, or one of us could move in with her and Pop."

Agnes looked at Tony and then at Luke and Duane. "I don't believe we need to discuss those two seriously, do you two?"

Both shook their heads. Agnes continued, "Luke will soon have Robert's children in Tennessee. He's not married, so it's not likely he can take care of two more adults. Duane, you work odd hours, and I don't believe your wife would appreciate quitting her job. So that leaves you, Tony. Are you prepared to take Pop and Mom?"

Everyone laughed. It was a well-known fact that Tony's wife managed to get along with us, but I couldn't call her a big fan of the family.

"It was just a suggestion," said Tony, ducking his head.

"Are we ready to face Pop in the morning?" I asked.

"Is anyone ever ready to face him?" added Duane.

Everyone was silent.

"I think we need to let Agnes conduct the meeting in the morning. She's done an excellent job tonight."

"Oh, thanks brother. I believe we should all pitch in and that settles the question."

"Well, you have done an excellent job, Sis." Duane continued, "What time do we have to be there. I need my beauty rest."

"Ten sharp. Homewood Suites has a great breakfast. Do you want to meet, eat breakfast, and go over there from here?"

"Sounds good to me." Tony headed for the door. "Come on, Duane."

"Okay, I second the motion to adjourn this meeting. All in favor?" Hands went up and I headed everyone for the door. "I'll see you at breakfast in the morning — eight, okay?"

"Sure, I may have my eyes open by then." Duane walked out followed by Tony. Both waved as they turned the corner down the hall.

"Sis, tomorrow's another day."

"Why do I wish it was over?" Agnes smiled, as she stood in the hall. "Hope the kids are in bed. See you in the morning, Luke."

"Night, Sis." I watched as she went down the hall. "I'm glad you're my sister," I called after her. She threw up her hand, but didn't turn around.

I shut the door and tidied up the room. Our discussion had been civil with some sibling banter. *"Dear God, I hope tomorrow's meeting will be that easy."*

My second prayer this afternoon.

Then I remembered I needed to e-mail Manda. My laptop sat on the coffee table in front of the couch. I settled down behind it and accessed my mail. Answering the most urgent ones, including one from James, I turned to the most enjoyable task of the day. My fingers raced over the keys.

Dearest Manda, I started. *Do you know how much I love you?*

❧ CHAPTER TEN ❧

Luke

It seemed like Marty's Mini Market, owned by Marty and Betty Sue Watson, had been across from the entrance of my parent's subdivision forever. On the way to school, work or town, it became a family tradition to stop there and pick up a slushy drink. Today was no different. Mike's truck steered itself into the parking lot. "Come on Agnes, let's do our thing."

We both laughed as we unlocked our seat belts and slid out of the truck.

"Some things never change," said Agnes. "How long has Betty Sue been behind the counter taking our money?"

"Since Noah built the Ark," I guessed, while I held the door for her. We chuckled again as we entered.

"Betty Sue," I addressed the pleasantly plump lady who operated the cash register. "Has Pop been here for his daily dose of today's news?" I didn't stop for an answer, but headed straight for the slushy machine.

"Surely has, Luke, and your two brothers stopped by a few minutes ago. I hear you guys are having an important meeting this morning and need fortification."

I turned and looked straight at Agnes, raising my eyebrows and wondering why they'd shared such intimate info with her.

"Your Mom is getting worse, I guess."

"She does have serious problems."

"I wonder how much she knows about Mom's situation." Agnes whispered as we poured our sugar drinks from a large machine which swirled its contents and grumbled at us from the counter.

"Dementia is a serious problem in older folks these days," called Betty Sue, as we placed lids on our drinks and pulled straws out of a container next to the slushy machine.

"Guess that answers your question, Sis." I said this as we walked back to the counter to pay for our purchase.

"I wonder what percentage of us will deal with it in the future?" Betty's fleshy hands took my ten-dollar bill, flew over the register keys, and handed me my change without pausing. I knew better than to count it. She was always correct. Her mocking glare made her customers very uncomfortable should any question her proficiency.

"There are many origins of dementia. When I went on the Internet, I couldn't find anyone who'd venture a guess on a percentage. My speculation is that any estimate would be wrong."

"Will you put your Mom in Nightingale Place?"

Good heavens. What didn't she know about our family? She was a walking encyclopedia about the community in general. "That decision hasn't been made, Betty Sue." My hand was on the door handle. "Are you ready to go, Agnes?"

As I pushed open the door and my sister passed through, Betty Sue continued, "I hope she gets good service. Nursing homes are notorious for their problems in this area."

The door closed behind me, cutting off her further comments.

"Whew!" exclaimed Agnes. "I didn't realize how much she knows about our family situation. Do you suppose Duane and Tony shared our whole conversation last night?"

"Some of it for sure. But in their defense, she does have a way of drawing out the most intimate details. She asks good questions."

Agnes stood sipping her drink.

I looked at her. My sister was almost as tall as I. Her lipstick matched her fingernail polish, and her makeup was immaculate. She had blue eyes, and the sunlight brought out sparkles in her blond hair. Although she wasn't the most beautiful woman I'd ever seen, there was a certain air about her. Accessible and caring, this made her a desirable and attractive friend.

Neither one of us felt an urgency to leave. I made the first move. "I don't want to, but we need to head on to Mom and Pop's house. We may need to be playing referee at this very moment. I'm praying our meeting will be a smooth one."

"I've been doing the same thing all morning."

～

"Pop, good morning." I stuck out my hand as I walked in the door.

"Is it?" he responded and ignored my intended handshake.

So, this was how it was going to be.

"Luke, you're here. Your father said you were coming." My mother got up, as I headed toward her. She welcomed me, kissing my cheek. She seemed the same—normal, like my Mom. For a brief instant, I wondered why we were here.

I looked around the room. For several years, nothing had changed in my former home. Duane and Tony sat on the traditional-striped, blue-beige couch in front of the window which overlooked the front lawn and porch. Baby-blue sheers with a cornice and curtains shielded the inhabitants from the stares of outsiders.

A pair of brass candlesticks with blue candles still sat on the piano, where I'd practiced my piano lessons as a kid. A picture of each child in assorted frames and ages sat atop. I walked over and picked up mine, disturbing a thin layer of dust.

Pop's red leather recliner with a brass table lamp— blue lampshade, of course—was near the hallway, leading to the kitchen. Why Pop chose red for his chair was anybody's guess. It looked showy and out of place in the nothing extraordinary room.

A full bookcase separated his chair from two beige fireside chairs. They framed the red brick fireplace. Agnes and I headed for them. As I sat, I noticed the arms were slightly soiled. We made ourselves comfortable. Today, I realized comfortable was a relative word.

"Luke, how is your church and music ministry?" asked my Mom who sat in an overstuffed chair near the door. Her needlework was pushed into a woven straw bag with the words 'Visit Dallas/Fort Worth' emblazoned in navy on the side. She hadn't stopped looking at me since I entered the room.

For a second, I closed my eyes, sucked in my breath, and mentally shook my head. The woman sitting across the room from me looked exactly like Mom and acted like Mom. She appeared to be normal, but I knew she was not normal. Pain, anger, and love followed each other in rapid succession as I answered her question. "Our church is growing. We have new people joining almost each Sunday, and my choir is progressing nicely." I went on and filled in more personal details. When I stopped talking, an awkward silence filled the room. I looked at Agnes.

She cleared her throat. "Pop, you know why we are here—to discuss Mom's problem and try to iron out the details of her immediate needs." Agnes listed the latest incidences pertaining to my mother's erratic behavior. She talked about problems which might arise if something wasn't done—burning the house down if she cooked, leaving the water running and flooding the place, or trying to drive the car unaccompanied.

I listened as Agnes talked about the possibilities open to us. She covered everything we'd talked about the night before and then told of our unanimous vote for Mom to go to Nightingale Place. Through with her comments, she opened up the floor for discussion.

Until then, my father hadn't opened his mouth, and the closed, obstinate look on his face hinted at his position. Now he cleared his throat. "What makes each of you think that your mother and I can't make our own medical decisions?" He emphasized each word. "What makes you think I can't take care of her?"

Another moment of silence, and then Duane spoke. He was the oldest child present, and by rights should have expressed his opinion first, but his attitude and interaction with Pop started our discussion off with unrestrained lack of respect.

"I can think of two reasons. One, you've hidden Mom's medical condition from us even though you knew she was having problems," Duane stated. "Two—"

"I didn't know you cared, Duane." Pop sat forward in his chair, uttering his words in a sarcastic manner. "And how do you know this? You never come to visit." He stared at my brother through his wire-rimmed glasses. Their mutual dislike for each other permeated the air.

"Okay, okay," I tried to defuse the friction before it escalated. "Duane's busy with his business, Pop."

Tony hurriedly said, "I'm not sure if Duane was going in this direction, but when you are living within a situation, there's a chance you don't realize the seriousness of the problem. As the old saying goes, 'Sometimes you can't see the forest for the trees.' I have that on my desk, because it's the same at NASA. We call in an outside person to assess a particular problem. Then we get answers—good answers. I believe our responsibility is to be that outside influence in Mom's life. To give you advice, because not living in the situation, we see the dilemma a little clearer, and we can come up with a good answer."

Pop turned his accusing eyes on Tony, but before he could chew out his youngest son, Agnes spoke up.

"Tony's right," she agreed. "We're worried about Mom. We realize you feel you can take care of her, but after her exploits of late, that's questionable."

"We love you both and want what's best for you," I was quick to say, thinking that love was a word we never heard when growing up in this house. I'd never heard my Pop tell Mom he loved her. Neither had spoken this word to their children. It wasn't likely he would understand my statement.

Suddenly, my mother asked, "Luke, how's Peggy? I don't remember when the baby's due?" I wondered how that switch got turned on, but I answered her question with a future date and she smiled, got up, and wandered out of the room. We heard water running in the kitchen.

"Should I go check on her?" asked Agnes.

"Might be a good idea," said Duane still staring at Pop who stared back.

I sat there looking at each participant in the conversation, wishing the meeting was over. The situation was tense.

Agnes came back. "She was going to start cooking for us. Sounds like Mom. I convinced her to take a nap."

My father turned his accusing face toward me and continued, "Luke, if you love her so much why don't you come home and take care of her. You were her pet."

At least his attention had turned from my brothers.

"What's preventing you from doing that?" he insisted.

I answered with a calmness I wasn't feeling. "Pop, I've considered that, and I probably could for awhile." I chose my words carefully and continued. "But Mom is a woman. Soon she would have needs that I wouldn't be comfortable handling—needs that are best taken care of by another woman. And I couldn't sit in this house all day. I love to work. If I'm working, I'm not helping Mom."

"Then Agnes should do it. She doesn't work, and she's female." Pop looked at her. "I'll even pay you."

"Pop, I wouldn't take a dime from you." Agnes rubbed her eyes and face with her hand. For months she'd been doing triple duty, tending her family, helping with our Mom's problem, and fulfilling her church obligations. "Haven't you listened to any of our discussion?"

"Dad," I pleaded, "please be reasonable. She has to take care of her husband and children. Mom needs someone to watch her 24/7. She doesn't need to be left alone, even now when she's supposed to be asleep in her bed."

"Good grief! Pop reasonable?" snorted Duane who couldn't keep his mouth closed. "I'm so sick of this. Pop was never reasonable in his life."

"Shut your mouth, young man. You haven't changed a bit, and the rest of you are meddling where you aren't wanted."

Duane jumped up and looked fiercely down at his father. "You can't tell me to shut up, old man. I don't live under your mindless rules now." He'd stopped restraining thirty years of frustration over his father's rigid rules.

I had no way of knowing what he would say or do next.

"Please, please let's don't call each other names." I was on the edge of my seat, and I noticed that Agnes had taken the same position.

Tony was leaning back on the couch. His eyes were closed, and he was shaking his head. "Unbelievable," he muttered.

Pop got out of his recliner. He and his oldest son stood nose to nose. "Why don't we just take care of this right now? I'm tired of your mouth and your disrespect. My age shouldn't make a difference."

A belligerent Duane shouted back. "Sure, what do you want to do about it?"

Out of my seat, I pushed them apart and stood between them. "Stop it. You're both being unreasonable," I said as loud as I could.

Duane turned toward me. "I know you. You're a tattletale and spoiled brat! I haven't forgotten our wonderful childhood together. Togetherness! What a revolting word. In our family, togetherness was you and Mom with your heads stuck together over your homework."

"What do you mean by tattletale?" I looked at Duane for an explanation. I gave him spoiled brat, and I never turned away Mom's attention. And, yes, Mom helped me with my homework.

"You were always going around revealing information that got us into trouble." Duane sneered.

"I never did any such thing. I've always defended you and the others." How on earth did this conversation get sidetracked to me?

At this point, Pop decided to settle the argument in his usual manner, by getting rid of the object of irritation.

"Duane, you aren't welcome in this house. I'm asking you to leave." My father jabbed his thumb toward the hallway.

"With pleasure, and don't expect me to come back." Duane threw his hand in the air in a defiant motion and walked out the front door.

I hurried, following him to the porch steps. "Duane, I never snitched on you, never."

"Sure, tell it to someone who cares." He stomped down the steps and sidewalk, started his truck, and backed into the road. His squealing tires announced his departure.

I felt like someone had pulled a plug and drained me of all energy. I leaned against one of the porches supports. Duane hadn't verbalized this irritation with me before, and when I felt his annoyance, I never asked the cause. While I was young, I was afraid of him as much as I was of my father. They both yelled.

How would I prove to my brother that I hadn't told anyone of his dealings?

With leaden steps, I went back inside where the discussion had become a little more relaxed and civil.

Finally, Agnes persuaded Pop to let her put Mom on the waiting list at Nightingale Place. When an opening became available, he and she would make a final decision. Tony and I agreed to this solution, because this was as far as Pop would go.

Back in Mike's truck, I said to Agnes, who sat between me and Tony. "Well, that went great.

What happened in there?"

"Luke, I talked to my pastor last week. I had a heavy burden concerning our meeting. He said to expect the worst in personality conflicts to emerge in family discussions about a crisis like we addressed today. I knew it could happen. I hoped and prayed for the best."

"Pop and Duane are much alike," Tony observed. "I don't think they'll ever resolve their problems."

"Pop's rules were ridiculous at times, and he knew Duane would buck him. I think he caused problems between them so they could argue."

"I've often wondered what Pop's growing up years were like. He never talked about them. Could his father have been the same?" asked Tony.

"Families are known to follow cycles like that — habits passed from generation to the next generation. Guess we'll never know for sure." I made a left-hand turn onto the main road leading from the subdivision and passed the playground where we played as children.

"I once heard him tell Mom, she should be thankful. He wasn't a drunkard or hitter like his father." Agnes went on, "He probably didn't associate tongue-lashings and rigid rules as abuse."

"Agnes you've never told me that before."

"I didn't realize until this moment that we don't know anything about Grandfather Avery. I'll try to ask some questions in the future."

We were at the intersection to the subdivision. I stopped for the red light. Marty's Mini Market sat across the street. Suddenly, it dawned on me.

"So that's the answer. That's where Pop got his information about Duane's exploits."

"What are you talking about?" Agnes and Tony looked at me.

"Duane accused me of tattling to Pop and getting him into trouble."

"Yeah, he always told me to watch what I said to you. That you always ran to Mom or Pop with the news."

"You're kidding me."

"No, I'm not. I used to act like a clam and shut my mouth when you were around."

I was flabbergasted. "I never did anything like that, and I tried to tell him this on the front porch before he squealed his tires as he left."

The light changed green, and I turned left onto the main highway.

"Duane always did have diarrhea of the mouth, bragging about his adventures. Betty Sue was one of his confidants. When Pop went to get a paper, all he needed to do was ask a few relevant questions, or maybe not. Betty Sue, being friendly may have provided the information." I slapped the steering wheel at my discovery.

"When we get back to the Suites, we need to find him and talk to him. His schism with Pop mustn't go on. We never know what might happen, and I don't like disagreements like this hanging in the air." This came from Agnes, the peacemaker.

"Duane was adamant. I doubt he'll come around that quickly. Give him some time to cool off," I said.

"It still won't hurt to try."

When we arrived at the Suites, Duane wasn't in his room. I called the front desk. "He's checked out, sir."

After hanging up the phone, I turned to Agnes and Tony. "We won't be talking to him today. He's headed to Dallas."

"Just like him, rash and rushing," Tony commented.

"I wish we could have settled this. My guess is that he won't take my phone calls. He's stubborn like that."

"Agnes, I always got the feeling Duane didn't think he was measuring up. Who was he not measuring up to?" Tony asked.

"Robert," both Agnes and I answered at the same time.

"Why?"

"I've asked myself that a hundred times. I think Robert was the perfect child—good grades, good looking, good athlete, good mannered. Put good in front of it, and that was Robert."

Agnes added, "And Robert never caused Pop an anxious moment. Duane pushed the limits all the time. Tony, are you staying tonight?"

"No, I'm headed for Houston. I have an important meeting tomorrow afternoon."

"Do you have time for a quick lunch? It'll be my treat."

"Sure, Bro. Anytime you pay, I'm ready."

"Agnes?"

"We haven't eaten lunch together in a long time. Of course, I'll go."

"Let me take a pit stop. How about you guys? Do you need a bathroom trip?"

Later, as we went out the door of my room, Agnes said, "Luke, you'd better go over to Pop's tomorrow and make sure the money is transferred for Robert's children. It won't be long until they'll be headed to Tennessee. Let me know when you're going, and I'll go over and stay with Mom."

In the struggle over Mom during the morning, I hadn't thought about the children, and she was right. I didn't plan on being back in Texas until December. She and Mike were bringing the children to Tennessee. I nodded in agreement.

"I'll plan on coming to see them tomorrow afternoon. By the way, can you go with me to the mall? I have a specific errand to run."

"Sure. Why don't we combine the two? Pick me up before the children get out of Vacation Bible School. We'll run your errand, and then you can take them out for dinner."

"Sounds like a great plan. I'm sure they will have questions to ask. I know I would. I want to spend the afternoons with them before I leave."

"Are you still thinking of staying until Saturday. Mike may come home in the morning. I know he'd like to see you."

"No. I think I'll head home on Thursday. At the proper moment, I have an important question to ask somebody."

❧ CHAPTER ELEVEN ❧

Manda

Luke's e-mail said he was coming back on Thursday; two days earlier than he had planned. I would be working when he touched down at the airport, so our pastor volunteered to pick him up and take him home.

I was excited and eager to see him. Our relationship had changed dramatically at the airport. How long would it be until he asked that important question?

"A classic courtship," June exclaimed, when I told her about our words at the airport. "A couple or three weeks and I'm positive he'll ask you to marry him. I predict a Christmas wedding."

"That sounds reasonable. I can't see any reason to wait longer."

"Of course, it's reasonable. When's he bringing the children to Tennessee?"

I started laughing. "Marriage and instant children! Do you know how funny that sounds? Children are usually a year away. Unless, you're Abraham Lincoln. I read a book which said his first child was born almost exactly nine months after he married Mary Todd. I bet everyone was counting on their fingers."

"Not this time, sweetie. If they do, they'll come up short. These aren't babies, and you're having triplets."

The word triplets sobered me up.

"Oh, I shouldn't forget James." June added. "That makes it a quartet. Are you worried about how you will handle four kids?"

"I am *wondering* about our interaction. I hope my participation in our youth programs at church will give me a basis to understand their problems."

"It won't hurt. It's like being thrown into the river when you can't swim. You'll learn fast," June paused from washing the dirty combs at the sink. "You'd better learn fast."

"Luke's last message said Agnes and Mike were bringing them just before school starts. That should be sometime toward the middle of August. Luke's idea was to keep them busy with school so they wouldn't get homesick."

~

On Thursdays, Suds and Styles was a beehive of activity. Four stylists were hard at work. Today, I'd leave Suds and Styles at four-thirty in the afternoon. Tomorrow was the longest day for me. I wouldn't leave the salon until after eight.

The day had been a scorcher outside, and each customer complained about the excessive heat and humidity. My normal trip to the next-door deli proved that.

It was almost my quitting time when the front door bells announced another customer. With my back toward the door, I didn't bother to look over my shoulder. June stood at the front, making an appointment for one of her regular customers. She'd take care of the walk-in patron.

I stood teasing Mrs. Whithall's gray-blue hair into its familiar position. Putting it into layers and pulling it toward her face. I couldn't remember how long I'd done her hair—at least ten years. Hard of hearing, I leaned over close to her ear and chatted with her about an upcoming senior event at the new Clayton Center on the Maryville College campus. She was my last customer, and I couldn't wait to finish her hair and get home. I was sure Luke would come by my house tonight.

I felt like a giddy school girl, anticipating seeing her boyfriend after they'd declared their love on their last date. What would we say? How would we act?

I stood and patted the back of Mrs. Whithall's hair into place, looking at her in the mirror. "How's it looking?" I said loudly, knowing there would be some little something I needed to rearrange. She always made a suggestion each week.

She smiled at me and turned her head from side to side. "Don't you need to make the bangs a little fuller?"

There wasn't much to work with on the crown of her head, but I turned her toward me and adjusted the hair resting on her forehead.

It wasn't until I felt two arms steal around my waist and his warm cheek on mine, that I realized Luke was in the room.

"Hi, Beautiful Lady," he said softly in my ear, his voice trembling with emotion. His arms held me tightly against him.

Guess that answered all my questions. "Luke, Luke," I exclaimed, struggling to turn around in his arms. His blue shirt became a blur within my vision as I pressed my face against the soft cotton surface. "I didn't know you were going to come here."

"I wanted to surprise you and ask you for a date tonight."

"You did, and yes," I said. "I'm almost finished with Mrs. Whithall's hair style."

Luke sat down in the closest chair, and I kept working as he told me about his flight home and his plans for the evening. When I was finally through, I handed my client a large mirror so she could see the back of her hair, slowly turning her in the chair. I was so excited at Luke's presence, I was trembling.

"It looks wonderful, Manda. You always do such a good job. Will you put me down for the same time next week?"

I walked over to the counter that ran down one side of my cubicle and penciled her into my appointment book. She handed me the exact sum to cover her hairstyle and then another bill for a tip. I noticed her gratuity was generous, as always.

"You're set. I look forward to seeing you on Thursday — same time, same station."

"Is this your boyfriend?" she asked, as she picked up her large, multi-colored pocketbook and placed her billfold back inside.

Luke jumped up and waited to be introduced.

"Oh, I'm sorry. This is Luke Avery. Since he just asked me for a date, I think you could call him that." I looked at Luke, teasing him with my eyes.

"It was nice to meet you, Mr. Avery," said Mrs. Whithall with a slight bow of her head. "Manda, I'll see you next week."

I gave her a quick hug and watched as she started through the work area, greeting each stylist politely as she passed.

"Here, Mrs. Whithall, let me help you to your car." Luke rushed to her side.

"Why, thank you, young man." She took his offered arm, and I smiled. She'd already forgotten his name.

While Mrs. Whithall left escorted by my *boyfriend*, I picked up a broom, swept the floor, and tidied up my work area.

"June, I'm leaving. I gave my space a quick clean. I'll come in a little early tomorrow and do a better job. See you in the morning." Grabbing my purse and extra shoes, I hurried to meet Luke at the door.

"Have a wonderful date, Manda." June whispered as I passed the front desk.

I flung my hand into the air to acknowledge her comment just as Luke opened the door. "I'm ready to go," I told him.

"Bye, June," he said, waving.

We walked toward the parking lot. The heat off the blacktop was unbearable.

"I hope we're going somewhere cool."

"How about your favorite place, the Smokies?"

The mountains were good for a ten degree drop in temperature. I always rolled my windows down as soon as I passed the park entrance sign. The difference was amazing.

"I'm not sure that would be cool enough today."

"Take your swimsuit. I've got mine. I believe a quick swim will cool you off."

I could tell he was chuckling at the thought of me shivering after a dip in one of the Smokies cold streams. He was right. The chilly water of a Smoky stream would do the trick.

"I'll need to take my car home. I assume were going in the Tahoe."

"Yes, we are, and I will follow you. Our dinner is in a warming bag in the back seat along with drinks on ice. James is at Mrs. Docksets for the evening. We aren't in any rush the rest of the day."

"Have you been planning this a long time, Mr. Avery?"

"Hmm, maybe." Luke eased into his truck. "See you at your house."

~

"You passed the entrance to Cades Cove."

"Yes, I did."

I rolled my window down and poked my head out just as the road led off to the right.

"We aren't going there?"

"No. It's cooler where I'm going."

I turned to look at him. The Cheshire cat would have been proud of the look on his face. "Okay, where are we going, Mr. Avery?"

"You'll see."

Metcalf Bottoms, Elkmont Campground, and the Sugarlands Visitor Center passed by. Luke turned right and headed for Newfound Gap. Several minutes later, he pulled into the Chimneys Picnic Area.

"My dear, we will eat and cool off here."

By now, I was hungry as a bear, *again*, remembering my struggle in Cades Cove after my former talk with Pastor Lane. "I am famished." I hopped out of the truck and went around to the other side to help. Before I would grab something out of the back, Luke encircled me in his arms.

"I don't believe I've welcomed you properly."

He hadn't. At my home, I'd gone in, rushed to gather up what I needed, and piled all into his truck, including me. I didn't say a thing. His lips were on mine. The kiss was long as we made up for the time apart. Standing within the circle of his arms was the safest and most comfortable place I could imagine. His cheek rested on mine as he said quietly in my ear, "I love you, Manda Weathers. I believe you wanted to discuss that with me."

I grinned, remembering our conversation at the airport. "Not yet. Right now, my stomach calls."

"Lady, you know how to deflate a man's ego. I thought you only cared for me." Now, he laughed as he handed me our picnic food. We headed for a table and spread our feast. Each time we touched; joy filled my heart. He was everything I wanted or needed in a man.

Sitting together on the same side of the table, we made ham sandwiches, spooned out hot German potato salad, and hot baked beans.

"This is delicious. Did you come home and make dinner?" I found his food making in such a short time hard to believe.

"Like old George W., I cannot tell a lie. Mrs. Docksets was kind enough to come to my aid. She cooked."

"This is her famous baked beans. I should have known, and the potato salad?

"Kroger's," he said and grimaced. "Found out, for sure."

"So, you *did* plan all this."

"Yes, my darling," he said, ducking sideways as I took a playful punch at him, and gave him a gentle nudge in the ribs.

After eating, we took time to catch up on the happenings of the last few days, details hard to put down on paper, which needed to be discussed verbally. I saw his hurt as he talked about his brother and father's rift and Duane's accusation of his snitching. There was hope in his voice, at his father's softening attitude, toward placing his mother where she would be safe. And the children, his smile as he talked about his hope for them said it all.

He cautioned, "Clint may prove difficult, but we'll address his problem — if it happens — one situation at a time."

We changed into our swimsuits in a nearby park restroom.

As I came out, the Chimney's stark and barren rocks stood out against the sky. I walked to the road's edge and craned my neck upward. The climb was straight up at the summit, and a hiker needed to be in good shape to reach the top. My father and I had hiked the mount, eating a mashed cheese sandwich and boiled egg in celebration of the finished climb.

Down the road from where I stood, a flicker in the sunlight made me turn my attention to a bunch of small, pale-blue butterflies, flying over a wet patch around the water fountain. They dipped and soared, lighting momentarily to poke their proboscises into the damp area, and then they were off again, flitting in the rays of sunlight, coming through the dense growth overhead.

Our swim in the stream, flowing close by, proved to be cold and quick. The river, shallow, because of no rain, made swimming out of the question. Stretching out in the water, allowed our bodies to cool off without the exercise of thrashing our arms and legs. After several minutes, lips turned blue and chill bumps appeared on our extremities.

"Whew! The water's like ice." I sat on a rock in the sunshine, drying off with a soft towel, watching the boiling white water as it tumbled over hundreds of rocks. Luke was close enough. I didn't have to shout over the noise of the rumbling water. "But it certainly does its job of cooling you off."

"Doesn't the water feel great? You won't find anything like this in Texas." Luke pulled himself out of the water and sat on a rock below me. The cascading water rushed over the rock he sat on, giving him a continuous shower, and sending thousands of droplets sparkling in the sunlight.

"Really? I can't imagine not being able to swim in ice water."

"We have lakes and swimming pools where I lived. That's all." Luke moved onto the rock where I sat. He grabbed his towel and started drying off. "The water's warmer, because the air temps are warmer. You wouldn't want to swim in our rivers."

"Let's go change clothes and drive to the top."

"How did you know the rest of my plan?"

"I didn't, but I like it."

A few minutes later, we were back in the Tahoe, heading for Clingmans Dome, refreshed and ready for the climb to the top. Over a mile high, it was a place I loved to visit—the highest peak in the Smokies.

The road from the Chimneys Picnic Area to Newfound gap is curvy, the scenery breathtaking, and the grade steep. We gained several hundred feet in elevation as we drove along. Reworked by the Civilian Conservation Corps in the thirties, many of the pullovers still sported their handiwork. Stacked and cemented gray stone walls acted as a safety barrier to keep uncontrolled motorists from plunging several hundred feet down steep embankments. Those same walls held the road banks and kept them from eroding.

We'd already passed the famous hiking trail to Alum Cave Bluffs and Mount LeConte before we stopped to eat. Chimney Tops Trail was just beyond the loop-de-loo, as my family called the circle where you drive over yourself, after we pulled from our eating area. Every hiking trail in the area was well used, including the Appalachian Trail. Luke and I would step on it at Clingmans Dome.

"I just read that nine million people visited the Smokies last year."

"Several of those are here today," Luke observed as the traffic snaked down the mountain past us from Newfound Gap, heading for Gatlinburg. "Guess it's time for the bright lights of the city after being in the mountains all day. Gatlinburg's always so crowded."

Minutes later, we passed Newfound Gap, where President Roosevelt dedicated the park after it was created and where the Charlies Bunion trailhead lead off into the dense forest.

"Luke, have you hiked to Charlies Bunion?" We'd found out walking or hiking was an activity we both enjoyed, although during our short courtship, we hadn't had time to do much but walk around my subdivision. Of course, with this weather, I preferred to walk in the spring and fall. The temps were much more pleasant.

"No. Is the walk strenuous?"

Luke bore right, onto the road leading to Clingman's Dome. Continuing on Route 441 sent you into Cherokee, North Carolina. The Dome road was a dead-end road.

"I thought it was, but someone in better physical condition would be okay with the steep elevation and rough, rocky, root-filled footpath."

"Guess I'd better not try it. My muscles are vegetating." He had both hands on the steering wheel as he negotiated the sharp curves.

I sat back in the Tahoe's comfy seat, and we continued for several miles, enjoying the scenery.

He broke the silence. "This is the most beautiful drive in the world."

"I think you mean breathtaking, don't you?"

"Yes, breathtaking is the better word."

Every curve spread a new vista before us. Mountains piled upon mountains, stretching to the horizon and beyond.

I'd seen it all before, but seeing it again was like reliving an awe-inspiring symphony, or inspirational movie, or the miracle of birth. I never got over the experience or used to the grandeur. Surely, God had enjoyed making these mountains as much as we enjoyed the experience of seeing them.

"Are you too tired to walk up to the tower?" Luke asked.

"I wouldn't think of not going, and I want to visit the visitor center. It's new, you know."

Clingmans Dome Tower sat on the summit of the mile-high-peak. Three hundred and sixty degrees of uninhibited viewing awaited those who walked the half-mile, steep trail to its position on the mountain.

"I doubt the welcome center will be open, and it may be dusky-dark as we come off the mountain trail. I brought my small flashlight just in case."

Parking proved not to be a problem, and Luke was right, the visitor center was closed. I borrowed his flashlight and used it to illuminate the inside. I could tell the store was well-stocked with books and other souvenirs of the East Tennessee area.

"Come on, Sweetheart," he said, taking my hand. We headed up the paved path side by side, walking at a slow pace, because the thin air tests your stamina and lungs. I wasn't in a hurry, and neither was he.

Along the trail and against the sky, the graying trunks of hundreds of once green-needled Frasier Fir Trees stuck their denuded, dark spires above and amongst the dark, laurel and rhododendron vegetation—a harsh reminder of the wooly adelgid invasion which was killing the graceful-limbed trees by the thousands in all parts of the Smokies.

"The park service is fighting a loosing battle at present when it comes to stopping the spread of that menace," Luke commented as he squeezed my hand. "Too many square miles to cover."

The park was spraying several thousand acres of timber in a valiant effort to contain the fuzzy, white invaders.

I didn't respond. I was content to listen to the sound of his voice.

At intervals, loud people, talking in an animated, happy manner, passed by us on the way to the parking area. Stopping at one point to catch our breath, we greeted an elderly couple from New Mexico. I stared at her. Amazingly, she was wearing a pair of yellow sweats with the state's name emblazoned in red on the front. A roadrunner ran nimbly in place where the state capital of Santa Fe should have been. It was the sweats and the *hot red* I couldn't get over.

"She's always cold," explained her husband, noticing my stare.

After a quick, disgusted glare from his better half, she immediately changed the subject. "We didn't realize there was such a green place in the world," said the wife, waving her hand at the expansive view of high, tree-covered, rolling mountains which continued into the State of North Carolina.

I chuckled as I responded, "Many people from the Southwest and even Florida are astonished and say the same thing. We should call them the Great Green Mountains, but we don't."

"Where did the name Smoky come from? The sky is clear and the view unencumbered." The man turned to look at the scene before us. "I think I see a lake off in the distance."

"Yes, Fontana Lake, built by the Tennessee Valley Authority."

"The sky isn't always this clear," added Luke.

"No, and there are many theories on how the name Smoky came about. Some say it came from the haze hanging over the mountains, which often restricts the view and causes a blank, bleached-out-green, or flat surface appearance. Others swear the clouds, hovering low like a protective, warm blanket, after a life-giving rain gave birth to the name."

"Whatever the reason, your Smoky Mountains are certainly beautiful."

"Thank you, we think so, too."

"Manda, we'd better go." Luke was tugging at my hand, inching me up the trail. "Nice to meet you both. I want to get to the top so we can see the sunset." Even now, the tall trees were casting long shadows over the trail.

"Be sure and visit Cherokee and Gatlinburg while you're here," I flung over my shoulder, wondering what was so important about seeing the sunset.

The trail was deserted, and we didn't pass anyone else the rest of the way.

The tower on top of Clingmans Dome has a circular, inclining walkway. Looking down, I noticed the slanted concrete was showing several decades of wear—metal rebar appeared on the surface. Hand in hand, Luke and I gained the top promenade. From this vantage point, signs direct you to the most important peaks in the distance. The wind blew gently and, since the sun was lower on the horizon, the air cool—as always in late afternoon.

Luke suggested we walk to the side where the sun was setting. The air warmed in its golden glow, and the direction pointed toward Maryville. Wisps of clouds floated on the horizon.

"Might rain tomorrow," I observed, pointing at the clouds.

"Hmm." Luke said as he stepped behind me and put his arms around me, bending his head to my cheek. We stood mesmerized by the scene unfolding before us.

I felt like a teenager, enveloped by a first love. I wrapped my arms around his and leaned against him. I wanted to say, "I love you," but disturbing our present intimacy wasn't an option. I let it enfold, permeate, and radiate outward.

Two other couples stood at a distance—each seeking the intimacy of aloneness with each other.

"This scene one never forgets," I whispered in Luke's ear as his lips brushed my temple. Anything above a whisper would have broken the silence of this special moment.

"You smell like river water," he said huskily.

"Oh, I'm sorry."

"Don't be. I like it." He loosened his grasp. One hand fished in the pocket of his walking shorts. "Manda, I have something I need to ask you."

I took a step to the side and turned to look up at him.

He grasped something in his curled-up hand. "You've been my friend and confidant for several years. Some weeks ago, I asked you to think about becoming the most important woman in my life."

He went down on one knee. "After that time, I've come to realize I've loved you for many months. My mother's illness and a drastic change in my life, opened my eyes. Going forward, I can't picture my life without you. Will you marry me, Amanda?"

I didn't gasp at his proposal, but my mouth dropped open at the ring in his hand, which caught the last rays of the setting sun. The sparkling diamond rivaled the sunset.

He hurried on as I looked at the ring in astonishment. "I will keep you safe within the shelter of my arms for the rest of our lives. I will hold you close, but not too close, because I admire your personal strength and your passion for life. That is my promise to you. I've told you the challenges we will face. Will you become my wife, and with God's help, we will confront them together? I love you, Amanda Puckett Weathers."

As Luke knelt on the concrete, I stood looking down at this wonderful hunk of a man—my eyes going from the beautiful ring to his handsome upturned face. How could I turn him down? No, I couldn't. He was everything I imagined a husband to be—worthy and acceptable in my eyes.

"Manda?"

"The answer is yes, Luke. I will be your wife. I'm honored you love and respect me and consider my needs important. I love you so much."

Luke slid the ring on my finger and taking me into his arms, sealed our pledge with a kiss. Sheltered in his arms, I stood watching the sunset turn from yellow to orange to red. He murmured in my ear, "Sweetheart, there are so many things we need to talk about, but right now, I want to stand here and enjoy our new oneness. You can be sure, any future decisions I make will include you."

Several minutes later, I asked, "Do you think we need to head back?" I looked around. The other couples had disappeared from the tower.

"Are you cold, my darling?"

"Yes, shivering."

"Gee. I thought my love would keep you warm. Isn't there a song to that effect?" he teased.

"Maybe," I said. "And without your love, Sweetheart, I'd probably be an ice cube."

My feet flew off the surface of the walk as Luke grabbed me and twirled me around underneath the dome's sheltering roof. "Aren't you getting a little old for this?" I asked. "You'll hurt your back."

"I'm so happy, I could lift my Tahoe."

"Now, that's something I'd like to see, but at this moment, I'm cold and getting colder."

He put me down. "Okay, but don't tell me you're burning up when it's one hundred degrees tomorrow." He held out his hand. "Manda, I want to say a short prayer, asking God to bless our engagement."

When he said amen, I took one last look toward the west. Where the sun had fallen from the sky, only a slight glow outlined the mountainous horizon. All around us was darkness and space—an emptiness, filled with His beautiful but now unseen creation.

We started back down the circular walkway. Was this the perfect time to address a concern which bothered me? I wondered if Luke had thought of it?

"One thing, troubles me, dear heart." We were at the bottom of the tower with his flashlight illuminating the path in the evening twilight. We kept walking.

"What's that?"

"I can't give you children."

Luke stumbled on the smooth blacktop, almost dropping the flashlight. In the dim light, he threw back and shook his head, roaring with laughter. The sound echoed through the darkness of the forest, demanding the attention of any bear within earshot. "Are you kidding? I don't think that's high on my list of priorities. Four is enough, and if we decide otherwise, we can always adopt more. Is that okay?" he said firmly.

"Yes." I was glad he couldn't see the relief on my face. I'd always wanted children of my own, but at my age, the medical profession advised against it.

"Let's walk faster," he said. "Our bodies will stay warmer."

We hurried hand in hand down the steep trail. Back in the truck, Luke turned on the heater full blast. "What's the first thing on the agenda?" he asked, as we warmed.

"We need to go by and see my mother and father."

"Tonight?" Luke questioned as he pulled from the parking lot onto the main road, leading to Newfound Gap.

"No, not tonight, they turn in early. Let's do it tomorrow. I work late on Friday, but maybe we can take them out to dinner. I think they'd go."

"Will you call them and make the arrangements, and I need to have a long conversation with James."

"What do you think he will say?"

Luke laughed and reached for my cold hand. He didn't hold on long, because the curves demanded both of his on the steering wheel. "He has an idea something's going on. Before I left for Longview, out of the blue, he nonchalantly stated you'd make a good mother. I have no idea what brought that on, but I think that means you're in."

During the rest of the drive, we discussed some of the changes our union would

necessitate in the future. Our wedding would take place the thirteenth of December, just as my working partner, June, had predicted.

When Luke pulled into my driveway, I was exhausted from the events, emotion, and exertion of the day, I fell asleep as soon as my head hit the pillow.

❦ CHAPTER TWELVE ❦

Luke

The next morning, I got ready for work and drove James over to Mrs. Docksets. Heading to Church-on-the-Hill, I pulled into the administrative wing parking lot. Today would be a quiet, easy day since I was the only staff member scheduled to work. I parked the Tahoe, got out, and stretched my arms skyward. Last night was the first time I'd slept comfortably in several weeks. Seeing Manda, knowing her answer to my proposal, was as relaxing as a hot shower, followed by butter pecan ice cream.

The sky was a clear blue, and the clouds gone after last night's rain. The grass still looked a dusty green, famished for a good two- or three-day soaking. The humidity made the heat unbearable with no relief in sight.

Using my keycard, I hurried into the beige-colored hallway. Stopping, I made sure the door locked behind me. Our security team demanded vigilance on the part of the staff. During the week, a buzzer by the outside door alerted our church secretary of a visitor. I flipped on the hallway and office lights. After the events of this week, I somehow expected the work area to be different. Everything else in my life had changed. It wasn't, and I breathed a sigh of relief.

Checking messages and mail in my office proved to be short work. I grabbed the portable office phone and headed for the music department. I hoped our Fourth of July cantata would be ready to sing on Sunday. One voice mail said the sheet music was left by my substitute on the music stand in the choir room. I headed there to look it over.

My footsteps echoed down the empty church hallway. I passed the main entranceway and several silent classrooms. Before I entered the music room, I stood outside, looking up and down the vacant passage. Was something wrong?

I felt an unexpected burden. I half expected to see a figure standing there.

Many time's, in periods of upheaval in my life, I've had a closer feeling of His presence surrounding me. I felt it now — stronger than ever before.

"Why now, Father?" I asked. My life was settling into place. Manda and I were to be married, my father was open to my mother's move to assisted living where she would be safe, and the children were within weeks of coming to Maryville.

But I couldn't shake the feeling. What was wrong?

Instead of entering the music rooms, I turned, and in a few steps came to the double doors to the sanctuary. I grasped a handle, and with the pull of my hand, the wooden door swung outward. In this holy place, I walked over to the altar and knelt on the carpeted step.

"I know you're here, Father. I feel You nearby."

For some seconds my mind was blank, as I rested in His presence. Then my lips started moving. I poured out my heart to the only real Father who'd declared His love for me. I did it loudly and entirely. First, I thanked Him for His hollowed name, Jesus—Jesus Christ—and continued with the many blessings He'd showered on me this week. I prayed Romans 8:38-39 where He said I can rest in His promise, *that neither death, nor life, nor angels, nor principalities, nor powers, nor things present, nor things to come, nor height, nor depth, nor any other creature, shall be able to separate us from the love of God, which is in Christ Jesus our Lord.*

Then I asked the same thing for Manda, James, my future children, and my immediate family. Several minutes later, I got up, turned around, and was surprised that I needed to wipe tears off my cheeks. I had no idea when they started, but I was refreshed and renewed.

Why had He sent me here to pray?

I didn't know, but whatever was coming, He would be with me. This was one of His promises. The burden that had pressed so suddenly upon me outside the music room was gone. Maybe not gone, just moved to other broader shoulders.

I pulled air into my lungs, and let it out in a ragged sigh. "I love you, Lord." I told Him. I knew He was listening.

Back in the music room, I checked over the music for our Fourth of July special. According to notes my substitute had made on a sheet of paper, I decided we needed another practice session during our Sunday school classes. That meant calling or e-mailing each choir member to warn them about my decision.

Hours later after leaving voice mails and talking to several on the phone, I sat at the piano, playing the melodies and singing the lyrics to the music, a tribute to the forming of our country. Playing the piano and singing always lifted my spirit. Soon, I was singing with enthusiasm and gladness.

During my hearty rendition of *America the Beautiful*, I didn't hear my pastor until he sat in a choir seat before me.

"Maybe you should sing a solo on Sunday," he suggested as I stopped playing and turned on the piano bench to face him.

"I hope the choir will know the music well-enough so that I won't have to." I returned, as I smiled at him.

My respect for this older man had increased each year I served at Hilly Church. He was my pastor, adviser, and friend.

"What are you doing here?" I asked.

"I came in to put the finishing touches on my sermon. Sometimes, it's not quiet enough at home — too many disturbances and too much honey-do list." He grinned.

I suspected it was the honey-do problem he was fleeing the most, but didn't express my thought. "An empty church inspires an effortless, clear, and creative atmosphere."

"Exactly. It's hard to explain, but I work here better than anywhere else. I believe everyone is like this. Your best place is at the piano, or lost in your music."

I nodded. Now was the time to tell him about last night's happening. "I have some news for you, Pastor."

"I thought maybe you would."

I chuckled. So, that was the real reason he was here. He knew of Manda's and my courtship. In fact, the whole church knew. On yesterday's trip from the airport, I had mentioned our increasing courtship and love—not giving him many details. I told him I was surprising her for a picnic after she got off from work. He must have read through the few words I uttered. "Last night, Manda and I went to the Chimneys Picnic Area."

"A-a-nd …"

I decided to prolong his agony. "We had a really nice time. Went swimming. Drove to Clingmans Dome. The traffic was heavy as usual." I shrugged my shoulders.

He shook his head. "Lu-u-ke!"

"Manda and I are engaged to be married." I blurted this out. So much for increasing the excitement of the announcement.

"Miracles haven't ceased," exclaimed the pastor of Church-on-the-Hill. He jumped up from his chair, rushed over, and extended his hand. "I've been praying for this to happen."

I got up from where I sat and shook his hand, giving him a pat on the shoulder and a hug. "I hope she doesn't have second thoughts. Our situation is unusual and laden with many drawbacks."

"Ah, God has brought you two together. I'm sure of that. I'm always amazed at the intricate tapestries He creates in some lives, while others are of simple design—no strife and, seemingly, no earthshaking events."

"I guess it takes all kinds."

"When's the wedding."

"On December 13. I hope you will be available. We both want you to perform the ceremony."

"Let's go check my schedule."

As we walked out the door, my pastor stopped and placed his hand on my shoulder. "My wife was saying yesterday, you two are made for each other. Wait until she hears about this." His hand slid off my shoulder. "It's okay to announce your engagement to the congregation on Sunday, isn't it?"

"I'll check with Manda and make sure. No one in our families know yet, and I haven't really said anything to James."

We continued down the hallway. I listened to two sets of steps. The other presence was gone.

CHAPTER THIRTEEN

Manda

Even though I'd gone to sleep exhausted after the long day, I had awakened just after two in the morning, taken a potty break, and returned to the bed's warmth. Tossing and turning, I couldn't go back to sleep.

I chuckled as I remembered another famous girl. *The Princess and the Pea* was a famous children's book. She couldn't sleep because a little pea under her mattress made her uncomfortable, and I couldn't sleep for the same reason. Instead of a pea, my engagement ring was the culprit. Of course, I could have taken it off, but that wasn't an option. Luke had placed it there only last night. No way was it going to come off my finger anytime soon.

Six o'clock a.m. The alarm clock hadn't even gone off. I turned on the light, but continued to snuggle in the warmth of my queen-sized bed, until I remembered my promise to June to come in early and straighten up my work area. Throwing the covers aside called my attention to the flashing diamond on my finger which felt strange after all the years of being bare. The embedded circle left by Todd's rings had long disappeared.

Luke and his sister had chosen a beautiful ring. I lay looking at the circle, which surely symbolized love and marriage, which after saying the I dos, should never end. Turning the circlet to catch the light, I noticed a yellow sparkle hidden inside, symbolizing the great joys bubbling to the surface as two, being joined to another, experience the oneness of their relationship.

I laughed out loud, saying, "Manda, you're making all that up." I sure was, but my thoughts *sounded* wonderful.

The yellow diamond sat at the center of a gold, swirl setting. It stood taller than the circle of small diamonds framing it. I couldn't have picked an engagement ring which suited me more. In the Tahoe's glove compartment, Luke had pulled out a velvet box and showed me the plain gold band he'd purchased to go with the gorgeous ring. We'd decided to go to the mall and buy his wedding band the following week, when things settled down a little.

I got up and busied myself with making my bed, tugging at my striped, teal-green bedspread which match my window treatments. Glancing around the room, with its beige walls, beige blinds, and trey ceilings, I noticed I'd left the light on in my walk-in closet. I jumped up, walked over, and opened the door. The smell of new potpourri met my nostrils, as I searched for the lavender, Capri outfit I'd bought at Foothills Mall last week. Today was new, changed, and life required a new suit of clothes. I wanted to celebrate my engagement and ring.

Bathroom chores proved to be the same as last night's sleep—weird. But along with the foreign thing on my finger was the delicious feeling of a decision made. Marrying Luke was no longer an option. Our union would become something I looked forward to with anticipation and longing.

Before I left for work, I called my parent's home. My sleepy mother answered the phone. "Mom are you and Dad going to be home tonight."

"What time is it?"

"Seven," I replied.

"Seven," she grumbled. "Hold on." I heard her yell at my father, the early riser. She asked him if they were going anyplace.

Then she came back to me. "Your father says we'll be home."

"Then Luke and I'll be over to take you out to dinner."

"Luke? Do you mean your church's music minister, Luke Avery?"

"Yes. He's the man in my life. He wants to come over and meet you and dad officially.

"I'm thrilled, sweetie, and I'm sure your father will be too. Doesn't he have a son? How old is he?"

"He does, and James is nine."

"Then I'll be a grandparent." My mother was laughing and excited as she spoke.

"Mom, I've got to go to work. We'll be there at seven." I hung up the phone and grabbed my pocketbook and work shoes. I was so excited about introducing my future husband to my parents, I almost missed the top step into my garage. My mother thought she was gaining a grandchild, wait until she found out it was soon to be four.

≈

The drive to Suds and Styles took forever, because I stopped at every red light on Lamar Alexander Parkway, before reaching the final turn to work. I pulled into my normal parking place, catching a glimpse of June standing just inside the front door. I should have known she'd be watching for me. I giggled, thinking she reminded me of a vulture, standing close to its expiring next meal. I decided to let her hover for a few minutes, as I rearranged several items in my center console and on my passenger seat.

When I looked up, June had opened the salon door and positioned herself outside on the edge of the sidewalk in the morning heat. Arms crossed, she stared in my direction. I ducked my head and chuckled. "Better get out, Manda, before June has a heart attack or heatstroke." I opened my car door.

As soon as June saw the top of my head, she called, "Hey, girl. Methuselah was slow, but he was old."

I acknowledged her comment with a wave of my hand, grabbing my extra shoes and purse from the back seat. Closing the rear door, I wrapped my hand around the shoulder strap on my handbag and buried the ring against my chest.

"What were you doing?" my impatient employer asked as I approached her.

"Rearranging my front seat and console. I mashed my brakes to stop at one of the red lights on the parkway. I didn't leave enough room to stop."

"Got your mind on other things, huh?"

"Must have. The screech was awesome, as the youngsters in my Sunday School class always say."

June held the front door open. "I want to hear all about your date last evening," she paused to let me by, and I headed for my station. We were alone for an hour before the other stylists arrived.

June plopped down in my styling chair. Obviously, she wasn't moving until she heard all the stimulating details.

"Do you want me to wash and cut your hair, my dear?" I asked while placing the load I was carrying in its customary places.

"Girl, I want a detailed description of last night's happenings—now. What did he say? Where did you go? When...?"

"Okay, okay, one question at a time." I snatched my combs and brushes from the counter, walked past my annoying boss, and filled the basin with water and soapy disinfectant solution. June followed me, sitting in her styling chair.

Picking up the stiff bristled brush on the sink's edge, I plunged my hands deep into the hair washing basin. I started scrubbing my work items, flipping bits of suds in all directions as I cleaned and rinsed them. Choosing a white towel from the stack nearby, I picked up a comb and patted it dry. Then I dried a brush.

June's eyes were on me, boring a hole in my backside.

Resigned to giving June a blow-by-blow description, I started with, "We went to the Chimneys Picnic Area and picked a table next to the stream rushing down the mountainside. We ate side by side and discussed his trip to Longview."

"Was it crowded? The picnic area I mean."

"Yes, it was."

"Did you walk the Cove Hardwood Trail? That's a good place to hold hands." During spring, this forest trail was gorgeous and covered with a blanket of wildflowers.

"No. Who's telling this? Keep quiet," I said feigning frustration.

"I haven't been there in forever. So, what happened next?"

"You already know that Luke e-mailed me from Longview, but he hadn't told me everything. He felt some of his information needed to be explained in more detail when we were together after the trip." I told June the highlights of Luke's trip, leaving out private parts I didn't feel crucial for her to know. "He thinks his father is open to considering his mother's being placed in a ward for those with mental disabilities."

"I hope so. I'd hate to see her get badly hurt, or worse still, hurt those she loves. Did you come home after your talk?"

"No, we took our swimsuits, so when we got through eating and talking, we went into the water to cool off. The water wasn't deep enough to swim."

"Ah," said June, "lovey, dovey in the water."

"No. No lovey, dovey in the water."

"Isn't that where he kissed you?"

"No-o!"

"I can't believe the man hasn't kissed you yet."

"He kissed me when we got out of his truck at the picnic area. He kissed me when he left for Dallas."

"You left that part out."

"Oh, you're impossible."

"No, I'm not. I want *all* the juicy details."

"I'm trying to tell you that. We went for a swim if you can call it that in the shallow water. Sure did cool us off, though. Luke suggested we change out of our wet bathing suits, because he had something else, he wanted to do."

"What was that?" June leaned forward, thinking another juicy spot was coming.

"He was trying to be mysterious, but I suggested going to Clingmans Dome and ruined his secret."

"Oh. What's the big deal about going to the Dome? Remember me telling you —"

"June!" I cut her off. Her "remember when's" usually took several minutes to tell.

"Okay, okay. Calm down. Wasn't it getting late?"

I was still cleaning combs and brushes as I talked. "Yes. We drove to the top." I held up my finger — the one without the ring. "But being late, it wasn't crowded when we got there. He and I walked the steep trail, arriving just before sunset."

"How romantic. I can see it now." June waved her hand from left to right above her face. "Hand in hand, you walk up the inclining ramp. In the yellow glow of the sun's last rays, Luke turns. His dark eyes meet yours, and bending he kisses you softly on the lips, declaring his passionate love will last forever. Am I right?"

"June, you read too many mushy novels. Unlike the romantic, passionate males in those books, Luke doesn't like to rush things. We stood quite a while watching the sunset. His arms were around me."

"Now we're getting somewhere."

I was laughing inside at her, but my next words were, "Then he whispered in my ear, you *smell* like river water."

"What!" June exclaimed. "You must have driven him out of his mind. River water, indeed."

"At that moment, he was loving and passionate." I explained to her, while she shook her head. "I was thrilled. He kissed me again."

"Really? Twice in one night. I can't believe it," she said sarcastically, getting a bit perturbed.

Ignoring June, I picked up my combs and brushes now wrapped in the drying cloth, walked back to my station, and put them into their individual drawers. She didn't need to know how many times Luke and I kissed. The time had come for me to tell her what else happened, and I needed to make it short and sweet.

She followed close behind me, like a bulldog sniffing a trail. Leaning on the counter of my booth, she said, "Mark my words, in a few weeks, he'll ask you to marry him."

"June, you may as well give up the book idea."

"Why?"

I held up my left hand. The diamond's yellow facets sparkled in the fluorescent lighting.

"Oh! You devious woman!" June took one step toward me and seized my hand, turning it right and left. She gushed, "It's beautiful. The most beautiful ring I've ever seen."

How many times had I heard that before? Every time one of our customers got engaged.

Grabbing me in a bear hug, she danced me down the room past the other stations. She stopped. "Bet I got the wedding date right, didn't I? Christmas?"

"Almost. We decided on December 13."

"I still can't believe you're getting married."

"We'll need a bigger home."

"You're going to sell your house?"

"Yes. We both decided a new house, and a new start would be best. My home has memories of Todd and his of Peggy. Whoever sells first will move into our new residence and the other will relocate after our marriage. This means our two households will remain separate. Maryb and Marcus will come to live with me. James and Clint will live with Luke."

"What kind of place do you want?"

"Luke wants to move outside the city. Maybe buy five acres and have a couple of horses. He misses riding like he did in Texas. Other animals—maybe. That's the children's decision."

"Tending animals is a good way to teach responsibility."

"Yes. I want the children to have separate bedrooms. At first, Luke suggested the two youngest boys could stay together, but I insisted, and he agreed. I don't think having someone in his room is fair to James. He's always had his own room."

"Having a separate bedroom makes perfect sense— less intrusive, having your own space. What does James think of all this?"

"Luke will talk to him today, and we're going over to my parents' home tonight. I don't think James or my parents will have any objections."

"This is so exciting."

"We'll have to have a gigantic garage sale to combine two houses."

"I'll help with the sale. You know how I love garage sales, and we can advertise to our customers— hand out flyers for them to share in their neighborhoods."

I couldn't help but laugh. "I was hoping you would."

June stood for a moment, looking at me. "You really love this man, don't you?"

"June, I don't think I loved Todd this much. I wonder if maturity causes you to feel more deeply, or maybe it's a different kind of love as you age. I don't know. But I would be devastated if anything should happen to —"

The front door bell jingled. Chattering loudly, the other stylists entered Suds and Styles.

"Girls, hurry. See Manda's beautiful diamond."

CHAPTER FOURTEEN

Manda

Telling James wasn't a problem. "Aw, I guessed it was gonna happen," he said, coming over to give me a big hug. He surprised me by looking up at me and saying, "Can I call you Mom?"

"I hope you will. I've never had a son before, and I can't think of any young man I'd rather have call me Mom."

"Are you ready to leave?" asked Luke, giving me a hug and a light kiss on the lips.

This was the first one James had seen us exchange. He looked at us and sheepishly grinned.

"I'm ready." I picked up my purse and hung it from my shoulder. James ran out the door and headed for the Tahoe.

Luke said in a low voice as I punched the garage door closer, "He asked me if he could call you Mom."

"It is a little premature to call me that. I mean, I love the idea, but what will everyone else think?"

"Here's what I think," Luke said forcefully. "I think it's perfectly okay, but I told him he'd better ask you. He was so eager, I got the feeling he liked the idea."

"Then it's settled. Are you nervous? Meeting prospective in-laws is supposed to be hair-raising, isn't it?"

"No."

"I wish I could say the same."

∾

When Luke, James, and I arrived, my mother answered the door. The smell of tonight's dinner wafted from the back of the house. I knew that smell—green peppers, and onions—sautéed in butter. I was sure baking potatoes were in the oven, and ground, sirloin steak was resting on the kitchen counter waiting to be grilled. "Mom, what have you done? We were going to take you and Dad out to eat."

"Good evening," she said. "Please come in. I decided to cook," she nodded, as a punctuation for her sentence and the end of that question. "I hope I've not upset your plans, Manda." She wiped her wet hands on her apron, which she took off and placed in a folded pile on a hall table. After shutting the door, she ushered us into the living room where my father put down the evening paper and rose from the couch to greet us. He never read the paper in the living room.

Hum-n, this is going to be formal, I thought, feeling awkward and out of place in the room with the best furniture and gold-framed, stiffly poised family pictures scattered atop the tables and in the bookcases. I noticed Todd's picture was missing.

Even my voice sounded strange, high-pitched as I said, "Dad and Mom, this is Luke Avery and his son, James.

My father gave me an are-you-okay glance and came forward. Shaking Luke's hand. He took over the conversation and broke the ice.

"Luke, I've seen you when my wife and I've been at your church for special programs, but we've never met you officially. And this is James?"

James nodded a yes.

"Son, why don't you sit with me on the big couch? Manda, you and Luke take the *love* seat." He cocked his eyebrows as he emphasized the word love.

Luke and I both caught his intention, and we laughed. My mother shot him a glance that could kill. So much for formal, I thought. Not with my father around.

"I guess you know why we're here," said Luke, taking my hand in his as we sat down on the *love*seat, exposing the beautiful ring on my finger. It flashed in the lamplight.

"Oh, Amanda," said my mother, throwing formality to the wind. She hurried over to look at it. Bending over my hand, she gushed, "Manda, it's just beautiful, probably the loveliest ring I've ever seen." She threw a "wow" glance at Luke.

"That's exactly what June said when she saw it this morning."

"So, you two are engaged," my father observed as Mom headed for a fireside chair. It was normal for her to claim a den recliner. She looked stiff and uncomfortable in the straight-backed seat.

"Yes, sir. One day exactly, that is if you approve. Since you don't know too much about me, I was hoping you would let me give you a little history of my relationship with your daughter."

"Please do. If Manda hadn't warned us some weeks ago about the possibility of a man in her life, we would have been very surprised — very surprised indeed."

I sat there thinking this meeting wasn't going as I'd planned, but Luke wasn't perturbed. He continued, "You must realize that Manda and I have known each other for several years."

I listened as Luke told them of his first wife's passing, his struggle to deal with her death, and raise his young son. He squeezed my hand as he mentioned my help with his music ministry at church and his eventual realization that I was more than a helper and friend. "I knew I was in love with your daughter. I wasn't sure she felt the same way about me, so I put off saying anything to her."

"I was the same way," my Dad interjected. "Except in my case, I was too bashful. I almost didn't propose."

"I found my tongue, astounded at his words. "You, bashful? I didn't know that."

"Hard to believe, isn't it," said my mother.

I sat forward on the edge of the couch, digesting this new information. "You mean I might have had a different mother, because you were scared to say anything?"

"Oh, no. Your mother was my choice. I was afraid she wouldn't say yes. So, I made up my mind not to rush her."

My mother was shaking her head and laughing. "He's changed a lot since we got married, hasn't he?"

Dad looked at her and then back at me. "Your mother gave me courage. I haven't had any trouble speaking up since that pesky proposal."

"That was so-o-o long ago." My mother seemed to be reliving the moment.

"I'm sorry. We've interrupted you, Luke." My father had pulled James to his side, during Luke's words of his wife's passing. James looked natural and at ease, leaning against him.

"In my case, it turns out procrastination wasn't a good idea." Luke told of his brother's children and of his mother's dementia and his intention to bring the children to Tennessee. "How could I ask Manda to take on their responsibility with me?"

"Do you mean three more children are coming to join James?" my mother asked, her eyes wide. The grandchildren were piling up.

"Yes, I can't let them be split up." Luke said this firmly. "My sister Agnes is taking care of them now, but she has two of her own and a full life helping take care of my Mom. Her husband, Mike, works out of town most of the time, so he isn't there to help take charge of five kids. Clint, Marcus, and Maryb have already gone through enough trauma in their lives. The best solution for them is to come here. The rest of my family agrees with me."

"When Luke finally told me of his plans for the children, I already knew of his problem."

"You did?" Luke looked at me in shock.

I saw the question in his eyes. "Yes, Sweetheart. I did."

"But how?"

"Our pastor…"

"That explains your lack of surprise." Luke threw up his hand. "I was amazed you didn't show some kind of shock or amazement about the whole situation."

"By the time Luke asked me to consider seeing him with the idea of a future with him, I'd had time to pray and think about the consequences of a future marriage. I felt God was saying "Yes," and my mind was made up."

"And there I was, sweating in the cold on Clingmans Dome, wondering how you would respond. Why did it take so long for you to say yes?"

I turned to look at him. "Because I knew when I uttered yes, there'd be no turning back. So, I hesitated."

"This sounds like quite an undertaking. Marriage, four children, and whatever else that'll come with it." My Dad wasn't smiling.

"James, I have some cookies and milk in the kitchen. Let's go get some and ruin your dinner."

After James followed my mother to the kitchen, Luke said, "Mr. Puckett, only God can pull this off. Manda and I can't without His help."

"I'm inclined to agree with you there. But you realize Manda's been by herself for several years. She's an independent woman now."

Luke looked at me and smiled. Turning back to my father he said, "That's one of the attributes I admire in her. I don't believe we'll have a problem with that. Ministers are gone from home a lot with the responsibilities associated with their many functions in the church, and her ability to make decisions will be a blessing. I'll back her up when she makes them."

"This has to work. Your position as a minister in your church will be jeopardized if it doesn't."

"I realize that you're right. Manda and I are both rooted in biblical principles. As long as we use them as a guideline, we'll be okay."

My father was satisfied. "Have you set a wedding date?"

"Yes," I answered. "It's December 13. That's a Thursday. We plan on spending five days in Texas to celebrate our marriage."

"When are the children coming?"

"We don't have a definite date, but before school starts. I don't want them to start school in Longview only to reenroll here in Maryville."

"What about housing? Manda's home won't hold that many people. How about yours?" Of course, my father would ask this question. He was a retired builder who piddled with a woodworking shop in his basement.

"We'll be buying a new larger home. I'd like to purchase one outside the city where we can have horses."

"I used to raise chickens when I was a young kid." My father was full of surprises today.

"Raise chickens. I didn't know that."

"Yep. I was in the FFA Club. One year, I won a blue ribbon for having some of the best-looking hens in our county poultry show. The show was held below the courthouse, and we had state celebrities there."

"If we decide to raise chickens, I'll be sure to ask your advice, Dad."

"Do you have any idea which section of the county you might head too?"

"No, we've not had a chance to start looking."

"Well, of course you haven't. Guess I'm getting a little ahead of you."

"Mr. Puckett, Manda and I would like to have your blessing on our future marriage. We'll need your advice, support, and love to make this work."

"It certainly sounds like you two have most of the near future figured out. You can count on my wife and me to support you both. Most of all, we'll be praying for your new, blended family."

"Thank you, sir."

Dad stood. "Let's go see if we can scare up some grub or at least cookies in the kitchen." He led the way down the hall.

Luke took my hand and pulled me to my feet. I leaned against him, too weak to stand on my own. The discussion with my parents was over, and I was glad.

❧ CHAPTER FIFTEEN ❧

Luke

The sounds on the other end of the phone weren't comforting. Someone was sobbing, crying uncontrollably. "Agnes is that you?" My caller ID had already verified this call was from her.

"Agnes, Agnes calm down." It was one week since I'd returned from Texas to conduct the Fourth of July special music. Only four days ago, I'd called her with the good news of Manda's and my engagement. What could have happened to upset my sister so much?

Agnes managed to squeeze out, "Luke, oh Luke, I have more bad news for you."

"What has happened to Mom?" I stood and started pacing the floor behind my office desk, carrying the portable phone and waiting on my sister to respond. Had Mom burned the house down, or was she missing again?

Agnes kept sobbing. "It isn't Mom," she cried out.

"Has something happened to Mike?" Could he have been attacked because of his work? Agnes had told me of his problems with the residents in his work area.

"No, Mike's coming home. I've already called him with the news. I had to hear the sound of his voice."

"Then what is it?"

"Pop's had a heart attack."

Stunned by her words, I couldn't say anything.

"Luke are you there?" Agony, frustration, and desperateness tinged her voice. "I don't know if I can stand this or not. It's too much."

"Pop? Pop? You must mean Mom. Nothing's wrong with Pop."

Ignoring my comment, she rushed on, "I can't imagine what's going to happen next, and the doctor's say it's a bad one, and they aren't giving me much hope. If he doesn't have another, he may survive. There's no way of knowing what kind of condition he'll be in if he does live, and, of course, he can't take care of Mom—even if he makes it—at least for some time to come. What are we going to do?" I heard her draw a deep breath.

"But Pop's healthy as a horse. He can't be sick. He was fine last week." My mind was going in circles, as I tried to picture him lying in a hospital bed—white sheets, IVs, the smell of disinfectants, nurses and doctors in long hallways with lots of doors into rooms. Somehow, I couldn't wrap my arms around the image.

"I'm sorry, Luke. I hated to call you with the news."

"Pops had a heart attack." Saying the words helped me to understand them, and understanding them caused me to return to my desk to sit in my office chair. "Dear God," I said, dropping my face into my hands while still holding the phone. What was my next step in dealing with the immediate situation?

Agnes' next words told me. "Luke, you need to come home. I can't sit with Mom and Pop and tend five kids even with Mike's help, and will you call Tony with the news. I'll call Duane."

"I agree, Agnes. Let me work this out. I'll let you know my plans." I hung up the phone and sat in shocked silence while going over the possibilities. I jumped up from my chair and hurried to the pastor's office. On Thursdays, he was always at his desk, I needed the comfort of his human presence. I knocked on his door.

"Come in." As I entered, the pastor of Hilly Church looked up from the work spread across his desk. My ashen face must have told him the stress and shock I was feeling. He jumped up and hurried to greet me. "Luke, what's happened?"

"Pastor, I'm going to have to resign my position here at Church-on-the-Hill." I blurted out, stating the first choice which had come to my mind after the call.

"Wait a minute. What's going on? Surely, there's some other option. Tell me what's happened." All the time he was talking, he was leading me to the couch in front of his desk. We sat down side by side — his steadying arm across my back.

I drew a deep breath and plunged in. "I just got a call from Agnes. Pop's had a heart attack — a bad one. The doctors don't think he'll live, especially if he has another. This is totally unexpected. Our family just resolved Mom's problem, and now this."

"What a shock to your family. My guess is your father has never been ill a day in his life. Some men are not expected to be sick. They're like rocks — immovable."

"No, he hasn't."

My pastor continued to talk, realizing I needed time to think my newest family situation through — to unmuddle or unclutter my mind.

"I had an uncle who was the same way. One day, my aunt came home from work. He was sitting on the front porch, waiting on her — or so she thought. He'd already gone to heaven. His heart, too, we guessed."

"That's the other problem. Pop never went to church, and when I mentioned anything about whether he believed in Jesus as the redeeming Savior of men, he would cut me off or change the subject. I have a tremendous burden for him."

"Not everyone is interested in hearing about the love of our Savior. Each person makes that choice, because God gives us the freedom to choose."

I nodded in agreement.

"Why do you think you need to resign?"

"The situation in Longview is grave. Agnes and her husband can't take care of five children, my Mom, and my Pop. Here's what came to mind first. I need to go to Longview, and I don't have any idea when this crisis will be over. The only fair thing to do is resign and not keep the church in a quandary about my return."

"Can none of your other siblings help?"

"No. Duane has a business and employees to care for. He shies away from sick people, and he can't stand Pop. They had a big blowup while I was at home. My guess is he would rather not be around Pop — or Mom."

"What about your other brother, Tony?"

"Tony gets along with Pop and Mom. He's a possibility, but his wife rules the roost, and she dislikes our family, especially Pop. Why, I don't know. I'll call, but if she says he's not coming, he's not coming."

"Okay. You make the phone call, and I'll start calling our church leaders." He stood. "I'm sure they've been faced with a situation like this before, and we need to get them involved. We'll find out the protocol and proceed from there. I don't want you to resign. So, your resignation is not accepted at present."

"Tony has a cell phone and a business extension." I looked at my watch as I arose. "He's at lunch right now. I'll call him and let you know, but I'm not getting my hopes up."

"Luke, let's pray about this." Placing his hand on my shoulder, he bowed his head and said a short prayer. Then he gave me a quick hug. "God's working in this. You can be sure of it. Right now, you nor I can see the end, but His mind will become apparent as days pass."

"Thank you, Pastor."

"Let me know what your brother says. Have you talked to Manda?"

"I didn't even think of her." In my shock, I'd forgotten to call her. And hadn't I promised to include her in every decision. "I'll call her as soon as I talk to Tony. She'll be off early tonight. We'll have time to discuss the situation then."

CHAPTER SIXTEEN

Manda

"Luke," I grabbed him and held on, too emotional to say anything else. James slipped by us into the house.

"Hi, Sweetheart. I'm sorry for today's upheaval." He stood shuffling the hot, take-out pizza, so he wouldn't drop it on the floor. We had decided to eat a fast dinner, because we had several things to discuss before he left tomorrow morning.

Stepping back, I took it out of his hand and noticed James waiting patiently with his suitcase of clothes. "James, put your suitcase in a bedroom. Pick the one you want, and it's okay to turn on the television. I'll have something for us to eat in a minute."

I headed for the kitchen with Luke close behind me. Sliding the pizza onto my countertop, I turned to find his arms around me. His kiss was gentle.

"What's going to happen, Luke?" I still held him close, letting the comfort of his solid presence soothe me. He was going to Longview, and I didn't know when I would see him again.

"I wish I knew. I talked to Agnes again late this afternoon, and Pop's condition hasn't changed. He hasn't had another problem with his heart, but he hasn't regained consciousness either. I'll know more when I get there and see for myself."

"You said Agnes found your father." I turned around and started putting green salad into individual bowls, watching him out of the corner of my eye.

"Yes, she went to see how Mom was doing on Wednesday afternoon and stayed with her while Pop went to the supermarket for groceries." Luke stopped and put his hand over his face. "I still can't believe this has happened." A ragged sigh escaped his lips.

"I know this isn't easy." I kept shredding lettuce, letting Luke regain his composure.

Some seconds later, he continued, "She said Mom was doing well—lucid the whole time she was there. When Pop finally came back from the store, Agnes helped him put up the supplies he'd bought, including a pound of ground chuck. He'd planned to make vegetable soup. Mom loves vegetable soup."

"So do I. We have that in common."

"Agnes said she left about five o'clock, telling Pop she'd be back today about three in the afternoon."

"Was that the time she usually went by?"

"Most of the time. It depends on her schedule, whether she's fixed food for my folks to eat, or the children's activities for the day."

"So, she went earlier than she'd planned?"

"Yes, it turned out Clint hadn't told her of his baseball game today at four. When she prepared lunch, she fixed enough food for her, the children, and my parents. After the children ate, she headed for my parents' home. For some unknown reason, she didn't call to tell them she was coming."

"Maybe she ran out of time and was in a hurry."

"Possibly. When she got there, no one answered the door."

"That would have scared me into calling the police."

"Most of us would have called them, but my gutsy sister knew of a key kept outside for just such an emergency. She got it. Opened the door and went inside."

"I can't imagine what she was feeling—scared, wondering what she would find, but hoping for the reason to be simple and explainable."

"When she found Mom sitting in the living room crocheting, she wasn't too worried. This was a normal activity for her. What Mom said was what alerted her to the crisis that followed."

"What did she say?"

"Mom told Agnes that my Pop wouldn't get out of bed that morning. He was sleeping in." Another big sigh. "And, she grinned at Agnes, saying she was happy he was resting, because he worked so hard at his job. Then she told Agnes she was hungry."

"Your Pop is like my Dad—he never sleeps late. So immediately, Agnes knew something was wrong." I nodded, as I went to place the salads on the kitchen table and returned to rummage through a drawer for my pizza slicer.

"Yes. He's up before it gets hot and outside to do his yard work. He'll come back to the house or go to the toolshed at the back of the garage. We always laughed at the old shed with the ridiculous, expensive Hunter fan he installed overhead to keep cool. My father is tight with money, and this was totally out of character for him. Anyway, Agnes ran down the hall to Mom and Pop's bedroom. You know the rest."

I'd finished cutting the extra-large into slices and stood holding it. After several minutes, the pizza was moderately warm. The whole time I'd been working at dinner and we were talking, I was thinking. Now, since I'd made the commitment to love again—not taken lightly for sure, I couldn't stand the thought of not being with Luke. What if he was ripped out of my life like Todd? What was God thinking? He'd brought us together.

I'd turned around to listen to Luke's narrative, and now I voiced my thought. "I was so scared when you called me today at work. I don't know what I'd do if I lost you."

Luke reached for me, but I had to get rid of the pizza which had come between us for the second time today. It went to the countertop. Luke encircled me in his arms and brushed the bangs from my forehead. "I'm not going anywhere." Looking into my eyes, he smiled and continued. "Let me qualify that. I am going to Longview, but darling, I promise I'll be back." We stood cheek to cheek for a moment, locked in the embrace, thinking our own thoughts.

"Are we going to eat? I'm hungry." James stood in the kitchen doorway.

Luke and I pulled apart, realizing this was James' entrance cue. He always seemed to catch us with our arms around each other. He had the biggest grin on his face.

"Yes, Sweetheart, we sure are," I said.

Luke went to the refrigerator and started pulling from the shelves the salad dressings and a two-liter soft drink. I grabbed the glasses, napkins, and paper plates from my cabinets.

"Sit down, son. We'd better eat before the pizza gets any colder." Luke ran ice into the glasses from the fridge door and poured our soft drinks. "James, what kind of salad dressing do you want on your salad?"

"Thousand Island, of course, Dad." He pulled out a chair and sat down.

When we were all seated, Luke asked the blessing and pizza was passed around the table. Luke leaned over and whispered to me, "We'll talk after we eat. There are other things to discuss."

I nodded, knowing our time together would not be long tonight.

~

Two pieces of pepperoni pizza remained in the box as James left the table and went back to watching television.

"Why don't we sit here and talk?" I suggested as I put the extra slices onto a paper plate and covered them with plastic.

"Sure, would you like more to drink? I'll get it." Luke pushed back his chair, went to the fridge and got out the two-liter bottle of cola. Bringing it to the table, he said, "We may be here awhile."

After sitting down beside him, I asked, "What did our pastor find out?" We were arm to arm, and the conversation became more intimate, and our voices were lower.

"I can take an extended sabbatical without pay. They agreed to six months. After this time, the situation will be evaluated again."

"Oh, Luke. Do you think you'll be gone that long?" My heart felt like it was being mashed by a gigantic hand within my body. "I guess I never thought about the time involved. We'll have to postpone the wedding."

"You mean you still want to marry me?" Luke was smiling with his arm around the back of my chair. "You can back out now if you want to."

I reached for his warm hand which lay on the table, holding his glass of soda. "Of course, I still want to marry you, even if it's a year from now."

"Manda, I need the time to cover all the possibilities while I'm there. I can't know what will happen to Dad. Mom's waiting on a room to open up at Nightingale Place, and right now Agnes has all the responsibility on her. Mike can help, but he'll need to return to work. He's the only breadwinner in the family. Monthly bills don't stop."

"You have bills to pay too. Won't your brothers help?"

"Agnes called Duane, and I called Tony—nada to both calls. In my experience as a minister, this is the way it happens when families are in crisis. The burden falls on one or two people—usually just one. I have to help her. She's been wonderful about taking care of Mom and the children."

"She has, hasn't she? You're blessed to have her as your sister."

"You said something about postponing the wedding. I don't think we should change the date until it becomes necessary."

I nodded, agreeing.

"What a mess," Luke stated. "We had it all figured out, didn't we?"

"In one neat small package and tied with red ribbon," I replied.

"If worst comes to worst, I guess Clint, Marcus, and Maryb can start school in Longview. I don't like the idea, because then they'll have to transfer to Tennessee schools when I return. James will start school here since he's staying with you."

I voiced the biggest concern I had about the situation. "How much chance is there you might remain in Longview?"

"Worse case scenario, and not in my plans," he shook his head. "My work is here, and you are here." He dropped my hand and took his to rub the back of his neck.

Did I hear a "not at present" in his voice?

A memorized quote from the King James Bible popped into my head—*For this cause shall a man leave father and mother, and shall cleave to his wife: and they twain shall be one flesh.* Manda that goes for the woman too, I reprimanded myself. Did I love Luke enough to move to Texas, leaving my parents and the mountains I loved? He needed someone who could do just that, and I should have a profound, devoted love with this intent in mind—no matter what happened.

"Manda?"

"Sorry, I was just thinking about you leaving."

"I've covered all the events and decisions for today, and I do need to leave. I didn't realize how exhausted I was until just now." He stared at me, etching my face into his memory.

"I'll be right back." I rose from the table and went to my bedroom, noticing James lay on his bed sound asleep with his clothes on. Taking an afghan from the end of the bed, I quickly covered him up and went to my bedroom down the hall past the bathroom. Retrieving a photo in a white frame edged with gold trim, I returned to the kitchen.

Luke was standing at the kitchen door.

"Here, take this with you. The picture was made two years ago at church."

"Darling, I don't think I'd forget you in a few short weeks, but it'll be nice to see your face. I'll talk to your picture every day, especially if a problem comes up. I'm sure you'll give good guidance," he teased.

Realizing he was leaving, I said, "You'd better e-mail or call me." Grinning, I looked at him with threatening eyes and demeanor. "What time is your flight?"

"Early. Six o'clock."

"You'll be one of the first planes out." My voice caught in my throat as I spoke.

"Yes, I'll be in Longview before twelve noon."

"It'll be different here without seeing you almost every day. I've come to expect you popping in at work or stopping by the house." My heart was feeling the giant squeeze, again. "Church won't be the same either."

"What can I say?" Luke dug into his pocket and pulled out a key. "I had this made for you today. It's to the front door of my house. Just in case James needs something or you need to enter in an emergency. Might be a good idea if you checked it once a week. The pastor has another key if you lose this one."

I hadn't thought about a key. I laid it on the table place mat. "Are you packed?"

"That was my next comment." Luke's arms were around me. "Why do you always know what I'm going to say?" His voice was low, intimate. "The answer is no."

He held me close. "I don't always know, Mr. Avery. I love you so much, and I'm going to miss you." Without warning, the dam I'd been holding back all night broke loose. Sobbing, I clung to him.

He rubbed my back to comfort me and pulled me closer if that was possible. I was crying so hard, I was shaking.

"I'm not leaving until you calm down," he said.

"Then I-I may keep c-crying awhile," I said, knowing I must be looking ghastly.

"It's okay, Sweetheart. Everything will be alright, you'll see, darling." He said quietly in my ear. "I'd better tell James goodbye." He let go.

"James is asleep on his bed."

"Then I won't disturb him. We had a talk while we waited on the pizza."

He took me in his arms again, and we kissed. It was a blessed moment, spent with the man I loved. I hoped the time would never end, but it did.

CHAPTER SEVENTEEN

Luke

The hospital elevator made clanking noises as I ascended to the third floor where the intensive cardiac care unit was located at Longview's hospital. The sharp smell of alcohol and disinfectant violated my nostrils as I stepped into the main hallway. A Caution Slippery When Wet sign was prominently displayed in the middle of the hallway, but no one with a mop or bucket was around.

The scene of horses grazing in a field of grass with a forest of trees in the background, hanging on the wall in front of me, did not soothe my anxious feelings for what lay ahead. An arrow directed me toward the wing where I would meet my sister.

The ICCU unit fanned out in a V from the nurse's station. I stopped to get directions, asking if I could go in.

The nurse said only two in a room at a time and waved me down the hallway to the left, "He's the last door on the right before the emergency exit," she advised.

Most of the doors to the patient rooms were closed, but those that weren't revealed machines with tubes and blinking lights. When I entered Pop's room, I could hardly see my father for the tubes and machines which covered him. My sister rose slowly from a chair by the window and walked toward me.

"Sis, you look like a wreck." I gave her a gentle hug; afraid she might collapse if I was too aggressive.

She took my arm and led me to the short hallway into Pop's room. From there we could still see him trussed up in his hospital bed. "I feel as bad as I look."

Agnes took no offense at my statement. I assumed she was too tired to care.

"I got here as soon as I could."

"I know you did. I've been here for thirty-six hours straight."

"Any change?"

My father's face, what I could see of it, was a strange, sallow, pale yellow-pink. I'd been in many hospital rooms where people were being kept alive by machines, so I recognized the noisy contraptions even if I didn't know most of their names. This was the second time a family member was trussed up with them. I shuddered as my mind flashed back to Peggy.

Before Agnes could answer, we were almost shoved to the wall by two nurses who rushed into the room. They hurried to my Pop's bedside and starting checking monitors, tubes, and breathing.

Agnes whispered, "Three hours ago, he had a mini-attack and they rushed in to check him — the first one."

We stood quietly to the side as they busied themselves in the room. The nurses, satisfied that Pop was resting again, nodded and left.

"How did they know he was in distress?"

"Monitors over their stations. They're alerted if something changes in his vital signs. They come running to determine if there's a need to call the emergency team. Only so many patients to each nurse means you get the best attention, and they get to know their patients."

"How is his heart?"

"His heart rate has been irregular since Thursday. Check out that screen." Agnes pointed to a box on a stand with three black lines running through the monitor. "This line." She indicated one where the needle jumped with mini seismic vibrations. "That is an abnormal heartbeat," she emphasized, "but not enough to start the nurses running to his room." She was pointing at the screen again. "This is a normal heartbeat. Sometime, his heart beats normally for a few minutes, then it returns to that." She pointed again as Pop's beat out of rhythm again. "I've been sitting here watching the line and needle move. It's hard not to."

"He hasn't opened his eyes or regained consciousness at all?"

"No. There's so indication he knows what's going on. Last night, his doctor said he didn't know how he survived the first attack he had at home. His comment was that Pop was in good physical condition, or he would have died. They ran all kinds of tests. His heart is the only problem they found, and he has significant damage to it."

I walked over and put my hand on the only arm which wasn't full of tubes. Warm to the touch, I rubbed gently. Except for a handshake, I hadn't touched my father in years. The contact was strange, as foreign as the sight of him in the stark whiteness of the sheets around him. As bizarre, as the rails confining a seventy-two-year-old man to this bed. I couldn't remember when I'd seen my father in a prone position.

Pulling in a lungful of air, I let it gush out. Hot tears burned my eyes, as I put my hand over my mouth and tried to swallow the giant lump, I suddenly found there. Anger followed the sadness. My Mom needed him. How could he get sick now? She'd tended to his needs for forty-eight years. Only once had I seen her buck him. That was another time when he and my brother, Duane, got into it. She'd flown at Pop like a banty rooster protecting its hen and eggs.

I was having a hard time sorting out my emotions. It hurt to see him lying there, knowing he might never know, never have the full love his children had wanted to give him.

The touch of my sister's hand on my shoulder brought me back to the present. "Let's go down to the coffee shop, where we can talk out of the hospital smell."

On the way down on the elevator, I stated firmly, "He's done his best to wreck our family."

"Luke, I don't think he was ever taught to love."

We stepped from the elevator and were soon seated comfortably with cups of coffee to drink.

I spoke first. "I can still put the blame on him, can't I? And anyway, how did he get Mom if he didn't love her?"

"Definitely a loaded question, but Pop was a salesman and a good one. He was also good-looking and a charmer."

"You've thought about this a lot?"

"Yes. I've seen this same scenario play out in women in my church. Pop had an air about him that said *help me*. Maybe Mom felt the need to save him with her love, to change him, and married him for that reason. Many women do this and wind up in divorce court when they realize it can't be done."

"Only our Savior can save."

"So true, but Mom stuck with him all these years. He didn't abuse her physically, but did with words, as he did us all."

"Sticks and stones may break my bones, but words will never hurt me." Do you remember memorizing those words from England? They certainly aren't true. Words do hurt."

"Yes, words can cut to the core of our being, and Mom took a lot of abuse from Dad's mouth. She hung in there. I've often wondered what would have happened to Pop if she hadn't stayed with him. She needs to be praised and honored for that." Agnes paused in reflection. "They raised some pretty hardworking and high-achieving kids even though our family was dysfunctional."

"Dysfunctional, that's a well-used word these days."

"Luke, conflict and misbehavior can be applied to many biblical families. Even to a king who was after God's heart. He had one certainly in turmoil."

"How did you get so smart?"

"I wanted to know the *why* of Dad and what his actions did to us as siblings and as a family. I haven't shared this with anyone, even you. Mike and I have had some rough patches in our marriage. *Why?* And, I've answered the question for myself. Have you faced the ugly specter of anger about the lack of our father's love? Because whether you know it or not, there is a portion of one's temper associated with this need. We tend to strike at those we love, because they are closest to us."

The more I thought about her question, the more uncomfortable I got, and I was starting to be upset with her for asking. I tried not to show it when I replied. "Agnes, I think I have." My answer was clipped and short.

My sister ignored it. "I used to fly off in anger at Mike. Everything had to be perfect, and when he failed, I let him have it. I knew my temper tantrums hurt him, but I couldn't stop myself. I started to be like Pop with my children, rigid—perfection ruled. Like father, like daughter."

"You never had a temper growing up. I can't believe this."

"I did a pretty good job of hiding it, didn't I. But oftentimes I would lay on my bed and beat my fists against my pillow. Dad was the best deterrent when it came to expressing our emotions in our household, except when it came to Duane."

"I'm glad you didn't take it out on me when we were at home."

"Luke, you were a mouse, running at every problem. Blasting you wouldn't have been much fun, and Dad preferred someone who stood up to him, hence Duane. He took all Dad's pent-up anger. Even I cowered in my room, wanting to go stand up with him—angry about Pop and his demanding ways. It hurt to see them fighting. We all let Dad take his anger out on Duane, even perfect Robert."

"Are you saying we aided our father in his anger toward Duane?"

"Yes, I am. We didn't stand up for him, and we knew, even Mom knew, that he was being unfair to Duane."

"I think I'm beginning to see. Is that the reason Duane's so angry with us, because we didn't stand with him?"

Agnes reached her hand across the table and touched my fingers. "I think it's definitely part of his anger, but it's not likely he understands exactly why he's so upset at us."

We stood, got rid of our empty cups, and headed for the elevator.

"You can't imagine my years of deep anger. I wanted to change, be different. So, I diligently searched the Bible, looking for answers, and I found secular books which helped to put my personal problems into perspective. One Sunday night, I went to the altar at church. I laid my hurt, really my hate for Pop, at the feet of Jesus. When I got up, I left it there."

"Why haven't we had this conversation before?"

"Aren't you the one who said a crisis brings out the best and worst in people? I'm convinced it also loosens tongues."

"That's for sure. Duane's already chewed me out." I nodded. "Thanks for the education and advice. I'm going to think seriously about what you've said. Do I need to head over and take care of Mom?"

"One of my church friends volunteered to stay with her today. But you will need to be there by six. I was hoping you'd spell me. I'd like to go home and clean up — take a nap. Mike's taking care of the kids today."

"Sure, go on. I'll have some time to spend with Pop."

As she went out the door, I called after her, "When you come back, bring me one or two of those books you've been reading. I'll have time to study them."

"Brother, let me leave you with this verse. Found in 1 Peter 1:6, it's been a comfort to me. *Where in ye greatly rejoice, though now for a season, if need be, ye are in heaviness through manifold temptations.*

"I might say testing. The next verse goes on to say our faith will be tried with fire, but in the end if we remain steadfast, our test will bring honor and glory to God." Agnes paused for a second to let her verse sink into my brain, then continued, "My Bible is on the window sill. I'll leave it for you to use."

She was gone and I stood with the noise of the machines in the room and quietness from the bed.

The hospital-green chair she had vacated had a folded, beige blanket and pillow on its arm. The seat was one of those which pulled out and made an uncomfortable but useful bed, especially when you got so tired there was no choice but to find a spot on it to rest.

I went over, shoved it away from the window, and sat down. Leaning back in the chair, I placed the pillow under my head, and wedged it against the wall. Tugging the blanket over me, I sat watching my Pop's chest rise and fall.

I sat for several minutes, fascinated by the action of his lungs. Or was his breathing facilitated by the noisy machine positioned close by — breathe in, breathe out. Breathe in, breathe out. My Pop was alive as long as I could observe this function of his body.

~

Before six Agnes returned, waking me from a deep sleep. "You looked really peaceful in that uncomfortable chair."

I stretched, finding aching parts as I moved my body. "Ouch. And you look better after your nap." Her face did look less haggard than when I'd seen her earlier.

"How's he been?"

"No problem, at least no nurses rushing into the room and stumbling over my sleeping form."

She laughed. "If you hurry, you can make dinner in the hospital's cafeteria."

"Isn't there anything in Mom's refrigerator?"

"I doubt it. There might be some baloney for making a sandwich."

"Pop's baloney sandwiches," I murmured, looking at him. Somehow, one of his favorites didn't seem too appetizing at present. "How many baloney sandwiches did we eat as kids? I thought I'd turn into a hunk of the finely, ground stuff."

"Baloney was a cheap and quick way of feeding five children—two pieces of bread, a slice of baloney, mayo, and a wedge of tomato."

"Wonder why we always had tomato wedges instead of slices?"

"Cause, I think Mom got tired of Pop yelling when tomato juice and mayo ran down our chins onto our clothes. He was a stickler about cleanliness and the juice of a tomato's stains were hard to get out of our cotton clothes. By the way that's another one of my faults I've managed to overcome."

"I wonder at the things Mom did to keep peace in our family—many we'll never know about."

If you're going to eat in the cafeteria, you'd better go. Oh, here are your books." She handed me a plastic grocery bag.

"Man, that's heavy."

"I don't want you to get bored at Mom's." She grinned.

"Does the cafeteria have takeout? Do I need to take Mom something to eat?"

"Yes, it does have takeout, and my friend took food for Mom to eat. Mom will be cleaned up and ready for bed when you get there."

I gave Agnes a bear hug. "We'll touch bases tomorrow. I love you, Sis."

"I love you, too. Thanks for coming."

CHAPTER EIGHTEEN

Luke

When I arrived at Mom's home, she was napping in her chair.

"She's been very content today," Agnes' friend, Faith Caylor, observed after I introduced myself. "She busied herself with gathering her knitting supplies and purse from the piano top. We've had a good time talking and working on our projects."

"Thank you so much for helping out with her today. Did she eat her dinner?"

"Oh, yes. I brought stew and corn bread. There's enough left for her tomorrow, if you don't eat it tonight." Faith was putting on a jacket. "I know this looks silly with the heat outside, but it was chilly this morning, and I don't like carrying the thing."

"Do you live close by?"

"Not too far. It only takes me a few minutes to drive, so call if you need me. I'm a widow, and part of our church ministry is helping when families have emergencies and need assistance. Here's my card. I'm available most of the time."

We said our goodbyes. With the door shut and locked, I walked back into the room where my mother slept. I said quietly so as not to disturb her, "Mom, I'm here to take care of you. That's a switch, isn't it?"

She sat in Pop's huge red recliner with her head leaning over, chin on her chest. Her salt-and-pepper hair was combed back firmly over her ears. I ran my eyes over her familiar face, still youthful with almost no wrinkles for her seventy-plus years. She appeared to have applied her makeup sometime during the day, because a hint of lipstick still framed her mouth. In her lap, blue yarn was twisted loosely, around a finger on her left hand; the other fell limply at her side.

I wondered how long she would sleep.

Being as quiet as possible, I went to the hallway and picked up my large suitcase and carry-on. Walking to the back of the house, I passed the rooms where I'd spent eighteen years of my life. Being the youngest boys, Tony and I shared a bedroom on the first floor, while the rest of my siblings slept on the second. My parents' bedroom was down the hall from us, separated by the guest bathroom which also doubled as my brother's and mine.

I entered the bedroom, putting my carry-on in a chair next to my old chest-of-drawers and unzipped it. I opened a small top drawer of the old chest I'd used as a kid, preparing to place my underwear in the compartment. The space was stuffed with newspaper clippings that were yellow or turning yellow with age. My mother had a habit of cutting out newspaper articles, recipes, or helpful hints she planned to use in the future.

Placed to the side, in the same drawer, were several scrapbooks stacked on top of each other. Picking the first one up, I sat on the twin bed I'd used as a child and teenager. The book wasn't titled. I opened it up toward the middle and turned the pages with a big smile.

My mother's clippings were cut from the local newspaper. They were of her children's activities in school and beyond. Some headlines read, *"Longview Native Works at NASA," "Avery Valedictorian of Longview High," "Sports Important to Avery Family,"* and *"Avery Graduates from Dallas Seminary"* — plus many others with pictures glued in no particular arrangement in its black pages. I realized she'd made a life within this rigid household, even if it was only escaping to cut out her clippings or crocheting.

The other drawers in the dresser weren't as full, so I combined some and unpacked my underwear and some T-shirts, which I planned to don around the house. No shirt and tie or suit for me — just casual stuff most days. I placed Manda's picture atop so I'd see it upon entering the door.

Going to the closet, I found the space filled with my father's clothes — work, everyday, and formal — if you could call what he normally wore during the daytime dressy. As long as they were clean, he wore them out to the gatherings of his few friends — the few times he went.

I pushed them tightly together and placed my shirts and pants on some empty hangers. Extra shoes I put in the closet floor along with my empty suitcases. On the airplane, I had worn my scuffed-up Texas boots. My toiletries I decided to leave behind my Sweetheart's photo, and take them as I needed to the bathroom.

Placing my Bible and the books Agnes had given me on the nightstand, I noticed the electric alarm clock was still running. Another leftover from my growing up days. Some one must come into the room and wind it.

Tiptoeing back to the living room, I found Mom was still asleep. I headed to the kitchen to check out food supplies. While rummaging through the refrigerator, I found Mrs. Taylor's leftover beef stew, and the ground chuck my father had bought to make vegetable soup. It needed to be cooked or frozen before it spoiled.

I decided to make the soup. Mom loved it and so did I. Pop had bought all the needed ingredients, and I needed to keep busy.

Soon the smell of frying meat mixed with the pungent smell of sweet Vidalia onions drifted through the house. While the meat and onions browned, I opened a quart of Mom's canned tomatoes and store-bought cans of peas, corn and lima beans—bought in small quantities just for soup. I chopped up celery and carrots which were in the crisper. After the meat and onions browned, and I ladled off the extra grease into one of the small cans, I added the tomatoes.

The assorted veggies, along with whole cloves and bay leaves soon followed. Mom always said the last two were her secret ingredients. Then to my surprise she would toss in two tablespoons of sugar, saying, "That's for good measure." She couldn't explain the comment except to tell me her mother had said it.

As a youngster, I supposed it took the sugar to make a full pot. Remembering her puzzling action, I'd done the same thing for years.

The last item I always added was the Irish potatoes. I rummaged around and found them in a container in the garage. Selecting four large ones, I returned to the kitchen.

Mom was stirring the boiling, steaming soup. Had she turned up the heat under the pot?

"Mom, I'll do this. You go sit down."

"Who are you?" She tightened her grip on the spoon. Her flashing eyes said, "I dare you to take this away from me."

"I'm Luke, your son. I'm going to stay with you a few days." I made a move to embrace her and hopefully turn down the gas under the kettle.

She stepped backward. "I don't know you. I'm scared. Where's Pop? It's dark outside."

"Pop and Agnes are together, and yes, it is dark outside. Are you hungry? I'm making your favorite— vegetable soup." I started to pare the potatoes, keeping an eye on the pot.

"Do I like it?"

"Yes, Mom. See, I'm peeling the potatoes. Then I'll cut them into cubes, and we'll place them in the pot together." Speaking to her was like talking to a child in an adult body. I said simple things hoping to keep her calm and prick her memory.

"Why?" she asked. "The soup looks okay without them," she peered into the Dutch oven, still stirring the mixture. She hovered over it in a protective manner, continuing to watch me out of the corner of her eye.

"But you like potatoes in vegetable soup. That's what you always told me."

"I did? I don't remember telling you that. Who did you say you were? Where's Pop? He wouldn't get up, and I was hungry."

"Yes, Mom. Pop got up, and he's with Agnes."

"Oh ..."

This wasn't the Mom I knew. If I insisted on putting the potatoes in the soup and turning down the heat, I thought she might hit me with the long-handled soupspoon.

I decided to change the conversation. "Mom, let's go into the living room. You can continue your crocheting."

She brightened up at the word crocheting and let me take her by the arm. Thank goodness she let go of the spoon, leaving it in the kettle. I led her to Pop's chair. Soon she was stitching away, and I headed back to the kitchen.

I ran to the stove and turned down the heat, putting in the cubed potatoes, and placing the spoon into the sink. The soup would cook until the potatoes were done, and then we would eat it. Or rather, Mom would eat it or Faith's leftovers, since I'd already had dinner at the hospital. I went back to the living room and made myself comfortable in her chair.

She looked up from her crocheting. "Luke, I didn't know you were here."

I blinked twice, taken aback by her statement. "Mom, I-I've come to stay with you for a few days."

"How nice. Your father left with Agnes. She said he was sick and needed to go to the hospital. An ambulance came with siren and everything. Is that where they are now?"

"Yes, Agnes is with Pop now."

"When will they be coming home? Shouldn't I go and check on him?"

"I think Agnes is handling the problem. I'm sure it won't be long until he's home. You need to stay here and take care of the house until Pop gets back."

She nodded.

I saw no reason to tell Mom the gravity of Pop's situation. Agnes advised me to stress the lack of an emergency and no need for her to leave the comfort of her home.

"I'm making some vegetable soup. Smells good, doesn't it? Would you like some? I'll go check and see if it's done."

She pulled the recliner up erect, put the footrest down, and prepared to get up.

"No, Mom." I put my hand on her shoulder. "I'll check. You rest. It's been a long day."

"Thank you, Son. I'm so happy you're here. There's so much to catch up on since you were here last." She smiled, her fingers flashing with single and double crochet stitches.

I looked at her and smiled back. She didn't remember my visit only day's ago. Leaving the room, I checked the soup in the kitchen, watching the corn, peas, lima beans, and potatoes as I stirred and swirled them in the pot. They didn't have anything on my confused brain. This was exactly what Agnes had told me. One minute Mom was fine. The next she wasn't.

I returned to the living room, not knowing what to expect. "The potatoes aren't done. Are you hungry?"

She put down her crocheting and thought about my question. "Yes, a little. I always put plenty of potatoes in the soup. I love potatoes, don't you?"

"We'll have a bowl as soon as it's done." I started to relax a little. Mom seemed to be asking good questions.

"How's James."

"He's having the time of his life this summer. He'll be in fourth grade this fall."

"I can't believe it. Time passes so quickly. Did you bring him with you?'

"No, he stayed in Maryville."

My mother continued to smile at me. It was time to tell her of my pending marriage. "Mom, I'm engaged to be married. Her name is Amanda Weathers. She goes to Church-on-the-Hill."

"Luke, that's wonderful. Peggy's been gone several years. We'll always miss her. Have you set a wedding date?"

"Yes, it's December 13. I have Amanda's picture. I'll get it." I hurried to my bedroom and pulled Manda's photo off the dresser where I'd placed it. I rushed back to the living room, hoping Mom was still lucid. I handed the picture to her.

"Why, Luke, she's beautiful. She has stunning eyes."

For the first time, I felt like I could give my Mom the hug I wanted to in the kitchen. "Mom, I love you," I said, leaning over her. I wanted to say this, and I intended to repeat the phrase every time she was coherent.

She looked at me and smiled.

"I'll bet the soup is done now. Let's go get a bowlful." I helped her get up and we walked arm in arm to the kitchen.

She went straight to the sugar bowl, and I followed on her heels. "I think I forgot to put the sugar in the pot."

Placing my hand on hers I said, "Mom, you did. I saw you. Here, sit down and let me serve you." I led her to a chair at the kitchen table.

"The ladle is in the top drawer to the right of the stove," she advised.

I turned my back and opened the drawer, pretending to pull the spoon out, when I already had it in my hand.

My mother and I sat and enjoyed a bowl of vegetable soup. She chatted away about her children's former lives at home. "Luke, I'm going to the bathroom. Would you pour me another glass of tea? I won't be long."

I watched her leave the room, thinking how wonderful it was to interact with her on a normal level. She was always interested in each of her children's activities, asking multiple questions and listening to our explanations.

I cleaned the bowls off the table and washed them. Putting more ice in Mom's glass, I poured in more sweet tea and sat down to wait on her.

Twenty minutes passed. I went to look for her.

The door to the quest bathroom stood open. My spray shaving cream sat on the bathroom counter. Mom stood staring at her hands. She had shaving cream on them, all over the cabinet, and the mirror. "Mom, what happened?"

She turned to stare at me. Her eyes were blank, unknowing. "I couldn't find the soap."

The bottle of liquid soap sat on the counter next to the faucet. It's here. Let me help you clean up."

She jumped back at my touch. "Who are you? I don't know you. Where's Pop? Did he get up?"

Instead of touching her again, I turned on the water and made handwashing motions, hoping she would follow me. "I'm your son, Luke. Did you go to the bathroom?" I stepped back to give her some room.

She nodded, but I had my doubts. "Where's Pop?" she whined, but she did approach the sink and rinse off her hands.

"He's with Agnes." I handed her a towel and moved toward the hall. "Mom, it's past nine. Don't you think you need to go to bed?"

"Bed, yes." She dried her hands and moved to the doorway, where I stood.

I stepped aside and let her pass, giving her lots of room. She walked down the hall and started into the guest bedroom.

I rushed to her side. "No, Mom. Your bedroom is down the hall. Here I'll take you."

She let me lead her to the last room at the end. Her nightgown was lying on the bed.

"Here's your gown, Mom. I'll wait in the hall." I pulled a kitchen chair outside of her bedroom and sat down, wondering if she'd remember how to change into her bedclothes. I'd never been privy to my mother without clothes on, and I didn't intend to start now. If worse came to worse, we'd figure a way.

It seemed like an hour before she got her gown on, but it was only minutes. When I finally looked into the room, she was standing by her bed, uncertain what should be done next.

"Time to get in bed, Mom." I went to her, and helped her under the sheets and quilt top. "Mom, I'm going to get my Bible, and we'll have devotions." I didn't wait for her to reply but hurried to my room.

Reading the Bible to my Mom was a new experience. One I intended to cherish for the rest of my life. I sat there until she was asleep. How many years had she done the same for me?

Leaning over, I kissed her good night. "I love you, Mom," I told her again.

I was emotionally beat when I got up and left the room. Walking down the hall, I stopped at the door of the bathroom. How long would it take to clean up the mess she'd made at the sink? I had to do it. Choosing a clean hand towel out of the hall linen closet, I set about wiping off the mirror and sink.

When I finished cleaning the bathroom, the kitchen was next, and then the living room. Grabbing Manda's photo, I walked to my bedroom, wondering if I should rig an alarm, so I'd know if Mom came out of her room during the night. I couldn't think of a thing as a warning system. Maybe some bells hung over her door would work—they worked at Suds and Styles, and Laney's Hardware was just the place to purchase them.

I got ready for bed and decided not to call Manda. I was emotionally exhausted and since this was her day to work late, I decided to send her a brief e-mail with a big I LOVE YOU at the end. Tomorrow was Saturday. Suds and Styles closed at six. We would have a long talk then.

CHAPTER NINETEEN

Luke

Mike arrived the next morning at eight. After I opened the door, I hugged him. "It's great to see you, man."

"Luke, how was your night?" Mike was grinning, anticipating my response.

"Interesting," was the first word that came to mind. "I can see what Agnes has been talking about—Mom comes and goes." I related the highlights of the previous evening, leaving out the bathroom incident.

Mike nodded, as I told the details. "She'll do me the same way today, but I hope she stays out of your shaving cream."

I laughed. "Really? She gets into yours, too."

"No. Into your father's. He shared this bit of information when I came over to relieve him one day. He needed to go to the store, and Agnes couldn't come. He and I were both mystified about her fascination with the stuff. Agnes and I've talked about it, and neither one of us can come up with an answer."

"Well, I hid it where she can't find it."

"She's snoopy. She'll look. How do caregivers supervise their charges day after day without burning out?" Mike wondered.

"I'm already feeling tired, and I've only been here less than a day. I always thought the tendency to nurture and care is innate, built or imbedded into our natures," I suggested.

"I feel for those working in our assisted living and dementia wards after leaving here. Have you talked to Agnes this morning?"

"No, I've been busy getting Mom up and dressed. Have you talked to her?" His wife had stayed all night with Pop.

"Yes, we ate breakfast together at the hospital."

"How was Pop's night?"

"Two more episodes of erratic heart rhythm. Whatever the doctors are doing isn't helping. It doesn't look good. Agnes sent me over, so you could relieve her and sit with him today. She needs the rest."

"Okay, I'd like to do that. When are you going back to work?"

"I *have* to go back on Monday."

"How's the drilling going?"

"We're at a critical time in the operation. By Monday, our well will be at or around six thousand feet deep. That's when we start looking for signs of gas in the Barnett Shale. When we find it, we'll take measurements of the gaseous quantities embedded there, and then determine when to start drilling horizontally."

"You're drilling for gas? I thought Agnes said oil."

"There's some oil, but where we are, the vast majority of the reserves are gas. What we're doing is called fracking."

"I see."

Mike grinned at me. "It's a tad more complicated than it used to be."

"I don't understand drilling methods, but I do understand complicated. Mom's up and dressed. I hope you can fix oatmeal. She's already suggested it for breakfast."

"Hey, I can handle it. Don't worry about her. Just go spend some time with your Pop." Mike paused and added, "Luke, I don't think he's going to make it. His heart keeps trying, but ..."

"After seeing him yesterday, I have my doubts, too."

~

When I entered the door of the hospital room, Agnes was sitting in her favorite green chair—head back and eyes closed. She got up and tiptoed toward me.

"I don't know why I do that. He doesn't know a thing that's going on." She nodded toward Pop, who looked like he hadn't changed positions since yesterday.

"Have they been in to move him, lately?" I knew lack of movement led to pneumonia.

"Yes, they have. Not too long ago as a matter of fact." She walked to the foot of the bed and pulled the blanket over an exposed foot.

"How's it going, Sis?"

"No change, except for two more episodes last night."

"I know, Mike told me. Why don't you go on home and rest? I'll take care of Pop today. Don't worry about a thing."

"Why do we even sit here? It doesn't matter to him." she seemed uptight, and I knew she was tired.

I'd had a good night's sleep. "Maybe we hope it would matter to him. Or maybe, we think no one deserves to die alone."

"I suppose there's always the expectation he will regain consciousness."

"That too, but I can't picture Pop without being able to move and tinker around the house and his workshop. He did keep the house in good shape. When we went to the bank to transfer Robert's insurance money for the children, he told me he intended to start repainting the kitchen."

"I'm so glad you took care of that."

"What?"

"Transferring the money. If Pop doesn't make it, the money might have been held up for months or years."

"He wasn't too happy about transferring the funds without the children being in my home. It's a control issue with him. But I explained I wouldn't be back in Longview. I told him you and Mike would bring Clint, Marcus, and Maryb to Tennessee."

"I saw him the day after you left. He tried to persuade you to move home again, didn't he?"

"Yes, he did his best. Even hinted I could bring James and live with them. Can you imagine a stickier situation, even though he would have loved to have my son in the house. The trouble would have started when he tried to control both of us. I wouldn't expose James to that."

"You told him you were engaged to be married?"

"I can see him now. He stopped in mid-stride and looked straight at me."

'"If you marry a woman from Tennessee, you'll never come home to Longview to live. I was hoping' ... Pop shut down like turning off the ignition of a car. Agnes, that's the first time I saw hurt in his face, but he quickly covered it up, and started walking again, taking longer steps. I could tell he was angry, and I had a hard time keeping up with him."

"Do you think he regrets the fact he's alienated his boys?"

"Or is he blaming us again? I'd like to think regret was in his mind, and he was having second thoughts about his life. Isn't aging supposed to mellow you out?"

"Yes, but old habits die hard. You could see it in action at our meeting with Mom."

"Speaking of Mom, have you heard anything from Nightingale Place?"

"I talked to Mr. Taylor three days ago. He said there's a possibility a room will open up around the middle of September. The son of one of his residents has been transferred to Waco, and he and his wife will take their father with them. The timing isn't definite."

"That's good news. I thought he had a waiting list."

"He does. He explained when there's and opening, he goes down his list, and some people have found other places to put their family member, or they've decided to keep them at home, or they're just not ready to make the move. The nation's economy has forced some to remove patients from his facility. He said residents are always in flux."

"I hate to think of Mom leaving her home, but the sooner we can get a room, the sooner I'll feel better about the situation."

"I forgot to tell you. Mom has a doctor appointment on Monday. It's in the doctor's building next door to the hospital. I think it's at one in the afternoon." Agnes dug into her purse. "Here it is." She handed me the card. "The office is easy to find. There's a directory when you go in the main door."

"I'll take care of it. I'd like to talk to him about Mom's case."

Agnes looked over at Pop. "He *wouldn't like* not being able to work in his shop or drive his car," she said quietly, echoing my former words.

"No. I wouldn't want to be the one to support him through a long recuperation. He's hard enough to deal with when he's not sick."

"One of us may have to," Agnes said.

I shook my head. Words did not come.

"Guess I'll leave him with you." She walked over and gave him a gentle kiss on the forehead. For a moment, she stood and patted his arm. "I love you, Pop." She turned toward me. "Just in case he does know what's going on around him."

"I'll see you tonight, Luke." She gave me a quick hug and disappeared into the hallway.

I walked over to the hospital bed. Could I articulate the words, "I love you" and say them to my father?

I couldn't do it, but Agnes could. My sister followed Jesus' words better than I, and I was a minister who counseled and consoled the grieving and sick. I needed to change. Hadn't she said the very same words?

One of the books she'd given me to read was tucked under my arm. Giving Pop a last look, I walked to the green chair and got comfortable. Opening it up, I started on page one.

～

"Mr. Avery, except for *probable* Alzheimer's disease and intermittent urinary track infections your mother is in relatively good health."

On Monday, Dr. Isaacs stood by the examining table where Mom sat. She leafed through a magazine he'd handed her, checking out the pictures as she went, not interested in the happenings in the room. For some unknown reason I couldn't explain, she trusted this man. There was no, "Who are you? I don't know you? Where's Pop?" The doctor did bear a slight resemblance to my father, and maybe she felt safe.

Dr. Isaacs gave me a brief smile. His face was weathered from many days in the sun, and his glasses sat precariously on the end of his suntanned nose. He looked over them at me. I guessed the man to be a little older than I, maybe fifties.

"I thought she had dementia."

"She does. Alzheimer's and dementia go hand in hand."

"Why did you say *probable* Alzheimer's?"

"There's no way I can tell whether a patient has dementia just by looking at them. In fact, the only way to determine for sure if one has Alzheimer's is to do an autopsy after the patient is deceased. That's why we say probable when we talk about the disease. But a doctor looks at four things when the diagnosis concerns reduced mental capacity."

"What are they?"

"First, we do a complete medical history. Some medications can cause confusion. Second, we conduct medical tests. We draw blood and check urine. These tests rule out medical conditions that might be causing dementia. Third, neuropsychological tests check memory. That's the patient's ability to solve problems, attention span, and other aptitudes associated with brain function. And finally, a brain scan determines the possibility of an abnormality such as a tumor which could cause strange, confused behavior."

"Let's say Mom just walked in here. I brought her because she seems confused. What questions do you ask to determine if she has serious memory loss? I wouldn't inquire, but I haven't been in on any conversation concerning her diagnosis. I'd like to understand her condition better."

"I appreciate your interest. Here are some questions I would ask. Why don't you think about your mother's condition and answer them based on her actions?"

"Fair enough."

"Does your mother ask the same questions again and again? Can she follow directions without confusion? Time periods and people can be foggy. Is she disoriented in places she should know well?" The doctor looked at me as if to say "Well?"

I smiled as he asked the questions, recognizing the symptoms he'd named. "Yes, to all your questions. Two days ago, she went to my bedroom for the bathroom and used my shaving cream for hand soap. When I found her, she had made it to the bathroom and had the foam on her hands, the sink, and the mirror. She just stood there surrounded by the mess she'd made, not knowing what to do next."

"Exactly what I'm talking about. Actions such as what you've just explained aren't normal for her. Some AD patients get belligerent, protective of their territory. This anger can be mild, or the sufferer can strike out at you."

"Confrontational behavior or hitting anyone would be completely out of character for my mother." Then I remembered the pot of soup, the spoon, and her standing protectively over it. "But, that's a possibility."

"There you go. All the things I've mentioned so far are progressive. They will grow worse. Finally, she will quit taking care of herself. She has to be led to the table and spoon-fed. She won't bathe, and she'll do things which will endanger herself and possibly others around her." Dr. Isaacs turned around and took my mother's hand to help her off the examining table. She handed the magazine to me.

"Must be horrible for those who love the patient, watching and waiting." I leaned toward the doctor and shook my head, hoping for words of encouragement. I wanted to withdraw into myself, do anything not to acknowledge my mother's disease.

"It's never easy on those who must endure the loss of a parent or relative, because you lose them, but not in a normal way. In many ways, death is preferable to living with Alzheimer's."

"The stricken one has no conception of the horrible condition of their life. I hate the thought of my mother being here in body but not her mind."

"I know how you feel. My mother is in the final stages. She hasn't known me in over two years, and she's in excellent health."

"Is there any hope for a cure?"

"Research and clinical trials are ongoing. But, at present, there's no cure, no preventative medicine that I know of, although donepezil and some other medicines seem to slow it down for a few years. They don't stop it. You mother's prescription is for donepezil."

"It's like searching for the proverbial needle in a haystack."

"Yes. The researchers will keep looking, and we'll keep praying for an answer."

"You said your mother has AD. Is she in assisted living?"

"Yes. My wife took care of her for three years. As my mother's dementia progressed, so did my wife's stress over the cruel assault on Mom's life. She was becoming an emotional, high-strung wreck." He sat down on the roll-around stool next to the small sink in the room. Taking off his glasses, he rubbed the impression they'd made on his nose. The expression on his face had changed. He looked tired.

I got the feeling Dr. Isaacs *needed* someone to talk to like I did. He was sharing his experience of AD with me.

"I can understand what you're saying. I've been in Longview only a few days, and I'm rushing around trying to tend to her every need." I indicated my mother, who was standing close to the door with her hand on the knob. "At night, I fall in bed and don't want to get up in the morning, because the day won't be any different from the day before."

The doctor nodded in agreement. "My wife and mother were best buds, going shopping at the mall, visiting friends, and attending concerts at LeTourneau University. I had to tear my mother away from my wife's nurturing. It took months for my wife to get back to normal, but she's okay now, and Mom has good care."

"I don't want to think about Mom leaving the only home she's known for most of her life."

"It's hard. We took my mother's furniture and her favorite things. Put familiar pictures on the wall and hung drapes from her bedroom at home. I was amazed and comforted to see how well she adapted to her new surroundings."

"Could you share where she's at now?"

"Nightingale Place. I highly recommend it. Mr. Taylor runs a very professional facility, and his caregivers approach the residents with compassion."

"That's where we hope to take Mom."

Dr. Issacs looked at his watch. "Back to work. I'm surprised my nurse hasn't tapped on the door. He got up and went over to Mom. "Mrs. Avery, I'll see you in two months." He patted her arm. "Luke, I've enjoyed meeting you."

We shook hands. "Thank you, Dr. Isaacs. You've just validated everything I've thought about Mom's condition. I deal with people in hospitals and nursing homes every day, but until a medical problem happens in your family, there's no reason to search for deeper answers."

He managed to move around Mom and open the door. His nurse was outside, directing him to another patient.

❧ CHAPTER TWENTY ❧

Manda

"If your bladder doesn't hold tight like it used to, I don't see how you can expect other body parts to maintain the *status quo*." My father said, on Thursday, without cracking a smile.

Although he didn't quite understand this comment, James laughed at the outrageous thought of a bladder holding tight.

Mom shook her head, knowing chastising her husband was to no avail.

But I opened my mouth and said, "Dad! You're terrible," although I agreed with her, saying anything to him was useless.

Mom had called earlier in the week to make sure I'd be over for dinner today. I'd picked up James after work from Mrs. Docksets, glad not to have to cook or eat a sandwich. Luke had been gone three weeks.

We were sitting on the enclosed back porch, around a small table in Mom's olive-green décor. The color, a reminder that the house had been built in the sixties. My parents were the second owners of the brick and vinyl sided dwelling where I'd grown up. Before he retired, Dad's crew had made many upgrades to the home, including a grill just outside this glassed-in, air-conditioned porch where we sat now.

Mom arose and headed for the kitchen to bring the rest of the food.

"Would you rather I was stodgy, straight-faced, and cranky?" My father made faces over a chunk of grilled meat he'd speared from a plate with his fork, causing James to laugh again. He always took a bite of his steak before the blessing. "Just testing," he would say. "I might need to pray for the meat, also."

Everyone laughed, and I chuckled with them. "No, I'd rather you were just exactly the way you are now."

My father could be serious. "I know Luke's father will receive the best medical care at Longview's hospital. James, we'll hope he gets better and is able to care for your grandma. Of course, our heavenly Father may have other plans. Let's pray."

~

"Has Luke's father improved since I talked to you on the phone?" My mother placed the last bowl on the table and sat down, wiping her hands on her apron.

"None whatsoever. Luke says the needle on his Pop's monitor continues to record many episodes of his heart's arrhythmia. The doctors seem to think it's just a matter of time."

Mom pointed discretely at James.

I put my arm around him. "He knows. I tell him first. Luke doesn't want anything held back, and if something happens there'll be no shock."

"I worry about Luke. How's he holding up?" My mother held a spoon over one of the many bowls on the table. "James would you like some mashed potatoes?"

Before he could answer, my mother gave him a heaping spoonful.

Her actions reminded me of my growing up years. "The potatoes are grown in Pop's garden."

"Mr. Puckett, I think gardening would be cool," said James. Do you think I could help you some this year?"

"Son, if you're going to call my daughter, Mom, then you have to call me Granddad. Okay?"

"Okay, Granddad."

"And, to answer your question, yes. I'll be glad to have some company and help." My father gave James a high five, smiled at his soon-to-be grandson, and dug into his food.

I grinned, knowing my father was enjoying this new relationship. A mutual bond was already forming.

"Eat up, Son." To me Dad said, "So, how is Luke?"

"He's surviving, even though the situation is stressful. It isn't often two people in one family are acutely ill at the same time, and Agnes' husband, Mike, returned to work a week ago Monday. Agnes and Luke are stretched pretty thin. He used the words 'a rubber band ready to break' to describe the state of affairs."

"Mrs. Avery, how is she?"

"Luke went with her to the doctor. He said the visit was interesting. He was able to ask Dr. Isaacs several questions about Alzheimer's, and he found out the doctor's mother had AD."

"I wonder what causes Old Timer's disease. More and more elderly people are being diagnosed with it."

"I asked Luke the same question. The researchers don't know, and medications won't prevent or stop its progression."

"I feel for Luke. I wish I could help with his mother." My mother's face showed her concern. "I imagine he isn't sleeping well at night. Manda, I remember when you were sick, dear. The slightest sound woke me up, and I would go check on you." She reached across the table and patted my hand.

I took it and squeezed it lightly.

"Luke's had some problems with this. His mother wakes in the night, gets up, and wanders around the house. James here, sleeps like a log, so keeping an ear cocked to every sound is something Luke's had to learn."

"I'll bet he rigged up an alarm."

James piped up, "How'd you know, Grandpa?"

"Just a lucky guess, but also, something I'd do."

"When I talked to Dad, he told me about my Granny's night walks, so I told him about Mrs. Docksets' dog. She attached a ribbon with bells over her dog door. She knows when he comes onto the porch, and then she can let him into the house."

"She's a smart lady, Mrs. Docksets," Dad responded.

"So, my Dad rigged up some bells on a ribbon and hung them over Granny's door. They jingle when she opens it."

Something in James' voice caused my mother to look at him. "You like your Granny Avery, don't you?"

"Yeah, I wish she wasn't sick." James dropped his eyes and placed his hands on the table.

I hadn't realized how much the faraway situation in Longview affected James. I put my arm around him and gave him a hug. We needed to have a talk on the way home.

James looked at me, hurt in his eyes. "My Granny was my friend. But Pop, he wouldn't let me go next door and play indoors with my friend. He had some cool toys and several Lego sets. Pop insisted we play outside in the front yard with him watching. I don't know why?"

"Anyone for some orange pound cake and orange sherbet?" Mom pushed her chair from the table. I knew from previous experience the conversation had taken an emotional and serious turn, and this was her idea of changing the subject, hoping to cheer up everyone.

Dessert changed a somber mood my father always said, and my mother agreed.

"James, why don't you come and help me?" They got up, taking some empty plates with them and went to the kitchen.

Above the preparations for dessert, Dad and I heard her tell him, "Don't you worry about your Granny. She'll be in safe hands, and your new Mamaw Puckett will be here to help you."

I was sure the next sound was her hugging and kissing James.

∾

"James, I'm sorry that your Pop and Granny Avery are sick." We were heading back to my home. The rain poured down, and my wipers swooshed as they worked back and forth on my windshield. "We must continue to pray they'll be better."

"I've been praying my Granny will be better— every time I think of her. And Pop needs to get well so he can take care of her. My Dad taught me to *"pray without ceasing."'*

I recognized the Bible's words. "You *should* do that. There's another option when it comes to your grandmother. Aunt Agnes and your Dad have found a really nice place for Granny to live. She needs someone who's experienced with her problem to take care of her day and night. Pop may need the same constant care. If this happens, your father can come back home. But he isn't coming until then."

James turned toward me in the front seat to ask his question. "How long do you think he'll have to stay in Longview"

I shook my head. "I can't say. He may be there another month, or it may be the end of the year." I hoped his stay wouldn't be prolonged, because he would lose his position at Hilly Church. If that happened, I didn't know where we would end up. I pulled into my driveway. The garage door went up with the touch of my opener.

"It seems like he's been gone forever."

"I know. How would you like to play a game of Battleship before bed?"

"Cool." James jumped out of the Avalon and headed for the door into the den. I followed him into the room. He rushed to his upstairs bedroom. I heard thumping and then his footsteps on the stairs. "Mom, where do you want to play?"

"At the kitchenette table." I breathed a prayer. "Lord, thank you for nine-year-old miracles." I threw my purse on the den couch. First things first. I'd put it up later. Right now, I needed to win or lose a game of Battleship. I went to the kitchenette and gave James a hug as I passed him.

～

During my break at ten the next morning, I called Hilly Church. Friday was not a day my pastor was normally there, but I hoped to catch him working in his office.

He answered the phone, Hilly Church, I mean Church-on—"

"I know what you mean, Pastor."

"Manda, how are you? Sorry about my greeting, my thoughts were elsewhere."

"I understand, and I couldn't be better. I guess you've talked to Luke this week."

"Yes, we talked on Wednesday. He was upbeat, but tired. Don't think he's getting much sleep."

"The whole family's under a lot of strain. I wish there was more I could do to help. Long distance support and prayer, they're good, but I'd like to be physically involved, active, participating—what's the adjective I'm looking for?"

"Present, maybe? Manda, I know what you mean. This kind of situation makes you feel so small and helpless. We can't solve the problem, can we?"

"No, so praying to Him is the best activity. Only the Father can take care of the present dilemma."

"God knows the needs, and I use the plural, of the Avery family. He'll use this difficulty to resolve them, or at least give the family a chance to work through them. How they cope and come through is up to each member. I'm praying for them to learn to love each other. I believe the greatest difficulty lies there."

I heard what my pastor was saying.

"How are the plans for the youth's summer mission progressing." I'd had to give this responsibility up after taking James to live with me.

"Bess Myers and her husband, Milburn, have wrapped up the details associated with the project. They'll leave in two weeks."

"It's great to have someone act as backup. I'm going to miss going this year."

"Your life is as hectic as Luke's. Letting the Myers' take over is the best solution."

"Pastor, I called for a specific reason. School starts soon, and I know Luke's concerned about Clint, Marcus, and Maryb starting school in Longview. I've been thinking about a possible solution. I'd like to go down to Longview and bring the children home to Tennessee. They could stay with me until we find a bigger home. Would I be taking on too much responsibility?"

"How are you and James doing?"

"James is a joy to be around, and my parents adore him. I've never met the other children. I guess that's where my apprehension lies."

"Manda, there's a lot of unanswered questions within Luke's situation, and he nor you have a time limit to go by. Think about these problems associated with his family. As far as children, you've always been wonderful with them. I can't recall one child here at church who doesn't love you."

"I think I've considered all the obvious complications. My principal concern is the oldest child, Clint. He seems to be a bit of a challenge, according to Agnes. He's almost sixteen, going on thirty, Luke says."

"Pop Avery was his only role model," I heard my Pastor say, almost to himself. He continued, "Of course, you couldn't bring one without bringing them all."

"No, I couldn't."

"He's not going to listen to a female after being in the Avery household so long. He'll want to run the show like his grandfather did, and he'll expect you to knuckle under like his grandmother did. I think, Manda, it would be better if Luke were here with the children. Your concern is warranted."

"That's exactly what I was thinking."

"Do I hear a but coming?"

"Yes, I wonder if I couldn't manage until Luke's situation is Longview is resolved?"

"Have you talked to Luke about this?"

"No, not yet."

"Am I helping you dredge up all the pros and cons before you do?"

He'd figured me out. "Yes."

"I believe you've already made your decision, haven't you?"

"Sort of. Luke may veto my idea. If he does, I'll let the whole thing drop. I suppose the children should have a little say-so in the matter, too."

"You have my support, and I'm sure my wife will do the same, no matter which way this goes.

"Thank you, Pastor." I hung up the phone, somewhat relieved. Two hours later, the whole situation changed.

CHAPTER TWENTY-ONE

Manda

Luke was on the phone. "Manda, Pop had another major heart attack about two hours ago. He's gone. I hurried to the hospital, but he passed almost as soon as I got there. Agnes has gone home to sleep, and I'm back at Mom's."

"I'm so sorry, Luke." I was standing with a comb and scissors in one hand and holding the phone in the other. "Do you want me to come down?"

"Would you, Sweetheart? You'll be able to meet the rest of the family. I'd like them to know what a lovely lady I'm engaged to."

In sympathy with my intended, silent tears rolled down my face. Every noise behind me had ceased in the beauty shop, where sound carried to the front of the salon. I mentally ticked off the details which would need to be done. First on the list was his son. "What about James?"

"I've thought about him. Ask him and let him make the decision."

"Okay, that's a good idea. He may want to stay with my mother and father. Oh, Luke, you should see them together. It's wonderful how they get along."

"That's a relief. I'm pleased he likes them. He loved my Mom, but he never understood Pop. Did anybody."

"James wants to help my Dad in the garden this year, and Dad agreed. I was proud of them both. Are your brothers coming?"

"Yes. They'll both be here tomorrow morning. They're coming with their spouses, and the grandchildren are staying at home. Agnes and I will go make all the arrangements for the funeral early in the morning. I'll let you know what we decide, and I'll call our pastor, and Agnes will touch bases with hers."

"Will you bury him on Sunday?"

"I think so. Then those who want to stay can, and those who need to return to work can leave."

"I'll book a flight and be there as soon as possible. Will there be room for me at your Mom's?"

"Depends on the arrangements my brothers make. I'll let you know, and if not, I'll get you a room at Homewood Suites. Either way, you'll be covered."

"I miss you so much. I wish I could be there right now to put my arms around you and comfort you."

"You will be soon, Darling. There's someone at the door. I'll see you tomorrow. I love you."

"I love you, too." The other line went dead, and I felt like I'd been cut off in the middle of the conversation. "Get over it, Amanda," I chided as I hung up the phone, while brushing tears from my cheeks. All eyes were on me as I turned around and headed for June.

~

After calling in one of June's standby hair-dressers, I headed for the airport to check on arrangements for the flight to Longview. My next stop was my parents' home.

A smiling Dad answered the door. "What'd you do, quit your job?" he boomed as he swung the door wide so I could enter.

"No." I said, as my mother appeared in the hallway. "Luke's father just passed away, and I came by to tell you."

Something in my face or voice caused my mother to hurry to me. She threw her arms around me. "I'm so sorry, Honey."

The emotional strain of the last few weeks hit me without warning. Tears flowed down my cheeks as I sobbed on my mother's shoulder. "Luke's been through so much. The whole family has."

"Luke isn't the only one, dear. You have too. I've noticed the strain in your face each time you've come by." She led me to the living room, where we sat on the loveseat. The same one Luke and I'd used when we announced our engagement. That thought caused more tears to come. So many things had happened in the weeks since then. Mom let me quiet down before asking more questions. "What happened to Mr. Avery?"

My apologetic and awkward father produced a box of tissues and handed me one.

I looked up at him. I was sure my mascara was running down my cheeks with my tears. "Thanks." I wiped by eyes and blew my nose before I responded. "Another massive heart attack. He didn't survive long after. Agnes phoned Luke as soon as it happened, and he arrived at the hospital not long before his father passed."

"At least, he isn't suffering now." My father sat down on the edge of a chair, arms on his knees and his head lowered. I knew he was praying.

"When will they make the arrangements?" Mom asked.

"Tomorrow morning, and I'll fly out in the morning. Hopefully, the services will be on Sunday."

"What about James? Will he go?" my father asked.

"I booked him a seat on the airplane, but it can be cancelled. Luke said to ask him, and if he doesn't want to make the long flight, he'd be okay with him not coming. I was hoping he might stay with you until I get back sometime next week. Of course, my coming and going is open-ended with no set time to return. If you and Mom have plans, there's always Mrs. Docksets."

"Oh, no," said my father. "He's very welcome here. That would be *cool*."

I looked at dad and smiled. "Good. I was hoping you'd keep him."

My mom added, "He needs a little fatting up. He's too thin."

My Dad nodded a yes at Mom.

"Please give Luke our love and condolences when you get there." She stood. "Lunch is almost ready. You'll eat with us." Her statement wasn't a question, but a fact. My Mom believed everything is done better with good, warm food inside you, and she made both.

I pulled into Mrs. Docksets driveway in the middle of the day. She knew I was coming, because I'd called her with the latest news.

She opened the front door before I could knock. "I'm sorry about Luke's father." She was whispering, echoing the works I'd said earlier on the phone. "I didn't tell James you were coming. He's in the den watching cartoons."

James knew something was wrong the minute he saw me.

"James, Manda's here to pick you up."

"Now? But it isn't time." He was looking from one to the other of us.

"I know, but we need to hurry home, honey. Something's come up." I watched as he put his library book, Chinese checkers game, and his DS into his school backpack.

Mrs. Docksets said goodbye at the door. "You'll let me know if he's coming tomorrow."

"Yes, as soon as I know our plans."

I helped James put his backpack in the car's back seat. He slid onto the front, closed the door, and fastened his seat belt. I went around to the driver's side and got in. Waving at Mrs. Docksets, I started the car.

"Is it Pop?" He looked at me with eyes as big as saucers, a questioning expression on his face.

"Yes, I'm so sorry, James. Your grandfather has passed away, only this morning. I talked to your Dad before lunch. I think you should call him when we get home."

I pulled out of the driveway. I lived only three miles away, but across town.

James was quiet, too quiet. "I knew this was going to happen."

I heard the hurt in his voice. "He was very sick, James. He could have gone either way. Heart problems aren't good."

"We could have been good friends." James declared. "Why did he act the way he did?" A low sob escaped the young boy's lips.

It shocked me. James was a happy—go—lucky child. I'd never seen him cry.

"Everyone is different, James. Your grandfather was just more extreme and in a separate category from most people. I didn't know him, so I can't tell you why." From what Luke had told me, this was an understatement.

How could I comfort James? He sat glued to the passenger side door, his head against the window. Then it hit me. "You loved your grandfather, didn't you?"

Out of the corner of my eye, I saw a slight nod. I had to smile. Who would have thought it? But why not? James was a young child when his mother died. He wanted to love everyone, including his grandfather. He needed his family.

James sat up straight in his seat. "Most of the time, I felt sorry for him. Mom, why do you think he didn't love me? I tried to be good."

I was stopped at a red light. The traffic was heavy. Turning, I saw the pain in his eyes as he looked at me. "James, you are good and lovable. I love you very much. I'm sure in his own way Pop did love you. He just didn't know how to show his affection."

"Do you really think so?"

"Yes. Some people are like that. They grow up in life, and they never learn to love or show love." How else could I answer his question? How could a grandfather not love and show love to his grandchild?

"Did you know, he once gave me something?"

"He did? What was it?

"A silver dollar made in the year he was born. It's in my dresser drawer at home."

"There, you see. He loved you by giving you something that was valuable to him."

We were home. I went to the den. "James, your Dad wanted me to ask if you wanted to come to the service for Pop in Longview. If you don't want to go, you can stay with Grandpa and Mamaw."

He looked up at me, tearstains still evident on his face, which was now bright with a smile. "I don't have to go?"

"No, you don't have to, but I'm going for a few days."

"I'll stay with Grandpa and Mamaw. Grandpa said he needed some help cleaning up the garden. He doesn't think I'll get my hands dirty. Can I call to see if he still needs my help?"

"Yes, you can. But first, call your father. Make sure your decision is all right with him."

"Okay, Mom."

I watched his slight frame disappear up the stairs. Part of my heart went with him.

Heading for my bedroom, I started packing for my flight to Longview. I had several things to do before my head hit the pillow, including calling Mrs. Docksets, helping James pack for mom and dad's, and seeing him safely there.

Sounds floated down from upstairs. A somber James talked to his father. And then there was an excited and happy boy, talking to his grandpa. At least, he wasn't crying, but his new Mom was.

I shook my head. It seemed all I'd done since Luke and I'd realized we were in love was cry. I hoped sobbing would be over soon. Meanwhile, I let 'er fly. As my Dad always said, "'Crying clears the heart and clogs the sinuses.'"

~

Much of the flight to Longview was clear flying, but as I neared Dallas, clouds from the west obstructed the view of the ground. Luke had told me the skyline of the city was unimaginable. I sure wasn't going to see it today.

My flight landed, and within minutes, straight-line winds delayed every aircraft leaving Dallas. No one would be going anywhere until this blow was over. I found a convenient seat near a window in the main terminal. The ragged lightning flashed, rain streamed by, and the wind lashed at gateways, overpasses, and planes sitting on the tarmac. Momentarily, hail hit the concrete, bouncing more than three-feet high.

The scene was surreal. Outside nothing moved. No people directing traffic, or checking on delayed flights out.

My cell phone rang. I heard Luke's voice. "Manda."

"Hi, Sweetheart. I guess you know I'm stuck here in Dallas."

"Yes, I do. Don't worry about a thing. Our news station said a line of storms was coming, so I brought a book to read. I've lived in Texas long enough to realize a delay is always a real possibility, and you must understand what you're going through at Dallas is coming this way."

I got up from my seat and started walking up and down the main aisle in the terminal, pulling my carry-on behind me. My shoulder bag kept threatening to fall off, so I looped it around my neck. "I have no idea when we'll be getting out of here."

"Whatever happens—happens. I'll be waiting."

"Did you get your father's arrangements taken care of this morning?"

"Yes, Agnes and I planned the whole ceremony. It's at three o'clock tomorrow. Her minister will speak and someone from the choir will sing. There isn't a lot to say, so the service won't be long."

"Where will you bury him?"

"He'll be buried in a local cemetery right after the service. We went ahead and bought two plots, so Mom will be beside him in the future."

"Good thinking, and something you won't have to do later."

"I didn't realize so many arrangements needed to be made, or if I did, I've forgotten. It took all morning. But now, I'm here at the Longview airport, waiting on you. I love you, you know."

I couldn't help but smile. "It calms me to hear you say that. How did I ever exist without your love?" I stopped pacing and found a place against the wall.

"Ah, it pains me to say I think you did very well, my dear."

"Hold on. There's an announcement." I listened but couldn't hear everything the man uttered. "Luke, I'm going to have to go. The speaker was muddled, and I'm not sure what was said. Some of the flights are leaving, and I'm in the main terminal."

"You need to take the bus to the smaller gates, where the prop planes and small jets take off and land—puddle jumpers I call them. Check with any agent, and they'll steer you right."

"I'll see you soon."

"Manda, you haven't said I love you."

"I didn't?" I teased. "Very well, Mr. Avery. I like you very much. I admire you greatly, and yes, I believe—I think I love you."

"Just wait until you get here."

"That sounds like a threat."

"Manda, have a safe flight."

"I will. I love you, Honey." I loved flirting with my future husband.

"I'm not saying it again. Goodbye," said Luke.

❧ CHAPTER TWENTY-TWO ❧

Manda

"We put an announcement of Pop's funeral arrangements in Hardanville's afternoon newspaper."

Agnes, Duane, Tony, and Luke sat in their mom's home. I sat on one of the fireside chairs, watching the group's interaction, but not participating.

"Do you think any of his relatives will come to the service tomorrow?" This was from Tony, who shared the couch in front of the window with Duane. Agnes sat in Pop's red chair, because no one else wanted to sit there. Luke sat forward in his mother's chair—elbows on knees. Mrs. Avery was already in bed.

"That's what we're hoping. Maybe someone will show up. We may not have another time to find out about Pop's past. I'd like to know the what or why behind his anger at all of us. Why couldn't he love or show love to us?" Luke looked at each of his siblings.

"Luke, have you ever met any of his brothers or sisters? I'm sure he had some, because Mom mentioned a brother at one time."

"Tony, I never knew he had one. I wonder if he alienated them like he tried to alienate us. Why was he so secretive about his family? We never saw his mother or his father."

"How far is Hardanville from here?" asked Tony.

"About two hundred miles to the northwest."

"Toward the panhandle?" Tony continued.

"Yes. It's small, maybe five thousand residents in the county. I looked it up on the Web, because I had no idea where it was. There's no phone listing for an Avery in the town." Luke was shaking his head.

"Didn't Dad's former sales route run through the area?"

"Yes, as a matter of fact it did. He might have seen any relatives when he was on the road."

"You guys are just speculatin'. It isn't likely anyone will come. Dad was just an ornery old coot. My guess is he was born with his disposition." This sarcastic reply came from Duane.

"Luke, do you really think Pop had a problem in his growin' up years which caused him to be strict and unforgivin' a lot of the time."

"A lot of the time?" Duane snorted. "Tony, he was in the rigid mode all the time."

"Not really brother. Some of the pressure was off after you, Luke, and Robert left, and maybe I was better at stayin' out of the way. Guess I learned from your mistakes."

"Duane, Agnes gave me some books to read. I've finished all but one. They've enlightened me on some of the reasons families are dysfunctional, and, believe me, traumatic experiences in your youth explain many of the problems. She and I have talked about it. We think if we can delve into his past, we'll find a reason. We should have done this years ago and confronted him."

Duane was not convinced. "Have at it, Luke. I'll believe it when I see the evidence."

"Agnes, one of your books contains excellent information on the problem of youthful traumatic experiences. I'd like to send it home with Duane. Do you mind?"

"Why no, Luke."

"I'll go get it." Luke disappeared down the hall.

"I won't read it," Duane called after Luke.

When Luke reappeared with the book, he offered it to his brother. "Try."

Agnes joined in convincing his brother. "Duane, you've always said you wondered why Pop was so hard on you. Do you really want to know? This is a good opportunity to find out. I dare you to read this book." She pointed at the one Luke held in his hand.

Duane took it from Luke like it was a hot potato. He read, "Family Lies—the History of One Dysfunctional Family. Is there a lot of psychological gobbledygook in here?"

"No. *It is* written by a therapist, but in a language you can understand and about a real family not a fictional one. I believe it will open your eyes."

Duane started to make another sarcastic comment, thought better of it, and didn't say anything. Instead, he turned the front page and started to read the forward. His eyebrows knitted together. Something in the first few lines got his attention.

"It would be wonderful if we could solve the mystery tomorrow." Agnes, preparing to get up, pulled her recliner footrest underneath the chair, sat up, and smiled at Duane. "If there is one. I'm not sayin' there is."

"People, I'm headed for my room at Homewood Suites. I'm bushed." Duane got up, tucked the book under his arm, and walked toward the front door. "When should I be back here?"

"My church will serve lunch at noon, so be here before they come."

"Duane, I'm sorry your wife couldn't come. I wanted her to meet Manda."

"Just one of those last-minute happenings, and we couldn't work it out. Brother Tony, you comin'?"

"I was just waitin' for you to ask me," Tony responded in a deep Texas drawl. He stood and stretched his long arms to the ceiling. He was a basketball player like the rest of the Avery family.

"Is my car parked in your way?" Agnes pushed from the red chair, went to the door, and turned on the outside light. Everyone followed her to the front porch.

"Manda, I'm pleased to meet you. Luke's gettin' a real gem in you." Duane ambled down the steps toward his extended cab truck.

"It's great to meet you, Manda. I'd like to come to the weddin', if that's okay." Tony shook my hand and followed his brother.

Luke came over and put his arm around me, calling after them. "We'd be glad for both of you and your families to come. Agnes and Mike will be there."

We stood on the porch and waved as they pulled from the driveway.

Luke looked down the road at the disappearing taillights, thinking Duane's leaving was an about-eighty from the last one. Evidence of his squealing tires, dark rubber marks, were still on the road. "Did you girls notice how clear the sky was this afternoon after the storm?"

"Yes, I think rain is God's way of laundering the dust out of the air, washing it dirt free. At home, the newly scrubbed Smokies stand out clear and distinct against the blue sky. Sometimes, from my front porch, I can see individual trees on the skyline of the Foothills Parkway." I smiled, remembering the last storm.

"After a storm, I love to breathe the air. It smells different—fresh," Agnes added, sampling, by pulling in two lungsfull.

"And, it's cooled off—a refreshing cool, I might add," stated Luke.

We stood for a few minutes in the Texas darkness, listening to the hum of the world around us. Dogs barked, a dove was disturbed from its perch in a long-needled pine, and cars hummed along the main road in the distance. Somewhere the faint whine of a siren meant an emergency. Longview's hospital might be filling up Pop's bed in the near future. I prayed no one was seriously hurt.

"Do you really think someone will show up at your father's funeral from his hometown?" I asked.

"We hope so, don't we, Luke?"

"Knowing about Pop might help heal our family."

"You're assuming he had a problem, of course." I couldn't help saying.

"Yes, I just can't believe there wasn't."

"Anyone for coffee?" asked Agnes.

"How about it, Sweetheart?"

"Sure, but only decaf." I was tired from the long trip to Longview, but a cup of hot, steaming coffee sounded good. "Did I see chocolate cake on the kitchen counter?"

CHAPTER TWENTY-THREE ⚜

Luke

Right after the burial, Tony and his wife headed home to Houston, and Mike left for work in Weatherford.

At six o'clock on Sunday afternoon, the rest of the family decided to return to the Good Shepherd Cemetery. The sun, lower on the horizon, cast shadows of the oaks and pines on the pathway to my father's grave. Manda, Agnes, Duane, and I walked in silence toward the slight mound of fresh dirt with cuts of sod on top.

After anticipating someone from Hardanville might show up, no one had identified themselves before or after the funeral. Agnes and I were disappointed.

A few sprays and pots of flowers, maybe fifteen in all, sat at the head of the grave.

"I didn't see who they were from," Agnes indicated the flowers and started removing and checking the cards. "Here's one from your Pastor, Luke."

"I'm not surprised," I said. "He even thought about coming, but I convinced him the trip was long, and I told him I'd remember he'd volunteered."

Searching one of the pots on the ground, she stood puzzled at the card's name. "Do you guys know a Pete Coffey?"

Duane shook his head.

"Let me see the card." I studied the handwriting, hoping I'd recognize it. Scrawled in large letters was, *Your Friend, Pete Coffey.* "Who on earth is Pete Coffey?" I turned the card over. "There's a telephone number on the back."

"Do you think Mr. Coffey wants us to call him?" asked Duane.

"Guys, Manda and I've decided to go and see that tall monument at the center of the cemetery. We won't be gone long." Agnes and Manda left arm in arm for the short stroll across the grounds, to the memorial rock.

Duane and I stood at Pop's grave, each thinking our own thoughts. "I read the entire book you gave me last night. Once I started, I couldn't stop."

I wanted to laugh, but didn't. Instead I said, "Okay?" In this way, Duane could continue the conversation without me saying anything to aggravate or upset him.

"That book was written about us, wasn't it?"

"It was a real eye-opener," I agreed.

"I was the one who took all the guff."

"Yes, and I was the one who stood by and let you take it. I'm sorry, Bro. I'm sorry I didn't take up for you, because Dad was wrong to treat you the way he did. I hope you'll forgive me."

"You weren't the only one. Everyone did the same thing, even Mom."

"That's true, although she tried at times. As a family, we found it easier to let you bear the brunt of his anger."

"Even if we'd all stood up to Pop at one time, it wouldn't have mattered. He wouldn't have changed."

"Not likely."

"We might have pushed him too far. I always wondered if he would strike me—even hit me with his fist."

I shook my head. "I don't know. I just wish I'd have stood by you. I'd feel better now."

"You were only a kid, a kid who talked too much." Duane was smiling as he said this.

"Duane, I need to tell you something. It's a theory."

For several minutes I related how I thought Betty Sue Watson was the tattle tale he'd accused me of being. She was the local news filter, spreading gossip throughout the subdivision.

"Luke, you're right. I remember Pop coming in and telling Mom stuff about our residents, and it was after going to her store for some small item. I always wondered where he got his information. You're absolutely right."

"It's good to be right about something."

"Oh!" Duane said this word with a gush of air. "All these years, I thought—I guess I'm the sorry one now, Luke—both ways."

"That's okay, Bro. Now were even. That is if you forgive me."

Duane came around the fresh mound of earth, and we embraced. Embarrassed at our brief show of emotion, we stepped apart.

"I'd still like to know Pop's past," I said looking down at the mound of dirt.

"Maybe your answer is coming toward us. What do you want to bet this is Pete Coffey?"

It turned out the man *was* Peter Coffey. I invited him back to Mom's home.

~

The story he told was horrible, more terrible than I even imagined.

"Alan Avery was my best friend in grade school. When I first met him in the second grade, he had two older sisters and one brother. When we were in the fourth year, the principal came to the class and took him to the office. A next-door neighbor was there. An accident on a local road had taken the lives of his two sisters, and his father—who was driving—escaped with cuts and bruises. Alan's father never got over the tragedy."

"Two sisters," said Agnes. "How terrible. If we went there, could we find their graves?"

"Oh, yes. I'd be glad to take you, if you'll let me know when you're coming.'

"So, Pop had a surviving brother?" I asked.

"Yes, but he passed away at least ten years ago. His family put his obituary in the newspaper. He was nine years older than your father. I think he had a massive heart attack, too."

"Was he married? Did he have children?"

"I believe so. He moved to Lubbock."

"No wonder I didn't find any Averys in the phone book. Go on Mr. Coffey. We've never heard any of this," said Luke.

"The elder Mr. Avery was known to take a nip or drink a beer, but after the wreck, he became a drunk—a mean drunk. He took the pain of losing those two girls out on Alan and his mother. I remember Alan coming to school with bruises on his legs and arms. Once, when he accidentally got out of line, while going to the cafeteria, the teacher grabbed him by the arm. I noticed he winced, and later, he showed me the big black bruise where she had touched him. He said his father had made it. His father lost his ability to love and showed no love or kindness to his son."

I looked over at Duane, trying to read his expression at these words, wondering what was going through his mind.

Manda caught my attention and smiled. She knew what this man's words meant to our family.

Mr. Coffey continued, "On weekends, Alan would come and stay Saturday night. He and I went to church on Sunday morning. During a revival, we made a decision to follow Jesus. We went to the altar together. I think we were in the sixth grade at the time. I loathe what I'm going to relate next. Ministers are supposed to be trusted and worthy of respect."

Pop's friend didn't even have to tell it. I knew what was coming. Hadn't the book said that most people with my father's problems were molested in their youth? I heard him from faraway, because I didn't want to listen close-up.

"Where could he go? He was caught in a web—the victim of his father and his pastor. Finally, someone else whom the man had molested came forward and his parents filed charges against the pastor. That ended Alan's abuse, but the ordeal wasn't over."

"He had to testify, didn't he?" Duane said, nodding.

"Yes, he was identified as a victim and called to testify in front of a jury and audience to the extent of the exploitation—a traumatic experience for one so young. The local papers plastered the news and hearing all over the front page. The locals put two and two together. They knew the young men's names even though they weren't mentioned in the paper. They knew Alan Avery."

"What happened to the pastor?" asked Manda.

"Oh, he spent some years in the penitentiary. Not enough, to be sure, since he ruined at least two boys' lives. The other boy and his family moved away. We were in high school during the trial. Alan, living with his demons, faced his classmates alone. His father, consumed with his own personal hate, never understood his son's hurt."

"Dear God, no wonder Pop was the way he was. It must have been horrible to live with this information buried inside all his life." This came from Agnes.

"Alan never came back to visit me after the trial and the drubbing of his classmates. He withdrew into himself. As soon as he could support himself, he moved away."

"Did you ever see him after he left town."

"Only once. He said he'd come to see his mother. I think this may not have been the first time he saw her. I never saw him again. When I read his obituary in the newspaper, I wanted to come and pay my respects. I left my card on the flowers with my phone number on the back. I started out of town, but at the interstate I turned around. Something drew me back. I needed to meet his children. I didn't realize you knew nothing of his history."

I couldn't think of a single thing to say, so Agnes spoke up, "Mr. Coffey, we'll be eternally grateful to you for turning around. We felt Pop had a problem, but we had no idea what the basis was. You've told us precisely what we were looking for."

"I'm glad I could share this information with you. It's getting late. I'd like to drive through Dallas tonight—less traffic than in the daytime and the lights from the overpasses are beautiful. My daughter and son-in-law live west of there. I'm going to spend the night with them, and leave for home tomorrow." He arose and headed for the door.

Agnes and Manda followed him.

I got up and paced the room, trying to do the impossible and not think about what I'd just heard. As my traitor mind turned over the sordid events, my heart cried out, "Pop, Pop, why didn't you get help?"

Duane, guessing what I was thinking, looked up at me with tears streaming down his face. "Pop couldn't get help."

In my whole life, I'd never seen my brother cry. He'd always been stone-faced through every circumstance.

My racing mind stopped, when I remembered something, I'd read years ago...*Tears are wonderful drops. They wash away hurt and grief and leave pleasing thoughts and memories to visit and enjoy.*

Duane wasn't the only one crying.

I went over, sat beside him, and put my arm around his shoulders. "He must have been so ashamed, and he came from an era when people internalized distasteful events, such as what happened to him. It was taboo to go to a psychiatrist. And he'd certainly never go to another minister for counseling."

"He became exactly what he despised in his youth — hurtful and verbally abusive."

"At least, he didn't hurt us physically."

"I'm sure he consoled himself with this thought, when he lost his temper — the fact he didn't abuse us physically, and he wasn't a drunk."

I looked up. Manda and Agnes were still talking to Mr. Coffey, who must have been an angel in disguise. His help would bring healing to our family. "Thank you, Father for bringing Mr. Coffey to us."

"Amen," said my brother, a tear rolling down his cheek.

"The book talks about breaking the cycle. That's exactly what we must do. We can't ever become Pop. Getting help to overcome any lingering problems associated with his rigid ways and verbal abuse is a necessity. What did the book say? *Hidden anger may swell to the surface at the least expected moment.*" I knew a little bit about hidden anger, but I didn't take mine out on anyone. In fact, I hid it rather successfully — internalized it. "Duane, we need to change. We need to react to what we now know."

He and I had calmed down by the time the girls returned to the room. Manda stood looking at us from the hallway. "I declare this is the cryingest family I've ever seen."

I couldn't help but smile at her comment. The Avery family was going through the throes of change — change which didn't come easy.

"We'll be doing a lot more of it thanks to Mr. Coffey. They'll be healing tears."

After Duane said his goodbyes and we'd embraced for the third time in our lives, he'd left for Homewood Suites. Exhausted after the long emotional day, everyone had gone to bed.

With my head on my pillow, I thought about today's tears, I realized those of my brother's and mine would wash the hurt and grief away, but the amazing memories would start now, and we would enjoy being brothers from now on.

In the new quiet of the sleepy household, I knelt beside my bed to offer a prayer to my Heavenly Father. Brief and to the point, I said, "Lord, please let the events of today bring my family together in the love we never had growing up in this house. Forgive me for not being the example to my family, which I needed to be, after becoming your servant. Help me be a great father to my brother's children, full of your wisdom and truth. Thank you for Manda—for her love and support at this time. I pray for Duane and his family. Give Duane the courage and strength to seek you first for the help he needs. May he know I'm here if he needs to talk."

I stood. The burden for my father I'd been carrying for years, I left at my bedside altar.

CHAPTER TWENTY-FOUR

Luke

Early in the morning on Monday, Manda and I decided to take Clint, Marcus, and Maryb on a picnic to Jefferson, Texas. We planned to spend the day, enjoy the area, and get to know our future children much better.

When I called Agnes, she said Clint had a baseball game in the early afternoon, but she was sure Marcus and Maryb would love to go. They were up, and she would get them ready. She suggested taking all three out to eat when we returned. In this way, Clint could be involved in part of the day. Manda and I loved her suggestion.

I wasn't sure, but I thought I heard Agnes breathe a sigh of relief before she hung up the phone.

I decided to go east on road 80, from Longview to Marshall, on the East Texas Heritage Trail. Then we would turn north to Jefferson. Along this route, we saw contemporary and colonial homes, many with beautifully landscaped, green lawns. We stopped to tour the large, multi-faceted pottery store at Marshall. Manda bought a small, fired piece of clay of a coyote, howling at the moon.

Maryb's eyes got big when she heard it was signed by a Comanche Indian. "Are there still Indians in the area."

Manda laughed. "Yes, they still live around here, but they are very nice people. In fact, the woman standing next to the window has a name tag which says she's of the same tribe. Manda pointed discreetly toward the lady, who was describing a desert painting to a potential customer.

Back in the car, we headed north, leaving the bustling town behind. The ride was not long until we approached the outskirts of Jefferson.

"Look, Uncle Luke, there's a place where you can ride a boat through the swamp." Marcus leaned over the front seat of the car and pointed to a rough-looking building beside the road. We were outside of Jefferson, where water stood on both sides of the highway.

"That's the Little Cypress Bayou. It might get mad if it knew you called it a swamp."

Everyone laughed at the suggestion of a swamp getting angry. "Do you have any idea why it's called Little Cypress Bayou?" I continued.

"Because of the cypress trees, silly." It was Marcus' time to get even. "Everybody knows that."

"What's a cypress tree?" asked Maryb—our question girl.

"I pulled over beside the road. "Everyone out. Time for a lesson on bayous."

Amongst giggles, laughter, and slamming doors, we were soon standing safely by the road. "Watch out for cars careening over the road, trying to miss alligators crossing to get to the other side." I cautioned, swinging my arms, making faces, and bringing more giggles from the group.

Maryb eased over and took Manda's hand. They smiled at each other as my future bride shook her head.

"Maryb, do you see that tree over there?" I pointed to one not more than twenty feet from where we stood, which grew in a deep ditch alongside the road filled with brackish-looking water.

"Yes, is that a cypress?"

"Yes, it's a bald cypress tree. It grows in the water. Not all cypress grow in the water. The trunk is large at the waterline and tapers upward." I made the shape of the tree with my hands.

"It has needles on its limbs," Maryb observed.

"Well, sorta. Look at the difference in it and this live oak." I pointed to a small tree standing by the road. "Check out the lobed leaves and the straight trunk, compared to the cypress' see through needles and tapering trunk."

Maryb managed a couple of cautious steps in the live oak's direction, looking from one to the other. "Uncle Luke, what's the green stuff floating on top of the water? It looks yucky." She grabbed Manda's hand again.

"It's called algae. It likes stagnant water."

"What's stag-a-nut mean."

Manda spoke up. "Stagnant, Maryb, means still water or not flowing. Look closely. Do you see the water moving?"

Feeling a little safer, she let go Manda's hand and stepped closer to the brackish water filled ditch. Peering into the water, she said, "No, I don't."

Mischievous Marcus decided at that moment to nip his sister on the leg. He pinched her before I could stop him.

"Eek!" screamed Maryb, swinging her hand at her laughing brother. She ran back to Manda and wrapped her arms around her waist.

"Marcus, you should be ashamed." Manda said, pretending to be upset, but smiling.

Maryb looked fearfully at her brother and at the black water where she thought the monster which bit her had emerged. "Look, there is something moving in the water!" She exclaimed and pointed between two cypress trees at the edge of a larger pond several yards away.

"I bet it's coming this way." Marcus made sounds and motions intended to be threatening and mysterious.

"Oh, Maryb," I walked over and embraced both Manda and her, giving my fiancée a light kiss on the lips. "It's probably a beaver or otter."

"Or a snake." Marcus chimed in, still in a teasing mode. "Slithering its way through—"

One of my looks, which said don't continue, stopped Marcus' words.

"Uncle Luke, I'm ready to go." Maryb didn't care what it was, she'd had enough.

We got back in the car and headed into Jefferson.

I took them to a historical museum on Austin Street, and we ate lunch at a small mom-and-pop restaurant at the end of the street with red checkered tablecloths and ladder-back chairs. Although they were out-of-season, crawfish were on the menu. Frozen ones aren't quite as good as fresh ones, so I decided not to order them. And, anyway, they are quite messy to eat, and I wasn't in a messy mood. I did ask for Southern fried chicken. It was delicious. The children ate jumbo hot dogs.

Back out on the street, a gentleman with a horse-drawn carriage invited us to ride through town. "I'd like to sit up front with the driver," this from Marcus.

I looked at the gray-haired man, who nodded. "I'm Henry," he told the young boy and shook his hand. "You're more than welcome to ride with me." Henry helped Marcus up to his seat, and then helped Maryb and Manda into the main body of the carriage.

I was the last one to get in.

"Everybody ready to go?" Henry craned his neck around, checking on his passengers. Before he could chirp to the horse to go forward, Maryb moved from the backward facing front seat and squeezed in between Manda and myself. Now, we were all facing forward. The bench was a little tight, but we rode through the town with Henry giving us a description of the antebellum houses and their occupants.

At the end of the horse-drawn buggy ride, we had to make a decision — take the boat on the bayou or steam locomotive ride. I knew which one Maryb would pick. She'd had enough of the water and its inhabitants.

Three bags of popcorn and four drinks later, we sat watching the Texas countryside go by as the steam belched from the engine's smokestack. The pungent smell of coal smoke blew into the car's open windows, along with a little bit of soot.

Big Cypress Bayou passed by on the right, while Spanish moss hung in clumps from the cypress trees. A long-legged, blue heron lifted gracefully from a cypress knee and winged toward the darker reaches of the vast watery, river bottom.

The conductor came down the aisle and stopped beside our seat. "Tickets, please."

I handed him our tickets and waited for him to make a hole with his puncher. He handed the tickets back.

Marcus observed to the man, "Jefferson must be surrounded by water."

"Oh, not quite," he said. "Did you children know, years ago Jefferson was the main river port for transporting goods down to the Red River?"

"What's a river port?" asked Maryb.

"Well, it's a dock where the people here in East Texas brought their goods to sell; like cotton, grain, vegetables, and other things. These wares were loaded onto flatbed boats and floated to the big river—the mighty Mississippi. There they continued downriver until they arrived at Nawleans, where they were sold to a middleman who delivered them to their customers."

"What's a middleman?" she asked.

"A middleman facilitates goods from the seller or grower to the manufacturer or person who sells to a retailer."

"What's a retailer?"

"Maryb it's wonderful you need to know so many things, but the conductor has other tickets to punch.

He did have other tickets to punch, but on coming back up the aisle, he sat down in the seat opposite us.

"Manda asked, "Your town is called Jefferson. Was President Jefferson a visitor at some time?"

"No, no one knows how the town got its name. But the president wasn't here."

"Did Apache Indians live here?" asked Marcus.

"No, the Caddo Indians did."

"That's a strange name," he said.

"It's shortened from the original one. You wouldn't want to say it. The Caddo Indians lived here, and in Arkansas, Oklahoma, and Louisiana. Not far from here is a body of water named after them, Caddo Lake. There's a story which says one of the largest towns of the Caddo Nation was buried overnight under its waters."

The steam whistle blew. "That's my cue. Our ride is almost over." The conductor got up and went forward to the front of the car. "All off for Jefferson Station," he said over the intercom. People started to the front doorway, preparing to disembark the train.

After looking at my watch, I realized we needed to head back to Longview.

"Must we head home?" asked Manda. "This has been such a beautiful day and so relaxing."

"Yeah, Uncle Luke. I'd like to take a boat ride on the Big Cypress Bayou," said Marcus, standing at my sleeve. "I won't bother Maryb another moment. I promise."

"We can't, Marcus. By the time we make the trip home, we'll need to pick up Clint at the ballpark and go get pizza at Angelo's. How about it, guys? Is pizza okay?"

"Sure," said Marcus, not too enthusiastic about leaving Jefferson. He kicked at a loose rock in the parking area.

"Pizza's cool," said Maryb. Marcus had cured her on going near the Bayou again.

My rental car was hot inside. I slid in, started the car's engine, and turned the air conditioner on full blast. "Too hot inside," I said, sliding out and shutting the door.

"Uncle Luke, may I ride up front with you? I never get to ride in the front seat." Marcus complained.

I looked at Manda.

"Perfectly all right with me," she nodded.

"Look, there comes Henry again." Maryb pointed to the white carriage with the black man on the high driver's seat.

We stood watching him maneuver the horses and carriage through the afternoon traffic.

"Whew, Luke. I'm getting all dewy." Manda was fanning with some literature picked up at the train station.

I opened my door and said, "Yes, it's hot. Marcus, pile in." If there was a problem over the boat ride, all was forgiven.

Maryb and Manda slid into the back seat.

The car wasn't totally cool, but the fan helped move the inside air. We headed out of Jefferson for Longview—an hour away. Buckled up in the seat, Marcus eagerly looked out the window at the scenery passing by and talked about the Indian artifacts we'd seen in the historical museum. "And, Uncle Luke, we went arrowhead hunting during the summer at one of my school chum's homes."

"If you like arrowhead hunting, you'll love Tennessee. The Cherokees left arrowheads in just about every field, and when the farmer's plow, they come to the surface after it rains. I know several men in my church who might let us come and hunt for them."

When my soon-to-be-son mentioned school, a question popped into my mind, "When does school start, Marcus?"

"Don't mention school. I don't want summer to end."

"So, you don't know?"

"I heard Clint talking to one of his baseball buddies about it. I think he said in ten days, but I'm not sure."

In the rush of getting to Longview, taking care of Mom, and Pop's funeral, I'd forgotten to ask. School was now the most important item on my calendar, besides helping Agnes with the aftermath of paperwork associated with his death, and hopefully, Mom's placement in Nightingale Place.

I checked on Manda and Maryb in the rearview mirror, and shook my head at the scene. The ride had rocked one of the car's occupants asleep. I caught Manda's glance in the mirror of the car and winked at her.

She sat with her arms wrapped around the little girl, who was locked in the center seat belt—sound asleep.

The miles flew by quickly, and I soon turned into the ballpark parking lot, where we would pick up Clint. Was the ballgame over, or would we be waiting for it to finish?

"Okay, everybody, bail out. Let's go see if your brother has finished his game." The raucous sounds coming from the ballfield make me think he hadn't.

The bleachers were about half-full when we arrived.

"Let's go to the top row," suggested Marcus.

I looked up at the tenth row and decided I wanted a backrest. I'll compromise with you — one row down from the top."

"Okay, Uncle Luke." He turned to Maryb and said, "Beat you, B."

Marcus, along with his sleepy sister, rushed up the bleachers in a headlong race to see who could break their necks first. Because he was two years older and long-legged, Marcus was ahead. Seeing his sister trying so hard, he pretended to stumble and let his sister win.

I reached for Manda's hand. We climbed the rows together, sat on the wooden seat, and looked down at our extraordinary view of the field. Maryb came over and wriggled between us.

"There's Clint." Marcus pointed to the batter's box. "He's next to bat."

The scoreboard said the bottom of the ninth inning, score tied at two, and Clint's team was at bat. If his team scored a run, they would win.

The sun was setting in the west, but the air remained hot and stuffy. Manda had kept her literature fan and was using it vigorously. I felt the rush of air each time she moved it.

"Maybe, he'll win the game." Maryb shaded her blue eyes with her hand. "Uncle Luke, I need a pair of sunglasses." She was shaking her blonde curls in a nod.

I chuckled and gave her the good hug I'd wanted to give her all day. Since she'd been attached to Manda, I couldn't, except the one time on the Little Cypress Bayou, where I was careful to squeeze gently. "We'll have to take care of your lack as soon as possible."

Marcus heard this exchange. "If Maryb gets glasses, I should too."

Our talk was sidelined by a groan, which went up from the Longview crowd. The batter had struck out. Clint was on deck. "Come on Clint," they clapped. "You can do it."

"It's up to you, Clint. We need a home run."

The sixteen-year-old, using the Clint swagger, walked to the home plate, tapped the tip of the bat on the irregular piece of rubber embedded in the ground, and took a few practice swings. Then he stepped forward and assumed his batter's stance.

The curveball whizzed past him. "Strike one," called the umpire.

Brother Marcus jumped to his feet. "Come on Clint. Knock one out of the park," he yelled as loud as he could.

The rest of the boisterous crowd took up the shout. "Yeah, Clint. Knock one out of the park—knock one out of the park."

Clint's next swing hit nothing but thin air.

"Strike two," called the ump. His call quietened the crowd.

Clint beat the end of his wooden bat against home plate, sending small wisps of dust from its edges, while taking a condemning glance at the catcher and the umpire, who had absolutely nothing to do with his failure to connect to the ball.

The pitcher made a fatal error. Clint's favorite pitch was a slider. The pitcher wound up and threw the ball.

CRACK! The bat broke into two pieces, but the ball soared over the heads of the pitcher and second baseman, in a low arc, heading for the outfield.

The center fielder called for the catch as he ran for the ball. The ball dropped onto center field and took a high bounce. In his over eagerness, the ball hit the center fielder's glove and dropped to the ground.

Clint stopped at second as the ball was fielded and thrown to the shortstop. It wasn't a homerun but a two-base hit.

Clint stood on second base, touching up and running six or seven feet off the base and coming back to touch up again. He continued this action, teasing the pitcher into thinking he was stealing to third base, which he could do if he caught the ball-thrower off guard.

Everyone in the stands stood, encouraging the new batter. "Come on, Chuck. You can do it. Hit a homer. Win the game for us."

Across the way, the rival team's fans were doing the same for their pitcher.

The noise was deafening.

The pitcher, his tension rising, and maybe seeing the possibility of his tie game slipping away, made a wild throw to the batter. The catcher flung his body to the right in a valiant effort to grab the wild pitch. A bounce off the catcher's mitt, sent the ball rolling.

"Run, Clint, run," the standing crown roared.

He did past the third base, heading for home plate. Thinking better of continuing, he retreated back to third, as the catcher threw to the pitcher, who would have forced his out.

On the next pitch, the batter hit a line drive between first and second. Clint headed for home base and scored the winning run. The batter was thrown out at first.

Clint and his teammate had won the ballgame. The players crowded around them, congratulating the two and slapping them on the back.

"Marcus, go down on the field and get your brother. We'll wait on you in the car."

When Clint appeared with Marcus, the swagger had become a disgusting strut, full of pride in achievement.

"Great playing, Clint," I congratulated, as the others gathered around him, patting him on the back.

Clint moved his hand as if to ward off the praise. "I always get a home run," he shrugged in return.

"But you got the winning run, and your team won. That's something to be happy about."

"I guess it'll have to do." Clint still wasn't happy.

Maryb stood looking at her brother, pleading with her eyes for him to change his attitude. She spoke up, "Clint, we're going for pizza. Aren't you hungry? I am."

"I guess I could eat."

"Okay, Clint. You ride up front with me, and everyone else in the back."

Angelo's Pizza Eatery was on the loop around Longview. The sign out front said, *With a name like Angelo's, the pizza is mouth waterin' Italian.*

"I'm even hungrier after reading their sign," said Manda as I drove up and parked. "Is it *that* good?"

"It's delicious," Maryb gave a resounding nod. "Yum, yum."

"Then my suggestion is, we go in and find out." Manda opened the car door and gave Maryb a little pat on the arm as they got out. Maryb giggled and ran for the door. Everyone else hurried up the rear.

The chatter around the table was lighthearted and cheerful. Even Clint loosened up and forgot about the lack of a home run, although he remained more reserved than the others. He did grin slightly when Marcus told him of pinching his sister and her loud scream at the bayou.

While waiting for our food, I sat watching the interaction of the group. This wasn't bad at all—my instant family.

Clint was the only unknown in the group, which I felt was due to teenage rebelliousness. Marcus was mimicking his brother somewhat, but not wholly. Clint needed to be a role model for his brother, but since he was so wrapped up in himself, he didn't realize his attitude was affecting his brother, and maybe he didn't care.

Was something bothering him? If I asked, would he tell me? The answer was probably no. Not until he realized he could trust me. Should I try?

Maryb was a sweetie. She was already attached to Manda, and I felt she and James would get along very well, since they were close to the same age.

Only James was missing at my table. Thinking of my son, I decided to call him. I excused myself, got up, and went outside. The sun had set and the air was cooler as I dialed the Weather's landline.

Mr. Puckett answered the phone. "Hi Luke, I bet you want to talk to a certain young man." I heard him call for James.

"Yes, sir. I do. How's everything going?"

"Great, we've worked in the garden all day and went for pizza for dinner."

"I laughed. "That's where we are now, eating pizza." It was unusual for Mom Puckett not to cook. The occasion must have been special for them. "Was this a special occasion and how was the pizza?"

"Aw, we were just celebrating having a grandson, and I wanted to give my wife a rest from the kitchen. The pizza was great. Here's James."

"Hello, Dad." Hearing my son's voice made me realize how much I missed him. We talked for several minutes, and then I told him to tell his Grandpa, Manda would be coming home on Wednesday.

"Okay, Dad."

"Maybe I'll be home before you start school."

"I'm fine, Dad. Grandpa and I are working hard. You'll be surprised at how nice we've cleaned up the garden. He says it's the best the *old dirt* has ever looked."

"I can't wait to see it. I miss you, Son. I love you. I'll be home soon. Mind Manda when she gets there."

"I will. Love you too, Dad."

I heard the phone click. Why did I feel an emptiness as the phone went dead? My footsteps were a little heavier as I returned to the table. The pizza had already arrived.

"We said grace." Manda informed me.

"Uncle Luke, we need some ranch dressing." Marcus was chomping on a piece.

"Ranch dressing? Whatever for? We don't have a salad."

"Aw, all the kids dip their pizza in it. It's cool," said Marcus.

"Okay." I signaled the waitress. "We need ranch dressing. Better bring several cups for this crew.

"You'll try it, won't you, Uncle Luke?"

"You'll have to drag me kicking and screaming. I'm a firm believer in not polluting your pizza with ranch dressing."

"Aw, it's really good."

"I'll try the ranch dressing, if Manda will."

All eyes turned to her. "You will, won't you Manda, pu-l-ee-z-e?" Maryb couldn't be denied.

"Sure, I'm game." She rolled her eyes at me. I knew she was hoping we'd survive.

After eating, we headed for Mom's home to relieve my sister.

CHAPTER TWENTY-FIVE

Manda

"Manda, let's have breakfast tomorrow. I'll come by and pick you up, say about eight. Luke can keep the kids. Between them and Mom, he'll be a frazzled wreck when we get back."

Agnes sat on the front porch steps of Mom Avery's house. In the yard, four children whooped and hollered, playing a game known only to them.

Clint, seemingly too old for such child's play, sat on the end of the porch under the overhang. I watched as he banged the back of his athletic shoes against the brick veneer below. Close enough to hear his aunt's plan, he let out an audible groan. Obviously, he didn't want to spend a boring day here at his grandmother's. He stood, ready to go, and headed toward Agnes' car. I wondered if his electronic games were calling his name.

We were tired after the excitement of our long day in Jefferson. At least, I was. Wishing I had the energy of the squealing, running children on the front lawn, I replied, "I'd love to, if Luke can spare me."

"Wonder where he is?" She looked backward through the glassed-in door, but turned around quickly as a louder than usual scream rent the air. Grinning, she said, "You never know when a yell means someone is seriously hurt."

"He said something about getting Mom Avery a cup of coffee. Isn't it rather unusual for people to drink coffee this close to bedtime?"

Agnes laughed, "Yes, and it isn't decaffeinated either. Mom and Dad downed a cup before retiring as long as I can recall—something about warming up or relaxing with the hot liquid. I can't remember exactly. None of the rest of the family has the same habit."

The screen door banged shut. "So, what are you two girls cooking up?"

"We aren't cooking up anything, but Cracker Barrel will." Agnes looked up at her brother and grinned.

"What?"

"Agnes and I want to have breakfast tomorrow morning, if you will keep five kids and your Mom."

"You're not inviting me?"

"No," spoke up Agnes. "This is girl time just for Manda and me."

"Oh, that ought to be fun, or as Marcus and Maryb say, 'cool.'"

"What do you say?"

"Of course, you must go. What time is this breakfast starting?"

"Eight o'clock. Is that okay, Manda?"

"I'll be waiting."

"Brother, you should know, there's no set time to have her back."

～

"Thank you for inviting me to eat with you, Agnes. No one knows the Avery children like you do, and I wanted to chat about each child. Then, there's an important proposition I intend to make to Luke about them. I need your input on both.'

We were sitting in the Cracker Barrel at one of the Tyler exits. Earlier the greeter at the front led us to a requested window table in a quieter part of the dining room. The restaurant was on I-20, and interstate traffic filled the place.

"My intention, exactly," returned Agnes. "All Maryb could talk about last night was the fun she had yesterday at Jefferson."

"We did have fun."

The waitress came, and we ordered drinks and breakfast.

When she was gone, Agnes leaned forward and reached across the table, placing her hand on mine. "I'm so happy you and my brother are getting married. I think he couldn't have found anyone anywhere who suited him better."

"Why, thank you. We worked around each other so long. I think love sneaked up on me. I certainly didn't plan on falling in love with him. And no one would think a typical Hollywood love-at-first-sight story—not a lot of bells, whistles, and sirens going off. I still can't get over this ring on my finger." I raised my hand, fingering the engagement band.

Our drinks arrived. "Your food will be out shortly," said the waitress, heading for another table with their order.

Agnes leaned closer. "Mike and I were the same way. We grew into each other. We were high school sweethearts. I went away to college, and he stayed here and went to technical school. We saw each other occasionally, and wrote even more sporadically. But we did keep in contact with each other. There was never anyone else for either of us."

"I think that's great. After my first husband died, I made a blue-print to use for the next few years of my life. I guess God had other plans. I'm excited at our engagement, but I'm also wondering how I'll handle caring for the four children, since I've never had any of my own. I've worked in our children's ministry at church, but we send them home each day—like grandparents. It's what happens then, you know, at home which I think about."

The waitress returned with our breakfast. As soon as she placed the food on the table and disappeared, Agnes continued our conversation.

She laughed, "I think it's a given, you're gonna suffer the reverse of empty nest syndrome. Forgive me for laughing. It's really not funny."

"Well, I hope it's not a crying matter either. We've been doing a lot of bawling lately."

"I can't promise you won't cry. But I can tell you there won't be a place in your house where some offending article of the children isn't found. My guess is your house is orderly and neat."

"You're right. James is a neat and tidy child. Luke has taught him well, and we get along great." Picking up my silverware, I started to eat.

"As far as four children, in the summer, by the afternoon, you'll look for a nice, quiet place where you can think and rest. Go ahead and plan one." Agnes forked a piece of ham into her mouth. "When schools in session, do it during the day, 'cause you won't find one after school lets out or on weekends."

"It's that hard? Much of the day, I don't know James is in the house."

"How do you think James will feel about a new sister and two brothers? He is the youngest. Do you think he'll feel like his territory has been invaded? Will he share his toys? Some children are clannish. The three new ones may gang up on him."

"I've thought about this very problem. I think it's important to provide each child a space—their own small world within the big household. I think James will experience the pains most children face in blended families. He'll feel overwhelmed, but he adapts easily. The noise factor may present a problem. I'd hate to think the others would gang up on him. I suppose it's a possibility. The four will establish their own pecking order, and I'll do my best to referee. Don't you think he and Maryb will be instant friends?"

"I can't imagine Maryb not being a friend to anyone."

"Yes, I agree. She has that disposition, hasn't she?"

"Maryb's sunny smile and helping ways will be part of the glue holding your future family together. But when there's a problem, she clings to you afraid to move without your permission and help. She needs to learn to let go, trust her instinctive abilities to survive, and become brave in the face of difficulty."

"I can see her need. Maybe I can teach her. There is one quality I love in her character. Yesterday, a sole pleading look at Clint got rid of some of his surliness."

"Speaking about Clint, has Luke told you anything about him?"

"Only a little."

"Clint is an island unto himself. He's entered the teenage rebellious stage with enthusiasm." Agnes book a bite or two and then made another suggestion. "Maybe he's only trying to grow up or establish his adulthood as most kids do. When he's playing ball, he's aggressive and loud. He wants to win, and he interacts with his friends by standing his ground. If he doesn't win, he's very unhappy—like he's a total failure, and the whole game was lost because of him. He doesn't realize, if you play your best, you've won, no matter the score on the scoreboard."

"Has he taken on some of Pop Avery's characteristics?"

"Exactly, I've been concerned about this for years. Clint's never had another role model so why wouldn't he be like his grandfather? Losing his father and mother, like he did, after being attached to and loving them both for several years, stunted his emotions. The proverbial rug was pulled out from under his young life. My father wasn't a good substitute for that underpinning. When Clint needed a father figure to love him and explain that loss, he had the added influence of a man who couldn't show love—"

Agnes let me think my own thoughts. "Of course, your Mom must have comforted him."

"Oh, she did, but my father's overbearing presence negated any good influence she had, just as it did in my family."

"So how do I approach Clint?"

"I wish I knew. I've been trying to show him what love means, but nothing I've tried has helped. He's an enigma. A puzzle I haven't worked out. He can be sarcastic to his brother and sister, especially to Marcus, who he thinks is a wimp. He has offensive pet names for both of his siblings. He says they are only pet names, but the tone in which he uses them ..." Agnes raised her hands to punctuate her sentence.

"Why does he think Marcus is a wimp?"

"Because he's not into sports of any kind. All Averys are supposed to be athletes, you know. Marcus will go and cheer his brother when he plays, and he understands the games, but as far as getting out on the field, batting a ball, or tossing a hoop, forget it. He's not interested."

"Luke says he writes."

"He does. Mom always thought he was very good at it. Short stories and poems are his forte."

"Does he let you read them?"

"Sometimes, he does, and I enjoy reading them. A couple of weeks ago, he wrote a poem about a deer, going to get a drink of water. Let's see if I can remember some of it. He said his idea came from a picture he'd seen in a magazine. Here goes ...

A pretty scene it was, the deer on the bank,
Standing still, very poised,
Waiting for the slightest motion,
To send it running to the woods
Or plunging to the river.
And then there were others, a doe and a fawn.

I can't remember the rest. I'm surprised I remembered that much. You'll have to ask him about it. He'll probably get the poem for you to read. He keeps a notebook of his scribblings."

"Wow, I like it."

Marcus draws very well, also. I think he would do well taking art lessons. He really needs to develop both talents. You don't have to worry about school. Marcus and Maryb made good grades. Clint—not so much. One other thing, the girls like him."

I know a local artist who takes students. I'll see if I can hook Marcus up with her."

"Even though Clint harasses his brother and sister, they look up to him. He sorta became their boss as the oldest sibling after the plane crash. If he gets into trouble, you may find one of the others involved."

"I understand."

We paused for a few minutes to eat the remainder of our food, so it wouldn't get cold and sip our newly refreshed coffee.

Then, I decided to broach the subject I'd discussed with my pastor before coming to Longview. "Agnes, I haven't talked to Luke about what I'm going to say next. I'd like to take the children home with me before school starts. That way they won't have to change schools right after they start this year. I'm thinking Nightingale Place will have a room for Mom Avery before long. Luke can come home when she's comfortably installed in her new home and help me with their care. Do you think I'm touched in the head to think I can do this?"

"Makes a lot of sense to me. When does your school start?"

"Almost the same day as yours. We'd have ten days to make the transition."

"Would you quit your job?"

"No, I'm sure June would let me adjust my hours to the schools' schedules."

"When do you plan on broaching the subject to Luke?"

"Tonight. I fly back tomorrow afternoon."

"You'd be taking on a lot of responsibility." Agnes shook her head.

"I know."

"I talked to Mr. Taylor yesterday afternoon. He'll definitely have an opening in four weeks, so Luke would be able to come home after we move Mom."

"I guess the important question is do you think I can handle these three children plus James until Luke comes home?"

"There's no doubt you can handle them, but you'll find the job isn't easy, especially if you continue to work with no backup to help. Luke will have to firmly tell Robert's three, you are in charge, and your decisions are final. That's what Mike and I did. It worked pretty well. Clint will try to buck any decision he doesn't agree with, but he may be more prone to follow someone he doesn't know well, or he may try to run over you." She added, "T-B-D, to be determined."

She was right about TBD. My whole life in the next few years was a big to be determined. But I said, "I understand the challenge in his case. I'll be calling you for advice."

She laughed, "Great. Do you want me there when you talk to Luke?"

"Yes, I think your input would be valuable to us both. Okay?"

"Let me know the time, and I'll come over."

The waitress brought the checks.

"Manda, there's going to be some drastic changes in your life between now and Christmas. Luke tells me you're selling both your homes and buying a bigger house."

"Yes. We want something large enough so each child can have a room, and he misses having horses. So, we'd like acreage to go with the house."

"Then there's a wedding to be planned."

"I haven't even started on it yet. I'm sure some of the church ladies will help. I may just turn it over to them—be surprised."

"It's nice to have friends you can trust with something so important."

"Everywhere change is in the air, and unexpected problems may arise. I'm sure there will be some. I just hope my faith in God is enough. One day at a time. I learned this after becoming a widow. I survived and became stronger. Oh, my goodness."

"What."

"We didn't say a blessing on the food."

Agnes, immediately bowed her head. She said a blessing on the food and for peace in the next few days ahead in the Avery family.

We went to the cashier and paid our bills.

"Let's browse the store sales," suggested Agnes.

We walked past the fall and Halloween selections to the discounted clothes racks. "I buy clothes here a lot. Strange to buy clothes at a place where you eat eggs and ham."

She and I laughed together.

"Manda you learned a good lesson when you solved problems and lived with your emotional conflicts each day, but now you'll go to the next level. It's called multitasking with multiple problems and conflicts. You won't have any choice but to deal with them simultaneously. Most of us grow into it rather slowly—one child at a time. Not you. You'll be plunging headlong into the chaos of a ready-made family, plus a new husband on top of it all. And Luke will be doing pretty much the same. He and James have been in their own world for several years since Peggy died. All this change won't be easy on them either." She pushed some clothes around the store racks while I mulled her comments. "Are you ready to go?"

"I am."

Outside the rustic, brown building, I pointed to billowing gray and charcoal clouds, which were almost amassed over the top of us. The front was coming from the west.

"Looks like rain," commented Agnes. "I have rugs drying on my outside clothesline. Let's hurry. I may get home in time to pull them off the line before the rain starts."

❧ CHAPTER TWENTY-SIX ❧

Manda

I'd stood in the living room, watching the angry, dust-laden wind blow limbs and leaves off the trees across the road. In an instant, hail pelted the earth, leaping up in shock at the blow of hitting the pavement and falling again.

The weather radio blared, "Take shelter immediately," and sirens wailed, circuitously in the distance over the ruckus outside.

Luke took his mother by the arm as she said, "Where's Pop, I'm afraid."

Her words seemed bizarre and yet right on in the face of the storm. I stifled the urge to laugh as we rushed down the stairs to their cellar—my adrenalin pumping at ninety miles an hour. One hour and thirty-five minutes passed before a battery-powered radio alerted us to the all-clear.

The afternoon rain was a leftover from the dangerous storm which passed through East Texas after lunch. The blow had knocked off electricity and threatened tornadoes. This was the first time I'd took shelter under a tornado watch.

Coming out of the small cellar, seeing the softly falling rain, was a relief for an East Tennessean, who frequently endured worrisome thunderstorms without tornado warnings. This scene was more like I was used to.

~

Tonight, the mood was more relaxed than any since I'd been in Longview. Agnes, Luke, and I sat in the living room at Mom Avery's home. Outside, the rain continued to drop gently from the dark night sky, after settling the western dust.

Mom crocheted in her favorite recliner; the red one her husband had vacated. Both Luke and I had marveled at this switch. Nothing we came up with could account for her change. The chair was simply empty, and she chose it.

"Mrs. Avery, what are you making?" She was wearing navy blue pants with a colorful, flowered top. Luke had told me it was her favorite.

Knowing her dirty clothes went to the home's laundry, she'd gone and retrieved the outfit from the room, insisting she was going to wear it. Since I'd come down to Longview, the task of choosing her clothes and dressing her for the day had become my responsibility. I enjoyed helping Luke's mother—one small service I could perform for her. She would never know me, and I regretted this fact.

"I'm making a sweater for Pop."

It seemed to me she'd been working in the same spot since I'd arrived. "Could I see it?" I walked over and squatted by the chair as she held up her work. The crocheted piece in navy blue had no form. I looked over at Agnes.

"She works so hard at it. When she's okay mentally, she rips out the bad part and continues on, not understanding why the piece is wrong."

I turned back to the misshapen sweater in front of me. "It's looking really good."

"I think so, too." She smiled at me. "It's my favorite color." Then, she looked confused. "I think it's my favorite color."

"Would you teach me to crochet?"

"She looked at me with a puzzled, or was it a frightened expression on her face. "No, I don't think so. Who are you? Where's Pop?"

"He's around Mom," said Luke, coming over and patting his mother's arm. He reached down to help me up, giving me a hug at the same time.

It was time to talk about my idea for returning the children to Tennessee.

I followed him to the couch and sat down, as he put his arm around me. "Sweetheart, I need to talk to you about an idea I have." The words and sentences followed each other in rapid flow. "I've been thinking about taking Clint, Marcus, and Maryb back to Tennessee before school starts. They can stay at my home until you come back, and they won't have to transfer from one school to another. Agnes says Mr. Taylor promises a room in a month, so you'll be home soon. Don't you think my idea will work?"

"Whoa, there!" exclaimed Luke, sitting up on the edge of the couch. "Let's take this one sentence at a time."

"I'm sorry. I wanted to get the whole plan out at once. I've been considering this possibility for several days. The only reason I haven't mentioned my idea before, is because I wanted to meet the children, so they'd get to know me, and I them. It's reasonable that if we liked each other, they be more apt to follow my instructions, without you there."

"I can see that you've been thinking about this possibility," he said. "I can't deny taking the children back to Tennessee before school starts hasn't entered my mind, but I was hoping to do it myself."

"Then, we are in agreement there."

"And, placing them in a school where they wouldn't have to transfer is a much better idea, but four children without my influence and help is a huge undertaking. They're my kin and not yours, Manda."

"Do you doubt my ability to do this—take care of them?"

"Honey, I believe you can do it, but what about them. What if they aren't happy with the move? Maybe they'll be homesick, withdrawn, stubborn …"

"They may be all of those anyway, even if you are there."

"But I'd be there to help. You know, cushion the blow between you and them. We'd support each other."

"I still think it's the best idea. Maryb and Marcus aren't a problem. The question is Clint." I nodded at Agnes, seeking assurance.

Luke who'd been looking at me, turned toward her as she spoke up. "Manda and I discussed this at breakfast this morning, and I've had time to mull this over. I believe Clint will not be a problem, not until you arrive Luke. He'll see you as an authority figure and rival, taking over his perceived notion of the alpha male of his other siblings. He'll court Manda, trying to get her on his side before his uncle, the head of the family, arrives."

"Thank you, very much, Madame Psychiatrist." Luke was laughing at his sister. "I hadn't thought about the situation in that light. Do you think he'll be a model child?"

"I think the waves he'll make will be small splashes on the beach."

"If you put it that way, then, the idea of Manda taking them back with her sounds very feasible."

I'd been sitting on the couch, listening with wonder at the conversation. I hadn't considered Luke's absence as a blessing. Would Clint behave differently if his uncle wasn't there in Tennessee? The thought made perfect sense. But, according to what I was hearing, I'd have to be on my toes with him at all times. "So, it's settled. They're coming?"

"Not quite. When will this transfer take place, and when should the children be told? I don't think it's fair to spring the move on them without giving them time to think about and plan for such a big change in their lives." Luke sat back into the couch's cushions—more relaxed, since the conversation was winding up.

The three of us soon had all the details ironed out. I would fly home tomorrow and ready my home for the children to move. James' room had twin beds, so he and Marcus could share his room. Clint would have a room by himself, and Maryb would sleep temporarily on a couch in my bedroom.

On Sunday, five days from today, I'd be back in East Texas, driving Luke's Tahoe, which was big enough to haul the three children with plenty of room for luggage in the back. I'd spend a day to rest and start back on Tuesday, arriving on Wednesday. Thursday the children would unpack and, on Friday, they'd register for school.

Luke stood, digging in the pocket of his pants. "Here let me give you the keys before I forget them."

"That's a lot of driving for one person," noted Agnes.

"Manda's indefatigable when it comes to traveling long distances, aren't you Sweetheart?" He patted me on the shoulder, and we held hands for a minute.

He walked to his mother, bent over, and prepared to help her out of the chair.

"What about James? He could ride shotgun as we say here in Texas. The old stagecoach can handle one more."

"I'd love to have him. He'd keep me company, and we could pack light, so our suitcases wouldn't take up much room in the Tahoe."

"Then it's settled," said Luke, pulling his mother from the red chair. "When do we tell the children?"

"In the morning, before you take Manda to the airport. Stop by the house for lunch and we'll tell them then." Agnes suggested.

"I'll need Mrs. Caylor to sit with Mom."

Agnes promised, "I'll call her when I get home."

Luke walked to the hallway and turned, "Your church's ministry for emergencies has been a God-send, Agnes."

"I'll be sure and tell them you said so. They don't get a lot of credit. Guess I'd better go." Agnes stood, and we both joined Luke and Mom Avery in the hallway. There were kisses all around before Agnes left.

~

I stood watching at the small Longview airport, as planes took off and landed. My airplane sat on the tarmac, waiting to load.

Luke was gone after a long, gentle kiss. I know he hoped we'd made the right decision. What if something happened, I couldn't control? Or, our assessment of Clint's actions was wrong? Thinking through these last weeks, I realized my serene, predictable existence had gone completely haywire.

Of course, the flip side of the coin was possible. The transition might be peaceful and totally uncomplicated, with a bond established and growing between the children and me. Taking them back to Tennessee could become the best thing for all of us—for our future bonding as a family.

I said short prayers on the flight to Dallas and on the way home to Maryville.

CHAPTER TWENTY-SEVEN

Manda

One of the last things I saw as I walked out of my bedroom was Luke's wedding ring in its box on my dresser. I picked it up, kissed it goodbye, and looked around the room with its dark wood and oriental influence.

My bed was made with decorative teal spread and matching, sham-encased bed pillows atop. Two chairs sat in a corner with a square table and lamp in between. A knickknack shelf contained multicolored souvenirs of my diverse vacations to states and national parks.

These included Yellowstone National Park and a cruise from Los Angeles to the Mexican Riviera. A large landscape with teal colors and dark wood frame, with the ocean at sunset centered the wall over my bed. Another was positioned over the three-cushioned couch on the longest wall in the room.

I'd chosen each piece in the room with care, making it a decorator's dream, straight out of *Better Homes & Gardens*, except for the painting. I'd purchased it in Orlando at a shop on the way to Disney World. The bedroom represented my life alone after my marriage.

"See you later, alligator," I whispered to the room and flipped the light switch off.

Unlike the two-week jaunts I usually took, my trip to Longview would be short. I should be back here in three days. Today was Sunday, normally a day I went to church.

I walked into the hallway, dragging my carry-on and looked upstairs where casual décor was the word. The children's rooms would reflect their own tastes. With the exception of making the bed and cleaning up after themselves in the bathroom, house rules were simple and probably subject to additions. My home was ready for its new occupants.

"James, are you ready to go?" I knew he was up, because I'd heard him thumping around upstairs and water running in the bathroom.

I picked up my road atlas from the kitchen counter, checking the route to Longview for the tenth time, remembering the conversation with Luke at China Cuisine so long ago.

Guess I'm giving up the road trip to San Diego, but I'm going to drive a good chunk of it, I thought. I put the atlas under my arm, my purse strap over my shoulder, and drug my carry-on to the garage. Looking around, I saw James with his bag right behind me.

"Good morning, sunshine," I kidded him. He was still groggy-eyed.

"Is it still dark outside?" He asked, peering around me and looking out the open garage door. He groaned.

It *was* five o'clock in the morning. "I'm afraid so, but the sun will shine in about an hour. You can sleep if you want to. I feel great, like I could lick tigers, and I'm so excited. Are you excited?"

He looked at me with what could be called disdain. "Yeah, can't you tell?"

He grinned, and I laughed. I loaded the bags in the back of the Tahoe, which had spent the night in my spacious garage—a first for it. I knew James was looking forward to the trip, because he'd told everyone about our journey, including his grandpa.

"Okay, jump in. We're ready to go."

I started the Tahoe, the assuring purr of the engine low and steady. The driver's seat sat higher than the one in my Avalon, letting me see over the hood. I liked it.

As I pulled out of the driveway, my lights flashed on the For Sale sign in my front yard. My real estate agent was showing my house. Because one of our large factories was transferring employees to Maryville, opening up a new division, jobs were available, and people were looking for houses. One prospective buyer seemed promising.

"James, your father and I need to start looking for a new home in the country."

He perked up a little. "You mean out of town? I have friends at school who live on big farms with lots of cattle, horses, and other animals. One has a creek with fish in it. He goes fishing any time he wants to. I think that's awesome."

"I don't believe we'll be raising cattle, but he wants to have at least one horse, maybe two—depends on the acreage we buy. Do you know how to ride?"

"Yes, one of Dad's friends at church has horses, and we've been there to ride. My Dad's really good. He can sit a horse as they say."

"My experience with riding isn't good. God hasn't made a horse that sits me. I ache all over when I get off, and one time I fell on the ground, because I'd ridden so long I couldn't walk. I was embarrassed until another lady did the same."

James looked at me and grinned. "In Texas, we call someone like that a greenhorn. But I'm not calling you that."

"Yeah, yeah." I reached over and punched at him.

I turned onto the four-lane heading toward Lenoir City and I-75. "Do you want a biscuit from Hardee's? There's one in Lenoir City. I'm going to get one."

"Sure."

"Okay, take your nap while it's dark outside. You can eat your biscuit when you wake up."

～

I-75 south was a familiar road to me. After several miles, I crossed the Tennessee River and soon the overhead signs at Calhoun alerted me to the possibility of fog ahead. This was where a multi-car pileup injured and killed people decades ago. The sun was up and the roadway clear as I headed toward Chattanooga.

I looked across at James, snuggled up in a lap blanket and sleeping soundly with his neck pillow between his head and the door. His biscuit would be cold when he woke up.

Traffic thru Chattanooga on Sunday morning wasn't heavy at seven o'clock, but interstate switching was tedious — a real bear. I pulled the road atlas off the dash and checked my route, during one slowdown, making sure of my next off-ramp onto I-24. After rounding the famous horseshoe bend in the Tennessee River, I soon reached I-59 and crossed the corner of

Georgia. That's were James and I would start the long drive thru the state of Alabama to I-20.

Sweet Home Alabama. I hummed the tune as I drove through Fort Payne, the hometown of the famous musical group, Alabama.

James stirred and sat up. "Where are we?"

"In Alabama. We've been in three states since you started taking your nap."

"Three states! You're kidding."

"No, I'm not. Are you hungry? Your biscuit is on the dash and probably very cold."

"That's okay. I'll eat it anyway."

"I'll stop if you want a cold drink out of the cooler. There's a rest area ahead."

"No. I can drink 'em without being cold." James corralled his cola from the center console and started to open the can.

I put my hand out. "No wait, partner."

"Why?"

"I need a potty break. We'll put the hot one in the cooler and get you a cold one."

"Okay. I think I could go to the bathroom, too."

On the way in, I noticed he had his biscuit. "Why did you bring your biscuit?"

"Maybe they have a microwave, and I'll have a hot biscuit to eat with my cold drink."

"Now there's an idea I never thought of before."

James went to the attendant at the kiosk and told her his dilemma.

Amazingly, she took the biscuit and winked at him. "Wash your hands and come get it after you use the bathroom."

He turned and looked at me with the biggest grin on his face — an I-told-you-so-smile.

Back in the Tahoe with the warm biscuit, I asked how he knew she would help him. "Dad and I stopped here before, and they warmed my biscuit in their microwave."

We rode for a while in silence, as he devoured his biscuit.

"Look, Mom, there's a cave we could visit."

Sequoyah Caverns went by on the left. "Do you think we can stop there on the way back?"

"Maybe," I said as we passed the exit. "Depends on the time we pass through the area."

I'd placed a small trash can just between the two bucket seats and in front of the rear bench. James put his trash in it and grabbed a wet wipe to clean his hands. He sat looking at the tree-covered, northern Alabama countryside. "Doesn't look much different from home," he observed.

"No, it doesn't. How many times have you traveled this route with your Dad?"

"Lots. We always went at Christmas and for a week in the summer. When Mom was alive, she and I sometimes went for Easter when school's out for spring break. At least that's what Dad said. I was too young to remember." James turned toward me. "Did you know my Mom was born in Louisiana?"

I shook my head. "Do you miss your Mom?"

"Not anymore. I can't remember her unless I look at her picture." James looked over at me. "You're my Mom now. I like that."

I reached for his hand. "We don't want you to forget your birth mom, but I'll be so proud to have you as my son. I love you, James."

"I love you too."

We were silent, watching the Alabama countryside whiz by. "Mom, there's a deer," exclaimed James, pointing to the right side of the highway.

Sure enough, a large doe stood beside the road. I slowed down. "I hope she doesn't decide to cross the road."

"Like the chicken," said James laughing.

"Egg-zack-ly!" Now, we were both laughing.

She decided not to cross, but watched us, as we drove safely on. "Grandpa told me another funny. Do you want to hear it?"

"Sure, go ahead."

"One golfer says to a friend, "I'm on a golf diet." James looked over at me, egg-spec-tent-ly.

"Really? What on earth is a golf diet?"

"Yep. I live on greens." James cackled.

"Gosh, that's corny. Get it? Corn — ey."

In Birmingham, Alabama's state capital, the traffic was heavier. "Look, James. Those huge buildings are steel mills, processing metal for use in American products."

"Are they empty?"

"No, they look empty because they're so cavernous."

"Are we going to take the bypass around the city?

"No. We'll go straight through, and you'll see the city center."

A few minutes later, he asked, "How come all the tall buildings have bank, insurance and phone signs on top?"

"I suppose it's because they make a lot of money and build buildings with it. Have you ever been to Nashville?"

"No."

"Nashville has many skyscrapers like Birmingham." Then I asked him, "Help me look for I-20 signs?"

Overpasses, underpasses, and through roads became a maze of twisting concrete on pillars, snaking into and around the city's skyscrapers. Within minutes the first I-20 sign came into view. Hardly any roads ran on the ground, as we turned left and right to keep from getting run over by the passing, speed limit-breaking automobiles.

I breathed a sigh of relief when traffic thinned out, and I could relax and again enjoy driving the highway.

"James, you can throw the road atlas on the back bench, because this highway takes us into Texas and to Longview. That is unless you want to follow the map and tell me the name of the next big city."

"Sure." He sat with the map opened to the state of Alabama. "I think the next big town is Tucka-Tuckaloos, I can't pronounce the name," he said.

"Spell it."

"Okay. T-u-s-c-a-l-o-o-s-a."

"Ah, Tuscaloosa, home of the Crimson Tide. They're one of our football team's biggest rivals. There's never a way of knowing if red or orange will come out on top. Do you like football?"

"Yes, I watch with Dad, but he yells at the players."

"He does?" This was a bit of news I didn't expect. "What does he say?"

"Aw, he just tells them they picked the wrong play or they busted a play. He doesn't like to lose. I think he's what they call a sore loser." James was nodding along with his words.

From what I knew of the Avery men, this sounded just like them. "Are you a sore loser?"

"Sometimes."

I couldn't imagine James as a sore loser.

At the welcome center, after the Mississippi state line, we stopped to eat sandwiches I'd fixed the night before. They tasted good with the sweet pickles I'd canned with my mother's help earlier in the summer.

Seeing the pint canning jar, James asked, "Did you and Mamaw fix these pickles?"

"Yes, we worked our fingers to the bone, making them." I held up my left hand and spread my fingers apart, "See." My engagement ring flashed in the afternoon sun.

"I hope Grandpa and I can work in the garden next year. We'll grow more pickles ..." James stopped and thought. "Where do pickles come from?"

"Mostly cucumbers."

"Oh, we'll grow lots of cucumbers to make pickles. I think I'm getting sleepy again."

James took a nap through the first part of Mississippi. When he awoke, we were far into magnolia territory, driving through its capital— Jackson.

"Another state capital," he said.

"Yes, the last time I came through here was after Hurricane Katrina. Of course, the brunt of the storm remained south on the coast, but tornadoes, high winds, and flooding were issues here in the central section."

"Did our church come down and help with the cleanup?"

"Yes, it did. I went down for a week. The southern coast was a mess. People were without homes, clothes, and food. Some lost their lives. Not much evidence of the disaster now."

About one hour later, we could see the tall bridge spanning the Mississippi River in the distance. "Let's stop at the Welcome Center. We'll take a potty break and take a look at the bridge from the ground."

Mississippi southern drawl greeted us as we entered the building. "Hi, you all. Welcome to our great state." A picture of the governor, Haley Barbour, hung on the wall. "Is there anything I can help you all with?"

"We'd like a map."

She didn't have to know we'd already been across her great state.

"Please sign our visitors' book."

I stepped up to sign her book, telling James to go to the bathroom.

"Ah, you're from Tennessee. Is it hot up there? It's been a scorcher down here lately."

We stood discussing the weather until James appeared from the bathroom. "James, you stay with this nice lady until I get back."

When I returned from the bathroom, the two sat in two folding chairs with a book between them. The greeter looked up. "We were checkin' out the Spanish moss in our plantation book."

"It's awesome. Did you know it was once used to stuff mattresses? People actually slept on it." James looked up at me with sparkling eyes. He'd learned something new.

"That's interesting to know. Would you like to have the book to look at as we head down the road?"

"Yes. Can I buy it with some of the money Dad left me?"

"No, I'll get it."

We purchased the book, walked around the area, and at two o'clock left Mississippi via the metal span over the expansive river. James tried to look everywhere at once. "Mom, there's a barge going up river. Looks like it's loaded with sand or gravel. Where do you think it's going?"

"Good question. I really don't know, maybe Memphis. I think it's the next biggest port on the mighty Mississip'."

"Where do they get sand?"

"They dredge it from the bottom of the river. It comes from upriver when it floods and falls out of the water in huge sand drifts. There are piles under the water."

The barge and the bridge disappeared from view. I estimated we were four or five hours from Longview — four across Louisiana and one from Shreveport. Shreveport being the last big city before our destination.

Because I was growing tired, those four hours were the longest of my life. We stopped once to get icecream, and I called Luke on the phone.

"Hi, Honey, where are you?"

"We're coming across the state of Louisiana. James and I just finished eating ice cream at Monroe."

"You're making good time. You should be here around six or seven. Is it okay with you to go out and eat? There's nothing here at the house, and I'm sure you'll be exhausted."

"That's music to my ears. Let's plan on it."

"How's James doing?"

"Here, I'll let you ask him." I handed James the phone and concentrated on my driving. He couldn't wait to tell his dad about the trip. Finally, he handed the phone back to me.

"Hey," I said. "I believe he's enjoying himself, and we've talked about everything, including your passion for yelling at the Tennessee team when they're playing football. Shame on you."

"I yell at Texas, too, if that's any consolation."

"That wasn't what I meant, and you know it."

Luke was laughing. "Sweetheart, I'd promise not to do it, but I'd break my word."

"Don't 'Sweetheart' me." I was only teasing. "How's Mom Avery?"

"There's no change. Thank goodness, Agnes comes to help with her bath and other female chores. And Mrs. Caylor comes when I need her. I found out she's distant kin of Dan Taylor who's the director at Nightingale Place. Definitely is a small world."

"Not much longer until James and I get to Longview."

"No, it isn't, since you're past Monroe, and at this time of day, you should breeze through Shreveport. Will you be glad to see me?"

"Yes, I love you."

"Me too. Uh-oh. Mom's calling me. See you soon." The phone went dead. At that instant, I decided I didn't like cell phones. They cut you off from those you loved.

❦ CHAPTER TWENTY-EIGHT ❦

Manda

The few hours I spent in Longview were like a whirlwind. Luke insisted I not be involved in the preparations. He wanted me fresh for the long-haul back to Tennessee. James and I slept late and upon rising, ate a breakfast of bacon, eggs, and toast. Refreshed and dressed, I went to watch the madhouse taking place in the garage.

Many of the children's toys and personal items were stored in Pop's shed. When the children weren't playing, they were hauling out items for taking back in the Tahoe. Soon, it became evident Luke's truck would not haul the stack rising in the Avery's garage. Agnes brought over a load from her house and went back for more.

Included in the stack was a desk and chair for Marcus, a small rocker for Maryb, and pitching equipment for Clint. The largest piece, a twin bed with mattress and frame, came with linens to go with it. Maryb had insisted on taking the bed she'd used all her life.

"I had no idea we'd have this much stuff. Do you think we could sneak some out to a second-hand store this afternoon?" Luke stood surveying the heap in his mother's garage.

"No, let's don't do that. This stuff, as you call it, is familiar and loved by the children. It'll make the transition to their new home much easier."

Marcus appeared from Pop's toolshed, carrying — of all things — a cradle. I knew there was a story behind this wooden treasure.

"It's the only thing left from my baby sister," he explained and looked at Luke, his eyes pleading with his uncle.

Luke stood, hands on hips, gazing at the large cradle, which had wooden spindles and rocked. How would he keep it safe from being damaged? "Put your treasure down, partner. We'll figure out a way to take it."

Marcus' smile said it all. He didn't need to say thank you.

After he left, Luke turned to me. "Imagine, being attached to the rocking cradle of your baby sister."

"Marcus is a sensitive young man. Has he shared the poem he wrote about her?"

"No, he hasn't."

"It's a eulogy in a way and very moving. I don't remember it but 'silky blond hair' and 'baby giggle' come to mind."

Luke came over and put his arms around me. "It seems the children are learning to trust you, future wife."

We ended up renting a trailer and attaching the metal box to the back of the Tahoe. By late afternoon on Monday, the truck and trailer were packed. "Are you comfortable with dragging this extra weight behind you?"

"Piece of cake. I always helped Dad with his utility trailer. I just have more miles to drive." I said this with more enthusiasm than I felt.

"Speaking of cake, I'm hungry."

"Why don't we take everyone out for pizza? Angelo's mouth waterin' Italian sounds good."

"Are you going to dip yours in ranch dressing."

"I don't think so."

～

At five o'clock, I was up and dressed. I finished packing my carry-on and started down the stairs. The smell of freshly brewed coffee greeted me in the hallway.

Luke bounded up the steps. "Here, I'll help you." He kissed me lightly on the lips, went back down, and disappeared through the kitchen and out the door to the garage.

"My, aren't you the early bird," I called after him. I already knew he was an early riser. He preferred the quiet darkness before dawn to study the Bible and pray. He said his thoughts came easier, the day was unspoiled, and the overnight sleep refreshed him.

I went over to the coffeepot and poured a cup of the dark brew. A small carton of milk sat on the table, along with his half-full cup of coffee, some maps, and his open Bible. I added milk to my mug and waited for him to return.

Being longer than I thought necessary, I took my coffee and looked out the kitchen window toward the driveway. He was on the other side of the trailer. I could barely see his feet next to one of the tires. Not understanding what was taking so long, I set my coffee cup down and went to see.

"There's a flat on the trailer," he announced with a disgusted look. "I'll call the rental company and see if they can come and fix it." Luke went into his Mom's house to get the telephone number and his cell phone.

When he came back outside, he wasn't happy. "The recording says they don't open until eight. I left a message. Guess you're stuck here with me until then. Why don't we eat breakfast while we're waiting?"

"Call Agnes, she may want to bring the children over. You know they're up." I nodded. "Have we got enough food for them?"

"I think so." Luke walked back and forth as he called his sister. "She coming over, and she's bringing some extra milk and buttered biscuits from one of the fast-food restaurants downtown. She won't be long."

Agnes arrived with a full load of kids and small bags of luggage, which were filled with pajama's and morning toiletries, to be stored in the Tahoe. Breakfast followed immediately.

At eight o'clock, Luke finally got through to the rental company. They couldn't send anyone until ten. "The owner said they've got several rental units which need to be prepped for pickup this morning." He ran his fingers through his hair, something he did only when he was frustrated.

Rustling down the hall meant his mother was up. "I'll tend to her," said Agnes. Manda, you fix her some breakfast."

When Agnes reappeared, she whispered to me, "She's having one of her I can do this myself days. I'll clean up the bathroom while she's eating."

She didn't leave her show of independence in the bedroom and bathroom. Mom Avery decided the eggs and bacon I'd fixed weren't to her liking. She ended up eating leftover pizza and cola for breakfast, making loud, smacking sounds with her lips. The obvious escalating of her dementia didn't help our deteriorating mood.

As promised, the mechanic arrived at ten, took the tire off, and left with it to get it repaired. "Why didn't they bring a new tire and change it out?" Luke threw his hands wide in a questioning gesture, while shaking his head.

Our whole plan to drive to Maryville in one day was a complete disaster.

"Luke, I'd rather not drive after dark tonight, especially pulling the trailer."

"Yes, I agree. Let's check the Internet and see what we can find. I think you can still make Meridian, Mississippi and be home in the afternoon Wednesday. That is if they get the tire back on the trailer by noon. Come into the kitchen, and I'll show you where the town is on my maps."

"Ha, I have a map of Mississippi in the Tahoe. I'll go get it." When James and I stopped in Vicksburg at the Mississippi Welcome Center near the river bridge, I had no idea we'd need the map I asked for.

~

We'd been gone about two hours when Marcus asked to use the bathroom, and at one o'clock my breakfast was gone. "How about combining a bathroom break with lunch?" I suggested.

"Yeah, I'm hungry," Clint agreed. I'd asked him to sit up front so he could help me watch traffic. "Let's have pizza."

"We had Italian last night. You'll turn into a pizza. Any other suggestions from the back seat?"

I listened to a chorus of ideas coming from the rear. I shouldn't have asked the question. Lesson learned, I thought. Number One: don't ask, pick it out yourself, and tell them what you're going to do. "The next town we come to, we'll stop at the first, fast-food place."

Turns out it was a burger joint. The children ordered chicken strips, all except Clint who ordered a barbequed, roast beef sandwich. Go figure! I was the only *oddball* out, ordering a double hamburger with fries. I needed sustenance for the rest of the day.

Back on the road, we kept up a constant chatter. Out of the blue, Maryb loudly exclaimed, "Look, there goes a hot mama in a Mercedes convertible."

Startled by her comment, I jerked the steering wheel. For a few tense seconds, I watch in the rearview mirror as the trailer cut didoes behind me. "Maryb, you scared me. I thought someone was going to hit us." My voice was sharper than I intended, and when I next looked in the rear mirror, she appeared ready to cry. I said more softly, "Try not to be so loud. Where did you hear that expression anyway?"

"Hear what?" She sniffed.

"What you said about the hot mama."

"Clint says it all the time."

"I'm sure there aren't many Mercedes convertibles in Longview," I replied.

Marcus spoke up, "She lived down the street from Pop's in the subdivision. We usually saw her in the afternoon."

"I see. Somehow, I don't think that's a proper way to address a lady."

I didn't single out Clint or Maryb with my comment. I know Maryb understood my message, because later in the day she sidled up to me and told me she wouldn't say it again. Clint never said a word.

We didn't stop elsewhere, as we drove through Louisiana. Around three-thirty in the afternoon, we crossed the Mississippi River bridge, and I asked if they'd like to tour the Civil War site at Vicksburg. By this time, they were ready to get out of the car and do anything.

I followed the exit signs for the military park and soon turned into the visitor center parking lot, pulling into a space marked for buses. A huge cannon outside the building fascinated Marcus and James. Jumping from the vehicle, they went to check it out.

"How'd you like to fire that thing?" I heard Clint ask them.

We went inside and walked through the exhibits and then viewed the video of the battle site. A separate exhibit of the USS Cairo, an ironclad gunboat, which plied the Mississippi during the Civil War, was just as interesting, including the video and artifacts from its sinking.

We headed back to the Tahoe. After taking several valuable minutes to tour the visitor center, I looked at my group saying, "Guys, I don't think we've got time to tour the battlefield."

"Let's do it," said Clint. The others chimed in.

I relented and spent almost another two hours letting them see the monuments and battle sites. At six-thirty, we started the three-hour drive to Meridian, Mississippi. Traffic was light on the interstate and we had reservations, so there was no problem with check-in. We each had our bags with overnight items, and while in Longview, I had rented two rooms. Maryb and I shared a room. The three boys made do in the other.

We slept in on Wednesday morning, getting up in time to eat the hotel breakfast.

Gathering our belongings, we went outside to restart our journey. I was thinking, we hadn't had any trouble with the trailer except for the shimmy after Maryb's frightening comment, but when Clint rounded the trailer's rear, he stopped in disbelief and said, "The tire is flat again."

At this moment I decided again was a notorious word. Again, again, again, Lord preserve me from hearing it *again*!

I called Luke. "What should I do?"

There's a 1-800 number on the paperwork. Call it. I hope you won't have to wait long to get it fixed."

I pulled the Tahoe with the fixed tired out of the motel at twelve o'clock on the nose, noticing the gathering clouds piling up on the horizon to the north. "Lord, please don't let us have more trouble." I sure was invoking His name a lot.

I should've known stomachs would be growling before long. "Okay, everyone. Here's the way it is. In about one hour, we'll be in Knoxville. It's the next biggest town. We'll see if we can find something to eat."

"Knoxville?" James responded. "It isn't possible."

"Knoxville, Alabama, that's the location, my dear James."

The truck was quiet inside, as we drove on. I assumed everyone was consumed with weakness from being starved to death. I've always snacked when driving, preferring to increase my mileage and not stopping.

Lesson Number Two: Children need to eat nutritious meals—on time.

We drove up and down the small town of Knoxville, Alabama. There were no eating places. "I'm sorry. Tuscaloosa is about twenty miles away. There'll be scads of places there."

Can quiet be quieter? I can confirm this fact.

When I pulled into the sub shop in Tuscaloosa, a cheer went up. "Yeah, we're here."

After eating, I had to admit the teriyaki chicken was good, but coming back outside, the sprinkles of rain, I found on the pavement and in my hair, were not. I didn't mind driving the Tahoe in the rain, but seeing the ill-fated trailer behind me—just thinking about what might happen gave me a slight headache.

We hit Birmingham before the start of the evening's rush hour traffic. We'd have breezed on by, but a four-car pileup in the drizzling rain, backed up traffic on the interstate in the heart of town. I could do nothing but sit and creep. By the time we left the city, I never wanted to see the neon signs of any large commercial company on a tall building again. There was that notorious word *again*.

Just when I was beginning to breathe a sigh of relief after leaving the bright lights of the city, my trip home from Longview turned into a Stephen King nightmare.

The sky darkened and the clouds opened up and threw buckets of water on us. Brilliant flashes of lightning followed by the boom of overhead thunder surrounded and shook the truck. Looking in the rearview mirror, I saw three children cowering together in the back seat.

Seeing my quick glance, Clint turned around in his seat and informed James and Marcus, "Remember the cannon at Vicksburg? This is the kinda sound which happens when it is fired." Then he turned back around in his seat and laughed.

I looked briefly over at him. Could he really think this was funny? I concentrated on my driving skills, stayed in the right-hand lane, and slowed from fifty-five miles per hour to forty-five. I was afraid to go any slower.

At this rate, we might be home by midnight. Before we got to Gadsden, Alabama, the children complained of hunger. Gadsden had a Cracker Barrel—a warm place I knew well, but first I needed to fill the Tahoe with gas.

Driving the vehicle into a truck stop on the same exit as the restaurant, I pulled my aching bones and muscles out and started pumping gas.

"Manda, I need to go to the restroom." Maryb was standing near the pump, shifting her weight from one leg to the other. "Now!"

At that moment the pump clicked off. I hurried to put the cap on the gas tank and get my receipt. "Boys, we're going to the bathroom. Anybody else need to go?" I called into the truck.

All three piled out, and we ran into the building.

I didn't see the restrooms so I asked the attendant. She took one look at Maryb, whose face must have said "emergency," because the cashier jabbed her finger to the front left of the building.

"Maryb, it should be right up there." I gave her instructions and paid my bill.

Assorted chewing gum and candy was displayed on the counter. I decided to buy some. This might save me from stopping later as, we continued our journey.

Maryb came back. She put her hand over her mouth and whispered, "Manda, am I a #1 or #2?"

"What on earth are you talking about?"

I took my purse and purchase and walked with her to the front of the building. When I saw the signs, I burst out laughing. Or was I hysterical? "Sweetie, you can use either one. Go." I pushed her towards the #1 door. She hurried inside.

Evidently, the place had built larger bathrooms with showers for truckers in the back. Since most drivers were men, up front, they'd left the two smaller ones for women. All truck stops have numbered doors. In busy times, you are given a door number. I explained all this to Maryb when she came out.

Laughter released part of the tension of the trip. The boys appeared from the rear of the building. We left the station, went to eat, and continued our journey. We were still an estimated three or four hours from home. The good news was, it had quit raining, but I still had to be careful. The roads were wet and a mist rose from the hot asphalt. Soon, my headlights were boring through intermittent patches of fog.

One hour later, I was humming Sweet Home Alabama, as I went through Fort Payne. All three children, stomachs full, slept in the rear seat. Clint nodded to my right.

Real darkness had descended on the state. I was driving in the inside lane, because the interstate north of Gadsden is rough in the right one, making my head rattle. With my slight headache, I needed a smooth ride.

There was no warning, but a flash from my side lights revealed a deer coming at a rapid pace across the left-hand lanes toward the interstate median. As in a dream, I saw it hit the grass and start up the bank on my side of the road. I didn't have time to react or get scared. Just as it was about to reach the shoulder on my lane and run in front of me, the deer sat down on its haunches, as if pressed there by a mighty hand. If it hadn't been misty from the rain and dark outside, I'm sure I would have seen dust and dirt flying from the force of its abrupt stop. The Tahoe flew by, and I breathed again. There was that word, *again*.

"Clint, did you see the deer?"

"What deer?"

"The one that almost hit us." I realized he was almost asleep himself.

"No."

My lips moved in silent prayer. "Lord, thank you for your traveling mercies. Is it possible the rest of the trip could be quiet and peaceful?" I pulled in a ragged sigh. I was ready to be home. I'd had enough problems and excitement for several days.

CHAPTER TWENTY-NINE

Luke

Manda's brief call at twelve-thirty was a welcome relief. They'd arrived at her home. "I'll give you the horrific details tomorrow," she'd said. Whatever these dreadful facts were, I knew they were safe and sound. I turned over in bed and went to sleep.

The next morning, I talked to her at eight o'clock, Tennessee time. "I kept praying the whole day for you to be safe," I said after her thorough account of the previous day's drive.

"Your prayers were answered."

"Are they up?" I ran water in the coffee carafe and poured the liquid into the water well in the coffee brewer.

"None, except James. We ate breakfast, and he's making a welcome sign. We're gonna hang it over the kitchen door so Clint and Marcus will see it first thing when they come down from upstairs. Maryb slept in my bedroom on the couch. Hey, I've got to go. There's the doorbell. Probably some help to unload the trailer. I love you. We'll talk tomorrow or before."

I hung up the phone and plugged in the coffeepot. Mom's morning needs were escalating, and I wasn't comfortable with, nor should I perform the morning tasks associated with her shower and bathroom duties. I remembered telling Pop this very thing when he suggested I move back to Longview.

Thank goodness for Mrs. Caylor, who insisted I call her Faith. "You make me feel like Methuselah," she exclaimed over the phone when I'd called her. We made plans for her to come each day at seven-thirty.

After rising, Mom's comings and goings were erratic. I might find her in the living room, pajamas on, looking at the many pictures atop the furniture, crocheting, or wandering around the house with a dusting cloth. Structure was what she needed. Agnes, Faith, and I established a schedule to follow, shadowing the routine she'd be required to adhere to at Nightingale Place.

While I was fixing breakfast and keeping an eye on her morning's progress, Faith was to get Mom up and help her to the bathroom. Then, she would see that Mom showered and assist in choosing and donning clothes for the day.

Sitting at the breakfast table to eat was a time for us to talk with Mom, blue bib on, participating on days she was still lucid. In my mother's condition, besides crocheting or napping in the living room, taking her on short walks in the yard, or on sunny drives in Pop's car, there wasn't much in the way of activities she could do. Forget games. Forget eating out.

At my age, this lifestyle would bore me to death. Both Mom and Faith seemed happy with it, chatting away in the living room.

Although my mother's answers weren't coherent at times, Faith didn't care. Mom kept her company.

Being around Mom for several days, I realized she was much worse than Pop had led us to believe. Even Agnes had tried to tell me this. I didn't want to believe her.

There were times I ached to hold my mother and tell her how much she'd meant to me in my growing up years. My mother recoiled from this touch of affection, and I would hear, "Who are you? Where's Pop, I'm scared."

Mom's periods of lucid recognition became fewer and fewer. During one of them, I told her of Pop's passing. She didn't shed a tear, in fact, her eyes weren't even moist. She was quickly slipping into the darkest regions of her mind.

I'd just finished cleaning the kitchen after breakfast, Faith and Mom were in the living room when my phone rang again.

"Honey, my realtor has a contract on my house. She was at my door when I hung up earlier."

"That was fast. What did you do? Did you accept the offer?"

"I thought it best to tell you first. But, yes, the offer was exactly the amount I stipulated when I put the house on the market. They have cash. I can't very well turn it down."

"Do I hear a but?"

"I don't have much time to move. They want the house in a month, and where do I move? I thought about asking for an extension, but I don't want to lose the sale."

Although one problem was solved, this created another. "We'll need to start looking for a new home.

Could you spend some time checking around until I get there?"

"I don't know how much time I'll have, since I'm settling the children in here, taking them to enter school, and returning to work on Monday. I'm sure June is ready for me to come back."

"See if the realtor can help you with properties. She knows what we want. Check the realtor's supplement in *The Daily Times*. Circle the ones of interest and find directions on the Internet."

"Sure, I'll do both. We'll drive around on Sunday after lunch and look." She paused, "Our lives are moving so fast. I need you to help. I miss you."

"Mom will soon have a room, you'll see."

"Hey, I hear footsteps on the stairs. One of our sleepyheads is on the move."

"I'll talk to you tomorrow, Sweetheart."

When I hung up, I went into my bedroom to pick up the last of Agnes' books and started out the door. No, there was something else I needed to do. I knelt by my bed and earnestly prayed for an answer to today's dilemma. I asked for extra strength for Manda. At the end, I apologized to my Heavenly Father for being such a problem.

Then I took it back. This was His to solve, and I was sure He was working it out for good. Remembering the promise of Isaiah 40:31, *"but they that wait upon the LORD shall renew their strength; they shall mount up with wings as eagles; they shall run, and not be weary; and they shall walk, and not faint."*

I prayed His words back to Him.

How much clearer could His promise be? None. I would wait for Him to do the work.

I got up from my knees, picked up the book, and returned to the living room entrance. I remained in the hallway watching as Faith and Mom sat crocheting — my mother on her misshapen blue sweater.

As I stood smiling at them, the cell phone rang again. I pulled it off my belt and looked at it. "Grand Central Station today, aren't you?"

What's it called when you start talking to your phone?

"Did you say something, Luke?" Faith looked at me with questioning eyes.

"No, it's Agnes. I'll go to the kitchen and take this."

She smiled at me as I left and kept on chatting with Mom.

"Luke! There's been a miracle."

"Seems like the Avery family has been blessed with those the past few weeks."

"Nightingale Place has an opening. I just talked to Mr. Taylor. He has a resident going into a nursing home, she's moving today. Isn't that great?"

"Sure is. So when can Mom move in?"

"He said the room will be cleaned and disinfected this week and ready on Monday."

"Why so long?" It wasn't that I felt impatient, but I wondered what they were doing to the room. "Is the room in poor condition?"

"No, I don't think so. He told me before, this is standard procedure. In this case, the resident has been living in the room three years, so there is some minor wear and tear. They'll paint the room, and he says they'll install new carpet."

"Blue, I hope."

Agnes laughed. "Maybe. Mom will move into a room which smells new and looks new. We'll need to decide what furniture to take and pack her clothes."

"How about tomorrow for a preliminary look? I'll take a measuring tape, and we can jot down the measurements. This will help us decide on what to move. Then we'll go ahead and start gathering things and put them in the garage."

"We don't have to pack everything, just the harder, larger stuff to move. Boxed items we can take last."

"Think Mike can help Saturday or Sunday with the biggest pieces?"

"I'll call him. I'm sure he'll want to come home and help. I'll call my church, also."

"I wonder if Nightingale Place has a staging area? It would be nice to go ahead and deliver the items while he's here. If need be, we could do it on Sunday afternoon."

"I'll check and see. If I remember correctly, there's a maintenance man who helps move the furniture, puts up pictures, and hangs shelves."

"Gosh, we'll have some decorating to do."

"Yes, we will. I'll call Mr. Taylor about visiting in the morning. The children can stay with Mom and Faith."

"Good plan. I'll see you then." I immediately phoned Manda with the good news.

I'd seen Nightingale Place from the road, but hadn't been inside or met Mr. Taylor. Unlike most residences I'd visited, his facility had plenty of places to park.

On Friday morning at nine o'clock, Agnes and I walked through the front door and into a spacious reception area. The business office was on the right and the game or activity room on the left. Four elderly smiling residents, sitting on couches or in chairs, greeted us upon our arrival. They sat almost in a straight line to the side of the entranceway.

Agnes whispered, "They're always here—the welcoming committee."

We greeted them as we passed. "The one with the red cheeks, does she always nap?" This gray-haired lady sat with eyes closed and her chin resting on her chest."

"She was here the last time I came. I think she sleeps most of the time."

"I heard that young people," she said, a sneaky smile on her face and one eye now half open.

Agnes and I burst out laughing, as the receptionist came to greet us. "Mrs. Phillips are you causing trouble?"

"Would I do that?" the grin grew bigger as we followed the receptionist to her office.

"Agnes, it's good to see you again. I'm so happy your mom's going to have a room here. Is this your brother?"

"Yes, this is my little brother." Agnes looked over at me and grinned. "Sherrie, I'd like you to meet Luke. And, Luke, this is Sherrie Lufkin."

"It's nice to meet you Sherrie."

"I remember you." Sherrie pointed her red-enameled fingernail at me. You played basketball with my brother, Lance."

"Lance Sherman?"

"Yes."

"Your brother. Great player. What's he doing now? We had some fun times together at school and church." Lance Sherman was responsible for my church attendance in high school, after an incident in my life. I hadn't thought about *that* in years. The occasion slipped out of my mind as quickly as it entered.

"He's coach at Del Rio High in West Texas."

"Why'd he go all the way across Texas to coach?"

"You'll have to ask him that question." The phone rang and Sherrie held a brief conversation with the person on the other end. When she hung up, she asked, "Are you here to see the room?"

"Yes, do you have time? I need to make some measurements."

"Oh, I can help you with that." She turned around, pulled out a file cabinet drawer, and took out a file. From it, she handed me a paper which had a room layout.

I looked the diagram over. "This certainly helps. But I need more detail than this."

"Okay, let me tell the resident associates I'm going back to our memory care ward. They're cleaning up the dining room area. It's on the way. Follow me."

I looked at the pictures on the wall as we walked behind her. Landscapes, interesting faces, and other art adorned the walls. While we were waiting outside the eating area, Dan Taylor appeared, walking down the hallway.

"Mrs. Freeman." He came forward and extended his hand. "And this must be Luke."

"Yes, it is. Luke Avery, this is Dan Taylor."

"I'm certainly glad to meet you. I met your wife on my flight down from Knoxville."

"Yes, I remember Joyce mentioning she met you."

Sherrie appeared from the dining room, explaining she was escorting us to Mom's new room to take measurements.

Dan promptly said, "Sherrie, I'll take them."

The three of us started down the hall toward what appeared to be a set of doors which we were going to pass through. A small alcove with a couch and potted plant, revealed a woman with a cell phone. She was having a loud and angry conversation with someone on the other end.

Dan noticed my interest. "Don't worry, Luke. She's not talking to anyone. The phone doesn't work. Her problem is imaginary."

"Why isn't she in the Alzheimer's ward?"

"Other than the phone problem, she causes no trouble. If she starts wandering into other people's apartments, causing a nuisance, we'll move her. She gets along well with our staff and complies with their instructions."

He stopped to punch a set of numbers into a box on the wall and pushed on a door leading out of the main building. "I'll give you the combination of the wing where your mother will be. There's a separate parking lot and entrance to it, so you don't have to come through the main one. Just remember the handicaps of the residents living here. Make sure no one goes out when you come in and the door is completely shut before you leave it."

Good advice, I thought, remembering my mother's recent escapades.

We were walking through a glassed-in breezeway, containing seating areas, green plants, and a bird-cage filled with colorful, Australian finches. "They lay eggs and hatch them," explained Dan, as we stopped to admire them. "Our AD residents come out here to look, and in this way enjoy the sunshine."

"Luke, Mom will love this area. Look at the outside bird feeders, and even dried ears of corn hanging from the Bradford pear trees."

"We have squirrels quite often." Dan continued to walk.

Turning left down another corridor, I smiled at an elderly woman carrying a doll, humming to it.

"They sometimes have disputes over their babies. Like the child in Solomon's court, we referee."

Dan stopped at a door and motioned us inside.

Mom's area was one large room. The layout of the room caused its shape to be a thick upside-down T— bathroom on the right—closet on the left, and short hallway between. If you walked from the hallway to the wall opposite, the large window was centered on the outside wall. It let in light and the outside world, which in her case was a forest of trees not too far from the building.

"Sometimes, we have deer walking around next to the trees. Do you need me to help with your measuring tape?" Dan asked.

"No, it's a thick one and easy to manage." While I maneuvered the tape around the room, picturing where different pieces of furniture could sit, he and Agnes continued to talk.

When I was finished, he took us to the staging area, dining room, and common TV room. As we walked into the common hall, Dan pointed out the men who were waiting to carpet Mom's room. "We'll paint tomorrow. You can move furniture after that."

"That's a day earlier than we thought," Agnes replied.

"Yes, everything fell into place. Do you have a preference on carpet color or paint?"

Agnes and I both laughed, "Blue, please."

"Blue it is."

"May we bring Mom over for meals, so she can get used to her new home-to-be?"

"Feel free to do so, Agnes. I'll set it up. We welcome family members at all meals except breakfast. There's always a rush to get everyone to the table in the morning. Let's go back to my office. There's a stack of paperwork to sign and a packet of dos and don'ts for our residents and visitors."

∽

Taking Mom to Nightingale Place on Sunday afternoon was hard on Agnes and I, but she didn't have a problem with it. She went over to her red recliner, sat down, picked up her crocheting, which we'd placed in a basket next to her chair, and started on her perpetual blue sweater for Pop.

Agnes and I looked at each other and shook our heads. "You never know how people will react to new surroundings," I observed.

My sister took me to the airport, so I could schedule my flight home. My ticket was open-ended, and this didn't take long. The first opening, unless I wanted to fly standby, was on Tuesday afternoon. I made the reservation.

On Monday, I went to Nightingale Place and stayed all day. Agnes came later in the afternoon.

"She seems perfectly happy," Agnes observed. The television was on to *The Andy Griffith Show* with Opie, Aunt Bee, and Andy's crazy deputy. Mom laughed when the audience laughed.

"Have you noticed she no longer asks where Pop is?"

Agnes nodded. "Wonder why?"

"I have no idea. It might be associated with new surroundings, different people, or a different routine."

Tuesday morning, I had to tell Mom goodbye. Finding the right words proved difficult. No matter what I said, she smiled at me. I tried to get through, but there was no change in her demeanor. I kissed her on the forehead and escorted her to lunch. She was eating when I left at noon.

My heart was heavy as I returned to pick up my bags at her former home. Former sounded final, as I knew it was. She would never return here again.

I walked to the living room, pulling my bags. Pop's chair was gone, and so was he.

Impressions in the carpet where furniture had been removed, her empty closet, and empty refrigerator only added to my sorrow. This was the house where I'd grown up. It didn't matter if some of those years were marred by my father's rigidness. It was familiar— loved.

I walked over to the couch in front of the picture window, remembering the scene I'd witnessed not so long ago between Duane and my father. It took Pop's passing to bring us back together as a family and clear up the mystery surrounding my father's early history.

I made sure the house was ready to be uninhabited. Agnes, Duane, Tony, and I'd discussed renting or selling it and the car. Renting was probably the best idea. The money would help with Mom's expenses at Nightingale Place. These charges would rise as her AD increased.

But first a power of attorney must be arranged through the court. I was okay with Agnes as my mother's POA.

My flight left in three hours, enough time for Agnes and I to eat lunch before takeoff.

I saw her car coming down the road in front of the house. Looking around one last time, I went outside to the porch.

"Brother are you ready to go home?"

"Yes," I replied. "Let's go eat."

Afterwards, at the airport, I hugged my sister goodbye.

"Remember, you're the matron-of-honor at my wedding." I called, as I headed through the door, preparing to enter the gate for my flight. I could see the plane on the tarmac.

"I'll be there," she called back and waved.

Was that a tissue in her hand?

CHAPTER THIRTY

Luke

At ten o'clock, my plane arrived at Knoxville's airport. I overruled a plan to meet me at McGhee Tyson, since the children needed to be in bed for school the following day. I grabbed a taxi home.

I wouldn't see Manda or the children until we met at her home for dinner. Spaghetti was on the menu. She and I had decided we'd keep to our earlier decision for James and Clint to live with me, and Marcus and Maryb would stay with her. They had been told of the plan, and this was the night of transition. I hated to break up the children. I knew this situation wasn't ideal, but I couldn't leave the full load of three children on Manda. She continued to work, while the children were in school. Today, Wednesday, was a week exactly since she'd arrived home.

I shook my head, thinking a lesser woman might have run the other way given the prospect of a husband and family in one day. Everyone in the two households was undergoing a major upheaval in their lives.

The summer behind me, I looked forward to the three quiet months before Manda and I were married —

plenty of time for the Averys to come together, get to know each other, and interact as a future family.

~

"Luke, welcome home." My pastor came out of his office, striding toward me, his hand outstretched. "I know you're glad to be back."

"You can't imagine how much. Seeing Hilly Church this morning as I drove around the corner made my heart sing. I'll be glad to get back in the swing of things."

"Is your mother contented with her new home?"

"Mom walked into her room, sat down, and started crocheting. My sister and I were amazed and grateful for her easy transition. She could have been the other way."

"And, how is your sister?"

"Although she wouldn't admit to it, I'm sure Agnes is relieved. Her life will go back to normal." I was quick to add, "This may take some adjustment on her part, too."

"My pastor nodded. It's good to have you back. You know where your office is located." He went back into his, and I continued down the hall toward mine, pausing only to check our board of sick and hospitalized members.

Seeing my desk in the middle of the room was wonderful. Two bookcases sat behind it, separated by an oil painting of horses grazing outside of Longview. I walked around the desk and sat down. My chair still fit me! Leaning forward, I placed the picture of Manda from Longview, which I'd brought, next to a picture of James, realizing soon there'd be others to join them.

Swiveling in my chair, I looked out the window. The Chilhowee Mountain Range, one of the first of the lines of shorter foothills of the Great Smokies, stared back at me. "It's good to be back, old friend." This transplanted Texan was home.

There was one or maybe two more stops I needed to make before visiting some of the sick on the board in the office hallway. I got up from my desk, walked out of the office suite, and headed down the main church hall toward the music room. On the way, I detoured to the auditorium. I felt the need to pray.

～

Maryb and James were the official door openers at Manda's home.

"Dad!" James flung himself into my open arms.

I lifted him up and hugged him tightly to my chest, kissing him on the cheek. "Are you happy I'm back? I missed you."

"Yes, I told Maryb we'd play games when you got here. She likes to play games."

I put James on the floor and picked up Maryb. She gave me a kiss on the cheek. "How do you like your new digs, Miss Maryb, quite contrary?" I inquired.

"I love my new home and Manda." She answered, wriggling to get down.

"Speaking of Manda, where is my future bride-to-be?" I directed my comment toward the only open door into the house.

"In the kitchen," the children chorused together, "making spaghetti."

"Yum, methinks me smells the delicious aroma of tomato sauce and baking bread. Methinks me arrived just in time."

James and Maryb laughed at my funny way of speaking.

My lightheartedness continued as I was hauled into the kitchen with a child on each arm. "Mom, look who we invited to dinner," said James.

"Milady," I said with a sweeping bow. "Do you need assistance in your endeavors? Your Knight, at your service."

We met each other halfway and embraced. The children giggled as I gave her a more-than-welcome-home kiss. For a few seconds, neither of us said anything, content to stand quietly holding the embrace.

"Are you okay, my darling?" I drew back and looked into her eyes, which were filled with tears. Taking a finger, I caught one before it spilled over and ran down her face.

"Much better, now, since you are here." Manda gave me another light kiss on the lips. "Oh, the sauce!" She ran to the glass topped stove eyes. "I just turned up the heat," she explained as she stirred the pot with a large-handled spoon.

"Here, I'll stir. You go ahead with the other preparations." I whispered as she passed me, "We'll talk later."

Ouch. She pinched me.

"Thanks. I need to finish setting the table. Maryb, where's Clint?"

"I'll go get him."

We heard Maryb's steps on the stairs as she went to call her brother. James went out the back door, where I saw Marcus with his Match Toys, playing on the deck.

Manda turned to me. "Clint's been helping me place the silverware and napkins with the plates," she explained, rattling the knives, forks, and spoons in their drawer.

"That's a coup," I responded, thinking this was a different young man from just days ago.

"He's been helpful since we arrived."

"So, Agnes was right. He's making nice with you."

"I don't know, and I don't find him obnoxious at all." She pulled the plates out of the cabinet. "Keep stirring. Don't let the sauce burn, and stir the noodles. Oh, keep check on the bread. Don't let it burn."

"Gee, do you think I can handle three things at a time?" I called after her, as she disappeared into the dining room.

～

"Dad, do you mind if I stay with Manda until the weekend?"

I was sitting in Manda's family room after opting out of playing games, reading the paper when I wasn't nodding. The emotional and physical exertion of moving my mom into her new home and the long flight home lingered throughout my first workday at church. Two plates of spaghetti weren't helping either.

I put the newspaper down in my lap. "What do you mean, stay here? Our house will be empty."

"Aw, Dad, you can make it without me. Maryb, Marcus, and I have some games planned for the rest of the week."

"What about school-work, instead of games."

Manda sat nearby, listening to our conversation. "School-work comes easily for the three. Let him stay. He and Maryb are helping each other with school lessons, and I'm sure he'll be ready to come on Saturday afternoon."

"Why the afternoon? He needs to put his clothes back in his room, and Clint needs to transfer all of his stuff."

"Did you look in James' room and in your backyard? James and I only moved enough for the weeks we thought he'd be here, and you'll find Clint's personal equipment and most of his clothes are already there." Manda continued, "James, are there plans to go to my father's on Saturday morning?"

"Yes. Maryb and I are going to Grandpa's to help dig potatoes. He said he could really use our help. He will loosen up the hills, and we will pick them up."

"Really. Are you going to be a farmer?" I asked my son.

"I might, if Grandpa teaches me all he knows."

"You can stay, son." The newspaper crackled as a delighted James jumped into my lap and gave me a hug. He ran from the room to tell Maryb and Marcus.

"I'm amazed at his interest in gardening," I told Manda. "He's never grown anything before in his life." I smoothed the paper and folded it up.

Manda came over and sat beside me. "There's a tight bond growing between him and my Dad, and now Maryb's getting involved. I think it's wonderful."

"Those two are becoming fast friends, aren't they?"

"Yes, an enthusiastic James leads, and Maryb follows."

"That's interesting since she's the oldest one in their group of two."

"So-o-o." Manda looked at me, wondering if I'd pick up her nuance.

"Okay, okay, I get it." I leaned over and kissed her. "You know what they say about older women."

"What's that?"

"They're better at everything."

"Really, Mr. Avery. What *specifically* interests you?" she asked in a low intimate voice.

"Hum-m, their ability to cook, take the children to school, clean house—ouch!" Manda had poked me in the ribs. I grabbed her and pulled her to me. She resisted, by squirming in my arms. "I also appreciate their ability to love deeply and show love." I whispered in her ear.

The struggling stopped. "It's about time," she said.

I leaned my head down and gave her a proper welcome. The one in the kitchen earlier had been more reserved because of our audience.

"Speaking of following, you'd better follow me to choir practice," I said looking at my watch as we both rose.

"I'll get ready. I can't wait to see how surprised everyone will be to see you back at work."

"Are the children going?"

"No, they'll be fine here with Clint."

The next weeks were busy ones for the Avery's and the soon-to-be Avery's. While Manda and I looked for a new residence, the children were adjusting to their new schools. Our schedule was so hectic, we often didn't see each other as a whole family, except on Sunday or late at night.

Our biggest concern was Clint, but he seemed to quickly adjust from Longview to Heritage High School. His baseball and basketball coaches were members at Church-on-the-Hill and Johnson's Chapel, respectively.

Both were glad to welcome a standout senior who was skilled at both games.

After a hit-and-miss last year, the high school started to win its basketball games.

To help Clint hone his skills, I bought one of those portable basketball goals and set it up on my concrete driveway. Several times, I went outside and shot hoops with him, but any attempt to coach him was rebuffed decisively. Soon, he was joined by three neighborhood boys. It didn't take me long to realize I was an old codger, and I wasn't welcome.

He and I placed his pitching cage in the backyard. The area was just wide enough for a good, hard cast.

Manda and I went to all his home basketball games. No matter our relationship, I loved watching him play. He was grace in motion: leaping, turning, and tossing the ball. Many times, when it came to sports, I thought he was every Avery rolled into one. He was good, very good, better than the rest of us at both games. I knew Robert would be very proud of him. I was proud of him.

His best friend at church and school, if you counted out Caitlyn Myers, turned out to be Chop MacGregor's son, Charlie. This didn't give me a warm, fuzzy feeling. But I overlooked my apprehension concerning their friendship, thinking Chop might be friendlier toward me.

The surprise relationship was Caitlyn. Seeing them together in a boy-meets-girl bond was startling. Obviously, they liked each other.

In September, the Hilly Church Hikers resumed their walks in the Smokies. Both Clint and Marcus joined the group. The first hikes were short ones of two or three miles. Soon, plans evolved to make an overnight stay at Gregorys Bald. Checking on reservations for the shelter, revealed the wooden structure was empty for the night in question. The members decided to go and sleep in the lean-to which could be securely closed to bear traffic.

Two weeks before the Friday night stay over, Clint informed us he'd found needed hiking equipment at a local secondhand store. "Charlie and I drove over to Second Treasures-on-Hand, where one of the other hikers bought his gear." He continued with a note of exasperation in his voice. "He told us we'd find backpacks, sleeping bags, and other camping supplies in stock. We can't wait any longer to buy what I need." His open hand made a short jab in the air to punctuate his remarks.

Manda and I looked at each other.

We stood in the kitchen, cleaning up the pots and pans after dinner. She and I had discussed Clint's need for overnight equipment, and we had a plan.

"Clint, let's go out to the garage." She put down her drying towel and walked down the short hall to the door. "There's something out here you need."

I stayed in the kitchen. From there, I heard the conversation coming through the open door. I knew it was open, because Clint almost never closed one.

This was a source of constant irritation to me. We'd had several discussions about "cooling the world." Often, he came home from school, carrying his book bag, athletic equipment, and the banana Monkey Mush he'd picked up at Weigel's on the corner, where he got off the bus. I'm sure his intentions were good, but he never returned to shut the door. He would kick at it coming through. The door swung into the frame and didn't close, leaving a crack.

"I'm sorry, I should have given you this several days ago," I heard Manda say.

Silence reigned, except for the rustling and scraping of boxes and bags coming from the garage. "Here, help me." I heard Manda say.

I finished wiping the sink with the dish towel, walked over, and turned off the hall light. In the darkness, I watched the interaction of the two outside.

The garage light revealed Clint climbing a two-step ladder and lifting a plastic wrapped bundle from a high wooden shelf. The parcel had been there a long time, because a layer of dust was visible on its top side. He placed it on a work-bench in front of Manda's car and waited for her instructions.

"Go ahead, open it."

Clint unloosed the heavy twine, which held the mouth of the sack closed and peeled the plastic away from the contents inside.

"This was my husband's." Manda said as the large backpack appeared. "Todd used all of this when we went hiking, and he carried it on the Appalachian Trail. Everything you need is inside. Some of the things may look used, but they're still serviceable, and they have history."

Just for a second, I saw a window into Clint's soul as his crusty, not-often-readable face softened and hidden feelings surfaced. At this moment, I knew he was reachable, but what would it take to get behind the barrier he'd built to his heart.

The curtain dropped just as quickly, but his voice betrayed him. "Thank you," he said huskily, ashamed of his turncoat emotions, as he looked at his new equipment. He reached out and pulled an emergency whistle and flashlight from an elastic net pocket, turning then over to examine them.

"You're welcome. I think Todd would love for you to have his gear."

"What's this?" Clint said, checking out a roughly made pouch, hanging from the bottom of the knapsack. It was about the size of his sleeping bag which was secured to the top of the pack. He loosened the draw-string atop the mystery bag and pulled the cover down far enough to reveal a piece of strange-looking, open cell material. "It sorta looks like polyfoam, but it's a lot rougher—the holes are bigger."

"That's called reticulated foam. It's used in outdoor furniture and goes under your bedroll, keeping it off the ground. I don't know if it works or not. We never got to use it."

"Where'd he buy it?" the old, deadpan Clint had returned.

"Todd knew a lot of people. One was a plant manager at a local business. They built upholstery for local boat companies. You know, lots of boats are manufactured around here."

I watched Clint nod.

Manda continued, "From what I understood, reticulated foam keeps regular foam from soaking up water or lets the water run out of waterlogged cushions—something like that. Seems the application proved too expensive, and it was discontinued. Todd's friend had samples left, so he suggested we try it camping."

"Why didn't you get to use it."

"Todd passed away," was Manda's simple answer.

"Oh."

"Would you get the other bag down? It's mine. I want Marcus to have it."

"Aw, Inkspot will never make it hiking."

That was another thing I intended to have a conversation with Clint about—his derogatory names for his siblings.

Manda defended Marcus. "You don't know that. He should be given a chance to try."

"If he doesn't, would you let Caitlyn have it?"

"We'll see."

I slipped back into the family room, sat down, and picked up the paper. James, Clint, and I would be heading home soon.

❧ CHAPTER THIRTY-ONE ❧

Luke

Two weeks after I returned home, Manda and I were ready to solve one problem. After checking out houses, she for three weeks, me for two, I'd settled on one. I hoped she'd settled on it too.

The house was built on a short prominence overlooking Walland Gap. Going to the Great Smoky Mountains National Park from Maryville, a visitor always went through this cut to Townsend, our gateway to the busy Cades Cove area, and the Sugarlands Visitor Center in the most visited park in the United States.

From the back porch, an almost unobstructed view of Chilhowee Mountain stretched north toward Sevierville and south toward the Little Tennessee River and the Alcoa Dams built along the stream. Straight ahead, flowing through the Gap was Little River, which ended at Fort Loudoun Lake, bordering Knoxville.

I knew this area was a plus for Manda, whose love of those hallowed Chilhowee hills bordered on covetousness, since her family of Tiptons had owned and lived on many of them. I had to admit they'd wheedled their way into my heart.

A blacktopped right-of-way led off the main highway to the secluded eight acres and residence. The property lay in a ragged triangle. The narrowest point, approximately fifty-feet wide, touched the road leading to the acreage.

Lush landscaping surrounded the home on every side but the back, giving the immediate area a garden effect. Behind the main residence, a patch of woods separated the front property from the sloping pastureland and small creek to the rear. The shallow creek split the last six acres from the main section. A bridge with iron girders and concrete abutments, large enough for a tractor or small truck to cross, allowed safe passage for accessing the back property. It was perfect, I thought.

I broached the subject to Manda on Wednesday after choir practice.

"What about the house we looked at off the Walland Highway? Do you think it might work for our future family?"

We'd taken the four children over to the Puckett's for the evening. I hadn't realized how valuable grandparents were before, and China Cuisine was supplying our menu for tonight.

"I do like it. The kitchen is spacious, and that's important to me. I love the two-layered deck and landscaping in the front. The fountain and water garden are a nice touch."

"Yes, I agree. Each child would have a large bedroom and the master is a dream with its trey ceilings and huge bathroom not to mention his and hers walk-in closets the size of my present study. I think we could have horses, and James and Grandpa might make a small garden next to the creek. Maybe we'll all take a turn at planting and hoeing."

"Sounds like you're already living there, Mr. Avery."

"I've been thinking about it a lot lately, considering your contract to move out of the house will expire soon, and nothing else we've seen compares to this property."

"I like it because the children won't have to change schools. Clint could probably walk to Heritage, or you could drop him off on the way to church. I was hoping we'd find something out on this end of town. I'd have a longer drive to Suds and Styles."

"Yes, that's the only drawback. So, what's your final thought? Should we make an offer? I've done some preliminary figuring, and we can swing it easily and reduce our house payments significantly, when my house sells."

"There might be room for a baseball diamond for Clint," Manda mused.

I wasn't expecting Manda to suggest a baseball diamond, but she was right. We'd have plenty of room.

She reached over the table and placed her hand on mine, reminding me of another time, a few short months ago, when I'd done the same thing. It wasn't easy, but I pulled her hand to my lips and kissed it.

She knew my relationship with Clint hadn't improved. We were at an impasse; reserved and polite to each other. "I don't have a problem with a baseball diamond. In fact, his birthday is in late October. If we hurry, we could buy the house and construct the field for his present."

"Let's go out and look at it again. Really give every room a good going over."

"And take the children this time. We need their input also. How about tomorrow, after school. We'll have until dark."

"Tomorrow it is," she agreed.

I looked at her. She was beautiful in a coral-colored outfit. "Is that my favorite outfit?"

She grinned. "One of them."

"Do you remember the last time we were here, Sweetheart?"

"How can I forget? I still say if it hadn't been for our pastor, my answer might have been much different."

"Do you have any regrets?"

"No, I trust you fully, and that's more important to me than anything else. I repeat, being trustworthy is so vital to me."

I gave a chuckle, "I remember going to the men's room and praying for strength to tell you how I felt. Those feelings have grown deeper since then. You're the perfect helpmate for me."

"I'm glad you think so, or we might have our first argument at this moment"

The waitress brought our plates of food, and we stopped talking until she left.

"Do you love me, Manda?" I smiled as I looked at her.

"With all my heart, my darling."

"Then why don't you ask the blessing?"

"What!?" Manda looked startled.

"We don't want the food to get cold again."

She burst out laughing and then prayed.

~

The next afternoon, we loaded up three kids for the ride to their prospective home. Clint begged off. He wanted to ride over to Charlie Mac's to help him pack for their overnight hike tomorrow afternoon. We dropped him off with the promise that Charlie would drive him home.

Ten minutes later we arrived at the driveway entrance of our dream home. I drove slowly up the concrete and got out. Our realtor had shown the house after lunch and left the key in a potted plant off the front porch. After locating it, I opened the front door.

The crowd trouped inside.

We walked around the kitchen and family room.

"Maryb, what do you think of this place? Do you think you could live here?" I stood in the formal living room, watching her dance through the vacant area. Marcus and James were already upstairs, probably picking out their rooms.

Manda came from the kitchen. "Let's go upstairs and see what the others are doing," she suggested.

The three of us went up the carpeted circular stairs to a landing at the top. The arrangement in a backwards L, which overhung part of the kitchen—hardwood-floored, upstairs den to the right and doors down a banister-framed hallway to the left. These open to the living room below with the master bedroom underneath. Looking off the balcony, and opposite the kitchen, was the main den or family room with a small bedroom leading from the dining room. A large kitchen bar was attached to the center counter where the glassed stove top rested.

Then we started dreaming. "Manda, one set of our den furniture could come up here for the children to use."

"Yes, bookcases over here. TV here and game table against the wall."

"My area rug would fit nicely here."

We walked around the room, designating the places for each item.

Marcus and James appeared from two open doors off the banistered hallway. "We've picked our rooms. We left the biggest one on the end for Clint," James told us.

"Then this must be my room," said Maryb, opening a door and walking straight into the bathroom. "Oh."

"Are you going to sleep in the tub, B," asked Marcus, laughing.

"Don't be silly," she exclaimed with a downcast face.

"Where is Maryb going to sleep?" asked James, his voice showing some concern.

"Come downstairs, and we will show you." Manda's voice was mysterious as she led the way to a previously unseen door, leading off the dining room, which was next to my future study and her library.

"Here." Manda flung the door open. "I believe the last occupant must have been a girl—a very loved girl."

The room had ruffled curtains with white castles, pink shells, and brown teddy bears on them, and the carpet was a muted pink.

"Oh, oh, oh," exclaimed Maryb, walking across the plush carpet and touching a teddy bear on the curtains.

"Aw, it's a girl's room for sure. Pink is a girl's color."

"Not always, Marcus. Luke has been known to wear a pink shirt with his suit on Sunday. He looks pretty spiffy."

"What's spiffy," inquired Maryb.

"It's the same as awesome, isn't it, Mom?" James answered the question.

"It sure is, and we're a pretty awesome family," Manda responded.

I stood beaming at them. Throwing my hands wide to encompass the house, I asked, "So, is it a go, awesome family?"

"Yes," everyone answered.

"Okay, let's go home so Marcus can pack for his overnight trip tomorrow."

~

On Saturday, it was dark outside when the church van pulled away from my home. Marcus burst through the door after the overnight hike. "Clint saved my life," he exclaimed in excitement, dropping his pack to the floor in the den with a thud.

Manda and I jumped up, imaging all sorts of wild things happening. "What do you mean, saved your life?"

"It was a bear. I was in my sleeping bag. It tried to eat me!"

"Where are you hurt?" asked Manda rushing to him and turning him around to expose his back side.

Hearing the excited voices, Maryb and James appeared from the direction of the living room, where they were playing Chinese checkers.

Marcus repeated his claim, and everyone started asking questions at once. Clint walked into the room, carrying his backpack, and shook his head at the hubbub Marcus' statement had made.

"Quiet, everyone! Quiet." I shouted above the din. Everyone turned to look at me. "Let Clint explain what happened."

Every eye turned to Clint. "Aw, it wasn't much. I need a shower." He turned to leave the room. Like a trained athlete, the game was over. A shower was the next activity on the schedule.

Maryb tugged at his arm, preventing him from leaving the room. "No, we want to hear about the bear, Clint."

Here's your chance to be the alpha male, I thought and decided to encourage him. "Clint, there must be a story behind his statement." I indicated Marcus. "Sit down and tell us what happened." I waved my hand at a chair close to the fireplace.

There was a rush to find seats in the room. Not often did you hear a bear tale in the year 2007. Marcus ended up sitting on the floor beside his hiking equipment.

Deciding against the chair, Clint walked three steps into the room and positioned himself next to the cabinet, holding the flat-screen television. As the center of attention, he looked at each one in his audience, carefully avoiding my location.

"We stopped at the lean-to, just before the gated entrance into Cades Cove." He looked at Manda. "You know where that is Manda. The large map and other info are there."

She nodded, and he continued.

"When the volunteer found out we were hiking to Gregory Bald, he gave Mr. Myers a yellow paper. It cautioned us about the presence of a possible hostile bear in the area."

Mr. Myers was Bess' husband and one of the chaperones along with his wife on the youth's mission trip out west. Like Manda, the couple was deeply involved in the young people's ministry at church. Two of their children were on the hike, Caitlyn and Benson. In all, ten people headed up the mountain. Normally, the group was larger, but our college students were at school, reducing the number which usually participated by eight.

"When we got to the bald, it was almost dark. We noticed five of the eight sleeping spots inside the shelter had supplies atop, so we cooked our food and ate our dinner. I helped haul water from the nearby spring, heated it in a kettle over the campfire, and we washed our metal dishes and our hands. Taking a longer route to the spring, I saw a bear trap in the thick laurel bushes."

"Bear trap?" exclaimed Maryb. "What does a bear trap look like?"

Clint stopped and looked at her. "Well, it's a large round barrel with a pull-up gate at the front."

Maryb asked another question. "How does it trap a bear?"

"The gate goes *bang* when it's tripped and closes." Clint emphasized the noise by clapping his hands.

Maryb drew back at the handclap and opened her mouth to ask another question.

Everyone groaned. When Maryb started asking questions, they could go on forever. I interjected, "Maryb, let Clint tell the story. You can find out about the trap later. We'll look it up on the Internet."

By this time Clint was enjoying his audience and being the center of attention. He continued. "After dinner, we stood outside the lean-to. We had reserved the shelter. But with the articles inside, we couldn't haul ours in. Someone suggested clearing it, but we were overruled by Mr. Myers. We waited for the owners to show up. Maybe some catastrophe had befallen them. Someone suggested the bear had gotten them or the group had run off."

"We all laughed," Marcus remembered.

"Yes, we did, but we were a little tense because of the bear trap and instructions we'd received earlier. Caitlyn's delicate ears were the first to hear noises, coming from the trail, leading up the ridge to the bald. We all jumped up."

Clint paused in his narrative to check out his audience, then continued, "Next we saw flashlights. Five large men appeared out of the semidarkness and grunted a greeting. After acknowledging their presence, Mr. Myers explained our reservation, but the rouge hikers insisted on keeping their places. If they were crass enough to take our places, we decided they were determined enough to defend themselves.

"Mr. Myers wasn't interested in a fight, so we spread our sleeping bags on the ground in a semicircle around the campfire, some, ending up in a double row. What else could we do? We couldn't hike off the mountain at night."

Marcus interrupted his brother. "Clint and Mr. Myers kept the fire going with a stack of wood left by other day hikers to the area. I was on the outside of the second row from the fire. Clint wasn't too far away from me on the other end of my row."

"That's right, and Mr. Myers and I did keep the fire going until almost sunrise. At that point, we fell asleep. Just before the sun rose above the hill behind the lean-to, Marcus woke everyone up, screaming, 'There's a bear here!' I jumped up, started yelling, and leaped toward him as a black flash flew by me. 'Bear! Bear!' I yelled even louder than Marcus. I guess that's where he gets the idea, I saved his life. The bear almost ran over me. I did see the bear stumble over a log we'd been sitting on earlier, and it vanished into the woods, running for its life."

Marcus was laughing. "Everybody went crazy."

"Those around the campfire jumped up, and the men in the shelter bailed out. After everyone settled down, we heard the bear crashing around and growling angrily near the spring. Mr. Myers threw more wood on the fire, illuminating the immediate area around the camp. Several of us looked for rocks. Throwing them was one option should the not-so-bright animal return to our camp."

"I sat back down, but I didn't go back to sleep." Marcus was grinning.

"No one went back to sleep. The sun rose and the sounds in the forest behind the spring quieted down. The men in the lean-to left without saying goodbye. All the rogues, campers and bear alike, were gone. 'Let's cook breakfast,' suggested Mr. Myers. 'Yep,' said my little brother here, 'I'm hungry as a…' You can supply the word."

"Bear," everyone said and burst out laughing to Marcus' embarrassment.

"Did you go to the Bald?" asked Manda.

"Yes," Marcus responded.

Clint picked up his pack. "We walked to the top." He threw over his shoulder as he headed for his room. "And Manda, the reticulated foam worked really good."

"Marcus, I suppose you're ready to go hiking again, *really* soon," said James, giving his cousin a friendly pat on the shoulder, as he passed him on the way out the door. He motioned to Maryb. He was ready to return to their in-progress checker game. They left the room, trying to decide whose turn it was to play.

"No, I don't think so. I think I'll stick to hoeing in my garden."

More laughter, this time from the adults.

"Did you report the hikers who hogged your spot in the shelter?"

"Yes, as soon as we got back to Cades Cove. Mr. Myers and Clint went to the Ranger Station at the picnic area and reported them. The ranger was walking outside the information booth. He stopped to talk to them."

"There's not much the rangers can do to eliminate ill-mannered people from being ill-mannered. Reservations do prevent most problems, like the one your group experienced, from happening."

"That's exactly what the ranger told Mr. Myers. He said we were the only registered overnight hikers in the area. We gave him a description of the men and a couple of names we'd overheard."

"Was he happy with your description?"

"Maybe. He told Mr. Myers they might have been a group of poachers the park service has been chasing.

He said we were correct not to confront them. They probably had guns stashed in the woods nearby."

I hastened to tell Marcus, "It's very unusual to see corrupt men on the trails in the Smokies. Most hikers are helpful, courteous, and mindful of other people's rights and territory. Don't let this one experience color your impression of the mountains."

Manda was nodding a yes.

"Even so, I can't imagine a tomato running over me at a campfire. I think I'll stick with gardening with Grandpa."

"I'm glad you're home safely," Manda said. "Is that my cell ringing?" She went to the kitchen to answer it.

"Was it important?" I asked when she returned.

"Yes, wonderful news. We've been given a reprieve from moving. We can stay another whole month."

CHAPTER THIRTY-TWO

Luke

In September, Tennessean's blood turns orange as football season at the University of Tennessee gets underway. The Avery and Puckett families were no different.

One week, after Clint and Marcus's hike to Gregory Bald, we sat watching Tennessee play Florida, while munching large bowls of popcorn. Our team, under the coaching of Phillip Fulmer, had won the national championship, beating Florida State's powerhouse team several years earlier. Florida State was Florida's instate rival. Their games were as hard fought and important as ours against Florida.

Because of a series of coaching staff changes, including our longtime head coach, we became the underdogs. A miracle, we needed to win this game.

At the least, we were mediocre, so I was surprised when Tennessee showed up to take part in the game.

Our family gathered around my big screen TV, watching the play-by-play action. Both teams fought hard, but the defense on both sides was weak. This caused the score to mount along with the tension in my den.

"Did you see that stupid play?" shouted Clint, who seemed to be on a roll today. His obnoxiousness was apparent from when he got out of bed this morning. "Why'd they call a pass? They shoulda run up the middle. They only needed a yard. I woulda called a quarterback sneak." He leaned forward, almost leaping from his seat on the couch.

My first instinct was to reprimand him, but I managed to keep quiet. Instead, I said, "Hey, they know Florida better than we do. I'm sure they watched a lot of film last week."

"That doesn't mean they're calling the plays correctly," he retorted, glaring at me from across the room, where he sat with Maryb on the small couch.

Maryb moved to Manda's side, and Manda lightly touched my arm. I bit my tongue and waited.

In the fourth quarter, Florida went ahead by a field goal. We needed a touchdown to win or a field goal to tie the game and go into overtime. The clock showed twenty seconds in the ball game. Tennessee had one time-out and four new downs—plenty enough time and downs to win the game.

Tennessee stood on their forty-yard line. We had to pass the football, and, we had to run out of bounds to stop the clock on each play. Florida knew this. Our only hope was to either get another set of downs or a touchdown pass.

Instead of passing, they ran the football up the middle of the field, hoping to catch Florida off guard, gain yardage, and receive a new set of downs. The opposing team stopped them two yards shy of a first down. Tennessee used their last time out, but not before ten valuable seconds came off the clock. Ten seconds to go and one down gone.

I didn't agree with the call but said nothing. It could have worked. Clint sat in glowering silence.

Now, Tennessee had no option but to pass. The first toss toward the sidelines sailed too long and above the head of the intended receiver. The incomplete pass stopped the clock with seven seconds left. With a break, Tennessee might have two more plays before the game was over.

Seven seconds and counting, I thought. The quarterback squatted in the huddle. The players broke the huddle and lined up to play—another passing situation. The front line held and the quarterback maintained his footing, dancing in the pocket. In the infield, one of the pass receivers came open. The ball flew sixty yards through the air.

"It's a hail maker," shouted Maryb, sliding off the couch into the floor as the ball soared downfield, holding on to her half-empty bowl of popcorn. She startled all of us with her unexpected comment.

I saw the Tennessee player leap into the air. Just as the ball arrived, there was a flash of orange and blue as a Florida player batted the ball down. A groan went up around our room, and on the TV, everyone grew quiet in the stadium.

"What did you call the play?" I asked Maryb.

"I said it's a hail maker." Everyone laughed except Clint.

Maryb looked sheepish and then indignant. "Well, what's wrong with that? You all say it all the time." She moved back near Manda, looking at all of us. She'd forgotten her popcorn, leaving it sitting on the floor.

"Igmo," said Clint, not missing the chance to deride his younger sister. "It's not called a hail maker."

"Clint, you don't need to call your sister names." I chided him, turning to Maryb, I explained, "It's called a Hail Mary. Do you know why?"

"No."

"Because it's an impossible pitch and it takes a miracle to catch it. Is that a good explanation of the situation, Clint?" I looked back at him, but his mouth was clamped in a thin line. He refused to respond to my question.

A load roar came from the television. Tennessee was back on the field.

"Maryb, this will be another Hail Mary," I told her quietly.

Tennessee and Florida fans were standing in the stadium. The team came out of the huddle, lined up, and the ball snapped to the quarterback. On the clock, time was up, but the ball was sailing through the air. In the end zone, several players went for the ball. The scramble left a heap of players on the ground. In the end a Florida player held it up. The game was over, and Tennessee had lost.

"Stupid play calling!" exclaimed Clint, jumping up from his seat and scattering Maryb's bowl of popcorn across the floor.

"Igmo, can't you hold onto a bowl of popcorn?" he admonished her.

She began to cry at the roughness of his manner, slid off the couch, and started picking up the scattered kernels.

He left the room. I got up to follow him.

"Luke," was all Manda said. She motioned for Maryb to come to her.

"Young man, I need to talk to you." I called after Clint.

He didn't stop, but went into his bedroom. He tried to close the door. I put my foot in it. He walked into the room, sat down on his bed, with a defiant look on his face.

I took a huge amount of air into my lungs and held it, letting it out slowly while collecting my thoughts. I stood towering over him. I wanted to shake the living daylights out of him. Instead, I pulled up his desk chair and sat down opposite him. All the time I was thinking, I will not be Pop, and this is where I start.

"He's got some of the same stubbornness like the rest of the Avery family," observed Manda. "And, you're all competitive when it comes to sports."

"And always right, when it comes to second-guessing plays?" I smiled at her. She hadn't known the rest of the Averys long, but she'd already figured us out.

"What happened in there? It got quiet really fast."

We were walking up the road in my subdivision, something we often did at night when we had family time at my house. The warm darkness closed in around us. The yellow harvest moon floated overhead. We held hands, swinging them as we walked. The night was perfect for romance, if we'd been in a romantic mood. We weren't.

"Clint and I had a long talk."

"Yes?"

"I was gentle but firm. No more name calling. No more belligerent attitude."

"How long do you think that'll last?"

"Probably not very long. I still wish I knew what eats him. I hinted, but he refused to address his problem."

"What did he say?"

"Nothing. He gave me one of those are-ya-kidding-who-do-ya-think-ya-are stares."

We walked for a few minutes in silence. "You know, Sweetheart, except for him, we have a great connection within our family. I'm at my wit's end. I don't know where to turn."

"That's not true. We both know where to go, and we'll keep praying for God's answer to this problem."

I shook my head in the darkness. Manda was right. I couldn't fix this situation. Only God could. I would shepherd until the problem resolved.

"Luke, one of these days, Clint will learn to trust you as I have. I think trust is the basis of all true friendships and love toward others. When Todd died it hurt. I never thought I'd love again. In fact, had decided not to love again. But you sneaked up on me, or God had other plans. I love you, Luke Avery. Don't you forget it and always be trustworthy."

What could I say back to that? I stopped walking and, in the darkness of the night gave her a long kiss. "I'll be glad when I can call you Mrs."

∼

By the last week of September, Manda and the children were in their new home. We used the formal living room of the new house as a staging area, pushing the furniture back against the wall, until we had finished all the bedrooms. What wasn't stacked in this room remained in the garage until needed.

Packing and unpacking all the boxes and bags proved to be a challenge, but we decided those would be done each weekend. Our plan was to spend half of each weekend day installing furniture, beds, and hanging pictures. As bedroom furniture moved from two houses to the other, sleeping bags became beds on the living room floor in mine and Manda's old house until the final moving day, when clothes would be hung in the new closets.

The move was not easy, especially with both of us working and the children in school. June and Manda's mom and dad came to help, along with several men in my church.

Laughing and joking, the men helped me tackle the big stuff. They set up bed frames, dollied furniture into bedrooms, installed drawers back into chests, and ate lots of KFC and pizza from our local convenience store.

Manda directed traffic, and we obediently followed.

When all the furniture rested in their new locations, hanging pictures, placing favorite articles, and personal items in each room was next. The women made the beds and added the bathroom accessories. The kitchen dishes, silverware, pots, and pans were placed in cabinets and shelves. The pantry stocked with canned and boxed goods and spices. The ice maker in the refrigerator rattled when ice dropped into the empty container or a cup.

At this point, in a moment of oneness, Manda and I moved from bedroom to bedroom, praying for each occupant — for their lives and future.

I wasn't shocked when she pushed for Clint to move into his new room. She knew the absence of his presence in my house would be a relief to me. "Are you sure about that?"

"Very sure," she responded, hugging me and giving me a kiss on the cheek."

I relented, although I had misgivings.

Clint moved with the others. He continued to pander to Manda, often suggesting ways he could help her, something he never did at my home, where he went into his bedroom and closed the door.

I wondered if he realized he was pitting me against Manda. What did he think he'd accomplish by his hostile actions? I didn't point this out to my sweet lady, only to say she had a rapport with him that I didn't have.

Since the camping trip, and my subsequent talk after the UT game, he avoided me. On occasion, I caught him looking at me with a furtive look. He'd turn away when I caught his eye. When this happened, I had an uneasy feeling. What was the problem? I couldn't put my finger on it.

With the move accomplished, Manda and I often slipped out the back door of our soon-to-be new home together, to check on the progress of Clint's birthday gift. His baseball diamond was nearing completion. The workers came each day when school was in session. The field would be ready by birthday time.

The real shocker to me was when James asked to join his cousins at Manda's. "But, Dad, I need to help Mom and Maryb," he explained. "They depend on me."

I looked at my almost ten-year-old son. Of course, he was staying out there most of the time already, we both were. At first, I was adamant. "James, don't ask me again." But I never said, "That's final."

There was a conspiracy afoot. James quit approaching me on the subject of moving, but Manda, Maryb, and Marcus plotted to gain my approval on the move.

"Okay, okay," I threw up my hands in surrender. "He moves," was all I said.

Maryb jumped up and squealed. She gave me a hug and ran to tell James.

Later, I walked through my empty house, wondering if I had a communicable disease. How many times had I wished for a quiet TV and space to think? Now I had it, and I didn't want it. My home was silent and lonely without my son. I wished someone *out there* wanted me to move. Of course, they did. I was just having a pity party.

Later, after having my devotions and prayer, I lay there thinking. What continued to amaze me was Manda's love of motherhood and her instincts for the children's needs. For someone who didn't have children of her own, she embraced our four with a bewildering compassion and deep love I guess I hadn't really expected. And, the children loved her back.

The question—what had I expected? Wasn't her interaction with the children in our ministry at church a prerequisite to the decision I'd made to confront her with my love? Exactly. I decided this when I realized my family would increase by three. I couldn't have approached another woman of my acquaintance with the same proposal.

Ah, the proposal. It seemed light years away since we'd stood on Clingmans Dome and declared our future as man and wife. I was more than ready to say the words, "I do." That made me wonder, what plans Manda had made for our wedding? Tomorrow I would ask her.

Clint's birthday was anticlimactic, considering all the activities in our lives. But it was obvious he loved his baseball diamond, especially when several of his baseball buddies showed up to eat his cake on the back porch and play ball. I'd made plans with Charlie Mac to bring friends from school.

Backslapping and cajoling each other, they ran down to see the new playing area. After cleaning the kitchen, Manda and I joined the others at the two-tiered spectator stand. The Averys yelled and stomped their feet, cheering the players on.

CHAPTER THIRTY-THREE

Manda

 W hy was I blessed with such happiness? My cup was full and running over. Like King David, I wanted to dance and sing before the Lord. This thought ran through my mind many times as I finished Mrs. Whithall's hair on Thursday afternoon. This second week of November, I'd adjusted all my appointments, and she'd agreed to move hers up earlier in the day.

From now on, I'd leave work in time to arrive home before the children came from school. Luke or I drove them to school in the morning, because the road to school was busy with cars. But our house was close enough for them to walk home in the afternoon, and I wanted to be home when they came through the door.

"Why am I blessed with such happiness?" I asked Mrs. Whithall.

"Amanda, I can't contemplate anyone who deserves contentment more than you do, my dear," she said in her correct societal manner—one I suspected which came from ancestors going back as far as the Mayflower.

June was close enough to hear. "Hey girl, she's right about that. You deserve it, kiddo." Good old June, totally down to earth.

Should I bask in the glow of their biased comments?

Except for Clint, our family days together were a daze of happiness. And Clint was helpful to me, not showing the animosity he projected on Luke. In fact, he seemed to go out of his way to be of assistance. When I told Agnes, during one of our numerous phone calls, she couldn't explain his actions. "Be glad life's going smoothly. I'm praying for you."

"Agnes, Luke's agreed to let Clint take beginning driving lessons at school. Most of his friends drive and have cars. I don't know about the car. Someone's got an old jalopy at church. We've discussed buying it for his first car. No decision has been made. I'm sure it'll be nice to have another person who can go to the store or take the car to get gas."

"He always wanted to get his license here. Pop wouldn't let him even touch the car after …Well, he just wouldn't. I bet he's excited."

"How's Mom Avery doing?"

Agnes gushed as she spoke about her Mom. "She's settled into her room without complaint. Manda, you should see the old blue sweater she's been crocheting for Pop. It reaches down to the floor with no signs of getting shorter. The boys tease her by attempting to take it from her. She turns her eyes on us and gives us a stare full of daggers. Then we all laugh, and she smiles back. She really seems happy at Nightingale Place."

After I'd hung up the phone, I realized we'd become a family in every way, except for marriage. Marriage—I was ready for that, too. A month to go and the plans were made—nothing extraordinary—no frills, no fuss. Just a slow walk down the aisle to the man of my dreams. Like the Bible said, a helpmeet—a Christ-follower and trustworthy in every way. My floor-length, ivory-lace dress hung, waiting in my closet at home.

June brought me back to the present.

"Earth to Manda," exclaimed June, laughing. "How are you going to get through the next few weeks? You're already in a daze."

"I know, but I'm so amazed every time I think about Luke, the children, and the pending marriage. Last year at this time, I was a carefree happy widow with plans made for a single life—no worries, no cares. Now, look at me. What a difference several months make." I paused and then continued, "Did I tell you the ladies are hosting the reception at church?"

"Only a thousand times," said June. "And we're going to be there with bells on, aren't we Mrs. Whithall?" June came over and patted the elderly lady on the arm.

"I'm sure the reception will be lovely." She nodded in response.

"Where will the children stay while you're on your honeymoon?"

"My parents will keep them. They bought old army cots from the surplus store in Knoxville, and the children will take their sleeping bags over. I'm sure the place will be a madhouse, and my parents will be exhausted when we return."

"Have you definitely decided on where to go?"

"Yes, we've decided to go to Gatlinburg for four days. Luke wanted to go to Texas and stay at a lodge near Weatherford, but both our schedules are demanding and with Christmas being near, going far away and staying longer isn't practical. At least, the Christmas Special at church will be over. I'm looking forward to relaxing, although I don't know if you can call Gatlinburg, for a honeymoon in the holidays, relaxing."

"I think the wedding, reception, and honeymoon will be glorious," said June, waving her hand, the one with the comb, in the air. "I only wish it was me. I'd quit working so hard and retire—let some man keep me up."

"You're always going to retire, June. You never do."

Before I drove home, I went to Food Plus and bought rib steaks for dinner. Knowing this was one of Luke's favorite entrées, and I felt like fixing his special meal tonight.

The children would be content with grilled hamburger meat, eaten like steak, but with catsup slathered over it. Instead of baked potatoes, which Marcus and Maryb didn't like, I'd serve garlic mashed ones and a tossed salad. Amazingly, all the children loved the "'rabbit food'" as they gleefully called it.

The store had carrot cake on special. I bought one for dessert.

Since I'd stopped for food, they'd beaten me home.

"Hey, Mom," said Maryb, coming into the kitchen. She'd started calling me this because her best bud, James, did. "Can you help with my lessons?"

"Yes, give me thirty minutes to put up groceries and start preparations for dinner. I'll call you when I'm ready."

Maryb hurried to her bedroom, and then she rushed upstairs to the communal TV room or C-TVR, as the kids called it. A sign at the top of the stairs with these initials and the admonition, "'Be Nice'" written in bold letters hung from the ceiling. We'd named the room this to differentiate from the others in the house, holding a TV. I heard the television come on and the Cartoon Network was soon playing a bit too loud.

I walked to the hall and called up the stairs, "Hey, are you hard of hearing up there. Turn the TV down a notch or two. I can't hear myself think." I heard a muted giggle, and the sound became much lower. She and I played this game each day, unless the boys got to the control first. It was our way of saying, "I'm home. I love you, and I'm glad to see you."

Maryb's homework turned out to be simple, and we were finishing up when I heard the garage door rise. Luke was home early.

"Hi, Sweethearts," he said, as he came into the kitchen. "What are we having for dinner — potato soup?" He sniffed the air. Coming over, he kissed me while raising the lid of the pot where I was boiling the potatoes, and sticking his nose in the steam coming off them. He licked his lips. "Yum, you taste good."

"I was testing the cream cheese frosting on the carrot cake. I pointed in its direction."

"It's definitely going to be good." He smacked his lips, making Maryb giggle.

"We're also having grilled rib steaks and hamburgers along with mashed potatoes and salad."

"What's the special occasion?" Luke walked around the kitchen island to the low bar where Maryb sat. He leaned over, gave her a kiss on the cheek, and looked at her homework.

"You're special. I felt like having your favorite meal tonight. That is if you'll grill the meat?"

"I will, I will. Let me wash up." He disappeared down the hall.

Maryb took her books to her bedroom. She reappeared and went back upstairs to the C-TVR, where I heard the television going. I heard voices and, in five minutes, she came back down the stairs.

"Mom, why does my brother call Marcus, Inkspot, and what's an inkspot?"

I knew Luke and Clint had talked about this problem, and I had a sneaking suspicion Clint was still using their names behind our backs. So, I tried to explain. "First, he shouldn't call your brother, Inkspot, because he uses the word in a derogatory way."

"What's derogatory mean?"

"The word means not a nice way or kind way. I think in your words, "He's putting your brother down. Your Aunt Agnes calls you Squirt, but she does it with love."

"Oh, I see. When Clint calls me Igmo, he isn't being nice."

"Not at all. Now, to answer your other question. Back in earlier centuries men like George Washington, Abraham Lincoln, and anyone who wrote, such as your brother, Marcus, used an angled-ended, goose feather quill, or wooden pen with a sharp metal tip."

"Didn't they have pencils?"

"Yes. But official papers and correspondence were written in ink. They dipped the metal or pointed quill end into an inkstand. That's a bottle or other container which held ink. Then they carefully wrote words on paper. Sometimes, if they got too much ink on their tip it made a smudge or spot on the paper—a blob or ink spot."

"I still don't understand why Clint calls Marcus that name."

"My guess is, it's because your brother is not an athlete like him. Your brother likes to write poetry, put his thoughts down on paper, and draw—use a pencil or pen. At least, this explanation makes sense. Would you agree?"

"Yes. What does a quill pen look like?"

Thank goodness, Luke returned to the kitchen. "What's going on in here?"

"We're having a discussion on writing with ink before the ballpoint pen was invented, when people used quill pens and pointed metal pens dipped in inkstands to write. Maryb just asked me what a quill pen looks like." I smiled at Maryb, and then did a slight eye roll at Luke, which said please come to my rescue or save me from a hundred-more-questions kind of look.

"Well, Miss Inquisitive, let's go look it up."

"See, Mom. He just called me a name."

"Yes, but I called you this one, because I love you, just as I do Manda here." He winked at me. "How's dinner coming?"

I walked over to check on the potatoes. "No more than fifteen or twenty minutes."

Luke took on a threatening posture and in a gruff voice said, "We'll be back!" He walked stiffly through the door to Maryb's giggles.

I called after him, "Mr. Terminator man, remember you have to grill the steaks, and how about a fire in the fireplace. It's chilly outside and in here."

I heard him tell Maryb they would look up feather quills on the Internet and in the encyclopedia in my library, which was also his new study. Shaking my head, I started finishing my salad. Those two had a special bond.

A few minutes later, I heard Luke's cell ring. I couldn't hear what was said, but Luke seemed preoccupied when he came back to the kitchen. I looked at him with a question on my lips.

"That was the Pastor. He needs to talk to me about something urgent. I'm to meet him at the church at seven, so where are the steaks? I need to start grilling them."

"He didn't say what was so urgent?"

"No, only that he didn't want to discuss it over the phone."

∼

At eight, Luke returned. He usually went home at eight-thirty, so he didn't have long to stay. I could tell by his crestfallen face what he was going to say was serious.

I was stirring up a cake in the kitchen, after cleaning the dinner dishes, and starting the dishwasher. I laid down my spoon and put the batter in the oven, while I watched him put another log on the fire and jab at it with the poker.

"Sweetheart, you need to come into the family room and sit down."

At his words, a chilling shock ran through my body. Had someone died? Had he lost his job or had Pastor resigned? What on earth was so important?

"No," my mind rebelled. "This has been a perfect day. Don't spoil it now."

CHAPTER THIRTY-FOUR

Luke

I sat on the cozy couch in our comfortable family room, realizing my next words would be painful and troublesome.

Manda eased down beside me, reaching for my hand. She squeezed it encouragingly.

How could I tell her the news our Pastor had shared with me, and how would she react to it? Coming home in my truck from meeting him, I'd concocted different scenarios to soften the blow. None of them were sufficient or satisfying.

I was thankful we were alone in the family room. Marcus, James, and Maryb were in their rooms, getting ready for their bedtime at nine. I heard the muted sound of the TV coming from the C-TVR. Allowed to stay up later, Clint was watching the tube.

Buck up, Luke. Manda will understand. Why wouldn't she? A nagging voice, I couldn't put my finger on kept nudging me. She won't understand. Don't you remember her words?

I didn't remember.

Her hand was warm in mine. Nothing to do but plunge in. "Manda, there's something ..." My voice came out in a strained whisper. I stopped and stood, letting go her hand and leaving her sitting there alone.

I, cleared my throat, and tried again. "Manda, there's something I haven't told you. It's not because I intended to keep it from you. I—I forgot it. I guess the best explanation is I put the situation behind me, erased the affair from my mind," I began lamely, wishing I could take the word *affair* back.

"What are you trying to say, Luke? I don't understand."

"When I was sixteen, that was over twenty years ago, and a star basketball player at Longview High School, I got involved with a bunch of guys on the team, who liked to run around the local jock joints and drink beer. We were underage, but if you knew the right people ..." I'd started pacing the floor, running my hands through my hair.

"What!" A startled Manda wore a look of incredulity on her face. "I didn't know you ever touched alcohol, although I'm sure most young men who play sports probably did drink at times."

"After our home games, we'd chose a player's house, buy beer, and go there to drink." I shrugged my shoulders. "We were jocks. We were entitled, and we strutted around our high school campus with that mentality. Most of us were from tough homes, and none of us could hold the alcohol. Some threw up, and the rest of us got drunk. I got drunk.

"On occasion, Pop let me drive his car, but not always, to my home games. When Mom attended, I went home with her and stayed there. Pop never came to the gym to watch our team play, but followed the live action on our local radio. He didn't have a clue." I shook my head.

"He trusted you." Manda drew in a long breath and let it out in a short burst. She didn't know the whole story, and already her head was down and her eyes wouldn't meet mine. "He trusted you," she repeated.

"He did. I betrayed his trust. Each time, after one of our binges, I slept over at a fellow player's house. If I drove Pop's car, and became too drunk to drive home, I didn't. I shudder to think what might have happened, if my imbibing had continued and escalated during my senior year. I don't know where I'd be now. But I assure you, I didn't continue.

"One night after our usual overindulgence, I broke my rule of never driving after drinking, and I started home in Pop's car. He needed it early the next day for some important function. He rarely told us of his business, and we weren't invited to ask." I paused, struggling to remember exactly what happened. "Everything's a little fuzzy for the next hour. I recall fighting to keep the car in the right lane. In my drunken stupor, I was sure the center line was moving on the roadway. I kept jerking the steering wheel and ended up in the ditch.

"Somehow, I managed to get the car out, but I still had enough sense to know I couldn't continue home. I pulled into a parking area in front of a local business, and I either passed out or went to sleep.

"That's where the patrolman found me. I'm sure I smelled of alcohol, and I couldn't walk the parking line in the lot. He took me to the police station and charged me with public drunkenness. The charge would have been worse, if I'd been driving when he stopped me.

"After hearing stories about my father, you can imagine the conversation we had on the phone. I was grounded. He yelled over the phone, 'Don't even think about driving the car the rest of the year.' I couldn't blame him. He was right. He asked our next-door neighbor to bring him to the station. When he picked me up, he never said a word, and never mentioned the episode to me again.

"My case was heard in court. Of course, I was guilty. I was so ashamed. I couldn't look the judge in the eye. All I could do was look around the courtroom and hope I didn't see anyone I knew. One man I did know was a reporter from the local newspaper. He'd interviewed me during the three years I'd played first string at Longview High. I sat there, imagining the headlines on the sports page the next morning. I couldn't concentrate on the proceedings, and I don't remember the sentence the judge handed me.

"What I heard were the words he said next. He was suspending the sentence, because I'd never been in trouble before. He went on to say the record of the arrest would be expunged if I didn't return to his court for another offense during the next year. I felt like someone had elbowed me as I came down from laying one up for another score in a basketball game—the wind went out of me and my knees were weak. I sat down in the chair behind my attorney's table. I was relieved and thankful.

"What the judge did next, I didn't expect. He called me up to his bar. 'Young man, I'd advise you to find another set of friends, because I don't want to see you back in this courtroom. Avery, you're a good basketball player. I follow you in the papers, as I've followed all you Avery boys. Don't mess up your life by doing something stupid like drinking again.'

"I listened to him. I changed my friends. One of my classmates, Lance Sherman, had asked me to go to church with him. This didn't get any brownie points with my Pop, but I went anyway. Because of Lance's persistence, I felt a tug to change my life. You know the rest." I looked at Manda. Her face was expressionless.

"When I applied as music minister at Church-on-the-Hill, I told Pastor about this episode, that it had been expunged, and no record existed of the charges. We decided the facts weren't vital."

"Why have they been brought up now?"

"I don't know how it happened, but Clint must have learned of my trouble from someone at Longview. He told Charlie MacGregor while on the camping trip to Gregorys Bald, and Charlie told Chop." I paused to let this sink in.

What was Manda thinking? She didn't say anything.

I continued, "This afternoon after I left church to come home, Chop and two of the elders caught our pastor walking out the door to his car. He was headed home. The belligerent three plus Pastor went back into his office and the men repeated what Clint had said, embellishing it, I'm sure. Pastor then admitted he knew of the problem and that the one digression had been expunged. They're demanding an accounting of the events surrounding Clint's remarks. I don't know where this is going from here." I waited, but she made no comment.

A silent Manda — this wasn't like her. I rushed on. "You know how Chop is, Manda. He's like a hound on the trail of a rabbit. He won't stop until this whole affair has been hashed to bits. He loves to stir up trouble." I stopped walking in the middle of the room, realizing the next step was up to her. I couldn't tell what she was thinking or if she was thinking.

Her head was still down, and her eyes closed.

"Dear God, what a mess." Manda rubbed her forehead with her hand in quick, short passes.

"I hadn't thought about the problem in years, not until I saw Lance's sister at Nightingale Place a month ago, and she mentioned him. It was and is in the past for me. Sweetheart, I'm sorry I didn't tell you." I walked over and sat beside her. I looked at Manda. From her few terse questions and words, I couldn't tell if she was upset with the problem or me.

She was withdrawn, and the emotional bond between sweethearts was gone. Even though she sat near me, I was alone on the couch. What was she thinking?

I needed to know.

I reached for her hand, "Manda, I…"

She jumped up.

I looked at her in surprise. Her words were measured and clipped as she spoke. "Do you remember the last time we were at China Cuisine?"

"Of course." Now those words — the ones I couldn't recall — started to push forward. I had a sinking feeling.

She looked up at the ceiling and drew a quick, nervous breath. Her face opened up, and the emotions she'd been controlling chased each other across it.

Slinging her hands erratically, she spoke through a sudden flood of tears, making wet trails down her face.

My first reaction was to get up and pull her into my arms. She was hurting, and I had caused the pain. I stepped toward her, "Darling…"

"No. Don't touch me." She drew back with such force I might have been a snake darting forward to strike. "Remember at the restaurant I told you I trusted you fully."

"Manda, I know this sounds—"

"I told you how important trust is to me. You've broken it, just as you've broken the trust of every church member who voted for you to become minister of music, including me."

"But Manda, this wouldn't have happened if—"

"Don't blame someone else for your actions."

"You're being unreasonable. There's nothing to be concerned about. I'll explain to Chop and …"

Now, I was talking to her back, as she ran from the room. Her steps echoed down the wooden floors, and the door shut decisively to the master bedroom. That thud was the most sickening sound I'd ever heard.

I followed, forgetting the C-TVR was open, the tube on and overhead, and anyone up there could plainly hear words spoken below.

Standing outside the door she'd just shut, I pleaded, "Manda, you've got to know I didn't do this on purpose. I never intended to hurt you." I listened. There was no response except the sound of water, running in the bathroom. Then I remembered her saying a hot shower takes care of many problems. I hoped she'd wash this one away. Somehow, I didn't think it was going to be that easy.

I walked back toward the kitchen and den. The upstairs TV was silent, and the lamp-light was off. I assumed Clint had heard the door slam and my comments afterward and gone to bed. I wondered if he knew what havoc he'd caused.

Something was burning!

I hurried to the kitchen. Pulled open the oven door. Smoke billowed into the room. The fire alarm sensor went off as I grabbed a pot holder and set the burnt cake on the glass stove top eye.

Taking the newspaper off the countertop, where it was placed for me to read each day, I grabbed a dining room chair, climbed on, and fanned the sensor until it quit making the shrill sound. I doubted anyone would eat the cake tomorrow.

Back in the family room, I didn't sit on the couch, but paced up and down in front of the fireplace, where glowing coals and piles of ashes rested. I stared at it, miserable and disgusted. I thought about what I'd said. Was there a way I could have softened the blow?

And the worst wasn't over. Tomorrow would bring more repercussions. Chop would come with several people all stirred up to do battle. I pulled in a quick lung-full of air, letting it out in a whoosh. Better not to cross that bridge until I had to, and now I'd have to do it alone.

No, that wasn't true. A couple of Bible verses popped into my head. The first was Romans 8:28 where Paul says, *And we know that all things work together for good to them that love God, to them who are the called according to His purpose.*

How would my Heavenly Father work this for good?

I had no idea.

But here's what *you* should do Luke, as a verse from Matthew 6:24 followed immediately, *Take therefore no thought for the morrow: for the morrow shall take thought for the things of itself. Sufficient unto the day is the evil thereof.*

To me the verse said, and I spoke out loud, "Live each day only, with the knowledge that God will work tomorrow's problems out."

Pop came to mind. He'd kept secrets from our family for decades. No, that wasn't my intention. Pop lived with his horrific problem until he passed, never confronting it.

I'd faced mine, made the right decision, and moved on. Somehow, I needed to convince Manda of this. I'd hurt her, but not intentionally. She could trust me. I had to reassure her of this. But how, and when?

"Uncle Luke, are you going to say prayers with me?" Maryb had walked into the hallway in her pajamas.

"Sure," I said, walking around the couch. "Let's go." I drummed up some enthusiasm and followed her to her room. Manda or I heard prayers each night. Tonight, I felt the need to join in.

Maryb and I knelt by her bed. Manda had taught her the prayers of her childhood. The ones of her mother and father and Tipton great-grandparents, who came from Old Chilhowee. I wondered which one she'd pick. Usually, she prayed "'Now I lay me.'" Tonight was different.

"Angels bless, and angels keep
Angels guard me while I sleep

Bless my heart and bless my home
Bless my spirit as I roam
Guide and guard me through the night
And wake me with the morning's light."

Maryb continued with blessings for those she loved. "God bless Uncle Luke and Mom, James, Marcus, Clint, Grandpa and Mamaw. God bless my teachers and school friends, especially Alice. Amen.

I tucked her in and, leaning over, gave her a good night kiss on the forehead. "Sleep tight. Don't let the bedbugs bite."

"Uncle Luke, what's a bedbug?"

"Later, gator," and I turned out the light to Maryb's giggles.

Marcus was ready when I went to his room. "Uncle Luke, I'm supposed to start art lessons next week. Did you know that?"

"No, I didn't. I knew Manda was supposed to check into lessons."

"We start Monday night. I'm really excited." I listened half-heartedly as Marcus kept talking about getting his art supplies tomorrow. "Manda will take me."

As I came out of James' room, I paused at Clint's.

No, this isn't the right time. I could feel anger inside of me. Righteous anger, maybe, but there was no need to unleash it on the young man. I needed to approach him when I felt calmer. I would wait until the full consequences of his words were known.

Deep in thought, I walked to the balcony rail and looked over the edge. The downstairs formal living room was decorated with colors of red, orange, and yellow—Manda's favorites. She'd done a beautiful job of bringing fall into the house.

I walked downstairs and paused in front of her door. "Good night, Sweetheart." I don't know if she heard me or not.

Heading home I thought of another possibility for combatting these rumors. I'd work on it in the morning.

CHAPTER THIRTY-FIVE

Manda

I stood in the darkness of my bedroom, alone with my thoughts. Twenty minutes under the hot cascading shower hadn't washed the tremendous hurt I felt down the drain. My tears disappeared into the small dark hole along with the water. Luke's confession tore my smug world apart. Words from a childhood nursery rhyme kept running around and around in my head as I pulled my nightgown from a drawer.

> *Humpty Dumpty sat on a wall.*
> *Humpty Dumpty had a great fall.*
> *All the king's horses, and all the king's men,*
> *Couldn't put Humpty together again.*

Like Humpty Dumpty, I didn't know if the pieces of my relationship with Luke could be mended. I remembered my mother's and father's caution when I dropped the bombshell of the possibility of a new man in my life. Did he meet my strict criteria for a husband? I had gushed he did.

My father was reminding me of another time. A long, high school boy-girl relationship had turned dreadfully wrong when I found out he was two-timing me. He'd spoken the same words, given the same friendship ring, and professed undying love to another girl at a different school. We'd even discussed our future in college and possible marriage afterward. I thought my life was over.

It wasn't. After that episode, my relationships with the opposite sex were guarded and so was my heart until Todd came along and proved he was trustworthy.

After that unpleasant incident, my father asked me to do something. I was to make a list of characteristics I wanted in a future husband. When I finished, trust was the first and most important to me—number one on the list, which I had taped on my dresser mirror.

A noise outside drew my attention. I dropped my nightgown over my head and walked to a half-open window, which fronted the road leading into the property. The light breeze of cold night air stirred outside and filtered into the dark room, ruffling the satin folds of the pale blue nightie which fell to my feet. The air felt good on my skin, after the hot shower.

For the first time after my engagement to Luke, I doubted. Uncertainty reared its ugly head, and I wondered at the folly of selling my lovely house, taking four strange children under my wing, and promising to marry a man who seemed to drag a heap of baggage behind him.

What if this relationship fell apart like Humpty? What if it couldn't be mended?

From the bedroom window, I saw the flash of the Tahoe's lights as Luke headed for home. Turning around, I started to crawl into bed when I suddenly remembered the cake in the oven. I ran out of the room barefoot, heading for the kitchen.

The cake was ruined, and the kitchen smelled of burnt flour.

I walked to the fireplace and turned my backside to the little bit of warmth coming from the coals still burning in the opening. Looking around the area, I pictured the scene as it was only hours earlier. What had happened?

I was in an exhausted daze.

Heading back to the bedroom, I crawled into bed, and turned onto my side. Pulling the pillow into a ball, I settled into its warmth.

After working most of the day, coming home to cook dinner, and listening to the narrative of Luke's former drinking problem, I was bone tired. "This day's had its mountaintops and deep valleys," I murmured, as I relaxed and fell into the heavenly oblivion of deep sleep. I was even too tired and mentally exhausted to pray. I knew my heavenly Father would understand.

The next morning, I went through all the necessary excitement of getting the children ready for school—glad that I could drop them off and head to Suds and Styles, where I'd be busy with Friday's work. There, I could pretend everything was just fine when it wasn't. My only break was at noon, and since my one o'clock had cancelled, I planned to go to Subway and drown my sorrow in a sandwich combo. The morning drug slowly on, and I did too.

June hadn't said a word, but I noticed her quick glances in my direction. We'd been friends long enough for her to sense a problem in my life. I knew she wanted to talk, but she had a full schedule like I did. At one point, she came over and gave me a quick hug.

Five minutes before noon, the bells on the front door tinkled. Luke entered the front door of the salon and stood talking to her. I heard him say he'd come to snatch me away for lunch. Other cheerful greetings were called to him from the rest of the work crew. He answered by waving his hand, but didn't make a move in my direction. I could do nothing but get my coat and go.

"I know you've decided on a place to eat lunch." Luke put his arm around me and kissed my forehead as we walked to his vehicle.

"Subway," I answered tersely. The sandwich shop was close enough to walk, but due to the cold weather and wind, I usually drove.

Nothing else was said until we'd ordered our food and carried it to our table. Outside the business, cars whizzed past on the four-lane, and a gasoline station across the road advertised soft drinks at a cheap price. The world moved along at a normal pace.

Luke leaned forward. When he spoke, his voice was sure and tender. "Amanda, I love you." He never used my full name, so what was coming was serious. "You know this without me saying it another time, but I intend to keep using those three words until I can't say them. My feelings for you will never change."

I knew he was serious, and his eyes were full of the love he professed.

"I never intended there'd be another woman in my life, but you sneaked up on me." Luke stopped and smiled at me. His food still wrapped in paper lay on the table.

I concentrated on my sandwich, glancing now and then in his direction. My heart ached when I looked at him. My emotions were still in turmoil, and even now, as during the morning, I held back the tears which threatened to overflow and run down my cheeks. I couldn't say a word, or I'd be blubbering.

"After my arrest many years ago, I became a Christ-follower. My life changed, and I never looked back. I looked forward to the calling I'd felt to become a minister. At first, I intended to stand in the pulpit. I entered seminary and studied to preach. During my second year, it became clear to me that music was dearest to my heart, and though I'd stand on the podium with the minister, I would lead the choir.

"I've been true to my calling, and the problem I experienced in my youth was forgiven years ago by the God I worship. Darling, I'm hurting with you, because I never intended to cause you pain. I don't want my youthful indiscretion to cause a rift in our plans. Amanda, what else can I say?"

The raw pleading in his voice unnerved me. My heart reached for him, but reasoning or pride said a resounding no—no, not yet. The battle raged between the three, as my thoughts whirled in a muddled maze. I opened my mouth, and closed it.

"Sweetheart, what are we going to do?"

I remembered another occasion when he'd pleaded his case in such a way that my heart melted at his question. I put down my tasteless sandwich and dropped my head into my cold hands. What were we going to do? I'd been struggling with that decision for several hours and hadn't made up my mind. What I needed was space. Yes, exactly! A timeout where I could find the answer—a period of calm within this tempest in my life.

Was that my voice? "Luke, give me some time. Right now, I can't think straight." This was true.

"I don't want to lose you. Take all the time you want." Luke straightened and opened his sandwich, satisfied with my answer. "For the sake of the children, don't you think we need to continue our normal lives?"

"Yes, I do." Keeping our regular schedule was reassuring to me at this rupture in our relationship. "There's no need for them to know something's wrong."

We sat finishing our meal, watching the other customers and lost in our own thoughts. Luke hadn't said to work through my hurt, but I knew this was something I needed to accomplish. He'd said he didn't want to lose me, and I didn't want to lose him.

Time? I hoped that was all I needed.

Friday was not the busiest day at Hilly Church. "Luke, did Chop come back to church today?" I needed to know.

"Yes. Pastor has called an emergency meeting of church leaders for Sunday afternoon."

"I see. What will happen?"

"I hope he and I can convince them that no avoidance was intended in my omission of this episode in my interview with the search committee."

I nodded. "I hope the meeting goes well."

Luke took me back to Suds and Styles and let me out at the door.

❦ CHAPTER THIRTY-SIX ❦

Luke

On Sunday afternoon, I sat in the front row and waited for the meeting to start. All but two or three of the men stopped to greet me as they came into the room. Don Jackson sat on my left, and Pastor Lane sat on my right. Chop and his friends commandeered the second row.

Bill Parks, head of the deacons, took control of the meeting.

"Men, we've called this special meeting to address a predicament which has recently come to the attention of several church members. But before we start, I want to ask Milburn Myers to pray that our discussion will be conducted in a Christian and a harmonious way."

After the prayer, Chop was given the floor to speak. Every person in the room had heard reports of Chop's accusations—some true and some bordering on or outright falsehoods.

Fifteen minutes later, the facts as he knew them were emoted, embellished, and punctuated with vigorous nods of the head and arm slinging. Chop loved grandstanding, and his captive audience could do nothing else but listen. "I demand the resignation of Luke Avery." Gripping the speaker's stand, he paused to let this sink in. Then he leaned forward, looking directly at Pastor. "And I demand the resignation of Pastor Lane, since he's as culpable as Avery in this episode."

There was rustling and murmuring in the chairs behind me as Chop included our pastor in his remarks. Demanding his resignation hadn't been mentioned in our discussions. This was a new wrinkle in the tempest whirling around me.

Bill Parks got up. "Pastor Lane will speak now."

I watched Pastor Lane rise and walk to the podium. His face was solemn as he said, "Good afternoon, gentlemen. I know you want to hear a full explanation of the facts in this case. Luke will give them to you after I sit down. This whole scenario has been blown out of proportion as to the alleged misconduct committed against our church.

"I use the word misconduct loosely, because in my opinion there's been no attempt to delude me, you, or our church members. Especially, if there is not a record of it in the judicial system, and certainly none in the spiritual realm, since Luke claims the right of all of us here as God's children."

Out of the corner of my eye, I could see nods. Don Jackson vigorously nodded, shaking his metal folding chair at the same time. His reassuring arm fell on my shoulders. For once in my life, I felt like hugging and kissing the man.

Pastor was finishing up. "I must remind you of the woman taken in adultery. Jesus defended her by saying, 'Let him who is without sin cast the first stone.' None standing nearby could attempt to even toss a pebble, let alone a stone. I think our Savior heard several rocks fall on the ground. I believe He would stand here, exactly where I'm standing, and say the same thing about each one of you, Luke, and myself." Pastor looked over the men sitting in the room. Then, he said, "Luke, you have the floor."

I walked to the front of the room, and as I'd been taught to do in seminary, I looked over my audience, making eye contact. This included Chop MacGregor and his friends.

Then I plunged into my narrative, telling these men almost word for word, the story I had related to Manda. "I believe my heavenly Father intended this sin to work for good in my life. Without this episode, I might not have become a Christian. I can't help but praise Him for it. I'm sure some of you can relate to an experience of this kind."

There were more nods in my audience, which encouraged me to go on, "During my freshman year at college, the record was cleared, and I put this life experience behind me. I didn't need to remember it, ever again. Pastor talked briefly of our sin being taken away by Christ's death on the cross. I like to think mine was wiped away twice—physically here on earth and spiritually in heaven."

Until this moment, I'd held onto the podium. Now, I came around to the front. "I didn't know Pastor Lane when I came to Maryville for my interview with the search committee. But the instinct to trust him was strong. I've learned to respect, love, and value his knowledge while serving here at Hilly Church.

"As I waited years ago, for my meeting to become your music minister, I shared with him the indiscretion of my youth. He agreed with me, there was no need to bring up this subject. I'm sorry if I've caused you pain or hurt you because of my omission. I'm pleading with you not to punish him for my actions. He doesn't deserve it, and I hope you don't think I do either.

"But—and this is a sincere, heartfelt but—if my presence here causes dissension or stands in the way of Church-on-the-Hill's different ministries, including the music ministry, then I will step down. What I need from you is a vote of confidence or not. Then I'll know what to do." I walked to my chair and sat down.

With deliberate steps, Bill Parks walked to the speaker's stand. "Thank you, Pastor and Luke. I believe we have a clearer understanding of the facts in this case. I want to make a few remarks pertinent to this hearing, and then I'll open up the floor to anyone who cares to speak."

"I've never known a more dedicated man of God than Luke Avery, and that's not because he's my sometimes fishing buddy." He paused as chuckles rippled through the room. My valiant attempts at fishing were well-known and sometimes used in jest by the minister during his sermons.

"He's a great minister of music and a valuable friend to each member here at church. We've shared many difficulties of church management. I realize this is not what he was hired to do, but he's willing and available to help. This includes washing church windows or sweeping floors if necessary.

"On occasion, I've seen him walking the grounds, picking up trash when I couldn't get to it. I know that's not my job, but neither is it his. Pastor and Luke have given us something to think about this morning." Bill stared straight at Chop and continued, "I, for one, do not believe the charges against these two men rise to the occasion of resignation."

I heard squirming behind me, and someone cleared their throat.

"In fact, not even close. Because of the extended hullabaloo and rumors surrounding the accusation, my suggestion is for Pastor and Luke to explain the situation to the congregation next Sunday. It's my hope that will be the end of the matter. I will entertain a motion in a few minutes, but first, is there anyone else who cares to speak?"

Three men, including Don Jackson, walked to the podium and spoke positively about my tenure at Hilly Church. No one had the courage to back up Chop and do otherwise. Not even the men he'd brought with him.

The first motion, not to ask for mine or Pastor's resignation, was brought before the group. It was affirmed by a thirty-to-three vote. The second one was for clarification of the facts to the church body, next Sunday during our morning service. That vote was unanimous. Because of Bill Parks wise leadership, a schism in the church was averted.

Much backslapping took place once the meeting was over. All I wanted to do was return to the comfort of my office. Only one hour remained until our evening services started, when Manda would bring the children to church.

I needed to call Agnes with a special request, which I hoped she would grant.

CHAPTER THIRTY-SEVEN

Manda

The following Saturday, when I saw Agnes walk through the door, I knew Luke had decided to use his biggest weapon to plead his case. I trusted Agnes. I didn't have any reason not to trust her.

"Manda," she came around the kitchen island and gave me a warm hug. "What a wonderful house."

I nodded and started to speak.

"Aunt Agnes," I heard Maryb's voice as she ran down the hall to greet the unexpected visitor, throwing herself into her aunt's arms.

"Hi, Squirt, let me look at you. My, the Tennessee hills are agreeing with you. I believe you've grown three inches."

"Mamaw says it's all the fresh vegetables we've been eating. Did you know we're going to have a garden next year? Grandpa's plowed it up. And James and I are going to take care of it. He's been teaching us how to hoe and weed. Do you want to go see it?"

"Whoa there, Maryb. Agnes just got here. Let her take off her coat, and Manda can show her your new home." Luke took her coat as she slipped it off her arm and draped it over the family room couch.

"Are you going to stay with us, Aunt Agnes?"

"No, she's staying at my house, but she'll be over here most of this weekend. She flies back to Texas on Monday afternoon." Luke had turned toward me as he uttered these words.

"Okay, let me lead the way so I can give you the grand tour." I linked my arm in hers, and we headed up the stairs.

"Manda, I'm going to corral the children and take them to the zoo in Knoxville. We'll be back in time to go out for dinner."

"Gr-g-great," said Maryb in fine Tiger-speak. "I'll go tell James and Marcus and Clint." She bounded past us up the stairs to their bedrooms, and I heard her tell Marcus and James they were going to the zoo.

"Cool," was someone's muted reply. Clint elected to stay in his room.

For several minutes, mayhem reigned. Chattering children went in one direction as Agnes and I slowly toured the house.

"Get your heavy winter coats," I called after them.

Soon doors shut, and laughter ceased.

Downstairs, she and I walked through the dining room, Luke's study which included my library, and Maryb's bedroom.

"Oh, to be a child again and have a bedroom like this one," exclaimed Agnes, testing the carpet, walking to the curtains to look at the animals, and checking out Maryb's small desk, where her schoolbooks lay atop.

"You should have seen her face light up when she first saw it."

Agnes and I ended up in the kitchen. "Are you hungry," I asked, as the time was approaching noon. "We could go out to the corner market to eat, or I have leftover meatloaf, mashed potatoes, and green beans from last night's dinner."

"I love leftovers. I think they're even more flavorful after an overnight stay in the fridge.

I'll help you fix them."

I pulled bowls out of the fridge, and we prepared our plates.

"How's Mike doing?" I asked, as I put her plate in the microwave.

"There was a problem with the oil drilling rig he was working on, so while it's being repaired, he's been doing paperwork in his Longview office. It's been nice to have him around, and he's been able to work on my honey-do list." Agnes smiled at me.

The microwave bell dinged. I pulled hers out and put mine in, plus added ice to our glasses. "And Mom Avery?"

"Not much change mentally." Agnes poured tea into our glasses. "She's settled down at Nightingale Place like she's always lived there. I don't go as often as I used to. She's okay."

The bell went off again. I grabbed my plate, two paper napkins with silverware, and led her to the dining room, saying, "There's more room, and we can spread out at the table."

After we were comfortably seated, I asked, "I supposed you've heard of Luke's problem at church?"

"He called me and told me." She took a bite of meatloaf. "Um, this is delicious. Tomorrow's the day he and your pastor talk to the church, isn't it?"

"Yes, I'll be glad when it's over."

Agnes put down her fork, leaned forward, and looked at me. "Manda, you can trust Luke. Out of all my brothers, he's been around to help me when I needed him. He's never wavered in his love or support for any craziness I tried to accomplish. I started in church because he invited me to go. I'd trust him with my life and family."

"It's just — well, the shock of not knowing when he could have told me, and the possibility of the revelation leading to insurmountable problems in our church."

"I understand your concern. We've had our share of overwhelming, horrific moments in the Avery family this year. Within its very foundations, life for all my siblings totally changed. In many ways, our family has healed and solidified, something we haven't had before. It's wonderful. We even phone each other."

I looked at Agnes as she talked. She was right. Finding out Mom Avery had dementia and Mike's former problems at work, along with Pop's heart attack, death, and revealed secret childhood did qualify as horrific.

I went on to explain to her why trust was so important to me, especially in relationships. "I've drilled this one aspect into my heart and mind. I guess I overreacted."

"I totally understand. I've learned more about relationships since I married and had to figure out my own problems. It's not easy when you grow up in a dysfunctional household. The Bible holds the answers, but sometimes it's hard to dig out the minute ones — the ones that aren't so simple."

She and I ate in silence for some minutes.

Agnes' matter-of-fact manner, concerning the mountain I'd made out of the molehill surrounding Luke's admission, was coming through plainly.

"These potatoes are delicious. What did you do to them?"

"Cream cheese."

My so-called problem was no more important than our discussion of mashed potatoes with cream cheese. "I also added garlic," I said, smiling back at her.

She always said the right thing. I got up, went around the table, and gave her a hug. "I love you sister-to-be."

"I love you right back. Will things be okay between you and my brother?"

"It's like I told Luke. I need some time to work through my feelings. But yes, I think so. Let's take our plates to the kitchen, and we can sit in the family room. The fire will be warm and we have throws to curl up in." She and I continued to talk as we cleaned up our lunch plates.

"My brother will be happy to hear that."

"Please don't say anything." I held up my hands to caution her. "This needs to play out in its own time."

"I won't. How's Clint reacting to this situation?"

In front of the fire, I answered her question. "Luke and I haven't approached him with our concerns, but he knows there's a problem, and he's withdrawn from us—both of us now. We've reached out to him, but he refuses to let anyone into his confidence. He goes to school, comes home, and keeps to himself. You don't know how many prayers have been prayed for his protection and safety."

"I understand your concern, and you can't push him." Agnes shook her head.

"No, like me, he has to work this problem out himself."

"Mothers always want to rush in and fix things."

"Agnes, how would you like to see my favorite place in the world?"

"I'd love to."

"Let's put the dishes in the dishwasher and head for Cades Cove. I haven't had a chance to visit in weeks. In fact, being alone has become cherished in my busy life. Oh, I'm not complaining. I can't imagine how I lived without four wonderful children underfoot."

"I wanted to ask you about their life-changing addition to your home. I know how it is to live with two busy children."

"It's been interesting, learning each child's personality and watching them change and grow. Did you know Marcus is taking art lessons, and Maryb loves for me to help her with her homework? Clint is a star basketball player on his high school team. We go to his games. And James, along with Maryb, is my helper in the kitchen and around the house."

"Sounds like you've adjusted very well."

I laughed, "Yes, I've changed also, and my parents are having another childhood."

"I'm glad your parents can show them the other, loving side of being a grandparent."

I knew Agnes was thinking of Pop Avery. "Me, too."

Shutting the dishwasher door, we headed for my Avalon. "Have you been to Cades Cove?"

"I've been to the Sugarlands Visitor's Center. Luke took us there on a former visit. We never seem to have much time when we come up. Is the cove close by the center? Seems like we passed the entrance."

"Not really close at all. We'll make a right turn long before we reach the center. The cove is on the Townsend side of the Smokies and the visitors center is in the Gatlinburg area, on the way to Newfound Gap, Clingmans Dome, and Cherokee, North Carolina. Have you been to Cherokee?"

"No. Luke told us there's a play called, '*Unto These Hills*.'"

"Yes, it's an outdoor drama and very good about the Trail of Tears. When you and Mike and the boys can get away, we'll have to plan on going. We usually stay all night in Cherokee, because the play is long and lasts late."

"I'll see what our family can work up. Mike does get some vacation time. What's so unique about your favorite place, Cades Cove?"

I took a minute to round up my thoughts, "Cades Cove is pastoral. For me, a calming place — a place to rest and reflect and look across hundreds of acres of serene pastureland and reflect on how things were and how they influenced my life today. The Tipton family, my mother's side, first came to the New World in the late 1600s. They migrated west, with a lot of the rest of the Chesapeake Bay area transplants, and turned south down the Shenandoah Valley, into northeast Tennessee to Rocky Mount and the Johnson City area.

"Many of my ancestors were land speculators as were most of the men who first traveled to Tennessee. One of my ancestors consolidated land grants and soon owned a great deal of Cades Cove. He never lived there, but many of his relatives came and established homes — really log cabins in what was a wilderness then.

"The cove is visited by many who come back just to ride around and make sure it hasn't changed, which is what we're going to do today."

"Sounds like fun."

"Usually it is, but during the peak of autumn leaves, cars are bumper-to-bumper. Not today. We're past that time. There will be some travelers. You'll see."

With plenty of time to talk, I told her of the high school, boy-girl relationship—the one which caused caution toward any male closeness.

"Trust Luke," she reiterated. "He's dependable and indispensable."

Halfway around the one-way road, we got out of the car at Cable Mill. I let Agnes take her time and explore the pioneer area of grist mill, water flume, and framed house with its outbuildings.

"Is that a gift shop?" she pointed to another building on our way back to the car.

"Yes. They have everything, including the kitchen sink stuffed inside. Do you want to shop?"

"Do we have time?"

"Always." She and I detoured toward the small building. "We'll take time. You go ahead and browse. I've always wanted to grab one of these rocking chairs and sit on the porch. I'll imagine another time and place while I wait on you."

I was bundled up against the cold, wearing heavy coat and gloves. Across the driveway, several deer grazed on the cold grass in a meadow probably used earlier for a pioneer garden. The floor of the porch creaked as people entered and exited the shopping area. I rocked as I waited.

Instead of dreaming of cove years gone by, I thought of Luke. Even though he was around most of the time, I realized I missed the affectionate bond of love between us. We no longer had that. He tried, but I resisted.

The schism must be mended. It was up to me. I was the one who'd caused the divide. I was the one to make the leap and ask for his forgiveness.

❦ CHAPTER THIRTY-EIGHT ❦

Manda

After the Sunday sermon, Deacon Parks got up to moderate the meeting. He called the special meeting to order and explained the reason for its business. Chop MacGregor was allowed to speak and then Pastor.

Luke had a surprise for the church meeting. He had copied a recent letter he had requested from the judge, who had presided over his case, to give to those attending the business meeting. The judge, now retired, had sent the letter back by Agnes.

"I have a couple of pages to be distributed pertinent to today's discussion."

Luke did not say another word as the deacons handed out copies of the letter, and then he walked behind the pulpit. "I think the letter will say it all as far as my escapade in former years. I'd like to give you the opportunity to read it before I speak." He resumed his seat and reread the two pages himself.

Agnes and I sat toward the back of the auditorium. We waited like everyone else, reading the letter, and finding the contents very interesting.

First, the judge explained his qualifications, role as a juvenile judge, and listed some experiences as a judge on the bench. Then, he went on to talk about the Avery family, and about their prowess on the football field and basketball court. He told of following them for years as they grew up in sports, and how he was surprised and unhappy to see one of the boys in court.

He wrote:

> *Luke Avery, was very embarrassed and sat staring around the courtroom as he pleaded guilty to the charges. I read the officer's report and, as usual, if there are no extenuating circumstances or other offenses in juvenile court, I pronounce sentence, according to the law. I didn't know Luke Avery personally except on the basketball court, but I believe in giving a young person a second chance to redeem him or herself. There was no record of another offence, not even a speeding ticket or reprimand, so I suspended the sentence. Then, I told him the record of his arrest would be expunged if I didn't see him in court for a year.*

> *After the official procedure, I called him up to my bar and gave him some needed guidance. "Young man, I'd advise you to find another set of friends, because I don't want to see you back in this courtroom, again."*

> *The letter went on, "Avery," I said, "you're a very, good basketball player, but not competent in your choice of friends. I've followed all of you Avery boys in the newspapers. Don't mess up your life by doing something unwise like this again. My advice is to find another group of friends." I watched as he walked out of the courtroom, wondering since he'd been given the*

chance to redeem himself, if he would take my advice.

There were others in his class who were given the same option. At least two that I can recall are now in the state penitentiary – one with a life sentence. Imagine my surprise when years later, I read in the newspaper, he's going to seminary to become a minister. He'd heeded my words, as I found out, when I received a kind letter telling me of my influence on his life.

His record was expunged with no need to record it in any transaction associated with living in our country. This means government, state, or city affairs – expunged from all legal records or court files.

I hope this sheds light on his present situation. Kindest regards.

J. Michael Stoneman

Luke arose to explain what happened next. "I did listen to him. I changed my friends. One of my classmates, Lance Sherman, had asked me to go to church with him. This didn't get any brownie points with my Pop, who wasn't a churchgoer, but I went anyway. Because of Lance's persistence, I felt a tug to change my life.

"After my arrest many years ago, I became a Christ-follower. My life changed, and I never looked back. I looked forward to the calling I'd felt to become a minister. At first, I intended to stand in the pulpit – like Pastor Lane. I entered seminary and studied to preach.

During my second year, it became clear to me that music was dearest to my heart, and though I'd stand on the podium with the minister, I would lead the choir.

"I've been true to my calling, and the problem I experienced in my youth was forgiven years ago, by the God I worship.

"I believe my heavenly Father intended this sin to work for good in my life. Let me say that again, *I believe my heavenly Father intended this failing to work for good in my life.* Without this episode, I might not have come to know Jesus and become a Christ-follower. I can't help but praise Him for it. I'm sure some of you can relate to an experience of this kind."

Nods in the audience encouraged Luke to go on, "During my freshman year at college, the record was cleared, and I put this life experience behind me. I didn't need to remember it, ever again. Pastor talked briefly of our sin being taken away by Christ's death on the cross. I like to think mine was *wiped away twice* — physically here on earth and spiritually in heaven.

"More than this, I don't know what to say. I hope you will give me a vote of confidence. Thank you."

I watched as Luke stepped off the platform, and, with Pastor Lane left the room.

Deacon Parks took over the meeting. Instead of a voice vote, paper ballots were handed out. Later, when they were counted, only one vote turned out to be negative. We assumed this one was Chop's. Even his supporters turned against the man and voted for Luke.

❧ CHAPTER THIRTY-NINE ❧

Manda

How do you say I'm sorry? Even though I knew what I needed to do, I found that pride stood in the way. I couldn't open my mouth and say simply, "I'm sorry." Even though I'd told Agnes everything would be okay between Luke and I, our situation hadn't improved very much.

Two weeks after Agnes went back to Texas, I headed for church under leaden skies. The weather station said there was a threat of snow. At thirty-two degrees and with moisture-laden air, we could have a good one, meaning inches.

The children in the car were bundled up in heavy coats, gloves, and Maryb wore her toboggan. Clint rode in the front as usual, and I looked at the rest in the rearview mirror. Most of them had no inkling of the problems Luke had faced within the church body, and I was glad of this.

At Hilly Church, Caitlyn waited inside the door for Clint. I watched them disappear down the hallway. They appeared to be in serious discussion over something. I wondered briefly what was going on, but dismissed their interaction as a personal problem between friends.

Marcus headed for his class, and I checked James and Maryb into theirs. I was trying to decide whether to go by Luke's office when he appeared in the hallway.

"Good morning, Sweetheart." He kissed me on the forehead. "I'm headed for the music room. Are you going to class?"

"Yes, I'm on the way. After church, let's go out to eat. I don't have a thing to prepare for lunch." What I should have said is, I don't want to cook.

"Pizza?" he questioned.

"Too bad, it's not Angelo's."

"Does that mean you want to drive to Texas for lunch? I'm game."

"No, silly." Some of the old banter was back.

"We'll let the children decide."

"You're asking for trouble." I raised my eyebrows and cocked my head, turned and went down the hallway. I felt his gaze following me as I left.

Sunday School seemed to be two hours long instead of one. For some reason I was antsy or maybe that was anxious, or … I didn't know what was wrong with me. I left my class early to get to the choir room, but Don Jackson and several others were already in their seats. I sat down in mine. Luke appeared from the music library. After the choir practiced, we headed for the sanctuary via a set of steps leading up to the choir loft. My feet and legs felt like lead.

The service before the sermon went on-and-on. The choir went down, and I walked through the hallway back of the sanctuary and entered one of the double doors to the seating area. My customary place was four rows down on the center aisle. The pew was almost empty. The threat of snow must have kept several of the congregation at home.

We had streamed live for several years, so they could view the service without driving to the building.

Across from me, a large group of the student ministry sat together. I could barely see Clint and Caitlyn sitting together on the far side. Closer to me and also in his group of younger boys, Marcus smiled at me as I sat down. Maryb and James were in another section of the large building in their own children's church.

After I got comfortable in my seat, and there was some question about that, I had time to look at the church bulletin. Pastor's sermon was directed straight at me. The verse, from Matthew's sixth chapter was on forgiveness found in the Lord's Prayer. My emotions grew tenser.

As the service progressed, the blue pad on my church pew developed lumps and bumps, and I couldn't find a happy place. I squirmed. I adjusted my legs. I propped on the pew arm. I moved my Bible in my lap, turning pages. Nothing helped to relieve my distress.

"Forgive men their trespasses." Pastor must have repeated a thousand times,

Or, was it reverberating in my suffering mind, along with hypocrite! Hypocrite! Hypocrite, my conscience yelled at me.

When the invitation was given and I arose. I found my fingers were locked onto the pew in front of me. I cast my eyes toward the floor and prayed. I knew what I should do. "Lord, give me strength to do it."

With my emotions in a whirl and before I could step from the pew into the aisle, a stir in the congregation caught my attention. From the right, I could see someone walking toward the front of the church. The person was Clint!

I remained rooted to the spot, knowing the confrontation taking place at the front in the altar was more important than me walking down the aisle at that moment. I'd wait a few moments.

❧ CHAPTER FORTY ❧

Luke

Earlier in the week, I'd stopped by Pastor's office. "Luke, read the sixth chapter of Matthew today. I'll be speaking on forgiveness Sunday. Our church needs to hear this message, especially after what's happened lately."

I started to apologize again.

"No, Luke," he said, holding up his hand. "That's behind you and me. But I just think our congregation needs a refresher course on forgiveness. I hope this message will do it."

∽

Now, I was at the front of the congregation, looking at the worshippers. The pianist was playing the invitational hymn. The first stanza was almost done when a movement to the left of me caught my attention. Someone was walking down the aisle.

An electric shock ran through me. It was Clint!

I took three or four steps toward him and let him walk the rest of the way. He threw his arms around my neck and sobbed. I held on, comforting him, waiting for him to speak.

"Uncle Luke," he sobbed into my ear. "I'm sorry. I shouldn't have done what I did. Telling Charlie was wrong, but I resented your authority. Once the words were out and Charlie told his father, I couldn't stop the hurt I was causing." He stopped and sobbed again. "You've been good to me, like a dad. I miss my father."

The hurt of many years fell with the tears rolling down the young man's face.

The collar of my shirt was wet with his tears. I hugged him close. "I want to be your father. Can you allow it?"

I felt him nod in agreement. "I want that more than anything."

"Clint, what you did was wrong, and I believe you know this. Right now, you feel guilty and your heart is full of sorrow. I forgive you. Do you understand what I'm saying? I forgive you."

He nodded and cried again.

The pianist played on, leaning closer to the ivory keys. I saw tears dropping from her eyes onto her fingers.

"Clint, when the judge expunged my record, he made a way for my actions to be forever erased. Christ did the same for every human born to man. By faith, we believe in His virgin birth and His sinless life on earth. Every sin that has been or will be committed was carried to the cross—hidden underneath His precious blood never to be visited again, expunged if you will."

"I know this."

"I believe the Holy Spirit is pricking your heart. Isn't there something else you need to do?"

Clint nodded.

I let him to the altar, where we knelt. "This is an act you must do alone, but here is what you must do. Confess your sins to the Father, and ask His forgiveness. When you do this, the Father has promised to forgive you. Thank God for sending Jesus Christ to die on the cross, making a way for our record of sin to be erased forever. The guilt you've been carrying around will be lifted."

I stood and left Clint there, starting up the aisle toward Manda. Whatever problem we still had needed to be settled. Today, I felt, was the day.

CHAPTER FORTY-ONE

Manda

I couldn't see what was happening from my position in the church. I did see Luke take Clint to the altar. He knelt, and then he arose, heading in my direction. I don't remember him reaching me.

I never faint, but the emotional upheaval of the last several weeks had built up until my body rebelled.

∾

From somewhere far away I heard, "Mom, wake up. Mom, please wake up."

I wasn't a mother. This child had the wrong person. I opened my eyes and Maryb swam into my vision. "What happened?"

"Darling, you fainted. I caught you before you fell. How do you feel?"

Putting my hand to my forehead, I replied, "Dazed."

Luke had carried me to the pastor's office, where there was a couch. We sat on the couch. His arms were around me, and Maryb was holding onto my hand for dear life. Several people were in the room, including Clint, Marcus, and James. All of them, looking concerned.

I closed my eyes to shut out the light.

"Clint, will you take the children outside so Manda and I can talk?"

"Sure, Dad."

I heard a rustle as everyone left the room. This had to be a dream. Did Clint call Luke, Dad? "Pinch me."

"What?"

"Pinch me, because I must be dreaming."

"No, you're not dreaming." Luke laughed. "Try to remember what happened."

I thought back. Something about forgiveness and Clint was at the altar. Several people in the audience were crying, including me. Luke was hugging me close. Now was the time.

"Luke, I love you. Can you forgive me? I've been such a fool." I wanted to make a hundred excuses to explain my actions. I decided to get lockjaw.

"Sweetheart, I forgave you days ago. I was waiting until you could forgive me. I'm sorry if I hurt you. What caused you to react so fiercely to my confession?"

I told him of my high school experience. "That's why trust is so important to me."

"I understand. Are you feeling better?"

"I think so. Let's see if I can stand up." Luke half-lifted me off the couch. My legs were wobbly, but serviceable.

He laughed at me. "I believe I can cure your problem, Amanda Puckett Weathers, soon to be Avery." He took me in his arms.

When he placed his lips on mine, I knew I was home and safe within his arms. The kiss was long and lingering. He whispered in my ear. "In two weeks, we'll be man and wife. I'm glad we got this cleared up. I'd hate to miss our wedding night."

"Mr. Avery, we're in the pastor's office."

"So be it." He said, laughing. We walked out of the office together. "Pizza, anyone?"

❧ CHAPTER FORTY-TWO ❧

Manda

Pink wasn't my color, but dusty rose worked wonders. I took the sweats outfit out of the closet, pulled the top over my head, and drew the pants on. Socks, plus shoes, and I headed for the kitchen. Three over easy eggs and three pieces of buttered toast, one with my own strawberry preserves, and I felt much better. My plans were to lounge around the house and do absolutely nothing. Tomorrow was my wedding day.

Luke's house was full of relatives from Texas. Agnes, Mike, and their two children were there. Tony and his wife had flown in from Houston. Duane and his wife had driven from the Dallas-Fort Worth area with the idea they were going to spend some time in the Smoky Mountains before returning home.

"Do you know how much I love you?" Luke had said, when he'd called.

"Not as much as I love you — never ever, no way." I'd answered his statement.

"Guess where I slept last night."

"In the Tahoe?"

"No. On the couch in the living room with all the kids in their sleeping bags. We had fun, but they kept me up half the night talking about their first flying adventures and catching up." He yawned over the phone.

We'd elected to have the young ones spend the night at his house. I could imagine the mad-house he was living in at the moment.

"You're suffering a lot to be with me. I feel so-o-o sorry for you." I kidded him. "Are you going to be here at eight?"

"Thereabouts, it seems everyone wants to come and see our new home. Guess we'll have a caravan coming up the drive."

"What are your plans for today?" I asked.

"The men will go with me, and the women will stay with you to pretty up for tomorrow. What time is June coming?"

"She'll be here at ten to do our nails. So much for my relaxing day." I groaned, realizing the house was eerily silent.

"I promise the men and children won't be there long enough to jeopardize most of your plans."

"Okay, I'll trust you with that."

"Right," he'd said and hung up the phone.

At fifteen after eight, the cars arrived.

Because we had a dusting of snow the night before, Luke took the group through the garage, where they could clean their shoes before coming into the house. Hellos and hugs came from all directions, and I met Tony's wife for the first time. She was willowy and tall—her clothes straight out of New York's society shops.

Children headed up the stairs to the boy's rooms and the C-TVR. Soon the television was blaring. Luke called up from downstairs. "We leave in ten minutes. Don't take your coats and gloves off."

"Well, future wife on the morrow," this was accompanied with a kiss on the check, "Don Jackson has invited everyone over to the hill behind his house to go sledding."

"Is there enough snow? We barely have the ground covered." I walked to the kitchen window and looked out to make sure.

"He phoned that he's got two inches and, being closer to the mountains, I'm sure the snow is deeper. We'll stop by Hardee's and get biscuits and orange juice on the way. And, if I know Don and his wife, I wouldn't be surprised if there's hot chocolate and cookies to keep the children warm." He went on to observe, as he hugged me. "Tomorrow's going to be hectic."

"Yes. I'm a bundle of nerves, even though the church ladies took care of everything. All I have to do is show up. I'm glad we decided on the bare necessities. Did the wives eat at your house?" I asked, hoping I wouldn't have to cook.

"Yes, they found something in the fridge, so they'll be fine until lunch."

While we were talking, all the men bunched together in front of the fireplace. Duane observed, "Why don't we stay here in front of the fire?" He shook his body and did a b-r-r-r.

"When the girls finish, send them over to Maggie's Restaurant. That's where I'll take the men and children to eat lunch. I plan on going to Fort Loudoun fort in Vonore and if we have time to Sequoyah's Birthplace

Museum. Then we'll pick up the pizza, spaghetti, and bread and head back here for dinner."

"Hey, kids," yelled Luke. "Let's go."

The herd came down the steps and milled around in the family room. Out through the family room hall and door to the garage they went. I didn't bother to go look at the mayhem outside as they piled into cars and left.

June came at ten, her manicuring set in her hands. "Okay, who's first?"

The next hours were filled with fun, primping, and talking.

～

Luke and I had set the time for our wedding at ten in the morning. This would give us time for the reception and to drive over to Mom's and Dad's to eat lunch where we'd leave the children. The rest of the Averys were left to their own pursuits at Luke's house until they left the area or flew home. The key would be left in a safe place for my father to pick up later.

Agnes arrived at nine, to ferry me, Maryb, James, Marcus, and Clint to Hilly Church.

As the children trooped downstairs from the C-TVR, I was amazed at how smart they looked. Suits and ties and Maryb's long purple dress were new, bought for this special occasion. "My, you guys are a handsome lot."

Agnes said, "Manda, where's your camera? We need to take a picture."

She arranged us on the stairs. Me in front, and the excited children behind, peeking over my shoulders.

"Are you ready to go?" asked Agnes, looking me over. "You're beautiful."

I swished my wedding dress. "Today, if I were an ugly duckling, I'd still feel beautiful."

We headed down the steps to the garage and out to her car. "Oh, Agnes. Get my bouquet out of the fridge, and Maryb's rose petals are in there, too."

Agnes returned in a few minutes with two boxes. "Now, we're ready."

Several cars were already in the parking lot at church. Luke's Tahoe wasn't in his regular space. He hadn't arrived yet. I could guess at the chaos at his home, getting three sets of relatives out of the house.

The ladies in our fellowship hall greeted me, as I came through the door. The tables were decorated with snow white tablecloths, bowls of pink and purple flowers, and crystal plates and silverware—the church's best dishes. "Did you stay all night to do this?" I was stunned at the streamers overhead and white wedding bells placed in their loops. "How wonderful!"

A small wedding cake to cut sat on a special table where I would lay my bridal bouquet.

They would have sheet cakes to serve along with a few condiments.

Someone came in the door. "Luke's arrived."

"Hurry Agnes. There's a small room back of the sanctuary for expectant brides. Oops, I mean …"

Agnes cut me short, laughing. "I know what you mean. Head out, I'm right behind you. Where's Maryb?" The children had headed in every direction once we came into the fellowship hall.

"Uh—oh, have we lost her? You'd better go find her. She knows which room it is."

Someone said, "Here comes Luke."

I rushed out of the room, to the laughter of the ladies preparing the reception.

The full-length mirror in the waiting room revealed a mature woman in a long, lacy beige gown. The V-neck was wide enough for my grandmother Tipton's pearls to rest comfortably in its opening—something old.

I pulled my bouquet out of the box. Purple, pink, and beige ribbons surrounded the nosegay, where a bee of beige and brown was almost concealed in the roses. This, as a joke from my father and his assistant gardeners—something new.

Maryb burst into the room. "Uncle Luke is so-o-o handsome. He said to tell you hello."

I could picture him in winter white for the wedding with white shoes.

"Where's your Aunt?"

"Oh, she's greeting the other Averys. She said to tell you she'd be here in a minute."

"Okay," I pulled in a long breath and let it out through pursed lips.

My mother rushed in to give me a kiss and hurried out the door to take her seat.

I wanted to pace the floor, but instead sat down in a chair next to a window, where I could look out on the parking lot. The lot was half-full. Resting my face in my hands was a thought, but smudging my makeup wasn't an option.

"Maryb, I'll be glad when this is over, and I can get back to my old life."

Then I remembered I hadn't gotten Luke's wedding ring off my dresser. "Maryb, go get Agnes, *now*!" The urgency in my voice sent the little girl flying out of the room.

Agnes hurried in. "What on earth's happened?"

"Luke's ring is on the dresser in my bedroom." At that moment, the preliminary wedding music started. We had fifteen minutes.

"Where's the key to the house?"

"Here in my purse." I grabbed it and opened it up. There was Luke's ring. I'd forgotten I'd placed it there the night before. "I think I'm going to collapse." I handed Agnes the ring.

"Not now." She grinned. "Wait until after the wedding. Maryb, where's your petals?"

"Here," she held up the carton.

"Let's take the basket out and get ready to go. I'll go check on our progress and come back.

When she reappeared, the last song before the wedding march was being played. "I think we're ready. Luke and Mike are in place."

I followed her out of the room. Someone opened the double doors into the sanctuary. I stood just out of sight of the audience. Maryb had her hand in the basket of rose petals. The wedding march started. Maryb went through the door, carrying her basket of rose petals and tossing them from side to side.

Then Agnes started her long walk.

I inched toward the open door. When Agnes was halfway down the aisle, I moved into the auditorium into full sight of the raised dais, standing on the white runner to the altar. The audience rose.

I must have taken ten steps before I had the courage to raise my eyes. Maryb was right. Luke was so-o-o handsome.

THE END, ALMOST

"Sweetheart, where are we going?" I asked, as my new husband turned right instead of left at the first turn after we left my parents' house. I snuggled up beside him, with the heater full blast in the Tahoe. Leaving my parents was the first I'd noticed how cold the outside world had become. Afterall, my mind had been on other things today.

"Maybe, I need gas," responded Luke, grinning at my question, his arm around me.

Four miles later, he passed the gas station—didn't even slow down.

The puzzled sensation increased. We were zipping along toward Maryville, past the turn for Hilly Church, past Blount Memorial Hospital. When we didn't turn right or left at Broadway Avenue, I realized we were headed for the airport.

"Okay, give," I commanded. "Are we flying to Texas?"

"There's only one other state in the union besides Tennessee."

"So, that's a yes. "But we have reservations in Gatlinburg," I protested. "And what about walking the streets decorated with holiday lights, looking into the stores, eating fudge, or hiking to Mount Le Conte?" I rattled off all the things we'd talked about doing.

"Cancelled." He laughed.

"Was everyone in on this?"

"Pretty much."

"So, give me the details." I wondered if I'd packed the right clothes.

"We are headed to Mesquite Lodge outside of Weatherford, Texas. I called and made reservations with Dr. Blind, the owner, and he says they have a Christmas theme throughout his house and cabins. We'll be treated to a chuck-wagon dinner around a campfire, ride horses, and — if we can stand the cold — he'll take us out on his pontoon boat, fishing in his big lake. I checked the weather. With sunshine, I think our honeymoon will be a forever thing to remember."

"Yes, glorious, for a man on a sports mission." I shook my head.

"I didn't forget you. Dr. Blind's wife will take you to downtown Dallas or wherever your heart desires. She adores shopping. He says she knows every nook and cranny where fashionable clothes and precious, exotic articles of interest can be found. Any extras, we'll ship back UPS."

"I see." My honeymoon was starting to sound more interesting.

We pulled into the parking garage and hauled our suitcases out of the back of the Tahoe. Our flights were confirmed at the Delta desk. Then, we rode the escalator up to the walkway on the check-in floor for the concourses, passing the water interests where we'd first said goodbye.

Luke stopped me. "Do you remember what happened here?"

I laughed. "You attempted to kiss me."

"Yes, I did. Didn't do a very good job of it, did I. I think I'll try again."

He did, and this time he was much, much better.

❧ EPILOGUE ❧

Manda

The crisp, cool air of autumn surrounds me, as I step from my five-bedroom home in the country. I pull my hooded jacket closer, hugging it to me as I walk to the deck railing. In the twilight, I can barely make out the gentle slope below the deck. It falls to the small creek running at the back of our property, where the bright harvest moon reflects in the two-acre pond one of our church members dug for us.

Our house, built on top of one of the foothills of the Smokies, reveals the dark outline of the Chilhowee Mountains in the east and the twinkling lights along the road to Maryville in the west. Luke and I had found a home in the rolling countryside and, just last year, after the sale of his house, we'd added another six acres of land to the back of our property.

Near their small barn, in the distance, one of our two horses neigh. Otherwise, all is quiet. Only the distant sound of a passing solitary car disturbs the peace I seek outside of my home. I still need the complete quiet, the aloneness of my own thoughts, at times.

"*I will lift up mine eyes unto the hills, from whence cometh my help,*" I whisper, my face upturned to the night sky, where the Big Dipper sits suspended above my head. Standing here in the dark, surrounded by God's love, I realize I depend on Him every moment just as the stars do.

Throwing my arms wide and looking at their brilliance overhead, I say, "Father, you are amazing, and I use the words of King David, *'You are great and greatly to be praised.'*" How many times I've uttered those same words—sitting in church, driving my car, or standing at my kitchen sink, washing dirty pots and pans from dinner?

Even King David's words fall short when I look at the miraculous scene before me. Here I am, standing on my back porch, but I am only a speck in the great universe God created—only a brief thought, among billions, perhaps trillions of thoughts in His mind as He contemplated its construction and spoke it into existence.

My earthly father always said his job with blueprint, hammer, and nails was easy compared to God's giant task on that momentous day. Imagine the earth, water, darkness and light in one day. Then my father laughed and said. "But God had help. The Holy Spirit and Jesus joined him at his wonderful, complicated task. I can't split myself into three people. Sometimes, I wish I could."

Thinking of fathers, a day of sadness comes to mind. Mom Avery lies beside Pop Avery in the Longview cemetery where he is resting. She was buried with her crochet needles, skein of blue yarn, and misshapen sweater she was making for Pop. Luke and I flew down for the funeral, promising Agnes to bring the children in the future for a visit. We'll go this year after school's out, because we want Texas to be part of their lives.

Reflecting back on the last three years, I am amazed at what God has accomplished in my life. Who would have thought two years ago that I would be married to the most wonderful man in the world, have four attractive and unique children, and enough bedrooms in a sprawling house in the country to accommodate them all? I smile in the darkness at these astonishing facts.

The sound of children's laughter brings me back to the present. Turning around, I can see them through the sheer curtains covering the French doors leading to our kitchenette. They hover around the table, playing a game with their father as overseer. I walk closer to the opening, so I can observe their interaction.

Clint is a sophomore at the University of Tennessee and a star player on the baseball team. His father and I think he might go to a minor team when he finishes school. He and Caitlyn are closer than ever. She attends a small college south of Maryville. On weekends when they're home, he picks her up in his old jalopy for dates at our home or Grandpa's. He's starting to remind his father the car may die on the road to school. Luke tells him to get a job, but I think there's a newer car in the works for Christmas. We haven't hinted at this to anyone.

Marcus, our resident artist and writer, won a competition at an art gallery in Knoxville. The winning entry of his hero, my father's portrait in charcoal, wearing his old work hat, hangs on a hallway in our home. We've told him this wall is his to fill with other charcoal, watercolor, and oil paintings. He makes excellent grades and loves English and geometry.

Maryb still brings her homework into the kitchen. It's not that I can help her, but she loves my company. At thirteen, she has blossomed into a beautiful young lady who makes blisters on her hands hoeing our garden.

James is eleven and my father's helper. Together, they work two gardens. My father told me, when he no longer needs his equipment, he wants James to have his tools. Luke keeps saying James will be a farmer when he grows up. I agree with him. His father and I join him in the evening as we walk about the place, checking to see if all's well and watching his garden grow.

My husband is at the head of the table, while our *Scrabble* game rests in the center on its turntable. Luke isn't participating, although he normally does. He's refereeing the play, turning the pages of a dictionary, and saying to Maryb, "There's no such word as herdle." Then he whispers to her, something I can't hear. As he speaks softly, with his hand over his mouth, I step closer.

Her face lights up. "Yes," she says. "I can make hurdle."

"Dad, you're not supposed to help her," complains Clint, teasing his little sister.

Maryb places the tiles on the turntable with a flourish. "It's your turn, Marcus."

Being married to Luke is everything I had hoped and dreamed. His tenderness and love, and steadfastness in the face of adversity are surpassed only by his willingness to be a servant-husband. I think this last characteristic has become the most important to me. I still get a thrill when he calls me "darling."

Our life continues to center around the church. Pastor Lane is resigning, effective the first of the year. There'll be a new minister and a new direction with his coming. Hilly Church Hikers still hit the trails of the Smokies. Luke and I often go on the shorter jaunts, enjoying the mountain vistas, sniffing the myriad flowers, and silently watching the wildlife.

Last month, we hiked to Clingmans Dome. Standing there with the sun setting in the west, Luke asked me to marry him, *again*. There was no ring, but a sealing kiss of lovers who are man and wife.

I shiver. It's time to go in. I'm getting cold in the moist night air. How often I've looked to the tree covered hills for comfort and help, and tonight before I step back into my busy world, I remember the words of Robert Frost and say them out loud ...

The woods are lovely, dark, and deep,
But I have promises to keep,
And miles to go before I sleep,
And miles to go before I sleep.

I crack the door. Clint moves his chair, so I can squeeze through.

"Mom, come and join us," says James.

Luke winks at me.

I enter and shut the door behind me.

THE END, AGAIN

P.S. Oh, I forgot. I'm no longer an employee at Suds and Styles, but I do pinch-hit and get June to fix my hair. She still threatens to quit. I'll believe it when I see it.

THIS IS IT, I PROMISE!

Books of the Tipton Chronicles

Butterfield Station – 1858 to 1859
Chilhowee Legacy – 1911 to 1930's
My Cherokee Rose – 1930's and Present
Tipton's Sugar Cove – Matthew – 1917 to 1921
The Six at Chestnut Hill – 2008

On the Way

The Tipton's at Tybbington, Before and Beyond – 550
 A.D. to 1690 A.D.

There will be sequels to some of my books. I can't write but so fast. Be patient. R.R.

The books are available at Amazon.com or may be ordered through your local bookstore.

Ms. Rhyne may be reached at rebarhyne@gmail.com.